PENGUIN BOOKS

Sky Dancer

Witi Ihimaera is descended from Te Whānau A Kai, Te Aitanga A Mahaki, Rongowhakaata and Ngati Porou tribes and has close affiliations with other Maori tribes.

His novels include *The Uncle's Story,* the award-winning *The Matriarch,* winner of the Wattie/Montana Book of the Year Award in 1986 and its sequel, *The Dream Swimmer.* He has won the Wattie/Montana on two other occasions - for *Tangi* in 1974 and *Bulibasha, King of the Gypsies* in 1995. His other fiction includes *Pounamu, Pounamu, Whanau, The New Net Goes Fishing, The Whale Rider, Dear Miss Mansfield, Kingfisher Come Home* and *Nights In The Gardens of Spain.* Ihimaera has also edited a major five-volume collection of new Maori fiction and non-fiction, called the *Te Ao Marama* series. His first play, *Woman Far Walking,* premiered in 2000 at the International Festival of Arts, Wellington. He was associate producer on the film *Whale Rider,* which premiered to international acclaim in 2003. *Sky Dancer* is his ninth novel.

Ihimaera is a former diplomat who has served with the New Zealand Ministry of Foreign Affairs in Canberra, New York and Washington. He now lives in Auckland and lectures in the English Department at the University of Auckland, specialising in creative writing and the literatures of New Zealand and the South Pacific.

Sky Dancer

Witi Ihimaera

PENGUIN BOOKS

PENGUIN BOOKS
Published by the Penguin Group
Penguin Books (NZ) Ltd, cnr Airborne and Rosedale Roads, Albany,
Auckland 1310, New Zealand
Penguin Books Ltd, 80 Strand, London, WC2R 0RL, England
Penguin Group (USA) Inc., 375 Hudson Street, New York, NY 10014, United States
Penguin Books Australia Ltd, 250 Camberwell Road, Camberwell,
Victoria 3124, Australia
Penguin Books Canada Ltd, 10 Alcorn Avenue, Toronto,
Ontario, Canada M4V 3B2
Penguin Books (South Africa) (Pty) Ltd, 24 Sturdee Avenue, Rosebank,
Johannesburg 2196, South Africa
Penguin Books India (P) Ltd, 11, Community Centre, Panchsheel Park,
New Delhi 110 017, India
Penguin Books Ltd, Registered Offices: 80 Strand, London, WC2R 0RL, England

First published by Penguin Books (NZ) Ltd, 2003

1 3 5 7 9 10 8 6 4 2

Designed by Mary Egan
Typeset by Egan-Reid Ltd, Auckland
Printed in Australia by McPherson's Printing Group

ISBN 014 301869 8

A catalogue record for this book is available from the National Library of New Zealand.

www.penguin.co.nz

for Jessica Kiri

Part One

[CHAPTER ONE]

– 1 –

The sea stretched brilliant and glistening to the horizon. High in the sky, a seashag hovered. It saw a fleet of tiny boats, nets straining with fish, bobbing over the rich kahawai grounds. Further out, a pod of whales was making its way northwards.

The seashag was preparing to relinquish its patrol and seek its lunch from a shoal of minnows broiling below. Suddenly, there was a flash from the coast, the border between sea and land, at the seashag's extreme right perimeter. Alert, the seashag circled towards the land, descending slowly to make a reconnaissance.

A beat-up Jeep shuddered around a bend and up to the top of the mountain road.

With a shiver of apprehension the seashag stalled, spilled air from its outstretched pinions, and dived. Like a stone it hurtled down to take a closer look. At the last moment it swerved, gliding parallel to the Jeep.

The hood was down. The seashag had a clear view. Two women. One older: the hen. The other younger: the chick. The young chick spotted the seashag. Its eyes grew wide and golden, and the seashag *knew*:

Yes. *Yes.*

The seashag opened its beak and uttered a gutteral hunting cry.

Kaa. *Kaa.*

Veering away, it sideslipped down the flanks of the mountain back to the sea.

– 2 –

The seashag had a greater effect on Cora than it did on Skylark.

"Oh my God," she screamed. She put both hands up to her eyes and covered them. The trouble was she was also driving.

"Watch out," Skylark yelled. She grabbed at the steering wheel and righted the Jeep. But Cora had also taken her high-heeled foot off the accelerator.

"Oh no you don't," Skylark said as the vehicle began to jerk to a stop, threatening to stall. "We haven't nursed you all this way up the road for nothing."

Quickly, she pushed her right leg over Cora's body and stamped down onto the accelerator. With her left hand, she changed gear. Surprised into action, the Jeep leapt ahead with a roar, crested the hill and, in a last gasp of petrol fumes and smoke, died.

"I'm sorry, honey," Cora said. "Did you see that crazy bird? It gave me such a fright, darting at us like that."

"At least we made it to the top," Skylark answered. "Otherwise, we would have rolled all the way back. From here we've got a chance."

Behind, the road twisted and turned back through thick green forest. In front, the road snaked like a roller-coaster down and around the contours of the coast. Tuapa, the small town Skylark and her mother were heading for, was just visible in the distance. The rest was sea, unrolling like a bolt of blue cloth to the horizon.

Skylark opened the bonnet and found the problem almost at once. "I'm going to kill that Zac," she said. A faulty petrol pump – or, rather, Zac's faulty replacement.

"Can I help you, honey?"

Skylark looked up, shaded her eyes against the sun, and saw that her mother was picking wild daisies further down the road. This was the way Cora always dealt with her problems: if you went wandering in the flowers long enough, by the time you returned somebody, usually a man, had made it all better.

"No, I've found what's wrong," Skylark answered – and her mother began sauntering back.

"Can we make it to Tuapa?" she called.

"Yes," Skylark said, slamming down the bonnet. "I'll just put the Jeep into neutral and we'll freewheel into town and –"

Too late, Skylark saw that Cora, trying to make amends, was already behind the wheel. Which was how, halfway down the mountain road, Cora had to overtake a big grader and, swinging widely, almost ran down two old Maori women who had chosen that moment to cross the road.

"Oh no," Skylark yelled as Cora, yet again, took her hands off the wheel, screamed and covered her eyes.

Skylark grabbed the wheel and pulled hard on it. Rigid with fright, she watched as the two women slid from the left side of the windscreen to the right. She saw two shocked faces, hair covered with scarves, dresses of a formless black. The larger of the two women pushed the smaller woman with a yell so that she would fall out of the Jeep's path.

Two bends down Cora asked, "Did we hit them?"

"No," Skylark said. "One of the women looked really angry, though. She was shaking a fist at us."

"We should go back."

"How can we? We've got no power and, anyway, it's too late."

"Well they should have been using a pedestrian crossing," Cora said. She reached in the glovebox for a cigarette and lit it.

"Mum," Skylark asked after a while, "do you think you could take the steering wheel again?" With Cora, you had to keep on joining the dots.

"The wheel? Oh! Yes, of course."

Puffing nervously, but still shaken, Cora guided the Jeep into Tuapa.

– 3 –

"Honey, please don't tell me that this is where we're staying," Cora said.

The main street led down to the small port. On one side was a pub, a fish and chip shop, a takeaway bar, a video rental shop and, interestingly, a massage parlour advertising in Korean and Japanese. On the other side of the street was another pub, a hall which looked like it offered Housie during the week and showed action and sci-fi movies during the weekends, a corner supermarket which also sold Lotto tickets and, next to it, an all-night diner. The diner had a couple of cars and a motorbike parked outside.

"Look on the bright side," Skylark said. "It's off season, so it's not costing us too much to stay here and –" she pointed to the all-night diner – "at least there are some signs of a pulse."

"You told me it would be a seaside resort," Cora wailed.

"There really wasn't that much time to organise this holiday," Skylark said. "I left it up to the travel agent."

"You mean we'll be stuck here for a week? In a place which doesn't look like it even has a mall?"

"Mum, you're such a fashionista." Skylark sighed as she stepped down from the Jeep. Just her luck – the garage, like a mirage, was down the other end of the street.

"Do you want to wait here?" she asked. "I'll get us a tow truck."

"Definitely not," Cora answered. "Who knows what might happen to a single woman in a place like this? One moment." She took out a lipstick to freshen her lips and flicked her fingers through her hair to give it sass and sex appeal. "How do I look, honey?"

An icecream on high heels wouldn't have looked any better. "Like the best thing to ever hit this town," Skylark said, knowing it was just the kind of soap-opera comment her mother liked. Which was why, when mother and daughter walked into the Tuapa Garage, Lucas, the owner, was immediately smitten.

"You've broken down, Miss?" he asked, all solicitous, as if Cora had stubbed a tiny red-painted toe. "I'll get Arnie to tow your Jeep in . . . Hey, Schwartzenegger!" he shouted, turning to the far end of the garage.

Arnie, the apprentice mechanic, did, in fact, look like a Maori version of Big Arnie himself. The hair was American crewcut. The face was handsome in a pretty-boy kind of way. The body was unbelievable. Even in his overalls, Arnie was a sight to see.

"The little lady's Jeep is just up the street," Lucas told him. "Bring it back here and fix it, okay? As for me and her –" He was suddenly painfully aware of the *Playboy* centrefolds plastered on the walls – "we'll be at the diner. Come and get us when you're finished."

"Hel-*lo*?" Skylark said. "Would you mind if I joined you?"

But Lucas wasn't listening. He motioned to the centrefolds.

"Arnie's," he told Cora.

Trailing after her mother and Lucas, Skylark took her irritation out on the disconsolate mechanic.

"If you think I don't know what's wrong with the Jeep, I do," she hissed. "It's the petrol pump."

Arnie gave her a dirty look but that didn't faze her one bit.

"Don't try to overcharge us either," she added.

The diner turned out to be a surprise. Clean, bright, with sparkling formica tables, plastic tablecloths and pretty little plastic roses in Marmite jars. Along one wall was a bar. On the other side of the bar a waitress – the peroxided Flora Cornish, who was fifty-nine but had been forty for the past twenty years – went about the business of dispensing very bad coffee to patrons who wouldn't have known the difference.

"Oh, how pretty," Cora cried as she picked up a handful of roses and sniffed them.

Flora Cornish looked at Cora, wondering what kind of dingbat she was, and her look changed into recognition.

"Here it comes," Skylark sighed.

"I know you," Flora screamed. "You're Cora Edwards. You used to be the weather girl on television, didn't you, love!"

The diner's other patrons stared at Cora, struggling to make the connection between a girl who had once been a nightly fixture on the six o'clock news and the older woman who stood before them. After all, her heyday had been five years ago.

"See?" Flora Cornish said, rummaging behind the bar and waving a dog-eared *Woman's Weekly*. There, in all her radiant youthfulness, was a colour photograph of Cora accepting the award for Television Weather Girl of the Year.

"It's true!" Skylark heard Lucas gasp. She saw the look on his face as he realised, hey, this was the best thing to have happened to him in years. He'd never been seen with, let alone talked to, a celebrity. His mind was already turning to romantic possibilities.

Meantime, of course, Flora Cornish just had to ring everybody else in the street to come and say hello to Cora Edwards.

"Time to bail out," Skylark said to herself.

Skylark stepped outside the diner and headed down main street to look at the port. Part way along, she came to a war memorial with a marble soldier pointing down a road that ran off to the left.

What was there to lose?

"Thanks," Skylark told the soldier. She followed his direction and it was like ripping through an old hoarding and finding another town behind the billboard.

Clearly, Tuapa was more substantial than at first sight. Not so long ago the main industry had been forestry, and workers and their families had flocked to the town. Now all that was left of their time here was the derelict railway station and yards. On the other side of the road the prospect was more encouraging. Immediately ahead was a medical centre and a primary school – two prefabricated boxes sitting in the middle of a paddock. Next to the primary school was a large college and technical training institute whose students, Skylark supposed, were bussed in from the surrounding district. Outside the college was a big poster:

BYE BYE BIRDIE
The All New American Musical
College auditorium
This Saturday 1 Performance Only

A shadow flicked over Skylark's head. She looked up. A skua, casting the serrated edges of its wings across the sun. Then another. And another.

There she is. The chick. There.

Skylark followed a circular road and happened on the port. It too was bigger than she had expected: coldstores, dry docking area, marine supply outlets and what looked like a fish packing plant; all evidence that fishing had supplanted forestry and stopped the town from becoming completely comatose.

The breakwater jutted out like a wishbone into the sea. Skylark decided to walk the length. One or two boats were still at anchor. The rest of the fishing fleet were out on the ocean and would not return until nightfall.

"Kia ora, kotiro!" A Maori fisherman, in Swanndri and woollen balaclava, called out from his boat. Too cross to reply, Skylark walked past him, right to the end of the breakwater. The waves had made the footing slippery. It would be easy to fall.

Now, the skuas cried. *Now.*

One among them closed its wings. Skylark heard a warning yell: "Watch out!" Surprised, she took a step backward.

The skua dropped like a stone.

– 4 –

"I've never seen anything like it."

The voice seemed to come out of darkness. Skylark cleared her head. Worried faces were looking down at her.

"When that skua hit her, she almost went over the side. Blood was coming out of her hair. I reached her just in time. Another second and she might have fallen into the sea."

Skylark sat up. "Where am I?" she asked.

She was back at the diner. Somebody had put a blanket around her. She looked from one face to the other. The man from the garage. The waitress. The Maori fisherman.

"Oh my baby," Cora screamed. "My baby, she's alive."

Skylark's head cleared. She saw her mother wringing her hands, reprising her role as a distraught parent on *Shortland Street.* "I'm definitely back on the planet," Skylark said to nobody in particular.

"You were attacked by a bird," Cora explained. "This lovely gentleman –" she pointed out the Maori fisherman – "he saved you."

"Call me Mitch," the man said, smiling. "Mitch Mahana."

"You could have died!" Cora wailed, as usual focusing all the attention on herself. Lucas took the opportunity to offer his arms and Cora's tears dripped down his hairy chest. He was leaning into her as if he owned her already.

"There, there, baby," he said. Skylark winced. Mum was at least ten years older than he was. What was this power she had over younger men?

Cora looked up at Lucas and then at the audience in the diner, as if she didn't know where she was. "It's been such a long day," she said. "And now this. You've all been so kind. But I think it's time Skylark and I booked into our lodge. Once we get there we'll be all right, won't we, honey?"

"Lodge?" Flora Cornish asked. "There's no lodge around here. Only the motel at the crossroads that the locals call the Passion Pit, and the hotel across the road which rents rooms by the hour."

"But Skylark's travel agent," Cora said, "made the reservation. Here –"

Flora pursed her lips. "Ah," she said. "You're talking about the old bach that Bella and Hoki rent out up the Manu Valley."

"Manu Valley?" Skylark repeated. She had a terrible feeling about this.

"I'll show you," Mitch Mahana said. He led Cora, Skylark, and the various hangers-on outside. "That's it. Up there."

Towering over Tuapa were two snow-capped peaks. Where they intersected was a dark, lush valley, the colour of greenstone. It was breathtaking, like the body of a great lustrous bird with wings spreading over the peaks. At that moment, sunlight flashed on two eyes of the bird.

"That's the reflection off the windows of Bella and Hoki's place," Flora Cornish explained. "The bach is just below theirs."

"But it's supposed to have views across the beach to the sea," Cora said.

"It surely has!" Mitch laughed. "Up there you can see to the end of forever. It's a front porch view on the rest of the world."

"How come it's so green?" Skylark asked. Not that she really wanted to know.

"It's Maori land," Lucas answered. "When the forestry came here everybody sold up and made a profit. Only the Maoris held out. People say that Manu Valley is one of the few places in New Zealand where you can see virgin forest as it once was. It's owned by Bella and Hoki now." He paused, and then turned to Cora. "Listen," Lucas said. "I can see you're distressed. There's no reason for you to wait around for Arnie to finish the repairs on your Jeep. By that time it will be too dark. He can deliver it to you tomorrow."

"But what can I do to repay you?" Cora asked.

Skylark gave her mother a sarcastic glance. "Lucas will think of something," she said.

Half an hour later, Cora, Skylark and Lucas reached the top of the valley, where a cattlestop announced that they had crossed over into private land. A NO TRESPASSING sign was posted at the gateway. Further on, two houses stood side by side, one an empty-looking bach, the other a large homestead blazing with light.

"Bella and Hoki must be waiting up for you," Lucas said. "Let's go and get the key to the bach."

He bounded up the steps and banged on the door. Cora took a moment to primp at her hair and touch up her eyeliner. She tried to do the same thing to Skylark. "Oh no you don't," Skylark said. She pushed Cora away and, taking her cue from a Dracula movie, made the sign of the cross.

"Honey," Cora sighed, "when are you ever going to start looking after your appearance?" She stepped down, straightened her dress and pulled Skylark up the steps to the front verandah. The door opened.

"Oh no," Skylark groaned.

"Oh you bet your sweet life, yes," said Bella.

She took a step towards them and glared at Cora and Skylark. Behind her was the smaller woman, propping herself up with two walking sticks.

"You could have killed us when we were crossing the road today. If it wasn't for the fact that my sister and I have already taken your money for the bach, I'd tell you both to shove it and shove off."

The other woman came forward. "Don't take any notice of my sister," she said. "She sometimes forgets about being hospitable to our visitors. My name's Hoki, and you must forgive Bella for being so impolite. Bella is the elder. I am the younger."

She turned to Skylark and smiled.

"Welcome, Skylark," she said.

[CHAPTER TWO]

– 1 –

Ahead, two snow-capped peaks jutted through morning clouds. The sun streaked the clouds with crimson. Approaching was a large wandering albatross, one of the largest flying birds in the world. All morning it had been catching one thermal after another to reach Manu Valley and the sacred mountains. The albatross had been assigned the reconnaissance because among all the seabirds its stiffly held wings, spanning 3.25 metres each, possessed great strength and power. Rarely did it need to flap them.

The albatross stabilised, looking for a gap in the clouds. It breathed smoothly through nostril tubes at the top of its long heavy bill. Those foolish skuas had botched the job and the human chick had escaped unharmed. Now it was up to the albatross to prepare for another attack. That morning, it had received from Kawanatanga, leader of all seabirds, its secret instructions:

Spy out the enemy territory and report back.

Seeing a gap in the clouds, the albatross dived. Immediately below was the valley. A waterfall was at the top, with a small river coursing from it.

Taking surveys left and right to ensure it had not been detected, the albatross silently slipped down into the valley. Its brief was not to be seen, not to alert the landbirds whose territory this was, or the two human hens who guarded the valley. The albatross was confident that by soaring out of the sun it would be invisible against the white clouds. All it needed was a few minutes to spy on the land below. Time enough to get in, do its job, and get out before the alarm was raised.

With a thrill of anticipation the albatross set about its survey. It registered the details of the valley: the forest, the two houses, the waterfall behind the two houses, the track to the cliff face where there was a tree, white boned, skeletal, like a hand with fingers clutching at the air.

Where was the chick?

The albatross spilled more air from its wings to make a faster descent. It caught movement. A small figure looking through glass doors.

Yes, the chick. In the smaller nest.

The albatross's thoughts flooded with hunger. Its huge beak overflowed with saliva.

Vaaa. *Vaaa.*

Ecstatic, it caught a swift downflowing air stream and descended the left flank of the mountains back to the offshore islands.

– 2 –

Skylark woke with a start, her heart racing.

"Has Zac found us?"

She looked around her and realised, no, she had actually managed to get Mum away from him. In this valley, so remote that even the travel agent didn't know where it was when she booked the trip, they were safe.

Skylark fell back on the pillows. But the sounds that had woken her persisted. She got out of bed, tiptoed past Cora's room and looked through the sliding doors. The bells were all around her, and they were making a kind of music. Some were high, shimmering, glittering sounds. Others were lower, mellow, sonorous. The wind, coming down from the snow, was cold. But Skylark could see the dawn was approaching, the two peaks pink as if they were blushing. The forest still stretched dark and lustrous on all sides, spilling down to the sea.

She opened the sliding doors. Below her the forest began to peal with the most extraordinary music. Snatches of descant. Bits and pieces of an indefinable tune. Fragments of other melodies drifting in on the playful morning wind.

"Of course," Skylark said. "The forest must be filled with thousands of birds."

At that moment of recognition, the sun flooded the mountain peaks with crimson. From every part of Manu Valley came birdsong, outpourings of liquid trills and runs swelling with unrivalled wildness and passion.

Cheet-cheet. Zit-zit-zit. Riro-riro riro-riro. Tweep-tweep-tweep-too-too-too. Swee-swee-swee-chir-chir. Bell-bello-bello-bell-bello-bello. Tok-tok-tok. Kita-kita-kita.

As the sun rose higher the birdsong approached fortissimo. Roulade after roulade of full notes cascaded in the air as each forest bird species tried to outdo the other, louder and louder.

The light touched the tops of the forest. The song reached its peak, a deafening orchestral magnificence that made Skylark put her hands to her ears. A hymnal to Tane. A gloria to light.

Tui-tui-tui-tuituia. Alla-alla-lala-alla. Atua-tua-tua. Io-io-io. Amine.

As peacefully as it had begun, the birdsong ended. A few random twitterings and silvered coloratura arpeggios later, it was over.

"Did you like the karanga of the forest birds, Skylark?"

Skylark turned in the direction of the voice. The smaller of the two Maori women, the one on walking sticks, was sitting on the verandah of the big homestead. What was her name? Hoki.

"Come, Skylark," Hoki said. "Let us enjoy the dawn together."

Skylark hesitated. "Okay," she said. She may as well try to get on with the natives.

She walked across the cold grass and up the stairs. Closer now, she could see that a hawk was perched on Hoki's left arm. It was long-winged and long-tailed. Its overall plumage was brown, barred and striped with reddish brown. As Skylark approached it reared its head and prepared to fly off. Hoki calmed it down and kissed the top of its head.

"You have done well," Hoki said to the hawk. "Thank you for your message. Reclaim the upper skies."

With that, the hawk leapt into the air and away.

Ka-hu, it called. *Ka-hu, ka-hu.*

Hoki unwrapped a shawl and gave it to Skylark. "You must be cold," she said. "Haramai. I suppose your mother is still having her beauty sleep? The same with my sister Bella. Not that it will do her any good. Her only hope is reincarnation."

The old woman smiled conspiratorially. She looked at the forest where the birds were beginning to ascend and go about their daily work. "Once upon a time, this whole land belonged to them," she said.

"To the birds?" Skylark asked.

"They were the supreme rulers," Hoki answered. "Not just over the forest in this valley, but the Great Forest which spread all over Aotearoa. You have to close your eyes and imagine, Skylark. Can you picture what it was like in those first days of our world after the Lord Tane, who made us, separated his parents, Earth and Sky? You know the story, don't you?"

"Yes, I've heard it." The scepticism in her words was obvious and Skylark saw a look of surprise flicker over Hoki's face.

"Sometimes, Skylark, you have to see stories with your heart as well as with your mind. You have to look through Maori eyes. You have to listen with Maori ears. Here, let me show you."

Before Skylark had a chance to say no, Hoki started to whisper to her. "Whakarongo koe ki au," she said.

It was the First Lesson.

"In the beginning," Hoki began, "in the days that have gone before us, Aotearoa was the Kingdom of the Birds. In those days our islands were completely covered with the Great Forest created by the Lord Tane. It was he who with other lords pushed up the Sky Father. He did this by doing a handstand and kicking with his feet at the Sky until it relinquished hold on the earth."

Oh no, Skylark thought glumly. Fairy tales at this time of the morning.

"In the space between," Hoki continued, "the lords all contributed to the world we now live in. Tangaroa, for instance, became Lord of the Oceans and guardian of all who lived in the ocean. Paia was Lord of the space between Earth and Sky. Tawhirimatea became Lord of the Winds. All together over seventy gods created all that is seen and unseen. And who was the supreme lord of all? Why, it was the Lord Tane, for it was he who created the Great Forest, verily, a Garden of Eden. The trees touched the sky. Palms and shrubs flowered underneath. Throughout, the Great Forest was laced with shimmering ferns and supplejack. The gateways were the titan kauri, the tallest trees in the world. The palisades were the totara, karaka, kahikatea, manuka, mahika, miro, matai, rata, kowhai and tawa. Over four hundred species of flora, rich with berries and fruits, thrived on the hills and in the valleys. The Great Forest was the wonder of the southern world, the lungs of the Earth, giving air to breathe, giving food to eat. But what use is a forest if it does not have a population to enjoy it?"

Despite herself, Skylark found herself piqued by the question.

"That's when the Lord Tane went up into the Heavens," Hoki continued. "There, the myriad birds were waiting for him, trillions of them, of all shapes and sizes. They were so eager to take possession of the land below that they crowded the gates of the Heavens. Laughing, Tane opened the gates and said to them: 'Go then, my impatient ones! Go down to the world I have created for you and live there.'

"Immediately the air was filled with whirring and jostling as one by one the various families of birds began to fly down to the world below. Indeed, in the great Book of Birds, that exodus is known as the Time of the Falling Feathers.

"Now, Skylark, you must never forget that Lord Tane made birds not just for Aotearoa but the entire world below. One after another, great fleets of them departed the upper Heavens and, as they descended, some flew north, south, east and west to all the lands beyond the horizon. The sun shimmered on their feathers like silver rain. First there were the curlews, godwits, sandpipers and snipes. Then came the stilts and avocets, followed by the phalaropes and pratincoles. Have you ever seen squadrons of birds in flight? They twist and turn as if they are dancing, and some of the squadrons can be many kilometres wide.

"Next descended the skuas, gulls, terns and noddies, followed by the pigeons, doves, parrots and cuckoos. It was as if ribbons of many dazzling colours were being thrown through the skies. And, as the birds descended, they filled the air with melody such as the world has never since heard. They soared down through the clouds – the swifts, the kingfishers and rollers – and the sun shimmered on their wings, creating rainbows of hue and colour beyond comparison. Then came the wrens, larks, swallows, martins, pipits and wagtails. Some of them had to carry down the flightless birds like the moa and the kiwi. Can you imagine, Skylark, how many birds were needed to carry the moa?

"Can you also imagine what they looked like, bursting through the clouds? How excited they were to see the land below? Indeed, the Time of Falling Feathers was similar to the exodus that the Bible speaks of when the Israelites left Egypt in search of Canaan, and it took many many days before the great migration from the upper Heavens was completed. After the pipits and wagtails came jostling the cuckoo-shrikes, bulbuls, accentors, warblers and flycatchers. The Lord Tane's laughter at the birds' great joy ricocheted around the Heavens. He had to step aside quickly to allow the thrushes, white-eyes, honeyeaters, buntings, finches, starlings and weavers to fly down. Finally, the least among them, the humble sparrow, became the last to leave – and the gates could be closed. But the Lord Tane hadn't expected there to be so many birds in the cages of the Heavens. Competition was already breaking out between those who arrived first and those who were still descending. Especially here, in his beloved land of Aotearoa."

Hoki stood up and walked to the edge of the verandah.

"That is how the Great Division was made," she continued. "The Lord Tane was very wise. He immediately realised that in Aotearoa the birds would need to be given different territories in order that they could all live peacefully together. He said, 'I will make half of you birds of the sea, manu moana, and your territory will be the sea and the coast. The other half I will make birds of the land, manu whenua, and your territory will be the land and the Great Forest I have made.' All the birds burst into a trilling of joy and thanks at the Lord Tane's wisdom. 'Just to make sure that you keep to your territories,' he said, 'I will appoint my brother Hurumanu as the guardian of seabirds and the Lord Punaweko as the guardian of landbirds.'

"Thus was achieved the setting apart of seabirds and landbirds. Ever since, twice every day, all the landbirds praise Tane's decision. The first time is at the first sign of dawn. The second is at sunset. So the Great Division has remained. Right up to this very day. But –"

Hoki shivered. She was looking across the land to the offshore islands. There, clouds of seabirds were gathering. "Be careful of the manu moana, the seabirds," she said to Skylark. "They know you are here. The seashags have been patrolling for a week, and you were lucky not to be harmed by the skuas yesterday. This morning, my hawk told me he saw an albatross on high-level reconnaissance. It was spying on us. Stupid seabirds, they grow arrogant and think they can come into the territory of the manu whenua with impunity."

"The seabirds should not be underestimated. Stay away from their territory, Skylark. Stay away from the beaches. Stay away from the sea."

– 3 –

It was mid-morning by the time Cora rose from her bed. The light was so bright that she automatically put on her dark glasses and went searching for Skylark. She found her in the kitchen. "Did you have to play the radio so loud?" she wailed.

"What radio?" Skylark answered. "That wasn't me, Mum. That was the birds."

Cora put up her hands in resignation. She looked at Skylark strangely – and pinched her.

"So this isn't a dream after all! I was hoping that it was and I'd wake up to find this had all gone away somewhere."

"You're supposed to pinch yourself, Mum, not me! Do you want a cup of coffee? I have to warn you it comes out of a can."

"Don't we have coffee beans? Or a grinder? You mean its instant?" Cora shuddered at the word. "This is even worse than I expected. God, pass me a cigarette and the cellphone. I'll get Zac."

"Zac won't know what to do."

"I know you don't like him but I'm going to tell him to get us out of here and back to civilisation. Now, why aren't I getting through?" Cora was having a panic attack. "Why isn't it working?"

Skylark sighed with relief. "I know you love your cellphone and can't live without it. And I know it's a really important fashion accessory for you, and a status symbol. But you know, life can sometimes be so unfair."

Cora stared at Skylark and then at the phone. Her pupils dilated and she clutched the cellphone like a drowning woman a straw. "My pretty purple cellphone doesn't work out here?"

"The telephones here are the kind that hang on walls, Mum, and they're connected to poles."

"No call waiting? No speed dialling? No screening of calls so that you can decide on whether to pick up? So we're well and truly stranded?"

Mum had never been the sharpest tool in the shed.

"It's a bummer," Skylark said.

The good thing was that Zac could not telephone them either.

Not only were they stranded, Skylark realised, but without their Jeep they had no wheels – and no luggage. Nor did they have food supplies to supplement the kitchen's minimal sugar, coffee, tea and milk. When Arnie arrived, they would just have to go back down the mountain with him to do a big shop at the local supermarket. Cora brightened at the prospect – shopping: coffee beans, a newspaper maybe – and hastened to the bathroom to make herself up for the trip.

Skylark, meantime, couldn't help thinking about Hoki's story. Was that why there were so many birds – landbirds, she was relieved to see – inhabiting Manu Valley? They were everywhere, circling in the sky or walking over the land. The bittern calling *'Ka Ka!'* controlled the marshland. The hawk squealing *'Kee Kee!'* was monitor of the upper Heavens. The wild duck honking *'Koekoe! Koekoe!'* ranged the skies from north to west.

What did Hoki call them? Manu whenua. Yes, that was it. Manu whenua.

If Manu Valley was like this, the Great Forest of Tane must have been awesome: a great confederation of bird tribes, interconnected groups of iwi, just like Maori had today, stretching kilometre upon kilometre from east to west, north to south. Within the tribes had been whanau groups of different birds occupying various levels of the forest strata.

No longer; only small parts of the Great Forest remained. Manu Valley was one of them. Bella and Hoki had kept it for the landbirds. They had created a sanctuary.

In an unsafe world, here birds of the land could find safety and protection.

"Just like Mum and me," Skylark said to herself.

Around midday, Arnie arrived – not on the Jeep but in a station-wagon. He stopped outside Skylark and Cora's bach, and Hoki came down the steps of the homestead to greet him.

"Kia ora, Nephew," Hoki said.

"Hello Auntie," Arnie answered. He saw Skylark glaring at him. "Before you start, don't shoot me, I'm just the messenger. There was something wrong with the petrol pump –"

"I told you so."

"And the carburettor and the pistons, and the engine was leaking oil.

But do you want to know what was really serious? Your brakes were just about gone. If you and your mother had been on the road a minute longer, you could have been killed."

Skylark shivered at the news.

"Anyhow," Arnie continued, "Lucas wants me to take you back to Tuapa so you can discuss what you want to do."

"Like *what,*" Skylark said crossly.

"We can repair it so you can get back north, but we'll have to send for parts, so you won't be moving from Tuapa for the whole time you're here."

"Oh no," Cora said. "What else can we do?"

"Well," Arnie answered, "if your Jeep was a horse I'd put it out of its misery and shoot it. But it's not, so there's another option. Lucas has offered you his station-wagon."

"But we can't do that," Cora said.

"Course we can, Mum," Skylark answered. If Lucas wanted to woo Mum with a car rather than roses, fine.

"In that case," Arnie said, "let's get back to Tuapa where you can talk to him. Then the station-wagon's all yours."

"We could do our shopping," Cora suggested, as if the thought had just popped into her mind. She turned to Bella and Hoki. "Would you like to come with us?"

Bella pondered this a moment. She nodded and then, for some reason Skylark couldn't fathom, said to her, "As long as *you* don't drive."

Arnie drove. Cora was squeezed between him and Skylark, looking as if somebody had sat on a tube of toothpaste. Bella and Hoki were in the back. "What did Bella mean about me not driving?" Skylark asked Cora.

"When we arrived last night," Cora said, biting her lip, "I was so embarrassed about running her and Hoki down. Anyhow, honey, you've always been better at taking the blame –"

"About what!"

"I told her you were driving."

– 4 –

Of course Tuapa hadn't changed, hadn't magically transformed into a great big city. No matter how hard Cora closed her eyes, crossed her fingers and hoped, when she opened them, she'd be in some MTV music video setting, it remained Tuapa. That made Skylark so glad. Serve Mum right for putting the blame on her.

However, news soon spread that Cora Edwards was back in town, and at their first stop – Flora Cornish's Tuapa Diner – the clientele increased quickly from five to ten and included the proprietor of the massage parlour, who was considering making Cora a job offer. Nobody seemed to remember Skylark's encounter with the skuas and nobody asked her how she was.

When Lucas arrived, it was clear to everybody that he had gelled his hair and substituted armpit *au naturel* with Old Spice. "I'm really sorry about your Jeep," he said. "I've tried my best to fix it –"

An offended splutter came from Arnie. Meanwhile Cora, utilising a little trick she had learnt from the Hollywood School of Bad Acting, bit her bottom lip so that small tears could appear at the corners of her eyes. "You're all so kind to me and my daughter," she said. "I want to thank you all from the bottom of my heart." Just to prove she meant it, Cora placed both hands on it. Everybody went "Aaah" but Skylark furrowed her brow. After all these years of trying to teach her mother, Cora still couldn't remember that her heart was on the left.

"I need a drink," Bella said. She wasn't fooled one bit. Off she stalked to the pub on the other side of the street for her usual shot of vodka.

"Looks like you and I are the only ones left," Hoki said to Skylark. "Shall we go to the supermarket, dear?"

"Don't forget," Cora whispered, "coffee beans, a carton of cigarettes, I'm out of make-up remover, ear plugs for those awful birds in the morning, a night mask to keep out the sun in the mornings and, oh, do try and get some lovely smellies for my bath."

Although Skylark wanted to make amends with Hoki, she wasn't at all thrilled at the prospect of company. Hoki would take hours to negotiate the aisles on her walking sticks. That plus Mum's little wee lie gave extra meaning to one of Skylark's favourite badges pinned to her jacket: I DO NOT WANT TO HAVE A NICE DAY.

However, when she and Hoki arrived at the supermarket the old lady wasn't a bother at all. Instead she placed her walking sticks on top of her shopping cart, put her withered left foot on the bottom rail and, with her good foot, propelled the cart along like a blackbird on silver wheels. Skylark couldn't stop laughing.

"Did you know you have such a lovely face when you laugh, dear?" Hoki asked. She had always been clever about getting people to open up to her.

Very soon Skylark was telling her about Mum, and about Dad. Eighteen years ago, Brad, Cora's first husband, had been a Canadian executive assigned to New Zealand to buy into an ailing television company.

"Your father's Canadian?"

"Yes," Skylark said. "He's living in the States now, and I sometimes go up to Los Angeles to see him. He and Mum didn't last very long. Long enough to have me and then they had different careers. When they separated I stayed with Mum of course. As for Dad –"

Darling Brad. He'd cracked the big time in the television industry. Recently he had married for the fourth time to some tummy-tucked pumped-up television starlet with lots and lots of hair who was appearing in a sci-fi series he was exec-producing. Daddy dearest, swearing undying love in the Chapel of Eternal Love, Las Vegas, to Vonda, Rhonda, Wanda, Sondra or whatever her name was.

"But he does send me a cheque every month and he does love me," Skylark said.

"So," Hoki asked hesitantly, "where do you get your Maori blood from?"

"Mum's real name is Korowai Whiria, but she took on Cora as her television name."

"Do you know much about your people?"

"No. I don't think Mum does either. She was adopted at some point when she was a baby. Lost contact with the whanau."

Hoki squeezed Skylark's arm. "And your own name? Where does that come from?"

"Skylark? Oh, I've always been called that. Mum and Brad thought it would stand me in good stead if ever I became an actor. Skylark has a kind of marquee ring to it. You know, your name up in lights: *Pretty Woman Strikes Again*, starring Skylark O'Shea."

Hoki paused to think about what Skylark had said. "Oh dear, who'd want to have people in the television industry as parents!" she said. Which was just what Skylark had thought all her life. "Well, Skylark, it's just as well you've turned out the way you are. It's lovely and a privilege to know you."

Their shopping completed, Skylark pushed her trolley into the sunlight. She'd load the back of the wagon, then return to help Hoki with her trolley. She only vaguely took in the fact that the once crowded carpark was now virtually empty. Just the station-wagon and lots of grey asphalt. She unlocked the back door, and didn't notice the shadows gathering above her. Even if she had, she wouldn't have worried – just a cloud passing across the sun.

There she is. We've got another chance at the chick.

A casual passerby would have assumed that the seabirds gathering above the station-wagon had been attracted by somebody feeding them crumbs of bread. But these birds were silent, feathering the air with menace, their wings whirring like blades.

Then Skylark heard a shout. "Stay where you are, Skylark. Don't move."

She looked up, and saw Hoki in the distance. The old woman had left her trolley near the supermarket exit and was advancing across the carpark. Except that the carpark wasn't grey any longer. Between Skylark and Hoki, the ground was covered with seabirds. Seashags. Black-backed gulls. Terns. Skuas. Hundreds of them.

All of a sudden, the ruler among them, king of all seashags, came flying out of the sun. The other seabirds set up a wild fusillade of cackles and screams, as if acclaiming his arrival. As soon as Hoki saw him, his name hissed from between her lips:

"Kawanatanga."

The seashag was bigger than the others. When he landed he immediately displayed his supreme position: tail erect, heraldic wings trembling, crest like a crown on his darting head. His top feathers were glossy black with an oily-green sheen. His undersurface was white. He looked at Skylark, his green eyes like a devil's.

So you are the chick, she of the ancient prophecy.

Kawanatanga's bill was slightly open, hissing, the sibilants like an evil sigh on the wind. His wings were outstretched, waiting only to get past Skylark's guard and administer the fast, killing strike through her eyes to her brain.

Hoki stormed across the carpark, black dress flapping like wings, flailing at the birds with her walking sticks. She interposed herself between Kawanatanga and Skylark. Kawanatanga wheezed, whined, writhed and swayed. Arrogant. Elegant. Demonic.

"E Kawanatanga, hoki atu koe ki to waahi," Hoki called. "Ki a koe he manu moana."

At her words, Kawanatanga squealed his rage. Hoki raised her walking sticks and advanced. She was seething with anger. "Didn't you hear me? Go from here, you and your seabird cohorts, and return to your territory. Do not dare to trespass on mine."

For a moment, Kawanatanga remained where he was, his long neck weaving, ready to strike. Then he stilled, nodded, and lifted.

Today the chick is yours, old hen. Tomorrow she will be mine.

As if of one accord, the other seabirds rose and wheeled away after their leader.

"Aue, Skylark," Hoki said. "I thought it was enough to warn you away from the beaches and the sea. But I now realise that the seabirds have already begun their incursion into the lands of the manu whenua."

Hoki's eyes were glowing.

"From now on, Skylark, you must never be alone. Ever."

– 5 –

A party was going on at the Tuapa Diner when Skylark and Hoki returned. Cora, of course, was in the middle of it, surrounded by Flora Cornish, Mitch Mahana and a gaggle of Korean sailors who, for some strange reason, were offering Cora wads of dollar notes. Lucas was trying to push them away.

"Hello, kotiro," Mitch said. He smelt of a thousand fish heads. "How's the head?"

"You're the only one to ask," Skylark answered. "It's fine. I –"

She was interrupted by a peal of laughter from Cora, who had turned her attention from the Korean sailors to a bespectacled young man who was blushing under her gaze.

"Skylark, honey," she called. "You must meet Ronnie Shore. He's from the local college. Ronnie? This is my daughter, Skylark."

Skylark saw the surprised look on Ronnie's face.

"I had no idea Cora Edwards was a mother," he said.

Skylark smiled sweetly. "There is a genetic match."

Ronnie looked startled. "We're putting on the musical *Bye Bye Birdie* at the college this Saturday night," he explained. "I heard Cora Edwards was in town, so I had this brilliant idea that she might like to join the cast. Your mother has the star quality that will really make the show."

"Ronnie is working out a specialty number for me to do," Cora said. "We start rehearsing tomorrow, don't we Ronnie."

"I just can't believe my luck," Ronnie gushed, as if Cora was Gwyneth Paltrow rather than an ex-TV weather girl.

Skylark saw that Lucas was trying to get back into the action.

"The drinks are on me," he said loudly. He might be just a mechanic and a bit of a rough diamond, but he wasn't about to let some other suitor, even if he was a high school teacher, spoil his patch.

"Did someone mention a drink?"

With a clatter and a stumble, Bella arrived back from the pub – and she was already full as a bull.

Hoki took one look at her and with compressed lips announced: "Perhaps it's time to go home, Skylark dear, before certain persons make public spectacles of themselves."

Hoki's disapproval set Bella off. All the way back to Manu Valley, she kept roaring with laughter, finding something funny everywhere she looked, and singing at the top of her lungs. Vodka fumes filled the car. Hoki kept on apologising for her sister's behaviour, but everybody else was hanging out the windows trying to breathe. By the time they arrived back in the valley, Hoki was seething – but Bella, blissfully unaware, was snoring her head off.

"I'll help you put Bella to bed," Skylark offered.

"Thank you, dear," Hoki replied. "That's definitely the last time I'm going to let her loose by herself."

She didn't realise that Skylark had another reason for wanting to be alone with her – and was surprised when, after they'd tucked Bella up for the night, Skylark let her have her question right between the eyes. Whenever there were questions Skylark needed answers to she had always gone on the offensive. She hated not knowing.

"I want to know what's going on with those seabirds," she said firmly.

Hoki took a step back. Looked frightened. The girl had caught her on the hop.

"I'll tell you tomorrow," she said.

[CHAPTER THREE]

– 1 –

What with the fuss about *Bye Bye Birdie,* Cora claimed all of Skylark's time next morning. Mum could be such a diva. Off on her own planet, her specialty number had escalated to a starring role. Up at ten, she was already putting on her makeup as if for a performance. By the time she finished, she looked like Bambi on beta-blockers.

"Mum, it's only a rehearsal," Skylark said, laughing.

"Yes, honey, I know that. But the rest of the cast are seventh formers and I don't want to appear – well, too mature." Which was Cora's synonym for old. "Now don't just sit there. Get the wagon."

Secretly, Skylark was pleased that her mother's time in Tuapa would be taken up with something she was excited about; all Cora's anxieties about being stuck in the wilderness would evaporate. She started the station-wagon and waited. Hoki was at the window of the homestead, telephone in hand.

"I'll deal with you later," Skylark said to herself.

"Hello?" Hoki said into the telephone. "Is that you, Arnie? Skylark and her mother are coming into town. I want you to do me a favour –"

– 2 –

Skylark drew up outside Tuapa College for Cora's first rehearsal. It was midday. The poster advertising *Bye Bye Birdie* now had a banner pasted diagonally across it:

WITH SPECIAL GUEST CORA EDWARDS

She saw a tow truck come to a stop on the opposite side of the road. Was it Lucas? No, it was Arnie. What was he doing here?

Ronnie Shore bustled over. "It's so good to see you, Cora," he said. He had assembled the headmaster, music teacher, head of the art department and the main cast of the production to greet her. The usual sycophantic sucking-up stuff began.

"I'm out of here," Skylark muttered. She gave Arnie a look as she put the station-wagon into first gear.

"Yeah, and I love you too, babe," Arnie said to himself.

Skylark didn't know Arnie was following her until she turned left into Tuapa's main street; he turned too. When she parked at a phone booth just outside the video rental shop, Arnie's tow truck stopped as well. But she had no time to worry about him right now. She took out her telephone card and inserted it. She hesitated only a moment before dialling.

The telephone clicked and a voice came down the line. "Hello?"

"You sleazebag," Skylark said.

"My favourite little girl," Zac laughed. "So you thought you could sneak away in the night and take my woman from me. Don't worry, I'll find you. How is she, by the way?"

"I'm not ringing you to discuss my mother," Skylark said "It's the Jeep. I should have known not to take it. It's a death trap and we could have been killed in it."

"My heart bleeds," Zac mocked.

"Listen, you no-account jerk! You have two weeks to get out of the apartment. I don't want you there when we get back."

"Is that what Cora wants?" Zac mocked. "Or is that what little daughter has decided? You do that to me, Skylark, and you'll be the one who pays. You kick me out, and Cora loses a lover and her supplier. And you, little girlie, you just might lose a mother."

Skylark tried to disguise her fear. "Zac, sweetie, if we promise to miss you, will you go away?" Then her tone hardened. "Mum's been in rehab for six months now. She's doing good. It's only when you keep coming back into her life that she goes back to her old ways. She doesn't need you any more. Pack your bags and get out. If you don't, I'm calling the police."

"But Skylark, I'm Cora's salvation," Zac laughed. "I'm the resurrection and the life. I saved her when she was down. I brought her to life again."

Salvation? Skylark thought back to that terrible night, five years earlier, when Cora had been fired from her position as weather girl. Nobody knew that she had already begun on a cycle of drug dependency. Her boyfriend at that time, Harry, had been a camera operator. They did a little coke here, a little coke there – but didn't everybody in the entertainment industry? The trouble was that Cora started doing it just before appearing on camera.

That night, Cora was on her mark when the light came on in Camera 3. The cue card came up:

Cue Weather Report.

The camera started to roll. Cora breathed in deep, polished her smile and got ready to beam its 300 megawatt perfection out to the whole of New Zealand.

Cue Music.

The recorded music came on. Lovely, slow, rhythmic, bringing images of an MGM movie in which Gene Kelly danced along a wet rain-streaked street.

For tonight's weather report, Cora had dressed in a plastic red raincoat with a hood on it. She was twirling an umbrella. Viewers adored her style. Sometimes she wore beachwear. Other times she held a tennis racquet or a golf club. She laughed, clowned, sometimes sang a short refrain from a popular song before launching into the weather information.

Cue Ms Edwards.

The words to the song Cora planned to sing began to roll down the autocue.

Action.

Cora began to skip to the beat of the music. She started to twirl her umbrella. The camera zoomed in on her as she sang:

"I'm singing in the rain . . ."

All of a sudden the coke *hit,* and before she could stop it Cora was laughing and laughing, pointing at the camera as if all the people watching from the comfort of their lounges were a hilarious joke. She dropped the umbrella and went waltzing around the set. The camera followed as she kissed anyone who happened to be standing in the wings. She was happy, so happy.

Then she tripped. Fell over. Wasn't that funny, viewers? Wasn't that simply the funniest thing you had ever seen?

The producer frantically signalled to get the cameras rolling on John Campbell. "Whatever Cora is on," John quipped, "I'll have some of that."

He took over the weather report, and television glided over the moment.

Cora was fired the next day. Boyfriend Harry didn't last much longer either.

Zac's voice spat its poison down the telephone. Salvation? The only salvation he gave Cora was a helping hand to push her right to the bottom.

"Zac," Skylark said, "protect the world and go put a condom on yourself. Don't even try to draw any more money out of Mum's account. Two weeks more of freeloading, you piece of shit. Then you're out."

She put the telephone down. Leaned against the glass doors, shivering.

What was this? Arnie was still parked outside on the road. Skylark wasn't in the mood.

"What are you doing? Stalking me?"

"Me? Stalking you? You think a lot of yourself."

"You know what I'm talking about. Well, just piss off."

"Jeez, what's your problem? What's with the attitude?"

Skylark levelled a look at Arnie. She thought about Cora and Zac and the notion that her mother might not be able to kick her habit after all. Knew that she would have to be strong for her mother as she had always been. The one who had been there when Daddy dearest left. The one who was always there whenever any of the men left. Poor Cora, who always needed a man in her life because she was scared of ending up alone.

"Do you think I like spending my lunch hour watching out for you?" Arnie continued. "I got orders from Auntie Hoki. She said not to leave you alone."

"Look," Skylark said. "I'm big enough to look after myself, old enough to know that the best person I can rely on is myself, and if I ever needed help I'd pick on somebody of my own intelligence."

"Cut me some slack, willya? You know nothing about me."

"Even if I did I wouldn't pick a man, least of all a Muscle Mary, even if you are perfectly formed, who goes to bad movies and idolises a movie star who speaks English with a German accent. Just leave me alone, all right?"

Skylark turned on her heel and went back to the station-wagon. Slammed the door. Floored the accelerator.

"You owe me big time, Auntie Hoki," Arnie said to himself. He took off after Skylark, tailgating her all the way to the crossroads and the Passion Pit motel.

Skylark however, wasn't having any of that. She put her foot on the pedal, roared past the motel – and, too late, saw the road to Manu Valley sliding past on her right. In an effort to swing the station-wagon around she put too much pressure on the brake. Next moment, it lost traction and was spinning and spinning off the road.

Arnie watched in horror as Skylark fought to correct the station-wagon; in a cloud of dust, it slewed off the road. He stopped the truck, ran over to the wagon and yanked the door open.

"Are you all right?"

Skylark was grim faced. "Don't talk to me, don't even think of saying anything to me, just leave me alone."

"Hey," Arnie answered angrily, "I'm the hero, right? I'm supposed to save you from the birds, not from yourself."

He slammed the door shut and walked back to his tow truck. He watched as Skylark managed to get the wagon back onto the road. She didn't ask for help and he sure as hell wasn't going to offer it, not even if she went down on her bended knees. Then he heard the wagon's ignition being switched off, and looked over.

Skylark walked across to where Arnie was standing. She took a deep breath. "I'm really sorry I hit the roof back there, but I want you to listen to what I have to say and not interrupt me until I've finished. Okay? We're not talking existential truth here, so this is simple. For the past year I've been looking after my mother. I was supposed to go to university but she was committed to a drug rehab clinic in February – and I chose to go with her. I'm the only one she has to rely on and she is the only mother I have. It's been a really horrific time for her, coming off drugs, but she's managed it, despite the fact that her boyfriend Zac still has his hooks into her. The reason why we're here is that I am trying to get Mum away from him. My mother always gets mixed up with the wrong men. I have to be strong for her. I've always had to be strong for her." She looked at Arnie, willing him to understand. "I know you want to be the hero but I'm not the kind of girl who has a squeaky Melanie Griffith voice and cries out, 'Oh save me, save me, I'm so helpless!' Do you understand?"

Arnie looked at Skylark and then he nodded. "Whatever," he said.

Which made Skylark so furious, because it could have been an admission that he understood what she had said.

Then, again, it could have been nothing like that at all.

– 3 –

By the time Skylark arrived at Manu Valley, the sun had gone behind the sacred mountains. Dark shadows enfolded the Earth like a wing. Evening's soft voices were murmuring in the wind. The flightless woodhens were beginning to call. Quails were whirring homeward.

Mac-wer-ta. Mac-wer-ta. Tek-tek-tek.

Skylark parked the station-wagon and suppressed her irritation when Arnie, stubborn as, pulled up behind her. He'd made no secret of following her from the crossroads and, now that he'd blown his cover, didn't care that Skylark was on to him.

"Why, Arnie," she said. "Fancy meeting you again. If you don't watch out I'll start thinking that you have romantic intentions."

"In your dreams," Arnie snorted.

Nor did Bella and Hoki seem surprised when Arnie turned up. Bella was on the verandah of the homestead, tending to an injured pukeko.

"Arnie, can you bring some wood in for the stove?" she asked. "Skylark, your mother telephoned to say she'd be late. Hoki's cooking, so you're having dinner with us. And just in case you might think it's funny to ask me if I still have a hangover, I wouldn't go there if I was you."

Skylark felt as if she had been fighting all day. She tried to be pleasant. "Can I do anything to help?" she asked.

Bella grunted, "No" and glared as if the pukeko's injury was all Skylark's fault.

"How did it happen?" Skylark tried again.

"Damn cars and trucks speeding down the coast highway." Bella gave her a meaningful glance. "If they can't score little old ladies, they like to use my birds as target practice."

Skylark just lost it. "Look, I know Mum and I almost clocked you and Hoki, and I know we were speeding and I'm sorry. I'll be big enough to apologise. But are you big enough to accept it? Because if you're not, you can stick your dinner."

Bella bristled and Skylark stiffened herself in preparation for an almighty blast of her anger. But Bella bit back on it, put a sock in it. "Hold the pukeko for me," she said.

"Does a 'please' go with that?"

"You sure push the envelope, don't you," Bella said. "Okay, please."

Skylark nodded and took the pukeko. The bird pecked at her fingers and wriggled as Bella fixed an adhesive bandage to its foot. Then Bella kissed the bird on the head and motioned to Skylark to put it down.

"Go home now," Bella said to the pukeko. "Return to your wife and to your loved ones."

The pukeko wobbled. It tried to rip the adhesive off and, when it failed, glared – not at Bella but at Skylark. "Go ahead," Skylark said. "Join the queue."

The pukeko hip-hopped and skipped into the trees.

"He'll get it in the neck when he gets home," Bella said, amused. "His missus will think he's been to the pub." Then she turned to Skylark. "Okay, so you've given me your perspective on what happened yesterday when you almost ran me and Hoki down, so let me give you mine. All our lives Hoki and I have protected Manu Valley and all the birds who live here. We're the only protectors the birds have got. It's our job, plain and simple, and I don't want to make a big thing of it, but I'm not about to see it all go up in smoke simply because one day you indulged in a bit of dangerous driving. I rely on my sister. She relies on me. We rely on each other for the strength we need to draw the line in the earth and say 'No' to all those people who want to cross it."

"I've already said I'm sorry. What else do you want me to do?"

"Do you think it's easy for us," Bella persisted, "to keep Manu Valley? To stand up to all those people who come to us and want us to sell it? They come because they want to harvest the timber. Or else they tell us, 'Look, you two old ladies are standing in the way of progress. Because of you we have to build our road around the coast instead of in a straight line from

Christchurch to Tuapa. You're costing us a lot of money.' Even some of our own people come to harangue us for keeping hold of the land. They say, 'This is tribal land but the only tribe living on it is you two old kuia. The rest of us live in the cities where life is very hard and hits us in the pocket. If you sell, the money will help to send our kids to school. You're holding us all to ransom. You are benefitting yourselves while we lose out.'"

Bella's voice was as firm as steel. "When everybody else is bending with the wind, very few people will lean against it. It has been very difficult, sometimes, for me and my sister to say 'No' to people who want to throw cash at us or get angry with us. Just as difficult is for us to keep on paying the rates so that we can keep Manu Valley. Our parents left us money, but that ran out quickly. Hoki and I were younger then, so it was easy to keep some cash coming in. I used to work with Mitch on the fishing boats and Hoki worked in the fish processing factory. As we've become older, making money has become harder. We rent out the bach. We live simply. Sometimes we go without. This is the price to pay, Skylark. You know why we do it?"

Bella couldn't stop herself. "Hoki and I are servants of the Lord Tane. We are his handmaidens, guardians of all the landbirds, nga manu whenua o Tane."

"Whatever gives you your jollies," Skylark muttered uneasily. She started to back away. This sister was as nuts as the other one.

"No, let me explain," Bella continued quickly. But she knew, even as she began to tell her story, that she wasn't going to tell it as good as Hoki. Once she started, however, she had to keep going.

"When the First Man came to Aotearoa some families were assigned to guard the land, to protect it, and to protect the birds who lived on it. However, when Aotearoa was discovered again, the Second Man was rapacious. Wherever he went he tilled the land and felled the Great Forest. Year by year, the Great Forest has diminished and the bird populations with it. No longer does the moa graze the southern grasslands. No longer does the huia sing in the forest. Of all the landbird species who once lived here, thirty per cent are now extinct. Many tribes of birds have been decimated, and only fragments of the Great Forest remain. The only reason Manu Valley still exists is because Hoki and I are descended from the original protectors, the women priests who set up our system of guardianship. It's a family thing. My mother and her sisters were the guardians of this sacred valley before me and Hoki. Before Mum and her sisters it was *her* mother and sisters. And so on way back generations. Just our luck –" Bella tried to smile – "but there has always been a prediction that in the generation of Hoki and my guardianship the manu whenua would face their greatest challenge. We have to face it together. We can't do it alone. Got the picture now?"

Skylark nodded. If this was Bella's little trip through la-la land, fine, as long as it didn't hurt anybody. "Pax?" she offered.

Bella grunted and put her hand out to seal the compact. But as they were shaking Skylark thought back to the seabird attacks and realised, with the chill of certainty, that there was a crazy logic to what Bella was telling her. "The seabirds have something to do with this, haven't they?"

"Me and my big mouth," Bella said.

– 4 –

"You told Skylark what?" Hoki asked. She was in the kitchen making dinner, and Bella was helping her dish out. Skylark and Arnie were sitting at the table, staring past each other.

"I'm sorry, Sister," Bella said. "My mouth ran away on me."

"Don't blame your mouth," Hoki scolded. "Next time you go to the pub, lay off the vodka shots. So what exactly did you tell Skylark? What kind of damage control will I have to put into place?"

When Hoki's temper was up, she took it out on anything that was to hand. She banged the pots and pans as if they were cymbals.

"Don't make me feel any worse than I do now," Bella said. "I told her about Manu Valley, about Mum and –"

"And?" Hoki waited.

"I told her about you and me being the handmaidens of the Lord Tane."

It was lucky for Bella that Hoki didn't have a serving spoon in her hand, otherwise she would have thrown it. "You had no right, Sister," Hoki exclaimed. "That was my job. I hate it when you do my job."

"It just came up. I took advantage of the opportunity. What's the problem?"

"The problem is that Skylark can't be rushed. She could be frightened off. She has to be brought to the understanding of what's happening in Manu Valley very carefully. I've only had time to give her the First Lesson. And what happens? You come along and tell her who we are, and she hasn't even graduated."

Bella never liked being backed into a corner and, in retaliation, could say things she really didn't mean. "Sister, you've always been too slow, you're forever dragging your leg."

Hoki gave a small angry cry. "Kindly keep my leg out of this."

"Well, you'd better hurry up with the lessons," Bella said. "There isn't much time. Can't you twiddle your knobs and get a better reception? Isn't it about time you went digital?"

"You shouldn't make a mockery of my gift," Hoki answered. "Nor do I need you to criticise the way I do my job, thank you very much."

Hoki gave Bella plates of food to take to the table. Bella put them in front of her guests, took a seat and made the silent duo into the silent trio.

"We'll eat when Hoki joins us," she said finally.

There was the sound of a smash as something broke on the kitchen floor.

"Should I help her?" Skylark asked.

"No," Bella said. "Hoki's perfectly capable of breaking the dishes all by herself – aren't you, Sister dear," she yelled.

"When Auntie Hoki's cooking," Arnie confirmed, "she doesn't like offers of help, because it draws attention to the fact that she's a –"

Bella mouthed the words: See Are Eye Pee Pee Ell Ee. Skylark got the picture. "The consequence is," Bella said, "that every month we have to go to The Warehouse to buy more crockery."

An ominous silence descended. When Hoki came to the doorway it was clear that she had heard Bella's remarks – and that war had been declared. Even so, she tried to appear calm for the sake of her visitors.

"Are you hungry, Skylark?" Hoki asked. She was balanced on one walking stick and pushing the tea trolley across the floor. On the trolley were two pots of stew. Somehow, she misjudged when to stop – and the stew sloshed over and into Bella's lap.

"Oops, I'm so sorry, Sister. And your best dress too."

Bella gave Hoki a suspicious glance but accepted the little accident. However, as Bella passed Hoki her plate to be filled with stew, Hoki miscalculated the distance. The plate fell between them and there was a second crash as it departed to the Great Kitchen in the Sky.

"You meant to do that, Hoki," Bella said.

Hoki beamed a smile of innocence and, changing the subject, turned to Skylark. "What I find interesting," she said, "is that all of us at the table are named after birds."

"Even Arnie?" Skylark asked.

But Arnie wasn't Hoki's target. Hoki was after revenge and she wasn't going to divert her aim from Bella. "Do you know about the bellbird, Skylark?" She started to dish the food onto the plates.

"Its Maori name is korimako," Bella said, oblivious of the fact that she was clearly within Hoki's sights. "When it sings it sounds like lots of beautiful bells are ringing."

Hoki gave her a wicked look. "I always wondered why, Sister dear, you never inherited such a beautiful voice. Your voice is so loud and raucous, especially when you've had a few."

"Is that so?" Bella parried. "At least I can sing in tune." She turned to Skylark and Arnie. "When Hoki was young people used to pay her not to sing." She dipped her spoon into the stew and grimaced. "Sister, dear, don't you think the stew is rather salty?"

Hoki took her place at the table, tried the stew herself and looked mystified. "No, Bella dear," she said. She cocked her head at Arnie and Skylark. "Do you two find it salty?"

"Keep us out of this," Arnie said. "I knew I should have gone back to Tuapa and had some nice and peaceful fish and chips."

Hoki glared at him and then returned to her target. "I'll give you a new plate of stew, Bella" she said, ladling the stew into a new dish. Then, not taking her eyes off her sister, she added three large spoonfuls of sugar to it. "You need all the sweetening that you can get, don't you, Sister dear," Hoki continued. "Now, where would you like your stew? In your stomach or over your head?"

"Time to bail out," Arnie said. But Hoki signed to him to stay at the table. She stood up and motioned to Bella to join her in the kitchen.

"Would you two proceed with dinner and excuse us?" Hoki asked her visitors. "There's a few things my sister and I have to sort out. For one thing she thinks I haven't got Ee Why Ee Esses and can't see her when she spells out Double-U Oh Are Dee Esses with her Bee Eye Gee mouth. Are you coming, sister dear?"

Bella gave an exaggerated bow. "After you, Sister dear," she said.

Skylark heard Arnie give a dismal sigh. His day had well and truly flatlined. He folded his arms and looked up at the ceiling. "Shovel it on, Lord," he said.

In the kitchen, a battle royal began.

– 5 –

Feathers were still ruffled when, a quarter of an hour later, Hoki and Bella rejoined the dinner table. Skylark didn't know who had won but she placed her bets on Hoki; she might be younger and smaller but there was no doubt that she was a determined old woman. Besides, Bella looked somewhat subdued, as if she had finally accepted her fault.

"Well, Auntie Hoki and Auntie Bella," Arnie said after dinner was over. "Thank you for the lovely dinner and the fun conversation. I really enjoyed myself. We must do it again."

He managed to duck just as Bella's hand came up to clip his ear. "You watch yourself," Bella said.

Arnie gave a brief nod at Skylark and beat a hasty retreat out to the tow truck. Hoki went with him to see him on his way.

"You mustn't mind us, Skylark," Bella said as she began to clear the table. "When you have two hens and they're pecking for the same seed there's bound to be trouble."

"Would you like a hand with the dishes?"

"No. You go and join Hoki. Otherwise she'll think I'm usurping her position again."

Skylark left the house and watched as Hoki embraced Arnie. In the darkness, Hoki looked different – so small and vulnerable, stooped there over her walking sticks. "Thank you for looking after Skylark, Arnie," Hoki said.

Arnie saw Skylark. "Yeah, well . . ." he grunted. As far as he was concerned, she was just another girl on an over-populated planet. He gunned the motor and skidded off into the darkness.

"He sees too many action movies," Hoki reproved. "It's a wonder he isn't brain dead."

"So what bird is *he* named after?" Skylark asked.

"Actually, two birds," Hoki answered. "His real names are Karearea Kereru, so he's named after the falcon and, unfortunately, the wood pigeon."

"Unfortunately?"

"For the wood pigeons, that is," Hoki winked.

"Now I know why he prefers Arnie," Skylark said.

Through the kitchen window Hoki saw Bella washing the dishes. What was it that Bella had said?

You're too slow, sister. You're dragging your leg.

"I think it's time for us to talk again about the birds," Hoki said. "Do you feel like a walk?"

"Yes," Skylark said. The sooner she got to the bottom of this, the better.

Above, the stars were like a million eyes staring down from Heaven. The moon was spilling milk among them. Hoki took the track up behind the homestead. The old lady moved with surprising speed, manoeuvring her walking sticks with practised ease. The track was very narrow and, every now and then, Hoki would stop, peer at something on the pathway and then flick it away with her walking sticks.

"You have to be careful," Hoki said to Skylark. "If you tripped on a stone you could fall."

The path took them up the side of a cliff. The moon flashed off it like a mirror. Looking up, Skylark saw the far reaches of the cliff face cutting into the edge of the black night like an axe. Not far away was the waterfall, cascading like mercury to the stream below.

"Surely," Skylark groaned, "we're not going all the way to the top."

No, halfway up the cliff was a small flat area overlooking the valley. Right at the lip was a bench. Hoki sat on it and motioned to Skylark to sit next to her. "Bella made this for me," Hoki said. "She knows I love coming up here when I need to have time to myself."

From the midway vantage point the view was breathtaking. The road down Manu Valley was a molten river, pouring as if from the moon. The liquid curved around the flank of the forested valley. Further away, the dark world stretched to the end of forever. Here, between Earth and Sky, you could believe that Manu Valley was where the world had been born. If you jumped, you would fall into the womb of the world. If you reached out you could feel the birth cord joining Heaven and Earth. Night birds were calling, filling the cup of the night with ecstatic song.

"Whakarongo koe ki au," Hoki said.

She began Skylark's Second Lesson.

"The Great Book of Birds tells us, Skylark, that the migration of the birds from the Heavens to the Earth took many days. However, it was clear to the Lord Tane, who had made the Earth, that his winged creations would need to be given different territories in order that they could live peacefully together."

"That's how the Great Division came about," Skylark said. "By it, we have manu whenua, birds of the land, and manu moana, seabirds. The God of landbirds is Punaweko and the God of seabirds is Hurumanu."

"Well done, tamahine," Hoki said. She pulled Skylark closer and, as a hen does with its chick, used her lips like a beak to preen Skylark's hair as if it were feathers. "The only bird that the Lord Tane didn't bring from the Heavens was the owl. That bird, as well as the bat, was brought from the realm of the Underworld. The point is that after the Great Division a balance was struck which allowed all the birds to live in harmony. They never questioned the setting apart of their territories. The landbirds, in their confederation of iwi, maintained supremacy over the land and forest; the seabirds were the territorial overlords of coast and ocean.

"The seabirds actually thought they had the better deal, which of course they did, but they have always been voracious of nature and always seeking to expand their ownership of all things merely for the sake of possession. As for the landbirds, they accepted the ordination of the Lord Tane. They became the first inhabitants of Aotearoa. The high-flying eagle and hawk took dominion of the skies. The moa grazed the plains of the southern islands. The graceful kotuku inhabited inlets near the sea. The kaka and kea held dominion of the craggy alpine terrain to the west. But by far the largest number – countless tribes – lived in the Great Forest that the Lord Tane had made for them. On the ground the flightless birds lived in burrows and fossicked for food.

"Then, one day, it all changed."

"Changed?" asked Skylark.

"It is not for nothing," Hoki said, "that the seashags, led by Kawanatanga, have been patrolling and waiting upon your arrival. From the very beginning they were the ones to bring avarice, desire and quest for domination upon the birds. Indeed, it was Kawanatanga's ancestor Karuhiruhi who, as Cain did with Abel, brought this bloodshed into the world. Landbirds still talk with fear of the Time When the Seabirds Hungered. Do you want to hear the story?"

Again, Hoki had cleverly manipulated Skylark.

"Okay," Skylark said.

One day Karuhiruhi, chieftain of the large black seashag iwi, decided to leave his cliff-faced pah and travel throughout his coastal domain. His wife, and royal consort, Areta, had just given birth to his first-born son and although Karuhiruhi loved them both, he felt the need to escape the royal rooms, husbandly duties and fatherhood. Flying low over the water, sometimes diving undersea in pursuit of fish and crustaceans, he reached a wide river estuary.

There, while wading in the estuary and reflecting on his life, Karuhiruhi was confronted by the Chieftain Kawau, lord of the rivershags.

"E tu," Kawau challenged, "who are you to trespass in my river domain?" He executed a haka of splendid jumps and swoops, flashing his sharply hooked bill.

Karuhiruhi bowed in acknowledgement. "E te rangatira," he said, "tena koe." He proceeded to mihi to Kawau. "I am sorry if I have strayed into your territory. It was not intended."

The exchange was elaborate and formal but, by the end of it, Kawau accepted Karuhiruhi's apology and his credentials. The atmosphere became more relaxed, so Kawau proceeded to extend the hospitalities of his estuary to Karuhiruhi. "Please rest as long as you wish before you resume your travels," he said.

"Thank you," Karuhiruhi answered. "But I think it is time for me to return to my pah. E hoa, since you have extended the courtesies of your home to me, may I extend to you the courtesies of mine?"

"I would love to visit," Kawau said.

So saying, he followed Karuhiruhi. The black seashag took off from the estuary in a long series of jumps before becoming airborne.

On the way back to his island fortress, Karuhiruhi proudly showed Kawau the extent of his domain and his tribe. His personality was invested with vanity and arrogance and he could not but boast about the vast coastal territory that he ruled. Kawau himself was not without pride and, as Karuhiruhi waxed lyrical about his possessions, Kawau became irritated by the boastful fellow. But he bided his time, knowing that an opportunity would eventually come to take Karuhiruhi down a peg or two.

Areta was awaiting her husband's return. "My Lord, your son is in his nest. You have arrived just in time for kai."

"My royal consort," Karuhiruhi answered, "I have brought a guest, Kawau, chief of rivershags. Let him be welcomed in the appropriate manner."

At this order, Areta and her female attendants called in karanga, and young warriors assembled to exhibit their skills at taiaha, peruperu drill and other martial arts.

It was time for kai. "Let it be only the best for our guest," Karuhiruhi said. He dived from the cliff, plunged into the sea, caught the choicest fish he could find and gave it to Kawau.

"Aue," Kawau grimaced. The spines of the fish had hurt his throat. He saw his chance to hang one on Karuhiruhi. In a slightly supercilious tone, he said, "Your food is no good, Chief Karuhiruhi. Where I live the food is much better."

There was nothing more humiliating than to have a guest belittle one's hospitality. "Much better?" Karuhiruhi hissed. "What food do you have that could possibly compare with ours?"

Kawau smiled, and his smile was not entirely guileless. "There are eels in my estuary which are so smooth that it is a pleasure to swallow them." He hung another one on Karuhiruhi. "Not like your fish which make me feel as if I have eaten razors."

If only Kawau had been more diplomatic.

"Is that so?" Karuhiruhi asked, beginning to take a dislike of this arrogant rivershag. "Prove it."

"Be my guest," Kawau said.

He led Karuhiruhi back to his river domain. Toroa the albatross, Karoro the chieftain of the aggressive and powerful tribe of black-backed gulls, Taranui the tern, Parara the broad-billed prion, Areta and other seabird courtiers accompanied them. Kawau was oblivious to the foreboding swish of Karuhiruhi's dark wingspan and the glitter of anger in his eyes. And he was also foolish! He took Karuhiruhi and the seabird entourage far inland, further than any seabird had ever been before, to a lagoon renowned for the deliciousness of its eels.

The lagoon was below. With a cry, "Taiki e!", Kawau plummeted from the sky, diving deep into the sunlit waters, pursuing the eels as they fled through the sunken logs and forests of their world. On returning to the surface, he nonchalantly tossed a gleaming eel to Karuhiruhi.

"Here!" he laughed.

Karuhiruhi arched his face to the sun. He saw the eel wriggling in the air, its sinuous length flashing in the sky towards him. "So this is better kai than my own?" he sneered. The gleaming eel fell towards him. He opened his bill, catching the eel. It slid down his throat, cool, wriggling, sweet.

Nothing had prepared Karuhiruhi for such joy. His green eyes widened with shock. "It is true." Even before the eel reached his stomach, Karuhiruhi knew he wanted more. He watched as Kawau offered eels to the other seabirds and observed in them the same swooning reaction. Always hungry, his mind immediately flicked to the ultimate possibilities: if this was the food in one lagoon, imagine the bounty in all the others. The seabirds stared at each other, speechless. Their sensory perceptions were in overload.

"So what do you think?" Kawau said.

The words flew out of Karuhiruhi's beak before he could stop them.

"One could murder for such sweetness," he said.

Murder?

"The Great Book of Birds tells us," Hoki said, "that this is how the battle of the landbirds and the seabirds began. It quotes a proverb that has since become famous in the literature of the landbirds: 'Over such things, eels, hens and land, are wars fought; he tuna, he wahine, he whenua, ka ngaro te tangata –'"

When Karuhiruhi returned to his cliff-faced pah, his mind was already whirling with a plan. Obsessed with the taste of eel, he got down to proposing a strategy. The voracious and cannibalistic Karoro was already his ally.

"I want to call a hui of all seabird chieftains," Karuhiruhi said. "It would be helpful if I had your support. Will you all give it to me? You, Karoro, kei te tautoko? Will you be my Second in Command?"

"Ae," Karoro nodded, his beak razoring the air.

"Count us in too," said Toroa, Taranui and Parara.

Karuhiruhi nodded. "Let emissaries be despatched to all the other seabird chieftains," he ordered. "All you who rule mollymawks, fulmars, petrels, shearwaters, gannets, boobies, pelicans, shags, tropicbirds, frigate birds and skuas, haere mai, haere mai, haere mai."

Three nights later, all manu moana chieftains had assembled at Karuhiruhi's island fortress. They were curious, excited, sensing that something revolutionary was about to happen.

"Timata," Karuhiruhi said. "Let us begin." In the firelit interior of the wharenui, with Areta looking on proudly, Karuhiruhi told the seabird chieftains of his meeting with Kawau. Never had Areta seen her husband act so powerfully, so like the ruler of the world.

"I have supped on kai so exquisite that I would give up all to have it again," he said. "Oh . . . that river eel was so smooth and so cool. When it slid down my throat I could not believe that food could bring so much delight. Even now, remembering it, I drool for more. It had no scales, brothers, and in its death throes it flicked its tail inside me. The sensation was exquisite, and lasted for days."

"How can such a food exist?" the chieftains asked. "No scales, you say?"

"None," Toroa confirmed. "Just think, brothers, of the other kai which must exist in the kingdom of the landbirds. Think –"

"All could be ours," Karoro added. "All, all –"

Karuhiruhi, Karoro, Toroa, Taranui and Parara swept the other chieftains along with the conviction of their words. Pathologically driven to eat, eat, eat, seabirds had always possessed appetites that could never be appeased. They gorged themselves even when full. Now they bore testimony to the aphrodisiacal nature of the food of the inland river lagoon. The vision they offered of limitless food sent all the seabird chieftains wild with delirium.

It was then that Karuhiruhi spoke what had until then remained unbroached.

"Why just stop at taking the kai of the landbirds," he hissed.

"He aha? What?"

The hui turned into a Council of War.

"Why should the manu whenua live in such luxury in the forest," Karuhiruhi continued, "where their food is within beak's reach, while we, the manu moana, spend all our hours scouring the coast and the sea for our paltry sustenance?"

"Ka tika!" the chieftains whistled, their heads bobbing in assent.

"Why should their food be so sweet while ours is salty? Their kai so smooth while ours is scaly?"

"Yes! Ae! Ka tika!"

Then Karuhiruhi voiced the Ultimate Heresy.

"Why should the landbirds have been given such bounty by the Lord Tane and the seabirds not?" he cried. "Why should the seabirds be denied the incredible riches possessed by the landbirds? Such division of bounty is unfair. The setting apart of the Earth into two territories was not meant to be!"

The chieftains whistled and screamed with horror. They waited for Karuhiruhi to be struck dead by Tane. They waited for Hurumanu's claws to descend and strike Karuhiruhi's head from his body.

Nothing happened. The seabirds tipped over into insanity.

"Let us take the land!" Karuhiruhi called.

Intoxicated by his rhetoric, the other chieftains roared their approval.

"Let us declare war on the manu whenua. Ka tika?"

"Ka tika," Karoro called in support, and he crossed his wings against Karuhiruhi's in an act of allegiance.

The chieftains roared their agreement. "Ka tika! Ka tika!" they cried.

Karuhiruhi issued the instructions. "War! War! War!"

[CHAPTER FOUR]

– 1 –

As usual in the morning, birdsong.

Skylark was asleep when the melody drifted through her dreams. Something was sighing in the wind. The trilling began, ornamenting the vocal line. The warbling came next, followed by a throbbing bass and a syncopated whistling. The sounds merged into a crescendo of wind chimes silvered with a scattering of bells.

"Not again," Cora wailed from her bedroom.

The sun flooded across the Manu Valley. The manu whenua repeated their age-old thanks to the Lord Tane.

Skylark awoke, wondering whether she'd been dreaming or whether Hoki really had told her about how the war between the landbirds and seabirds began. Her head was throbbing with it all. The seabird attacks, the stories Hoki and Bella were putting into her head – none of it made sense, yet she couldn't shake off the impact.

"No, no, no," Skylark said to herself. "I will not be caught up in someone else's psychodrama." She got up, put on her bathrobe, went to the kitchen and made herself a cup of coffee. A couple of pieces of toast with peanut butter later, and she was sitting in the sun looking across the valley.

What was that shadow over the sea? Was the weather changing?

Bella and Hoki were also up early that morning. At breakfast Bella made up with her sister.

"I'm sorry I overstepped the mark with Skylark," Bella said. "From now on, I'll leave you to do your job."

"You'll zip your lip?" Hoki asked sternly. She cocked an eye and made a threatening peck to make sure Bella got the picture.

"Consider it done," Bella answered. Better to have peace in the henhouse and to smooth ruffled feathers.

Satisfied, Hoki put an arm around her sister to show she'd been forgiven. "Good," she said.

Bella left the house in the direction of the toolshed, aware that she'd got out of that one lightly. Sometimes Hoki's temper could go on for days. Meanwhile, in the kitchen, Hoki got on with the breadmaking. She looked out the window, saw the shadows over the sea, and paused a moment to watch the weather front coming up from the south. She returned to her breadmaking. Then she looked again at the approaching southerly.

Her blood froze. "I have to find Bella," she said.

Far off she heard Bella banging and crashing away, preparing the traps to catch the wild dogs, stoats, ferrets and feral cats that roamed the forest, killing the birds and destroying their nests.

"Bella?" Hoki called. "Bella!"

The sound of fear in her sister's voice was enough to make Bella stop in her tracks. One look at Hoki's face and she came running.

"Are you all right, sister?"

"Look!" Hoki pointed.

The shadows weren't clouds. Seabirds, hundreds of them, were coming across the sea, making for the offshore islands.

"The Book of Birds told us this would happen, but I never thought we'd see the day," Hoki continued.

"It's an early warning call. Sister, you must bring Skylark up to speed. Rev up and put yourself into third, okay?"

Out on the *Sea Queen*, Mitch Mahana didn't take much notice of the seabirds arrowing overhead. He'd been aware the numbers had increased over the last few weeks, but merely put it down to seasonal migratory patterns. The offshore islands had always been the staging post for seabirds heading north for the winter. Of more interest was the movement below water. The boat's sonar system was pinging and it was clear from the screen that a huge shoal of kahawai was moving beneath them.

Within an hour Mitch and his crew — his son Francis and nephews Hori and Vic — had the nets out and were trawling the shoal. Soon after, they were scooping the catch from the bottom. The net rose and the kahawai began to stipple the surface of the water with froth.

Mitch and his crew were jubilant. It was a good catch. They began winching the nets in, unconcerned by the darkness of the clouds over the sun.

Then harsh cries split their eardrums and seabirds fell from the air.

Kaa. *Kaa.* Kee *law.* Kee *law.*

Mitch was accustomed to seabirds following his boat and skimming some of the fish from the nets. But this was different.

"Dad? Dad!" Francis came running along the deck. "What's going on, Dad?"

Hundreds of seabirds were hurtling down on the catch. Hungry after their long journeys to the offshore islands, they relished the opportunity of easy kai. Again and again they hurled themselves into the nets, slashing at the fish and tearing the flesh from throat to tail, stripping the kahawai to the bones in seconds.

Just as quickly as it had started, the feeding frenzy was over. The seabirds resumed their slow procession towards the offshore islands. All that was left was water stained with blood and bits and pieces of the catch.

The crew, open-mouthed, began to haul in the net. Nothing.

Mitch thought of Manu Valley. He thought of Hoki and Bella.

"We have to go back to Tuapa," he said.

– 2 –

Skylark finished her coffee. She saw Bella heading off to set her traps. A few moments later, Hoki appeared and began walking up the cliff path. She had binoculars slung around her neck.

Hoki must be going to the lookout point, Skylark realised.

For a few moments she watched Hoki's ascent. Then she took a deep breath and turned her mind to the most difficult mission of the morning: giving Cora her wake-up call.

"Mum?"

Cora was lying with a sleeping mask over her face. She was also wearing her high heels; they were sticking out of the end of the bed. She had got back very late last night.

"Go away," Cora moaned.

"I haven't made you a cup of coffee for nothing."

"I didn't get any sleep at all," Cora wailed. "Isn't there some way we can turn off the birds?" She reached grumpily for the first cigarette of the day.

"Mum, do you have to smoke?"

Cora frowned. "Let's make a deal today, honey. You don't talk about my smoking, I won't talk about your weight."

"Whoa," Skylark said. Cora was rocking today. Well, there were two ways of handling Mum's ultimatums. One was to rock on with the issue; the other was to be kind to the dear. Skylark chose to be kind. "So how did the rehearsal go?"

"The rehearsal? Oh! The re-*hearsal*!"

Immediately Cora was awake, sitting up in bed, plumping the pillows around her, reaching for her coffee and ready to dish Skylark the goss. "Honey, all I can say is that Ronnie is very lucky that I happened to be in town. I mean, it's not his fault that the girl who plays the lead can't sing and the boy who plays the hero can't dance and has no sex appeal whatsoever – but after all it *is* a college production."

Skylark always loved it when her mother played the star who comes in the nick of time to save the production.

"I watched the run-through," Cora continued, waving her hands to indicate it was so-so, "and then Ronnie and I got down to business. Ronnie – he has such lovely brown eyes, just like a puppy – asked me what I had in mind for my specialty routine. You know the story, don't you? It's set in the 1960s and famous rock star Conrad Birdie is drafted into the army. Just before he gets his hair cut he makes his final appearance on *The Ed Sullivan Show.* Well, a light went on in my head and I remembered something –"

Cora was in full flight now. She gulped at her coffee, took a long drag on her cigarette and brought Skylark into her confidence.

"Can you remember, honey, when I did my Madonna number at the TVNZ Christmas party a few years ago?"

Who could forget it, Skylark thought dismally. Mum was trying the comeback trail and chose to sing "Like a Virgin". Unfortunately, all that her frenetic, excruciating performance showed was that underneath her makeup was an ordinary and desperate woman – and certainly not a virgin – trying to hold on in a world that had grown young.

"I said to Ronnie, 'How about this! Not only is Conrad Birdie in the show but also –'" Cora was winding up to her big idea – "Madonna!"

"But Madonna wasn't around in the 1960s," Skylark said.

"A mere trifle," Cora sniffed. "Since when did you become so pedantic?" Lost in a vision of her own cleverness, Cora burst into song: "I wanted everybody to love me . . ." She forgot the words half way through, saw the look on Skylark's face and hastened to explain. "Luckily, Ronnie has the song on CD, so this time I'll lipsync it."

"That'll help," Skylark said, without meaning it.

"It'll all come together this time," Cora went on. "I even had a fitting for my costume, and one of the girls over at the massage parlour has a blonde wig – you wouldn't believe how many times Korean sailors ask her to put it on – and I'll sing the song, and then I'll turn to Conrad Birdie and give him the sweetest kiss."

Cora closed her eyes and pursed her lips. Skylark winced, embarrassed, and then was cross with herself. Mum was one of the world's courageous souls. She put herself out there, in the spotlight. What you saw was what you got. How many people were that brave?

"So what do you think, honey?" Cora asked.

Skylark knew she could never let her mother down. After all these years, when the audiences had slowly dwindled, she was still there to clap.

"Great, Mum. Just great."

An hour later, Lucas turned up to take Cora down to a dress rehearsal.

"What are you doing here?" Cora laughed. "Where's Ronnie?"

"I told him I'd collect you," Lucas said, which was a more polite version of the words he had used to warn Ronnie off his patch. In his hand he had a small bouquet of plastic roses. "These are for you," he said. They looked suspiciously like the ones Flora Cornish had on the tables of her diner.

"Don't do anything I wouldn't do!" Cora laughed.

Cora accepted the flowers and then, with a rush and a roar she and Lucas were off.

No sooner had they gone than Mitch Mahana turned up.

"Hello, Skylark," Mitch smiled. "Home alone? Is Bella or Hoki around?" He seemed anxious about something.

"I don't know where Bella's gone," Skylark told him, "but last time I saw Hoki she was walking up the cliff path."

"I know where to find her," said Mitch. "Catch you later."

Curious, Skylark watched as Mitch ascended the path. He reached the midway point and paused, looking out to sea. There was something so frightening about his stillness that Skylark turned and followed his gaze.

What was that shadow over the sea?

Then she realised: seabirds, hundreds of them, circling over the offshore islands.

"That does it," Skylark said to herself. "I'm going to get to the bottom of this, and I'm going to do it now –" With that, Skylark took off after Mitch.

When she reached the summit she saw Mitch and Hoki talking earnestly. She also saw something she hadn't noticed before:

A tree. But no ordinary tree. This one was skeletal. Bony, with many branches but no leaves. It looked like two hands, cupped like a bowl, with fingers clutching at the sky. There was something grand about the tree, something profound, and had Skylark been receptive she may have *understood.* But she had other bones to pick.

Hoki and Mitch didn't hear Skylark arriving. They were taking turns to look at the gathering birds through Hoki's binoculars.

Hoki's voice was grave. "Thank you for coming by with your news," she said to Mitch. "You are right to be anxious and to tell me off for not involving you earlier."

"Don't blame yourself," Mitch said. "I should have worked it out myself. I should have realised that the heliacal rising of the planet Venus is only two mornings away. No wonder the seabirds are arriving."

The heliacal rising of the planet Venus?

"Two mornings left to stop what has been prophesied. Skylark is the key. Only she has the power to lock the seabirds out so that the prophecy is not fulfilled."

I'm the key? What prophecy?

"Ae," Mitch nodded. "Don't forget – call on me and my son Francis if you need our help."

"I will."

Skylark felt her temper rising. "I hate being talked about behind my back!" she shouted, striding over to the pair. "What's this prophecy you're talking about?"

Hoki gave a gasp. She turned to Mitch. "Leave me alone with the girl, would you? We have an unfinished conversation."

"Okay, Kui," Mitch said. He looked at Skylark and his eyes twinkled. "Good luck!" he said to Hoki. "You'll need it."

Hoki watched Mitch start his way back down the track. Then she hobbled over to where Skylark was standing. "Follow me, child," she said.

She walked straight up to the strange tree and began to sing to it as she approached. "E te kaumatua, tena koe." There were tears in her eyes as she placed her nose against it in greeting. "This tree was once a giant kauri, the largest in the Great Forest of Tane," she told Skylark. "It was the first tree ever, like unto the Tree of Good and Evil that stood in the Garden of Eden. It isn't familiar to you, Skylark? Nor this place, the twin mountains?"

"Should it be?" Skylark answered. She was still trying to get over the astonishment of an old woman singing to a tree, good grief. Now she was on her guard, suspicious of Hoki's tears, and the way Hoki had of not answering the question to hand and, instead, tacking like a yacht in another direction. "Don't think you can fob me off again," Skylark warned. "What's the tree or the twin mountains got to do with the planet Venus!"

Hoki sighed and wiped away her tears. "Skylark, dear," she began, "not every question can be answered by going straight down the middle. Sometimes you have to take the long way home. This is why Maori like to answer by going in a circle. So humour a little old lady, because what you want to know about is all part of the same loop."

Oh, it was so sneaky, really, how Hoki eased Skylark back into the spiral of storytelling.

"The twin mountains are renowned," she began, "because Maori people regard them as being the closest point between the earth and the moon. In the time of the birds, they marked the very heart of the Great Forest. That eternal icon, the rainbow, arched overhead and, if ever you wanted to find the twin mountains, all you had to do was to look for the brightest rainbow in the sky. Why was it so bright? The celestial colours were made richer by the mist which was the very breath of the trees. Every morning the dew dazzled like emeralds. By afternoon the sun gleamed like greenstone. Came the evening and the Great Forest wore a garland of stars."

Hoki looked at Skylark. Was any of this getting through or was she still off-line? Hoping for the best, Hoki turned to the tree – and a sense of awe and reverence flooded her voice.

"As for the tree, it was immediately acknowledged by all the landbirds as representing the Lord Tane, as being unto the image of Tane himself. Over those years it became their Jerusalem, if you like, venerated as a sacred site. Here, they congregated whenever they had issues to discuss, disputes to settle or matters of grave concern to vote on. It therefore became the venue for meetings of the Runanga a Manu – the parliament of birds."

Hoki pointed at the branches of the tree. "The landbirds realised that their loosely linked confederation of different iwi needed a system of central governance. They appointed Chieftain Tui of the parson-bird clan to be their paramount leader, their prime minister as it were, and the ultimate arbiter of all things to do with landbird political, economic and cultural affairs. Along with Chieftain Tui, the landbirds also established a system of high-ranking ministers: Chieftain Ruru of the morepork clan was appointed because of his wisdom; Chieftain Kahu of the hawk iwi was appointed because of his warrior skills; and Chieftain Titi of the muttonbird clan was appointed because of his diplomatic experience. Below them, in hierarchical order based on whether they had wings or not, were all the chieftains of the other bird iwi. Of course, women were not regarded as having the same mana as men, so those women who led their iwi, like Te Arikinui Kotuku of herons, Te Arikinui Huia of huias, Te Arikinui Korimako of bellbirds and Te Arikinui Karuwai of robins, had branches lower to the ground where the wingless birds were.

"The most important branch," Hoki continued, "was right at the very top of the sacred tree. It was called the paepae, the perch of chiefs. If you wished to speak, you spoke from there in the pecking order determined by your rank. Speak out of turn and you were howled down. Thus, when the seabirds began to mass against the landbirds it was only natural that –"

"That?" Skylark asked.

"Whakarongo koe ki au," Hoki said.

She began the Third Lesson.

"Can you remember, Skylark, how the battle of the birds began? It started when the chieftain of the seashag clan, Karuhiruhi, was able to persuade all the other seabird chieftains to join him in a war to overturn the Great Division, a war against the birds of the land. He told them to assemble their troops on the offshore islands –"

The steady procession of manu moana to the pah of Karuhiruhi did not go unnoticed by the landbirds. The forest tribes lining the coast wondered about the squadrons of seabirds which blackened the sky from dawn to dusk. But it was Kawau, the rivershag, noting the sudden departure of the gulls and skuas from his bordering territories, who was the first to start putting two and two together.

"I must go and speak with Chieftain Tui," Kawau thought. He wheeled away from his lagoon and flew inland toward the twin mountains.

"Tena koe, Kawau," Tui said. He was a handsome chieftain with a feathered cloak of fine mazarine blue clasped at the throat with tufts of white curled feathers. He also had an eye for the ladies and, when Kawau found him at his official duties – on the paepae of the sacred tree – he was plucking the feathers of some very pretty constituents.

"Sir," Kawau began, "I have grave news. The seabirds, led by Karuhiruhi of the seashag clan, are assembling at the offshore islands to attack us. I think they mean war."

"War?" Tui asked.

Nothing fanned a cock's ardour more than sex or the prospect of a fight. Tui had just enjoyed the former, so he was quick to turn his interests the latter.

"What is your evidence? What proof do you bring to me?"

Kawau was reluctant to tell of his own involvement in the story but was unable to avoid the chieftain's probing questions. After all, Tui was the bird whose long beak could suck the deepest honey from the most challenging clematis flower.

"You have been a foolish rivershag, haven't you," Tui said. He pondered Kawau's news. Not for nothing was he regarded as Commander-in-Chief of landbirds. He claimed his wisdom and mana from being a direct descendant of Parauri, one of the brothers of the Lord Tane, and one of the three guardians charged with the welfare and fertility of the Great Forest.

"Your report is serious. Similar intelligence has been coming in from other landbird clans throughout the Great Forest. What was missing from their reports, and what you have now given me, is the missing piece of the puzzle: the motive for the seabird movements. Put together, the movements and the motive – and greed is the only motive that makes sense – indeed add up to war."

"What can we do about it?" Kawau asked.

Tui came to his decision. "We must call an extraordinary meeting of the

Runanga a Manu. Let all assemble on the Longest Night before the Winter Solstice sunrise."

He stood on the perch of chiefs, stretched his throat and with a cry sounding like a trumpet he called:

"Tui! Tui! *Tuia*!"

– 3 –

"Chieftain Tui's calls passed through the length and breadth of the land," Hoki said. "Each dawn it was passed during birdsong:

"'Haramai nga rangatira manu whenua ki te Runanga! Tui, tui, tuia!'

"Throughout the confederation the message was passed from one iwi to the next, from one whanau to another. It was called through the Great Forest. It was called across the straits separating our islands. It was passed from small thrush to high-flying hawk. From kingfisher to wingless weka. From grebe to the mountain citadels of the kaka and the pastures of the moa.

"'Haramai, haramai, haramai.'

"The Book of Birds tells us, Skylark, that it was to the paepae, to this sacred tree here, at the juncture of the twin mountains, that the birds journeyed –"

The chieftains came from the myriad pah, the many nesting places, of Te Tai Tokerau in the north, Te Tai Rawhiti in the east, Te Tai Hauauru in the west and from Te Waipounamu in the south – from the Hauraki, the Waikato, the Arawa, the Mataatua, the Kahungunu. You would have thought that because they had wings – well, most of them – the journeys of the manu whenua would have been speedily accomplished. Not so. Over the years they had developed intricate and highly sophisticated protocols which, by acknowledging ownership by the various landbird species of specific tribal territories, required rituals of encounter at every border before visitors could cross them. Their various fabulous and grand processions as hundreds of travelling parties through the whanau groups of the Great Forest were therefore slowed by the necessities of observing customary protocol. You never moved from one group to the next without paying the appropriate respects to that whanau, their dead, their living, and without due attention to your own whakapapa. Not only that but you also had to partake of kai, always a risky business as it meant you got fatter as you journeyed further. When you realise that the movements were further complicated by happening at various levels – on the ground, within the lower, middle and upper parts of the forest canopy, and in the open sky – you understand why the time taken for assembly in the twin mountains was dangerously overlong.

High above, quartering the land with upswept wings, was Chieftain Kahu of the hawk iwi. Proud and magnificent, protector of the upper skies, he kept lookout on the landbird processions below. "Come on, people," he called to the stragglers. "Make greater haste, kia tere, kia tere." Sometimes he sent his beautiful daughter, Kahurangi, or one of his virile sons with a more peremptory command to move it or lose it.

Eventually, one by one, the landbird chieftains arrived at the twin mountains closest to the moon. Chieftain Kuku of the pigeon iwi was showing the effects of eating too well during his travels; the puku of his white breast bulged over his dark plumage. He saw the sacred tree in front of him and wondered how on earth he was going to get to the top.

For Chieftain Kakariki of the parakeets, however, ascending the branches was a breeze. "Torete! Kaurehe!" he cried as he leapt from one branch to the next, chattering and spreading juicy gossip.

Chieftain Kakapo stayed on the ground, making up for his lack of flight by being his usual aggressive and male chauvinist self. There, he struck poses of superiority and cast angry looks at the women chieftains present – Te Arikinui Huia, Te Arikinui Korimako and Te Arikinui Karuwai.

"The parliament is the place of men," Kakapo muttered. "A hen's place is behind her man."

Always on the prowl, Chieftain Pukeko was making a nuisance of himself, trampling over Chieftain Kiwi, the shy hidden bird of Tane. Seeing this, Chieftain Kokako of the crows flew at him: "Hie! Hie! Haere ki te huhi, haere ki te repo! Go away! Leave him alone! Go back to the swamp where you came from!"

As for Chieftain Kea, he was lording it in his multi-coloured magnificence, strutting his stuff before his many wives.

Chieftain Pitoitoi of the robin whanau wasn't impressed. "That Kea is all blow and no go," he said.

Chieftain Kaka, Chieftain Koreke of the quails and Chieftain Parera of grey ducks all agreed. They noted that Kea had made a throne on his branch.

"Those Te Arawa customs are being taken up by everyone," said Chieftain Piwakawaka of fantails.

Chieftain Stitchbird of the native thrush iwi tittered; and so did Chieftain Popokatea of the whitehead whanau and Chieftain Brightbird of the silver-eye iwi.

It was an impressive sight to see the chieftains of the manu whenua hopping and flying among the branches of the sacred tree and taking their places. It was to be expected that there should be squabbles as some of the birds pretended to forget their lower status and tried to ascend to somebody else's branch; the upstarts were sent packing down to lower branches where they belonged. The roll call revealed that Chieftain Tui's command to come had indeed been heeded by all landbird chieftains. There was shy Chieftain Pakura of the swamp-hens, Chieftain Matuku of the bitterns, Chieftain Koekoea of the long-tailed cuckoos, Chieftain Pipiwharauroa of the shining-cuckoos, and Chieftain Kuaka of godwits. Chieftain Ruru of moreporks and Chieftain Whekau of laughing-owls waited for complete darkness before taking their places.

Chieftain Pekapeka of bats also waited until night fell, hanging from his own special upside-down branch. His participation was by special agreement of the birds, who had never been sure of his avian status but were persuaded by the fact that he flew.

Last to arrive at the Runanga a Manu, because they had come furthest, were Chieftain Titi of the southern muttonbirds and the graceful Te Arikinui Kotuku of the white heron colony at Okarito. They brought apologies from Chieftain Moa, which was a relief to all because he took up so much room when he sat down.

Kotuku was always one to make an entrance, gliding in like a glistening dream, her long white feathers raking the moon. She took her branch beside the other women chieftains.

"We're so glad you're here," Te Arikinui Korimako said. "Kakapo is being such a teke."

Kotuku fluted a silvery voice. "Not to worry, dear," she said. "Me and Huia can fix him any day. What do you say, Huia?"

The gorgeous Te Arikinui Huia sighed a delicious sigh. She preened her white-tipped plumes and adjusted her fabulous white-feathered choker. "My dears, he lives on the *ground*," she said throatily.

The assembly was complete. Within the amphitheatre of the twin mountains, sitting in the most ancient tree of the Great Forest of Tane, the extraordinary meeting waited to come to order. Whistling, trilling, cooing and warbling, the chieftains settled down.

Chieftain Kahu reported to Chieftain Tui. "All present and correct, sir."

Tui coughed, preparing to speak. He flew to the perch of chiefs, folded his wings and hopped, strutted, tap-danced and two-stepped his way along the branch.

"Show-off," whispered Te Arikinui Karuwai, who had been one of Tui's many conquests.

A glow came up behind the twin mountains, illuminating the sacred tree with unearthly beauty. The moon arose, full, belling out into the night. A great sigh of wonder came from the throats of the landbirds as they watched it ascend. Higher and higher it rose, dimming the stars with its awesome radiance. Tui lifted his voice:

"Whakarongo ake au ki te tangi a te manu nei a te ma tui, tui, tuituia!"

The Runanga a Manu, the Parliament of Birds, was in session.

– 4 –

"E nga rangatira," Tui began, "tena koutou, tena koutou, tena koutou katoa." He adjusted his mazarine blue cloak. "As we all know it was the great Lord Tane who with other Lords pushed up the Sky Father. In the space between he created his Great Forest as the home for us, the birds, his children. As our guardian he appointed the Lord Punaweko."

"Ka tika, ka tika," Chieftain Kuku interjected. The assembly murmured in agreement.

"The Lord Tane also set aside the coast and the seas of our whanaunga, the seabirds, under the guardianship of the Lord Hurumanu. This setting apart of manu whenua and manu moana has been enshrined in Divine Law and, in our history, as the Great Division."

"That is true, that is true," Chieftain Kokako assented.

"Now," Tui continued, "the alarm has been raised about the seabird troops that are gathering at the island fortress of Karuhiruhi, Lord of seashags. The troops have been training under the generalship of Karoro, chieftain of black-backed gulls. Special frontline squads under the command of Chieftain Toroa, Chieftain Taranui and Chieftain Parara have also been observed in specialist military activities."

The landbird chieftains began to murmur, shifting uneasily and hopping along their branches.

"How are we to respond to this challenge?" Tui asked. "This is the question you must debate. This is why I have called you all to this extraordinary meeting of the Runanga."

Tui flew back to his branch.

For a moment there was silence.

Then, rather prematurely, Kawau the rivershag flew from his low branch up to the perch of chiefs. There was an instant ruffling of feathers as the other birds expressed their displeasure at Kawau daring to fly past others of greater mana and take the perch before they did. Not even his showy display of strutting footwork and beakwork pacified them.

"E nga rangatira," Kawau began. His tone was pompous as he endeavoured to ingratiate himself. "It was I who brought the word to Chieftain Tui, and it was on my intelligence that he decided to call the Runanga. I –"

"Typical, typical," Te Arikinui Kotuku called out. "It is only the rivershag that cries out its own name. Ko au! Ko au! Ko au!"

The other chieftains laughed good-humouredly. But Kawau extended his neck in an arrogant gesture, dismissive of Kotuku. "It is easy for Kotuku to challenge me. After all, she has only one small inlet at Okarito to defend, an insignificant stretch of tepid water that nobody would want, whereas I have a lagoon famed for its food supplies."

Kotuku veiled her yellow eyes. "Silly shag, to think you can cross me and get away with it." The other women shivered. Kotuku was not one to be enemies with.

"I believe the seabirds plan to take my lagoon," Kawau continued. "It was there that Karuhiruhi tasted my sweet river eels, famed for their deliciousness and for their aphrodisiacal powers. Many of you have bickered over them. Now, the seabirds want to take possession of them. No doubt exists in my mind that the seabirds are therefore planning an all out war. I ask that our response be to deploy a strong landbird force to defend my lagoon."

"Self-interest as usual," Te Arikinui Huia murmured.

The landbirds swayed, weighing Kawau's words.

With a whirr of wings, Chieftain Titi of the southern muttonbird clan took the perch. A kapa haka expert, Titi was small in stature, but was well-practised in crowd control, twirling and gesticulating, doing the pukana, and winning the admiration of all. The landbirds settled down again.

"E nga rangatira," Titi said, "the issue is not whether we are at war but whether there will be a war. Certainly, the mass movements of seabirds to Karuhiruhi's island fortress seem to imply this possibility. However no declaration of war has yet been delivered to us."

"Can I believe my ears?" Te Arikinui Korimako asked. "Does Titi really expect Karuhiruhi to be so honourable as to declare his intentions? No way. Hey, Titi, whose side are you on?"

The question was reasonable enough. Titi, after all, was a member of the shearwater family, a seabird clan. His iwi had been included in the landbird confederacy by special dispensation: their burrowing sites often stretched inland from the beaches. It was to be expected that he, with the blood of seabirds in his veins, would incline to diplomacy and conciliation.

Titi responded by playing the injured party. "My loyalties may be split," he conceded, "but that does not undercut my argument that until there really is war we cannot say we are at war. For instance, if the seabirds saw us gathering, as we have done tonight, might they not think the same of us as we are thinking about them?"

"Ka tika," some of the landbirds nodded. "That is true."

Others, like Chieftain Kahu of the hawk iwi, however, were having trouble with Titi's line of reasoning.

"Might I say something?" Kahu tried to intervene. "Of all landbirds I am the one who has the greatest overview. I also know more than anybody the psychology of the seabirds. It is my clan's responsibility to maintain the borders and, from our high reconnaissance of the seabirds, my opinion is that they are certainly deploying for some major offensive. Over the past few days my iwi and I have had more sorties with intruding seabirds than ever before. I know Karuhiruhi. He is my implacable opponent. Words are wasted on him. What we need to do is to spring into action. If we don't prepare for war now, we will be overrun without any chance at offering resistance."

The chieftains began an anxious chattering. Kahu's words could always be trusted. But, the very idea of war was difficult to contemplate. There was, after all, no precedent.

Titi seized on the landbirds' indecision. "I agree with Kahu that the seabirds probably do mean to wage war. However, we must be prudent. To this end, I am prepared to lead a mission to the seabirds and, through my cousins, the shearwaters, seek an understanding of their intentions. If they truly are planning a war, let me have your approval to resolve any tensions through diplomatic channels."

Titi's voice was persuasive and as sweet as his own delicious flesh. His words held the landbirds spellbound. He was one of their top ministers. His words came with the weight of the mana that his office held. He offered them a way out of a military confrontation. Having lived with security of tenure for so long, they had grown complacent. They wanted the way of things to remain but preferred, if at all possible, to expend only minimal effort to maintain it. They were relieved to hear such reason being uttered by one as benevolent as Titi.

Even better, he had offered to do the work.

"Can you credit these men?" Te Arikinui Karuwai whistled.

"Kahu tried his best," Huia nodded, "but it is not his fault. His fellow chieftains are bound to take the easy option if they are offered it."

Kotuku became anxious. She was certain she could smell a rat. From the corner of her eye she saw Chieftain Kaka preparing to speak. What was that? Did he give a surreptitious wink in Titi's direction? Her eyes narrowed. "Ladies, it's a jack-up," she said.

With a harsh cry, Kaka flew up to the perch of chiefs. As if being swept up by the passion of the hui, the brown-cloaked chieftain attacked the branch with his beak. "This is what we would do to the seabirds if they dared to war with us," Kaka screamed.

"He kaka wahanui!" Chieftain Kuku called out with approval.

"He kaka kai uta, he mangaa kai te moana!" cried Chieftain Kokako, drawing a comparison between the kaka on land with the barracouta at sea.

With the light of theatrical anger in his eyes, Kaka struck a warrior position.

"Why do we even bother to worry about the seabirds when we know that we are better and stronger than them? Why do we worry ourselves over what they are doing when our own superiority is without doubt?"

"Kaka sure knows how to play to the gallery," Huia said. "Just listen to them."

The Runanga a Manu was roaring with approval and smug satisfaction. What a brilliant fellow Kaka was to remind them of their superior status.

Kaka modulated his voice, spreading a soothing mood of self-congratulation. "Let us not forget that we are an intelligent and humane species. We have the capacity to be forgiving, to be magnanimous, to be understanding. Is this not the trait which most sets us apart from the seabirds?"

"Ka tika, ka tika!" the chieftains called.

"Therefore," Kaka continued, "I support what my colleague Titi has suggested. Let us talk to the seabirds. Let us negotiate if we have to." He paused and lifted his left birdwing like a pointed finger. "And in our magnanimity and generosity, let us offer the seabirds – a treaty."

There was an inward gasp. A silence. A murmur as the suggestion passed from beak to beak. A treaty? A treaty? Yes, a treaty!

Kaka pushed his recommendation home before those pesky women could voice any objection. "In my humble opinion, we should not, unless absolutely necessary, plunge our people into a war which could devastate our lands. Does it really need to come to a fight? No. A treaty would be infinitely preferable."

Titi looked at Chieftain Tui. "I would like to propose, my Lord," he said, "that we take a vote on this matter."

Te Arikinui Korimako and Huia, alarmed, turned to Kotuku. "Do something, Kotuku," they said. "You hold rank over us."

"Yes! Yes! Let us vote!" came the cries from all the branches of the sacred tree. Chieftain Kahu tried a last-ditch effort. "No, my Lords, I cannot stand by and let you do this. I know Karuhiruhi, I know his ultimate ambition, I –"

Chieftain Tui cut across Kahu's words. "A vote has been called," he said, "and I am obliged to put it before our parliament. We will abide by the consensus."

"But –" Kahu tried again.

Tui put the vote. "All those in favour say ae."

"Ae! Ae! Ae!"

Kotuku stood up. "Oh, bother," she said, preening herself and tossing her head, "why am I always the one to have to do this!"

"All those against say no –"

"Wish me luck, ladies," Kotuku said. She opened her wings, glided like a dream up to the perch of chiefs, and made a perfect two-point landing on the branch.

"No," she said.

Chieftain Kaka was still sitting on the perch. Before he could stop her, Kotuku accidentally on purpose swept him off it with one of her gorgeous white wings and began her address.

"Ka tangi te titi! Ka tangi te kaka! Ka tangi hoki ahau –"

Immediately, there was an uproar from the male chieftains.

"Your neck should be wrung," Chieftain Kakapo screamed, jumping up and down on the ground. "It is only the cock who crows."

Kotuku looked down at him with scorn. "Get some class, Kakapo," she said. "Whiti koreke ka kitea koe. Find yourself some wings and transform yourself into a real bird."

But Chieftain Kakapo had support from Kawau. "You have no right to the paepae!" he cried. "Leave it immediately."

Kotuku regurgitated a seed and spat it at Kawau with derision. "You, of all people tell me to mind my place? It is you who caused the seabirds' hunger."

Yes," Te Arikinui Huia asked. "How did Karuhiruhi know about the lagoon?"

"I-I-I –"

"Ko au! Ko au! Ko au!" Te Arikinui Korimako mimicked.

"Because you showed him, didn't you?" Kotuku intervened. "You couldn't stop yourself, could you? You had to show you were better than he was, that yours was bigger than his and, because you did –"

Kotuku realised that this was the moment to drive home her point. She spread her wings, executed some movements of intimidation, lifted her beautiful throat and let everyone hear her warrior woman karanga.

Kra-*aak*. Kra-*aak*.

Even Ruru shuddered and closed his hooded eyes.

Kotuku began her korero of warning. "Listen! All of you! Ka maro te kaki o te karuhiruhi! The seashag's neck is already stretched out." The assembly gasped at her words. They knew very well their import.

"That's telling them," Huia muttered to herself as she saw the male chieftains lose colour.

"It is too late to negotiate," Kotuku continued. "It is ridiculous for Titi and Kaka to promote the idea of a treaty. A treaty is tantamount to giving in. It is a position of weakness, not a position of strength. It indicates that we are prepared to accommodate. Both Titi and Kaka have forgotten that things of value must be fought for or defended, not negotiated. Stop sitting on your mana. Have you all grown too smug and fat for war?"

Kotuku showed her scorn for the idea by attacking the perch with her beak and tearing strips off it.

Titi made a plea to Chieftain Tui to intervene. "Point of order, my lord, point of order –"

Like all women, Kotuku carried on regardless. "And why is the idea of a treaty stupid?" she asked, strutting her stuff. "Because there is already a treaty! Don't you remember? The Lord Tane made it when he gave us the land and his Great Forest. We are the Lord Tane's ordained children. The seabirds intend to break this contract. Are you all blind as a bat?"

There was an outraged splutter from the branch where Chieftain Pekapeka was hanging upside down.

"No offence intended," Kotuku apologised. "But don't any of you trust the evidence of your eyes? You have all seen the seabird squadrons leaving their nesting places and assembling at the offshore islands. What else are they doing if they are not plotting war?"

The sound level of the gathered birds increased, evidencing their nervousness at Kotuku's words. When the chieftains were like this, not knowing what to say or what to do next, their natural inclination was to pass the buck to their leader. Hadn't he been appointed to sort out such problems as this?

Tui found himself in the hot seat.

"What do you say, Prime Minister?" Kahu asked.

"I must admit," Tui began, "on second thoughts, with the benefit of hindsight, bearing in mind all the angles, having the best interests of all uppermost, given the circumstances –"

"Yes? Yes?"

Tui coughed, having run out of his usual stonewalling phrases. But he was not a supreme politician for nothing. "Kotuku has reminded me of two crucial points."

"What points are those?" The male chieftains hung on Tui's words.

"The first has to do with the magnitude of the seabird threat. Not only do we have to worry about Karuhiruhi. We also have to consider Karoro, Toroa, Taranui and Parara. Collectively, they are a formidable foe. Why would they all band together if they were not thinking on the big scale? And then there is the second point –"

Tui knew how to keep the chieftains in suspense. He paced his branch. Back and forth. Back and forth. "Kotuku is correct," he concluded. "It is too late for a treaty."

Everybody gasped. Tui spoke as the Supreme Commander. His sanction of Kotuku meant that he agreed with her assessment.

Kaka and Titi tried to object, but Tui waved them to be silent.

"Why is Kotuku correct?" Tui asked. "I will tell you why. She quoted a proverb about the outstretched neck of the seashag. But she quoted only the first part of it. The second part warns us that once his neck is stretched out, he cannot be stopped. He is already primed for battle and –"

"Ka tika," the chieftains murmured. "Yes –"

"No fish has any hope when the seashag has seized it. Nor bird."

At that, the noise of the landbirds grew into a loud hubbub. The divine Te Arikinui Kotuku launched herself into the air and returned to the women's branch of the sacred tree. She affected a simple, glorious, bow.

"Why didn't you stay up there!" Huia scolded.

"And make the decision?" Kotuku asked, fluttering her eyelids and preening her long filamentous plumes. "Oh no, let one of the men do that!"

Tui had already reclaimed the perch of chiefs. "The seabirds are hungry," he warbled. "The seabirds are voracious. The seabirds are power hungry. They have already committed the Ultimate Heresy. They have already broken the treaty –"

Birds were hopping up and down and scratching marks into the branches in their frenzy.

"If we don't stop them now they will overturn the Great Division. Today Aotearoa, tomorrow the rest of the world. Do you want this to happen?"

"No!" the landbirds screamed.

"Then is it agreed? Is it to be war?" Tui asked. "Kei te tautoko?"

"Yes! Yes! Yes!"

– 5 –

"So there was a war?" Skylark asked.

She was sitting with Hoki beneath the sacred tree, looking across the Manu Valley to the sea.

"Yes," Hoki nodded, "and the seabirds were the aggressors. They should have remembered the dictum 'Ko Tane mata nui', Tane sees everything, but they were so arrogant. They flew even in Tane's face when they decided to overturn his Great Division. They thought they could get away with it. More seriously they had caught the landbirds hopping. They were way ahead in terms of preparations for war –"

It was Te Arikinui Kotuku who realised that the odds were favouring the seabirds.

"Aue," Kotuku said to Tui, "what a big job you have now. How, my Lord, can you possibly bring our troops up to speed? The only iwi that is battle ready is Kahu's. It is hopeless –"

Kotuku let out a theatrical sigh but, under cover of her gorgeous plumes, winked at her sister leaders. They knew very well what she was doing: appealing to Tui's vanity by implying, in ever such an indirect way, that his chieftains just weren't up to the job.

"Don't worry, Kotuku," Tui answered, puffing out his breast feathers in a show of manliness. "I will order Kahu to begin compulsory military training, and to put our young warriors through a strict physical fitness regimen. Look at them! They've all grown so weak and plump from living the good life for so long. A war will do them good."

"He should talk!" Huia said to Te Arikinui Korimako. "Has he looked in the river lately? Even his puku drags along the ground when he walks. It's no wonder that he has trouble getting it up – I mean, getting his weight up into the sky –"

"Sly one," Te Arikinui Karuwai. "Sly one."

"Be reasonable," Chieftain Kaka interjected. "When was the last time any of us led a raiding party on an enemy? We've lived peacefully all these years and we've lost our skills."

"That may be true, but the seabirds won't be as reasonable as us," Kotuku said. "As far as I'm concerned, a long peace in our landbird history is not an acceptable excuse."

She turned to Tui, flirting with him again.

"Kotuku is right," Tui intoned. He lifted his voice to the assembled birds. "Let all landbird chieftains of all bird iwi and clans assign taiaha tutors to teach the ancient arts of warfare! All young men who have achieved mature feathers are to be called up. It is time for them to sharpen their beaks and claws! Time to get fit, start some serious wing ups, weight training, claw boxing, route flights and battle drills! Timata! Begin!"

Over the following week even Te Arikinui Kotuku was impressed at how quickly the chieftains achieved a level of battle readiness. But did she ever let up? She sidled up to Tui again, and honeyed words dripped from her beak. "Your leadership is of the highest quality," she said, stroking his feathers. "You have managed to get our warriors to an acceptable military standard. But, e rangatira, you need a battle plan to go with it."

"Who are you to tell us what we should be doing?" Chieftain Kawau interjected. "Let the men do what men do and let women do what women do."

"Don't be so complacent, you teke," Te Arikinui Korimako said. "Are you so ready that you are prepared to be in the front rank? After all, it will be your lagoon over which the war will be fought."

"I-I-I –" Kawau quailed.

"What's your battle plan, Tui?" Te Arikinui Kotuku repeated. "What sophisticated military techniques and stratagems are you going to deploy?"

Tui saw her point. He turned to his other chieftains, Titi and Kaka in particular, and gave them a withering look. "Hoi! Do you fellas think we can just turn up at the battlefield and expect our superiority to win the day? And what is that superiority anyhow? If any of you think that the seabirds will recognise our divinity, our mana and our chiefly status and retreat, think again. They won't, and we all know it." Tui puffed out his lacy collar and the double tuft of curled white feathers at his throat. "Kotuku is right," he said. "We need a plan."

There was a rustle in the trees and Chieftain Ruru came flying into the discussion. You think his going to sleep during the day was a natural inclination? Get a grip. It was all because of boredom. Ruru relished the idea of a battle. "Did somebody mention my name?" he asked.

"So it was," Hoki said, "that guided by Te Arikinui Kotuku's cool and measured hints the landbirds were able to set up their defensive system – and they had a battle plan to go with it."

Worked out by Ruru, the plan called for the strongest landbirds to lead a defensive war party. Chieftain Kahu, of course, was Chieftain Tui's left hand man and Second in Command. Among the other leaders were Chieftain Kuku of the pigeon clan, Chieftain Kaka of the parrots and Chieftain Kokako of the crows. Chieftain Pitoitoi was assigned to forward sentry duty. Straws were drawn for the great honour of sending out the three challengers in the first battle against the seabirds. The honours went to Chieftain Koekoea of long-tailed cuckoos, Chieftain Piwakawaka of fantails and, joy of joys, Kahu himself.

"A strong team," Tui approved. "Solid. Ace."

With increasing confidence, the landbirds practised their drills. All the while, far off, they could see the seabird ranks circling above the offshore islands and hear the savage chants and haka coming across the sea.

One afternoon, the chanting of the seabirds stopped.

An uneasy silence fell across the Great Forest.

"Well, boys," Tui said. "I think the time's come, ready or not. We should expect a dawn attack. Let everyone be in their positions. Is everybody clear on the battle plan? The war party will be at the forefront of the defence against the seabird army. They will engage the seabirds and then –"

At that moment, Hoki's lesson was interrupted by a flash of sunlight. She shaded her eyes and looked down from the clifftop to Manu Valley below. A car was coming up the valley road. Cora, returning home after her rehearsal.

"And then?" Skylark asked. She didn't want Hoki to stop telling the story of the war. But the mood was broken.

"We'd better get back home," Hoki answered. "Your mother will worry about where you are. We'll resume the story later. And by the way –"

"Yes?"

Hoki looked at the sacred tree. Rebellious, Skylark followed her gaze – and took a step back. For the first time she felt the mana and power of the tree. She saw it with new eyes, glowing, utterly commanding, and she felt she should kneel before it.

"You should never have followed me up here," Hoki said. "Only a few people know of the tree's existence. We who have guarded it all these years have a commitment to defend it unto the death. On no account must you come up here without my and Bella's express permission."

"You still haven't told me about the heliacal rising of the planet Venus," Skylark called as Hoki started her walk back down the track. Did Hoki really think she would let her get away so easily? No way.

Hoki stopped. "I was afraid you would ask me that," she said. "It's a special conjunction of the rising of the sun with the appearance of the planet Venus. Only at such conjunctions can extraordinary events beyond human understanding occur. All ancient cultures who watch the skies for new stars, comets and any astronomical disturbances to time and space know this."

"When is it supposed to happen?" Skylark asked.

"Actually, Skylark, in two days' time."

Skylark became very cross. "Well don't look at me," she said. "I'm just here with my mother on holiday."

That night, Skylark dreamt of the tree. It looked like the claw of a bird. When she looked again, the tree turned into Hoki's withered left foot. Then the tree caught fire, and Hoki's claw curled into itself, grabbing at the sky.

[CHAPTER FIVE]

– 1 –

With a start, Skylark awoke to a red sky.

The manu whenua were rising to the penultimate dawn. Their song was a brilliant, shining cantilena, soaring across Manu Valley. This morning, however, the song was sharp, uneasy, shrill, like stones being scraped together.

Skylark's memory immediately turned to Hoki's words. One day to go to the heliacal rising of Venus. She flung the blankets off her bed and stepped to the window. "Read my lips," she shouted to nobody in particular. "Not my problem, okay?"

"Oh why did I ever agree to go back to show business?" Cora asked.

The landbirds weren't the only ones feeling fractious that morning. So was Cora, having second thoughts about *Bye Bye Birdie* opening that very evening. She sat on a lounger in the sun drinking cup after cup of coffee, trying to learn her lines. She'd die of lung cancer or drowning one way or another.

"I'm never going to be ready in time. Really, Skylark honey, it's all your fault. You should have stopped me from saying yes."

"Can't you just relax and enjoy the view?" Skylark said between gritted teeth. "Can't you forget the show for a moment?" Skylark had decided that today she was going to be just a tourist.

But somebody had snapped Cora's elastic. She reached for her sunglasses, though even they could not diminish the glare from her eyes, and had a hissy fit. "If I wanted to enjoy the view I'd watch television," she answered. "At least I'd have a remote and a choice of channels. What have I got here? Just one view over a forest to a sea. And it's not even framed."

"What about all this fresh air –"

"Honey, you can buy fresh air in a can from the supermarket. 'Country Glade', 'Meadow Fresh' or 'Spring Flowers'. It might be full of fluorocarbons but at least it doesn't come mixed up with manure smells and bird dung."

Skylark picked up one of her mother's magazines and tried to bury her nose in it. "Oh no you don't, Skylark," Cora said, taking the magazine. "I'm not going to let a perfectly good tantrum go to waste. I need an audience and you're it!"

In fact, if Cora had bothered to look around her, she would have noticed that her outburst had attracted a bevy of curious multi-coloured parrots. They sat on the terrace, watching Cora carefully, and then began to imitate everything she did. When she paced to the left, they paced to the left. When she muttered, they muttered.

Kita-kita-kita. Nag nag nag. Boring boring boring. Yeah yeah yeah.

Cora was deeply offended. "I may have had one or two bad notices," she spluttered, "and some people might have switched channels to watch the other weather girl, but I have never been upstaged by birds of any colour or persuasion whatsoever. Go away, you awful things, go away."

Instead, one of the parrots flew at Cora as if she was the interloper. "Save me!" Cora wailed, as she fended the parrot away. "And don't you dare laugh, Skylark, don't you dare –"

It was too late. Skylark began to snort – huge trumpeting sounds of hilarity.

"Oh no more, Skylark honey," Cora said, seeing the funny side at last, "otherwise I'll wet my knickers."

That only set Skylark off on another round of laughter, and she collapsed into her mother's arms. Surprised, momentarily, by how big Skylark was, Cora's first reaction was to push her off. Then something was triggered in her memory – and she pulled her daughter closer to her instead.

"You've always been there for me, haven't you Skylark?" Cora began. "You save me from parrots, from trouble, from all the men who come into my life. Who's there to pick me up when they leave? You." Skylark tried to move away but Cora only tightened her embrace. "You're the only good thing to have come out of my marriage to Brad. How could I ever have fallen for him?"

"He's been a good dad," Skylark said, "and you've been a good mum. The best mother in the world."

"Have I really been that good?" Cora asked. She took off her sunglasses. "I mean, look at you –"

"No, Mum," Skylark answered. "Let's not go there." She hated Cora's self-pitying moods.

Cora was undeterred. "The way you are is all my fault. You should have been pretty. You should have been skinny. Instead you had to look after me. When your father left me, you had to become the head of the household. All that responsibility, Skylark honey."

"I'll say," Skylark answered, trying to change the focus. "How many of your boyfriends did I have to throw out of the house. Who was it after Dad?"

Skylark's strategy worked. "Don't get me started," Cora said. "Rick?"

"That's the one. Rick, Rick, thick as a brick. George was next, wasn't he? I quite liked him. He was replaced by Jock."

"He doesn't count," Cora sniffed. "Jock by name but certainly not by nature. I came home one night and found him in one of my frocks."

"Jock, Jock, the one in the frock," Skylark chanted. "One thing's for sure, you could certainly pick 'em. Then there was Harry –"

"Don't remind me," Cora shuddered.

"He was the one who started your little *problemo,*" Skylark said.

"What was he thinking of, giving me some stuff before I went on to do the weather!" Cora growled. "No wonder I got fired. If you hadn't stood up for me, I'd have been on my way to prison for possession of a class-A drug."

Skylark had rung darling Daddy in Canada and asked him for enough money to employ the best lawyer in town. Realising that having an ex in prison was not a good look for an upwardly mobile television executive, Brad instructed the lawyer to arrange a hearing for Cora. There, Skylark sought guardianship of her mother. The judge was another of those men who could never resist Cora's tears, and when she intervened with an impassioned "Please, sir, I'll be good", his heart melted. Surely a weather girl, the darling of the nation, should have a second start at coming up sunshine. So Cora was given in care to Skylark, who guaranteed that her mother would check into a rehab centre. The trouble was, that was where Mum met a certain slimeball called Zac.

"Forget him, Mum," Skylark said. "He's so low on the evolutionary scale, his only hope would be if somebody put a microchip in him so he can gain artificial intelligence."

Cora bit her lip, chewing at her lipstick. Tears were threatening. "God, I've made such a mess of my life," she said. "I've made a mess of your life too, of everybody's lives."

"I like trench warfare," Skylark said, trying to console Cora. "Look on the bright side. You beat your drug dependency. That gives you a gold star."

Cora nodded, but then her eyes widened with something that looked like sheer terror. Her face stilled, became calm with a chilling acceptance. "But I've still got another dependency," she said. "I'm not as strong as you, I've always needed a man in my life. I get frightened of being alone."

– 2 –

Midday came along and, with it, Ronnie to take Cora to the final rehearsal for *Bye Bye Birdie*. He too was feeling harassed. The sound system was playing up, and the lighting had been sabotaged by Lottie, the music teacher, who had wanted *The Sound of Music* instead. Not only that, but the boof-headed boy playing Conrad Birdie had come down with laryngitis.

"How are we going to manage?" Ronnie asked Cora. "Perhaps we should cancel tonight's show."

Did Cora take up the offer? Get real. Better to give a bad performance than no performance at all.

"One never cancels," she said, striking a pose. "The show must go on." Quickly, before Ronnie had a chance to think again, she turned to Skylark. "Now don't forget, honey, it's too far for me to come back after the dress rehearsal, so I'll stay down at Tuapa and have a bite to eat at Flora's. There's only a couple of hours between the rehearsal and the performance anyhow. I've arranged with Bella and Hoki for you to have dinner with them and for them to bring you down to the show. Please, Skylark, wear something attractive. And do your hair and put some lipstick on. If for nobody else, do it for me. All right? See you later, then!"

Cora hastened Ronnie to the car, and they drove off. "Peace in the valley at last," Skylark sighed.

Skylark made the most of the time alone to stay tucked up reading in a chair by the window. The only irritating matter was that she was constantly aware of Bella and Hoki as they took turns to stand sentry at the top of the cliff. They were looking across the sea.

At three o'clock Hoki completed her duty. Skylark watched her as she carefully descended the cliff path, using her crutches to manoeuvre herself past the waterfall and then down to the homestead. A sense of something heroic stirred Skylark's sympathies. Soon after, Bella called it quits for the day.

"Oh what's the use," Skylark said to herself.

Muttering crossly, she got up from her chair and stomped over to the homestead to see Hoki. How could she chill out with all this stuff swirling around about wars between birds and premonitions of a doomsday that would come with the next dawn. At the doorway she bumped into Bella coming out with that look on her face. She gave a brief nod to Skylark and yelled back over her shoulder.

"I am not getting all gladwrapped in that old dress!"

Uh-oh, two more people having a bad day, Skylark thought. I may as well throw a triple.

She walked into the room. Hoki looked up.

"So you're next, are you?" Hoki asked. She had a needle and thread in her hand, and was stabbing tiny stars onto a black dress.

"Don't take your anger out on me," Skylark said.

"Why shouldn't I? Isn't anything getting through to you? About the rising of Venus tomorrow morning? The battle of the birds that led to the prophecy?" Hoki's fingers were simply flying over the dress. One false move and she could prick herself. "You know, it happened not far from here. Down there, just below Manu Valley, that's where Kawau's river lagoon was."

Hoki pointed to a place halfway between valley and sea.

She began to give Skylark the Final Lesson.

"On the morning the battle began," Hoki said, "all the seabirds were gathered around the three offshore islands. There were so many of them that they smothered the sea completely like a white carpet. All eyes were looking toward Karuhiruhi's fortress. They were waiting for the dawn to tip the islands with the red colour of blood —"

Remarkable, really, how quickly the sun came up on that morning. The Great Book of Birds says that the fireball erupted with a hiss from the sea, ascended quickly, its light cutting quickly across the black night water. The surface of the sea became a mirror. The dawn travelled fast, and when it glowed upon the seabirds, that unholy Sea of White Feathers, it wanted to turn back, to retreat from such unnatural order. But it was too late. Already the sun's forward edge had drenched the offshore islands with crimson.

Kee-law, *kee*-law. Kaa. *Kaa. The Day of Days has come.*

The sun flared, burning all colour away, and it was day. There was no turning back. Karuhiruhi stood on the ramparts of the island fortress. Beside him was Areta, her baby son in her wings. On either side of the royal pair were the co-conspirators Karoro, Toroa, Taranui and Parara. The seabird army opened their beaks and began to hiss, creating a whirlwind of menace.

Karuhiruhi stepped forward. "Today, my fellow birds of the sea, is our day of liberation." The hissing grew louder. "Today we overturn the Great Division. If the Lord Tane disapproves, then let me be the first to be struck down. Oh, Lord Tane, do your will."

Karuhiruhi offered his breast to the heavens. But where was the bolt of lightning? Where was the death-dealing blow? There was none. None! The hissing became ecstatic, triumphant, ascending into the Heavens. "The Lord Tane has spoken," Karuhiruhi cried. "Let the war begin."

As one the seabird army lifted from the sea. They beat the air, keeping formation, and watched as Karuhiruhi and Karoro took positions at the spearhead of the seashag squadron.

"Forward – *fly*!"

"Meantime," Hoki said, "Chieftain Kahu of hawks was on forward surveillance. He sent his daughter, the beautiful Kahurangi, back with the message that the seabirds were on the wing.

"'Kia hiwa ra, kia hiwa ra!' Kahurangi shrilled. 'Be alert! Be watchful! Be alert on this terrace! Be alert on that terrace!'

"Duly forewarned, the manu whenua were in position. Chieftain Pitoitoi of robins was the first to see the black and grey cloud arising from the sea. He had never seen such a phantom menace and, for a moment, his voice almost deserted him. His throat seized up, so he took a quick sip of nectar, gargled and that did the trick. 'Pitoi toi toi!' he called. 'They're coming!' Hearing his call, Chieftain Koekoea of the long-tailed cuckoos, limbered up for action. How proud he was that he had drawn the straw to be the first challenger. How lucky, too, that he happened to be in Aotearoa and not wintering over in the Marquesas. Koekoea loved a good fight. Psyched up for action, he took to the air –"

Chieftain Tui saw and heard the manu whenua cheer as Koekoea streaked upward. He saw the light flash on Koekoea's long reddish brown tail feathers and watched with approval as he climbed swiftly to a height that would give him advantage. There, Koekoea took an aggressive position, flying backwards and forwards before the approaching seabirds.

Karuhiruhi sighed with contempt. He turned to Toroa, the albatross chieftain. "Despatch that bothersome bird," he said.

Toroa nodded his head and, propelled by his powerful wings, soared up to engage Koekoea.

At the enemy's approach, Koekoea felt battle excitement surging through his loins. He knew it was imperative for morale that the landbirds draw the first blood. Koekoea dived, planing down from the sky, calling his wild, long, drawn-out cry: "Shweesht *kik-kik-kik-kik*! Come no further! *Kik-kik-kik-kik*!"

For a moment Toroa hesitated. He recalled the times in the past when he and Koekoea had encountered each other during the long-tailed cuckoo's migratory flights between New Guinea and New Zealand. He had forgotten how evil-looking Koekoea, a carnivore and predator, was.

Toroa's hesitation was his undoing. He stalled and, stationary, became an ideal target.

"Cross the border between land and sea," Koekoea said, "and you do so at your own peril." He moved his head in a sinuous reptilian manner, drilling Toroa with his baleful yellow eyes. Then he struck. With a cry, Toroa reeled back, air spilling from his wings.

"I-ah-ha-haa!" Koekoea screeched in triumph. He had done it. He had drawn the first blood. High in the sky he heard Kahu, chieftain of hawks, calling, "Well done, you of the long-tail tribe which braves the sky."

Toroa returned to the seabird war party. Karuhiruhi was furious with him and slashed the albatross's face with his beak, drawing blood.

"But you said our attack would be a surprise," Toroa said. "You never said that the landbirds would put up any defence."

Karuhiruhi whistled scornfully. "You call one long-tailed cuckoo a defence?" Before he could pour more scorn on Toroa's pathetic display, Karoro plucked at his left wing: "Sire, the second challenger comes."

Karuhiruhi looked to the front and almost fell out of the air with laughter. Spinning and twittering through the sky came Chieftain Piwakawaka of the fantail clan.

"Do my eyes deceive me?" Karuhiruhi asked. "Is that really a bird in front of me?"

Now it must be admitted that a fantail – at best, the size of a human hand from the wrist to outstretched fingertips – does not convince as a worthwhile opponent. But Piwakawaka had drawn the second straw and was determined to claim the right given to him, whatever others might say. "You can't possibly send him," Kawau had moaned. "He will be made a mockery of by the seabirds." Te Arikinui Kotuku had disagreed and Te Arikinui Huia, who knew a real bird when she saw one, intoned an ancient proverb. "Ahakoa he iti," she said, "he pounamu." Roughly translated, Huia's words meant size wasn't everything.

Chieftain Tui therefore watched with some admiration as Piwakawaka flitted up to meet the army of manu moana. He raised a cheer for the valiant fantail. "Although our second challenge will be unequal, similar to David's battle with the giant Goliath, what Piwakawaka lacks in stature he makes up for in bravery – or foolhardiness. Go, Piwakawaka! Stick it to the seabirds."

The loud cheering buoyed Piwakawaka's spirits. His heart was thundering in his little breast. Pae kare, those seabirds were big fellas all right. Still, he was up here in front of the whole world, not to mention his wife and tribe, so there was nothing for it but to start doing his thing. He glared, grimaced, capered and double-flipped across the front line of the seabird attackers. "Tei! Tei! Tei!" he challenged. "Tei! Tei! Tei!"

"What an upstart," Karuhiruhi said, "what a clown." With a lazy gesture he ordered Taranui, chieftain of terns, to respond. "Make whatever morsel you wish of the miserable midget."

"Must I?" Taranui asked. Handsome and vain, he considered the challenge of a fantail beneath his dignity. Nevertheless he raised himself on his toes like a ballet dancer, did a lazy pirouette and a couple of jetés, and on upward-angled wings gained the upper air. There he sighted on Piwakawaka, wheeled, yawned and plunge-dived.

Piwakawaka ought to have been an easy target. But you should never underestimate an opponent simply because he is slow as well as small. At Taranui's first pass, Piwakawaka made an erratic jinking movement to the right and, insult of insults, showed his contempt for the tern in the age-old gesture of whakapohane – mooning Taranui with his bum.

"Oh, I wish he wouldn't do that." His watching wife, Waka, blushed.

Enraged, Taranui wheeled and squealed his anger. The action unsettled him, which was precisely what Piwakawaka wanted.

"Okay, you silly little shuttlecock, playtime is over," the tern called – and he made his second attack.

If there was one thing Chieftain Piwakawaka disliked, it was remarks that diminished the royal nature of his person. When Taranui called him 'little' he saw red. Taranui might be bearing down on him like a jumbo jet, but no way was Piwakawaka going to give air.

"Wait for it," he said to himself. "Not yet, not yet. *Now*." With a quick flip of his tail, Piwakawaka did a forward somersault over Taranui's head and landed on the tern's back. Fantails are insectivores, and catch their prey by hawking from a perch. Piwakawaka settled on Taranui's neck, gripped, and with one peck severed the tern's jugular. Like a jet plane trailing petrol from a ruptured tank, Taranui fell to his death.

"The landbirds let out a roar of elation," Hoki said. "However, their joy turned to dismay when they realised that Taranui had managed to twist his neck and catch Piwakawaka in his beak. 'If I go to my death,' Taranui yelled, 'you're coming with me.' Tern and fantail fell into the forest.

"Waka, Piwakawaka's wife, let out a cry of grief. 'Aue, taku tane, alas, my husband.' She sought solace, and Chieftain Tui quickly opened his wings and embraced her. Around them the landbirds fell silent, stunned at Piwakawaka's death –"

"Now's our chance," Karuhiruhi said. "Quickly," he ordered Karoro and Parara, "mount a two-pronged attack."

Before the gull and the prion could execute the order, winged vengeance came swooping from on high. Chieftain Kahu, angry of eye, his wingtips raking the sky, stalled in front of Karoro and Parara. "Going somewhere?" he asked. Two prion guardsmen came to protect their chieftains. Kahu's revenge was sweet. A sudden clawing movement and the prions were decapitated.

Kahu's intervention brought the landbirds back to reality, to the seriousness of their situation. Chieftain Tui began a haka of defiance. "Let not Chieftain Piwakawaka's death be in vain," he chanted. Very soon, Chieftain Kokako of crows joined him, followed by Chieftain Teraweke of saddlebacks and Chieftain Pipiwharauroa. "Avenge Piwakawaka's death! Kui! Kui! Kui whiti ora!"

Then, Chieftain Ruru of the owls blinked and sought Tui's instructions.

"Well, Chief," Ruru said. "Is it time to make the counter-attack?"

"Yes," Tui answered. "Lead your attack right through the middle of the seabird army."

Ruru bowed to Te Arikinui Kotuku and the other women. "Excuse me, ladies," he said. "There's a battle to win."

Uttering loud dismal shrieks he beat his wings and gained the upper winds. He looked as if he had come from the bowels of hell. His eyes, powerful for binocular judgement of distance, completely filled the sockets. As he advanced on the seabirds he uttered the call which, for all men and women, is a premonition that their last breath has come:

"Mor-*por*! Mor-*por*!"

The cry resounded across the sky. The Great Forest seemed to move, to shimmer, to seethe as thousands of landbirds flew upward to the battle.

"Taka rere! Taka rere!" they called. "Kia iro! Kia iro!"

"The landbirds and the seabirds began their bloody battle," Hoki said. She described the battle with her hands, sweeping them back and forth, swish, swish, swish, like a sword. If Skylark had been closer she'd have had to duck for cover.

"The Great Book of Birds tells us that the sky dripped blood as skua fought parrot, gull fought heron, prion fought wren. The seabirds thought they were crazed for battle: their passion was as nothing to the landbirds. The seabirds had made one very big mistake. They had underestimated the landbird numbers. They were totally unprepared for the manu whenua large and small who pitched in to fight against them. The mollymawks engaged in wing-to-wing combat with the pigeons, and soon found that the pigeons could outmanoeuvre them by swooping upwards, stalling, and diving in another direction. The fulmars came up against the awesome duck clan; the ducks were belligerent, aggressive and brooked no trespass. Out in the sky they had a habit of climbing high, then closing their wings and plummeting earthwards onto their target. A squad of petrels found themselves being used as low-level target practice by quails who, running fast downslope on twinkling legs, took off at the last moment, glided on stiff wings and hit them like swift, deadly bullets. All over the sky, prions, shearwaters, gannets, boobies, pelicans, shags and tropicbirds found themselves battling with myriads of landbirds. They soon learned to beware of the clownish kaka; their beaks could tear you apart. The kea clan, with their heavy bills, could not only dig in deep but could also kill by introducing a form of blood poisoning that could take effect in two hours –"

Karuhiruhi called in albatross reinforcements: "Toroa, now is the time to redeem yourself. Order your battalions into the air."

Toroa, glad to have a second chance, led the albatrosses into the fray. His strategy was to rise high above the battle and over Manu Valley. He had forgotten, however, that Chieftain Kahu and his squadron of hawks were waiting in the upper battlesky to thwart this very tactic. Their raking hind claws were lowered to slit open the enemy from head to stomach.

Nor was there any safety for the seabirds if they fell wounded into the Great Forest. There, the wingless forest birds trapped them and killed them. Even so, for a time the outcome of the battle hung in the balance. The fight was long. The fight was desperate. The uproar across the battlefield created such a din that it was heard on the other side of the world.

Then it was that Te Arikinui Kotuku decided to pitch in. "Don't you girls get tired of knitting, waiting at home for our husbands to return from whatever crusades they go on?" she asked Huia, Te Arikinui Korimako and Te Arikinui Karuwai.

"Nothing to do," Huia sighed, "except paint our clawnails Magenta Magic or Scarlet Desire."

"Our job just to wait," Korimako yawned, "for them to return battle-scarred and wounded –"

"To soothe and bandage them and to take them to the nest," Te Arikinui Karuwai fluttered.

"And while we're at it," shuddered Huia, "we have to listen to all their boring tales of heroism and courage." She preened down her ruffled feathers. "So what's your suggestion?" she asked Kotuku.

"I think it is time, girls, for us to have some fun ourselves." She launched herself from her branch. "Kia whakatane au i ahau!" she cried.

That's when the tide of battle turned. And at that very moment when the new combatants were entering the field, something else happened. Karoro of black-backed gulls saw a black seashag falling to the sea. He thought it was his leader, Karuhiruhi, and his courage deserted him. "The day is lost!" he called. "Retreat! Retreat!"

His call echoed across the sky. Other seabirds took it up. One of them, Karuhiruhi, very much alive, cried out: "No! Maintain the attack! Press on! Press forward!"

It was too late. All around Karuhiruhi the seabirds were breaking off. Above the battlesky came the mocking laugh of Chieftain Parera. "Ke-*ke!* Ke-*ke!* Yes, run, run away from the women!"

That's when Karuhiruhi knew he was defeated. Gone was his chance to dine all life long on cool, smooth river eels. Gone was his opportunity to become emperor of the world. He led his squad of seashags from the field of battle, vowing to whip that coward Karoro until he begged for mercy.

At the sight of the retreat, the landbirds gave a huge cheer. The kiwi came out and danced with the kaka. The owl clan celebrated with loud hoots of joy.

"Let there be a great feast of celebration," Tui said. To prove how glad he was that his inlet was safe, Kawau ordered his iwi to provide as many eels as all could eat. The merriment, feasting and dancing lasted many days, and all were happy – except for Te Arikinui Kotuku.

"Something's wrong," she said. "We've forgotten to do something. There's something important that we have overlooked."

"And what was that something?" Skylark asked.

"Well," Hoki continued, "Karuhiruhi happened upon it and his luck turned out to be to his advantage. This is how it happened:

"After the battle, Karuhiruhi brooded over his defeat and became afraid of the divine retribution that might come down upon him from the Lord Tane. He ordered his clansmen to make a huge altar to the Lord Tane, and on it he made many sacrifices. 'Forgive me, Lord Tane, for I have sinned. I tried to put myself above you, I tried to put myself in your place. I am unworthy of your protection.'

"Karuhiruhi stretched out his neck, waiting for the divine blow which would take his life. Instead the voice of the Lord Tane came down from the heavens: 'I forgive you, my disobedient servant and I shall give you another chance. For you have done what my landbirds, whom I love dearly, have not done. You, Karuhiruhi, have made sacrifice to me whereas they, in their pride at their victory, have forgotten to honour me with similar offerings.'"

"Oh no," Skylark said.

"Oh yes," Hoki sighed. "The manu whenua won the battle of the birds but they were as the Israelites who, when liberated from Egypt, did not praise the Lord their God and instead made a golden calf and worshipped it rather than their Divine Deliverer. And just as happened with the Children of Israel, so it happened to the landbirds. They were vain. They could only think of their victory, their triumph. Because of their arrogance, the Great Book of Birds tells us that the Lord Tane chastised them. Because of it, the Lord Tane said, he would test them again in a second battle of the birds."

"A second battle?" Skylark asked.

Hoki nodded. "It's all written in the Great Book of Birds, Revelations, Chapter Four, Verse Five. I know the words by heart."

Hoki closed her eyes and recited the verse: *"And it shall come to pass that in the latter days the sky will open. Then, oh birds, the Lord Tane will allow the great battle between those he loved, his landbirds, to be fought again with the seabirds, for the landbirds hath not respected his love and, indeed, shewed arrogance and did not make appropriate sacrificial offering unto him as Karuhiruhi did. So unto him, Karuhiruhi and all his descendants, Tane will offer up this opportunity as a lesson to be learnt by his birds of the land. And Armageddon shall begin in the third year of the second millennium as it is counted by Man. In that year, at summer solstice, the rising sun at dawn will be in conjunction with the heliacal rising of the planet Venus. And what will be will be."*

"So that's how Venus comes into it," Skylark said. "But what about the prophecy? What about tomorrow?"

Hoki opened her eyes. She was staring straight at Skylark, hypnotic, probing into her as if searching for something.

"The Great Book of Birds also mentions, two verses later, that the Lord

Tane received a delegation from the landbirds. The delegation was led by Te Arikinui Kotuku. 'Oh Lord Tane,' Te Arikinui Kotuku pleaded, 'forgive us, your creatures of your Great Forest, for our sin of pride. Revoke, we beg you, this agreement with the seabirds.'

"It is written," Hoki continued, "that the Lord Tane was not unmoved by Te Arikinui Kotuku's entreaties. 'What is done cannot be undone,' the Lord Tane answered. 'My word is my word and I will not go back on it. However –'"

"However?" Skylark asked.

"The Lord Tane said he would give the landbirds a second chance also. In the latter days, he said, just before the sky opens, he would send a chick, and she would have the power to deny the prophecy's fulfilment."

So that's it, Skylark thought. She stared at Hoki. Her mind was whirling but she was icy calm. "Oh no you don't," Skylark said. "This is the 'uh-oh' part, isn't it? The 'hel-*lo,* is anybody home?' part. You think I'm the chick, don't you?"

"You're the only one who's turned up," Hoki answered. Surely, now that Skylark knew the whole story, she would know who she was and what she was supposed to do.

Skylark dashed these hopes. "It's crazy," she began. "How can you even think it? Before my mother and I arrived here, we'd never even heard of Tuapa or Manu Valley. Don't you think that if I was the chick something more than chance would bring me here? Something like a sense of destiny or a quest? I don't feel as if I have been on either. My name is Skylark O'Shea and I'm just an ordinary girl."

"But the seabirds recognise you," Hoki said quickly. "They –"

"They recognise the threat," Skylark answered. "I just happen to have turned up to coincide with that threat. The girl who was supposed to arrive has taken a wrong turning and ended up somewhere else. Maybe she's had an accident on the way or something. Maybe –"

"No, Skylark, you are the girl," Hoki persisted. Her eyes were shining with conviction. "You're the one we've been waiting for. You're the one who can stop the sky from opening and the seabirds from fighting the battle of the birds again."

Skylark shook her head. "This has got to stop," she said grimly. "You're only hoping it's me. If I was the chick, don't you think I would know? Don't you think you'd have hit the jackpot by now? But no bells are ringing in my head and no lights are flashing like they do at the Sky City

Casino when all those dollar signs line up in a single row. Nobody is running up to congratulate me for winning a million dollars. I'm sorry, Hoki, even if I did believe your story, I'm not the girl you're looking for. Let it end here. Let it end now."

Hoki did not know what to say or what to do. All she could feel was a tremendous sadness, a heaviness that took her to a place of pain and heartbreak. She thought of all those handmaidens of Tane going back to the very beginning of Time. Was all their work for nothing?

"Leave me, child," she said. "It's time you got dressed for tonight anyway."

She kissed Skylark on the forehead, but held back her tears until the girl had left. Then, taking the blame on herself, she wept for the past, for the present and for the future. And she waited for her sister's return.

"We're in big trouble, Sister," Hoki said to Bella. "I thought that having told Skylark all I know, she'd know what she's supposed to do. She doesn't. In fact, she doesn't even believe me."

"Can't you tell her what to do?" Bella asked.

"No. I don't know either."

"What do you mean you don't know? You're supposed to know everything!"

"All I know is what is in the Great Book of Birds and what we're supposed to do. All it tells us to do is prepare the chick so that she can prevent the seabirds re-litigating the battle of the birds. But the Great Book of Birds doesn't say how."

"You mean there's no set of magic words, no 'open sesame' that she has to say? Or a magic wand that she can wave?"

"If there is, I don't know what the words are or where to find the wand."

"Skylark *is* the one, isn't she?"

"I don't know that either!" Hoki wailed. "She doesn't think she is."

"But she must be," Bella answered. "You must be doing something wrong, Sister."

"What can it be?" Hoki asked. "I've done everything in my power to open her mind so that she can walk into it and find the answers to her and our questions. But she is still on the threshold, the paepae, hesitating, and she doesn't even want to go in."

Bella was silent for a moment. "Well, there's only twelve hours to sunrise," she said finally. "All I can say is you'd better give Skylark a big push – and quick."

– 3 –

The day had been bad enough with its criss-cross currents of frayed tempers and wrong signals; the night was worse. With countdown already begun to dawn – not to mention the *Bye Bye Birdie* opening – everybody was on edge. So it was only to be expected that when Skylark went to Hoki and Bella's for dinner, wires were still fizzing and crackling like electric circuits looking for connection. One look at Hoki's face was enough to tell Skylark that the stubborn old woman hadn't taken any notice of what she'd said earlier.

"I'm telling you," Skylark said, "don't even think about it. I'm not the girl you're looking for, and that's final."

"If I were you," Hoki answered, the glint of battle in her eyes, "I wouldn't speak too soon, Miss Skylark O'Shea."

"What she means," Bella translated, "is that your conversation went in one ear and out the other."

"What I mean," Hoki corrected, glaring at Bella, "is that you may know you aren't the chick, I may think you are, but it's not up to us."

"What she really means," Bella translated again, "is that you shouldn't tempt fate, because you could end up with mud in your eye."

"Who is it up to!" Skylark asked.

Hoki drew herself up to her highest height. "It's up to the Lord Tane," she answered. "And do you," she said to Bella, kicking her, "always have to be my echo?"

Hoki's attitude left Skylark floundering for a response. In the end she just gave up. After all, how could you argue with a god? "Oh, suit yourself then," she said.

When Arnie arrived he found himself caught in the cross-currents. He'd poured himself into slimcut jeans and black leather jacket, and, man, his boots must have cost him a month's wages. Skylark had to admit he was an awesome looking dude.

"Hey," she said, "you scrub up well." Unfortunately she laughed, and Arnie assumed she was being sarcastic.

"Yeah?" he said. "Well, now that I'm closer up, my view isn't so hot either."

"Quit it, you two," Bella reproved. "And you, Arnie, you should be more of a gentleman. Can't you see how pretty Skylark is?"

Skylark was looking more presentable than usual. She had taken a serious look at herself and against her better judgement had decided it was time to renovate. She had put on her best jeans and a nice top, and she'd even added a plum-coloured vest. Not only that, but she had managed to get some curl into her hair – and was that just the hint of lippy? Not for long.

"I'd be a gentleman if Skylark was a lady," Arnie said.

Skylark stormed back to the bach and into her bedroom. Off came the vest and back on went the favourite jersey. Next, splash, and the curls disappeared, and while she was at it, wipe, and gone was the lippy too. Just to make sure that nobody messed with her, jab, on went a badge: I'M AGAINST ANIMAL TESTING (STICK YOUR HYPODERMICS INTO HUMANS).

There, that should do it. Enter the harpie from Hell.

"I didn't know it was Halloween," Arnie said as Skylark got into his ute. "Who's your date tonight? Festus Munster or Frankie Stein?"

"Get a life," Skylark answered.

Tuapa College was ablaze with lights. The street in front of the auditorium was packed with cars. "Goodness me," Hoki said, "the whole of Tuapa must be here. I've never seen so many people."

"Well what else is there to do on a Saturday night?" Bella answered. "At least coming here will mean two hours of enforced birth control for everybody." People were hurrying up the drive and past the sign announcing that *Bye Bye Birdie* was SOLD OUT.

"It's because your mother's in the show," Hoki said to Skylark. She was trying to thaw the frozen continent that had lurched out of the sea between Skylark and Arnie by making happee happee talkee.

"Yep," Skylark answered. "Star power. Mum was always big in the burbs. Pity that quality is wasted on some of the dumb ass locals, right Arnie?"

"What are you saying here?" Arnie asked, angry.

"Oh," Skylark answered in mock innocence. "You didn't wents to this college?"

"Quit it, you two," Hoki interrupted. "I don't know what's got into you, Skylark, nor you Arnie. Behave, both of you."

Further along from the auditorium the football field had been turned into a carpark for the evening. Arnie, hunched back in the driver's seat, looked like he was tempted to score a few of the squeaky-clean attendants with the ute. "Don't you dare," Hoki said.

"Why not?" Arnie growled. He parked the ute, leapt out and slammed the door. "I'll go and join my mates. I'll see you all later."

That was it. Hoki's eyes narrowed and she compressed her lips. "You just come back here, nephew," she ordered. "And don't think you're getting away so easily, Skylark." She pointed one of her walking sticks at her. "You two are not children. You're supposed to be two thinking adults, so act like adults. You, Skylark, you started it. Apologise to Arnie. Say you're sorry."

Skylark gave an incredulous laugh. "I will not say I'm sorry."

Did Hoki give a toss? No. As far as she was concerned, legally speaking, Skylark had said the word required. She lifted her other walking stick and waved it at Arnie. "Skylark said sorry, so now it's your turn. Say sorry."

"It didn't sound like sorry to me," Arnie mumbled.

"Perfect!" Hoki barked. "Now let's try to enjoy the rest of the evening, shall we?"

She marched off as quickly as her sticks would allow, leaving Skylark and Arnie gaping.

"I wouldn't argue with her if I was you," Bella whispered.

Reluctantly, Skylark nodded. Even so, as she watched Hoki negotiate the stairs to the auditorium she felt a mean idea enter into her head.

"Oh, topple over, Hoki," she whispered.

The vestibule was in a state of bedlam. The ticket booth was thronged with people trying to buy tickets. Bella and Hoki found Mitch and Francis. Mitch spotted Skylark and mimed a bird coming out of the sky towards her. Skylark ducked and Mitch roared with laughter. In a corner Flora Cornish had swapped her apron as proprietress of the Tuapa Diner for an apron as chairwoman of the Tuapa College Parents Association. She was presiding over the refreshments area, dispensing Coke, lemonade, coffee and tea with soggy biscuits to the masses. No wonder there was so much bad skin in Tuapa. Not that that seemed to matter to a group of Korean sailors, who were taking an inordinate interest in a group of sixth formers in uniform. Were they schoolgirls? When Skylark took a second look she realised they were girls from the massage parlour.

"Excuse me," Skylark said as she walked through the crowd. Her badge was doing wonders. People parted before her like the Red Sea.

Right in the middle of the crowd was Lucas. He had a young woman with him, and he didn't seem too happy about it. "Hello, Lucas," Skylark said. "Is this your sister?"

"His sister?" the young woman asked. "I'm Melissa, his fiancée, though he –" and she kicked Lucas in the shins – "seems to have forgotten it."

"Oops," Skylark said.

"Melissa's just come back to Tuapa for the weekend," Lucas said. He hustled Skylark aside, speaking in a hurried whisper. "She's been hanging around my neck like a smelly possum and I haven't had a chance to explain to Cora. Will you tell her that –"

Skylark stopped him. "Tell her what! That you've got another girlfriend? Sort it out yourself, Lucas." She turned, and pushed and jostled her way back through the crowd.

"We're right behind you, dear," Hoki said as she and Bella rejoined her.

"Am I a tug?" Skylark asked herself.

Across the vestibule she saw Ronnie, waving their tickets in his hands, and made for him.

"Did you see the 'Sold Out' sign?" he exclaimed. "We've never had such a crowd at a college production ever. And just to think that Lottie –" he pointed to the music teacher – "didn't think I'd pull it off, the cow."

An excited student came rushing towards him. "Sir, the headmaster has asked if we can put more seats into the auditorium. Sir?"

"More? They want more?" Ron was ecstatic. "Then give my audience more!" He turned to Skylark. "It's all due to your wonderful mother! Now will you all follow me? You have special VIP seats with me right at the front."

"Oh no," said Skylark and Bella in unison.

Hoki laughed. "Just as well you wore your lovely dress," she said.

"How did she persuade you to get into it?" Skylark asked Bella.

"We compromised," Bella said, pursing her lips and pulling up her hem ever so slightly. Underneath she was wearing gumboots.

"Now –" Ron hesitated. "There's just one more of your mother's guests to come and we're all set. Meanwhile, I'd better get backstage where I'm wanted. Do enjoy the show!"

Before Skylark could ask who the other guest was, Ron had disappeared backstage. Skylark stared afer him and saw Cora signalling her from the stage door. Her mother had on her blonde wig and her eyes were sparkling. She looked like a colour facsimile of Madonna herself. "Skylark, honey –"

Members of the crowd saw Cora and a great gasp of admiration went up. "There she is! Cora Edwards!" Cora laughed and, briefly, waved. She looked so gorgeous. Bursting with beauty. But Skylark knew there was something wrong. Her mother was too gorgeous. Her eyes were too sparkling. Something shifted behind Cora – and Skylark realised why her mother's manner was too animated.

All the ills and spites of the day came crashing down at her feet.

"Zac," Skylark whispered. Her first instinct was to protect her mother. She shoved through the crowd. "Get out of my way. Coming through." When she was close enough to Cora, she pushed her through the stage door and shut it. She turned to Zac. "You lowlife, how did you find us?"

"Skylark, honey! Be careful!" Cora laughed and, giddy, fell against Zac. "You'll mess me up and it's taken a whole day to look like this." Her arms went around Zac's neck and she sighed dreamily.

"I asked you, you sicko," Skylark raged, "how did you know we were here?"

Zac gave Skylark a mocking glance. "You always did have a mouth on you, didn't you, girlie." He kissed Cora but kept his eyes on Skylark, taunting her. "Have you ever heard of caller ID? When you called me from the phone box, it was oh so easy to trace the call."

Skylark felt the blood leave her face. She stepped back, angry with herself for being so stupid. She heard Cora laugh again. Up close, her mother did not look gorgeous at all. The wig was really bad and her face was absolutely caked with makeup. Where Zac had kissed her, the lipstick had smeared.

"Oh, Mum," Skylark said. "Of all the things I've ever lost, I miss my mind the most. Why did I ever let this happen to you?"

She had seen that beneath the false eyelashes Cora's eyes were unnaturally wide. She pulled at her mother's left arm. Found bruised skin. Punctures as if a snake had bitten it. Needle tracks.

"What are you doing, Skylark? Keep her away from me, Zac," Cora whimpered.

"How much have you given her, you loser?" Skylark screamed at Zac. "When will it kick in?"

It was too late. Skylark heard the overture starting up.

Of course Cora insisted on going on. The show must, mustn't it? Hadn't all of Tuapa turned up because she was starring? A star never let down her public, did she? And even though the two people she loved in the whole world turned her dressing room into a boxing ring for most of the performance, let nobody ever doubt that Cora Edwards was a professional.

"What's Zac made you do?" Skylark shouted. "Have you signed anything? You know I'm your guardian so anything you've signed won't stand up in court. Why do you need him, Mum? Why –"

"Why?" Zac interrupted. "Because I give her what you can't. You want some of it too, girlie? You want some of Zac's action?"

"Keep away from me, you creep. Go back to the swamp where you came from and do everybody a favour and die."

Cora kept smiling and smiling through it all. Family squabbles? Boring, boring, boring. The stuff Zac had given her was just great. It was like feeling something bubbling under you like champagne, keeping you afloat. It made you want to spread your arms and flyyy –

Skylark and Zac were so busy arguing they didn't know Cora had left the room until they heard her entrance music. "Onstage Miss Edwards, take your position please."

"Mum?" Skylark called.

Cora wasn't there. "Mum, *no.*" Skylark pushed past Zac and ran towards the wings. It was dark, she tripped, and there were so many people in the way. "Let me through," she called. Her heart leapt with hope when she realised Cora had missed her cue. The curtain was still down. There was still time to stop her. But the entrance music had started again.

"Cue Miss Edwards."

"Where is she!" Ronnie asked. He had been backstage, stage managing the amateurs. It hadn't occurred to him that the famous Cora Edwards would miss a cue and he was tearing his hair out.

There was a nervous rustle in the audience. Hoki and Bella looked at each other, puzzled. "What's going on?" Flora Cornish recalled the awful scene that had finished Cora's television career. Arnie, standing with Francis at the back of the hall, remembered what Skylark had told him about her mother: *I have to be strong for her. All we have in the world is each other.* Lucas was on tenterhooks. As for Melissa, she was hoping Cora would trip on her entrance and fall flat on her face.

For the third time, the entrance music started up. With a sigh of relief,

Ronnie caught a glimpse of Cora climbing the backstage ladder which would take her to the top of the set – a near-exact replica of one Madonna had in her music video.

"Stop her," Skylark yelled. Her voice was drowned in the orchestral introduction.

Cora reached the top of the staircase, found her mark and took up her position. She saw Ronnie and blew him a kiss. With a sigh of relief, he nodded to the headmaster, who was standing in front of the curtain playing Ed Sullivan. Then he caught a movement on the far side of the stage. Who was that? Cora's daughter? She was trying to get his attention. What was she saying?

"Don't raise the curtain. Don't –"

It was too late. Cora was ready. Everybody was ready. Cora struck a provocative pose.

Ed Sullivan gave a grin. "Ladies and gentlemen, not only do we have Conrad Birdie tonight but the girl all you men would most like to meet on a blind date. She's that superstar of our times, Queen of Pop, Maadonna!" he ad libbed.

The curtain went up. Exposed at the top of the stairs was a dazzling apparition. Applause, wolf whistles and cheers went up in the auditorium. This was what they had been waiting for all night. It was true after all. Cora Edwards, as Madonna, had really come to town. She looked sensational.

Cora began to blow kisses to all her fans. And after that entrance, who cared that Madonna's appearance in a 1960s musical was an anachronism?

She saw the boy playing Conrad Birdie standing at stage left. Remembered her lines. "Hey, Conrad, how's it hanging?"

With a roar, the audience lifted the roof off the auditorium. Quickly, Ronnie ran the tape of "Like a Virgin". There were a few bars of introductory music before Cora's lipsync. She began to work it, baby, strutting her stuff, flaunting her body, and pouting her lips as if she wanted to kiss everybody in the world. They loved her, they really loved her. But, at that moment, somebody dark knocked on her head, wanting to come in. Cora shook her head, willing the dark intruder to go away. *Can't you see I'm busy?* Perspiration was building up beneath the wig. She almost lost her place. Then, there they were, the bars leading up to the beginning of her lipsync. Thank God Ronnie had suggested it; free of having to sing the song, she could concentrate on dancing the steps. She tapped out the beat with her shoes. One two, one two three and:

"I went to New York, I didn't know anybody
I wanted to dance, I wanted to sing –"

Cora took the first step down the staircase. That's when whoever was knocking on Cora's head broke down the door. *Coming ready or not.* Before she knew what was happening, she was tumbling down the staircase and:

Cue Weather Report.

Explosions popped in Cora's brain. This had all happened before. Where was it? When was it?

Cue Music.

Cora tried to stand up. *Where aaare youuu*? Her outfit was ripped. One of her shoes had come off. Conrad was trying to help her up. She pushed him away. She had to get herself together to read the weather, yes, that was it.

Cue Ms Edwards.

Cora stumbled to the footlights. She made ready to beam her 300-megawatt smile out to the whole of New Zealand. But then she heard voices, or thought she heard voices, and they were whispering, laughing, mocking her.

And, all of a sudden, Cora felt a huge rocketing pain. The dark intruder leapt out at her. *You didn't think I'd let you get away that easily did you?* Cora screamed. "No, no, no, nooooooooo –"

Action.

Cora fell to the stage, put her hands up and pulled the golden wig from her head. With the wig went all illusion, all hope, all redemption. All that was left was a woman made up of sticks and straw, sugar and spice and everything nice, pitilessly exposed in the harsh light.

And where was lovely John Campbell this time, when she really needed him?

– 4 –

"Mum. Mummy?"

They were back at the bach in Tuapa Valley. Skylark was sitting beside Cora, trying to revive her. Hoki and Bella were hovering nearby, looking on.

"Hello, honey," Cora whispered. "I really messed up, didn't I? I messed up big time."

"Thank God," Skylark sighed. "You didn't mess up, Mum. All you did was trip on the stairs. It's the stuff that legends are made of. Nobody will remember *Bye Bye Birdie,* but they will certainly remember the night Cora Edwards fell."

"I heard the audience laughing. Somebody laughed."

"No, Mum, nobody laughed. Truly." She was trying to keep her mother's mood upbeat. She knew how quickly depression followed a drug-induced high. Once it wore off Cora would go down with the elevator.

Suddenly, Cora looked around, frightened. "Where am I? How did I get here?"

"Don't worry, Mum," Skylark said. "As soon as you fell I asked Bella to help me get you off the stage. Ron wanted to call an ambulance to take you to hospital."

"They would have found out about me . . . I would have been sent back to rehab . . ."

"I had to tell Bella," Skylark said.

Bella had once been a nurse aide. She recognised Cora's symptoms. Told Arnie to get the ute out to the front – and quick. The local news reporter had managed a lucky snap as Cora was being carried out by a grim-faced Lucas through the milling, shocked-looking crowd.

"Where's Zac?" Cora asked. "Is Zac here?" She looked from Skylark's face to Hoki and Bella.

"No, Mum, Zac's gone." At the first hint of trouble he had burnt rubber getting out of town.

"He's done another runner on me, hasn't he," Cora said. Tears were streaking down her face, and she began to shiver. Next moment she was convulsing.

"This won't be pretty," Skylark said, turning to Bella and Hoki.

"I'll say it won't," Bella answered. "Why didn't you tell us about your mother's habit? Are there any more skeletons in her cupboard that we don't know about?" She ticked them off: "First she's a dangerous driver. Second she's got an addiction . . ."

"It's not Skylark's fault," Hoki said. "Don't blame her for her mother."

Skylark gave Bella an angry look. "I haven't got time to cope with your aggro," she said. "I've got to concentrate on Mum. You and Hoki should go now. Leave me with her."

"Hoki can go. I'm staying," Bella said.

"This isn't like repairing the damaged wing of one of your birds," Skylark flared.

"Don't you think I know that? It's going to take the two of us to handle it." She turned to Hoki. "You go, Sister. I'll keep an eye on things here. But one of us has to watch out for the dawn."

And it was the Longest Night before the ascending of the sun and, with it, the heliacal rising of the planet Venus.

Hoki went to the homestead and got a thick, warm blanket. Behind the homestead was a small grove of fruit trees; beneath one of them was an old armchair where she liked to sit whenever she had a spare moment. She made herself comfortable in it, wrapped the blanket around her and kept watch on the spinning night.

"Lord Tane," Hoki prayed, "your humble servant seeks your help. As prophesied, you have sent us a chick. But is she the one we have been waiting for? If she is, what guidance can I give her to prevent the sky from opening? Help me, oh Lord, I pray you."

A loud scream interrupted her karakia. She shivered and wondered what was happening in the bach.

Cora was going from one screaming jag to the next, from one hallucination to the next. Screaming, laughing, crying. Bella was trying to hold her down. Skylark was sponging her forehead. Cora's head kept whiplashing back and forth – lash, lash, whiplash. "Oh Zac –"

"God, she's strong," Bella panted. "I don't know how long I can keep her down."

Skylark was concentrating on her mother.

"For once and for all get Zac out of your life! He's slime, Mum."

"This isn't about Zac," Cora laughed. "I don't care about Zac. What I care about is what he can give me." She spat a huge gob of spit into Bella's face.

Taken by surprise, Bella let go – and Cora sprinted into the next room, to the chair where Skylark had piled her clothes. "Zac left me some extra drugs. Where are they?"

"Oh no you don't!" Skylark was hot on her heels and wrested the bottle out of her mother's hands.

"Give them to me you little bitch." Cora reached for Skylark, snarling, clawing at her with her fingers. Skylark pushed her mother away. Cora fell to the floor, a shocked look on her face. Then she doubled up as the first cramps hit her. Her voice took on a cajoling whine: "Skylark, honey, please, just one tab? Skylark? Please?"

"I'm sorry, Mum, no. They're prescription poisons."

"Just one, please? That's all I need. Just one tiny tab? Please?"

Skylark shook her head.

Cora was on her feet again. Furious. "Zac brought them for me, they belong to me, give them to me." They started to fight again.

Then Bella was there, standing behind Cora, feeling for a pressure point in her neck. She pressed. Cora slumped to the floor.

"Go and fill the bath," Bella ordered. "Is there any ice in the fridge? Get it now and fill the bath with it. There's some more ice in the freezer in the homestead. Do it. Now."

And Hoki was watching the sky spinning, spinning, spinning with stars. The stars were chasing each other, dancing to some quirky lopsided rhythm, popping and cracking and sizzling like bizarre fireworks. Somewhere in the middle of the Southern Cross, something strange was happening.

"What is that?" Hoki said to herself. It looked like a black hole opening up and moving above the twin mountains.

Fearful, Hoki looked at her watch. Two hours to dawn.

During the midnight hours she had seen Skylark hurrying between the bach and the homestead and, through the bathroom window of the bach, Skylark and Bella struggling with Cora. There had been a piercing scream – "It's so cold, so cold" – followed by moans and shouts of such plaintive, begging quality that Hoki had to put her hands to her ears to shut them out. Then there had been more ruckus, Bella shouting, and next moment Cora was being wrapped up in blankets to get her warm. "I'm on fire," Cora screamed. "I'm burning up."

For the rest of the time, Hoki had been racking her brains, trying to find an answer to the problem that confronted her. "Where is the key to open the door so that Skylark can step across the threshold and into her own understanding?" She had a brainwave. She walked back to the homestead, opened the big walnut cabinet and took out the Great Book of Birds – a set of three ledger books into which her great-grandmother had painstakingly transcribed the words from the previous copy of the original Great Book of Birds. That original copy, written by the very first handmaiden of Tane, had long succumbed to old age, brittle paper and the ravages of sun and wind. Even the transcription copy made by Hoki's great-grandmother had to be handled with care.

Hoki opened the third ledger book and turned to Revelations. The sight of her great-grandmother's squiggly handwriting, done in fading pen and ink, made tears come to her eyes. She had a vision of all those handmaidens of Tane, keeping the faith alive, looking after the manu whenua, passing the job down from one generation to the next, making sure the primary imperative was maintained.

There will come a time when the Sky will open again. At that time, then will the reigning handmaiden be required to fulfil the task to which we have all been ordained.

Hoki wiped angrily at her tears. This time, when she prayed again, she aimed her prayers at all the former handmaidens. "Well, thank you all so much for dumping the task on me," she said. "You had the easy job. All you had to do was pass the message on like a parcel. But you forgot to mention how I was supposed to accomplish the task and what I was supposed to tell the chick." Hoki opened the third ledger book. In it was the Book of Revelations. "If the answers are here,"she continued, glaring into the past, "for goodness sake show me."

Skylark and Bella, meantime, were struggling to stabilise Cora.

"This is the worst I've ever seen her," Skylark said to Bella. "How much longer do we have to do this?"

"As long as it takes," Bella answered, as she pushed Cora down on the bed and kept her there. Somewhere inside Cora was a succubus. "Come out, damn you," Bella said. "Come out."

Then, around four in the morning, exhausted, Bella thought it was all over. Cora vomited yet again, and passed through the crisis point. Skylark recognised the signs and gave Bella a hopeful glance. She'd been sponging Cora, coaxing her through the withdrawal symptoms, forcing her to drink water, trying to help her to adopt the breathing techniques she had learnt in rehab, sponging her down again — and she was really beat.

Finally, Cora opened her eyes. She gave a grateful smile to Bella. She pressed Skylark's hands.

"Thank you, Skylark honey," she said. "Who'd want to have a mother like me, eh?"

"You're the only mother I have," Skylark answered. "It's not as if I can go and pick another one off the shelf."

Cora lay back on her bed. "I love you, honey." Very soon her breathing evened out.

With a sigh, Bella started to clean up. "You get to bed now," she said to Skylark.

"Thank you for being here," Skylark answered. "I wouldn't have been able to do it by myself."

Hoki snapped the Great Book of Birds shut. Nothing. She could find nothing in it to help her. "Well, that's it," she said.

She was beyond despair. Beyond anger. Beyond frustration. She began to shiver. A cold wind had begun to blow from the sea. Dawn was approaching. She heard a door slamming and saw Bella leaving the bach and walking wearily back to the homestead.

"Shift over and give me some of the blankets," Bella said as she came over to the bed. "If you think your night has been difficult, man oh man, I've been to Hell and back."

"How is Cora now?"

"We finally managed to bring her down. They're both asleep. And you? Any luck?"

"No," Hoki answered.

"Well, whatever will happen will happen," Bella said philosophically. "Hey, maybe we've got the date wrong! Maybe something has happened to change things between the time the Great Book was written and today. Maybe the sky isn't going to open at all."

Hoki gave Bella a questioning glance. "Since when did you change into a cock-eyed optimist? I like the old grumbly Bella better."

"Easy on the old," Bella said. "I suppose there's nothing for it but to take our medicine then." She fumbled in her kit and brought out a bottle of vodka.

"You know I never drink spirits," Hoki said.

"Oh go on, live a little," Bella answered. She poured a shot, lifted it to her mouth and threw the vodka against the back of her throat. "Ah, just the ticket," she said. She poured again and gave the glass to Hoki. "Be a devil," she said.

In the bach, Cora's eyes snapped open. Thank God, the old bitch had finally left.

She leapt out of bed and tiptoed carefully past Skylark's bedroom.

Where had she put that damn bottle of tabs? There! Grab her smokes too and a can of beer, and out of the house before Skylark could stop her. Now get away somewhere Skylark wouldn't find her.

What was this? A pathway. Leading up the cliff. The dawn was coming up, lighting the way.

"I worked very hard and my dream came true,

I went to New York and became a star . . ."

Cora tripped lightly up the pathway. She was feeling triumphant. Victorious. She reached the halfway point where there was a lookout and a bench to take advantage of the view. She hesitated but decided to go on.

Yes, go right to the top, Cora, dear. Find your mark. Then begin your song. One two, one two three and:

"I wanted to make people happy . . ."

She made it – to the top of path, the top of the cliff, the top of the world.

Now find a place to sit and watch the sun come up and have a smoke and get going before those damn birds start their singing.

"Mama's got her own plans for a party."

Giggling to herself, Cora sat down. She lit a cigarette and threw the match away. She took a few puffs and then got down to the serious business of feeling good. Good about herself as a woman. Good about herself as a person. Good about herself as a mother.

One tab. Two tabs. Three tabs. Hell, make myself a cocktail.

Where is that can of beer to skull it down with? Ah, that's better. "May as well trash myself for good and get it over with."

Oh no, the match was smouldering in the grass. Reach over, stamp it out. Too far, too far.

"Who gives a damn anyway."

The tabs took effect. Something began to tickle her. Whatever it was, Cora was giggling as if the whole world was a laughing matter.

Suddenly, whatever was tickling her stopped. It became angry and jumped on her. It was big, black and it was growling, and it bit her head off.

"Oh, Cora Edwards," Cora said to herself, "you're going straight to Hell."

Finally it was the dawn.

With a deep inward breath, Hoki realised something was wrong. For a moment she couldn't put a finger on it. Then she knew.

"Where's the birdsong?" she asked Bella.

Bella shrugged her shoulders. She stood up and looked across Manu Valley. Everything appeared normal. It was a day just like any other day. Then she looked up at the cliff, and her face blazed with grief.

"Well, nobody can hold back the dawn," Hoki said.

Bella kissed her on the forehead. "We tried, Sister. We tried."

The sun had come up, shockingly bright. Silhouetted against the sunrise was the ancient tree. All its branches were on fire.

"Look, Sister," Hoki said. Her voice was hushed. Above the sacred mountains, Venus was shining in its heliacal rising. The conjunction of dawn, Venus and burning tree made the sky glow. Within the glow was an imperfection, a place where the sky was thin.

Suddenly the fire from the ancient tree found that place of thinness. It found a seam, invisible to the naked eye and began to track along it until, with a sudden flaring, the sky ripped apart. Behind was a black opening, so dark and disturbing that Hoki gave a cry and fell forward. Bella caught her.

Hoki's attention turned to the sea.

Yes. There it is! As was prophesied, the sky has opened!

The first wave of seabirds was riding the thermals and ascending up the Manu Valley.

With a cry, a seashag hurtled toward the rip in the sky and in.

"It's started," Bella said.

Part Two

[CHAPTER SIX]

– 1 –

For thousands of years the seabirds had been promised this dawn. They smothered the offshore islands and the ocean around it, waiting for Kawanatanga to appear on the ramparts of his island fortress and lead them to their deliverance.

"Ka-wana-tanga! Ka-wana-tanga! Ka-wana-tanga!"

There was a roar as, from out of the eye of destiny, Kawanatanga appeared. His plumage was like armour, flashing metallic in the early light. Some of his plumes were ornamental, glinting like knives. His head was crested and the red side panels of his face gave the appearance of an iron mask. Protruding from the mask was a long, sharply hooked bill.

He quivered and shrilled with anticipation. From generation to generation the legend had been passed of the time when seabirds fought landbirds, when the sky dripped blood and when – oh, shame of shames – the seabirds had retreated the sky of battle. Then had come the promise from Lord Tane to Karuhiruhi his ancestor, that the seabirds would be offered the opportunity of a second battle of the birds.

Kawanatanga flapped his wings for silence, and a hiss came up from the sea. All eyes looked to the east, to the rising sun.

"It comes," Kawanatanga cried. He pointed to the horizon.

The dawn was there, travelling fast towards the land that the Lord Tane had made. Lo, it passed quickly over the offshore islands and made of the ocean surrounding it a simulacrum of another ocean in another Time – the sea of legend, the unholy Sea of White Feathers. But where was the open sky? In his impatience, Kawanatanga called out:

"Oh, Lord Tane, give unto us that which you promised." The bitter bile of anger surged within his stomach. It was almost on his beak to curse the Lord Tane for not fulfilling his promise. However, Kawanatanga saw another conjunction had appeared. "The planet, Venus –"

Red as a ruby, Venus ascended in its heliacal rising. Like a baleful, angry eye it looked down on the earth. Its gaze struck the twin mountains and flared across the valley beneath. The words of anger stilled on Kawanatanga's beak and he counted his lucky stars, because if the Lord Tane had heard them he might have penalised the seabirds for their arrogance.

The dawn was over. Venus disappeared. Kawanatanga saw something flickering red at the top of Manu Valley.

"The paepae," he whispered in awe. "The holy tree of the landbirds. It is on fire –"

Suddenly, one of the branches of the holy tree sizzled like a match and lit a seam in the sky, burning it open. Behind it, Kawanatanga saw the dark tunnel back to the Beginning of All Things. He gave a cry of triumph. The air around the ocean erupted into a maelstrom of harsh squealing as seashags, mollymawks, fulmars, prions, shearwaters and petrels communicated the news to each other. Albatrosses swooped joyfully in the sky.

Huge, black and avenging, Kawanatanga stepped forward. "Today, the long-waited prophecy has come to pass," he said. "Let us begin our great task."

He took wing. Following him came the first wave of seabirds, silent, intent, beak ready, riding the thermals of the sun-warmed morning, ascending up to Manu Valley.

– 2 –

That same morning, Cora was front page news in the *New Zealand Herald*:

Ex-tv Star, Cora Edwards, Falls From Stage

Below the headline was the dramatic photograph taken by the local reporter of an unconscious Cora being carried from Tuapa College in Lucas's burly arms. The caption read:

Ex-television star, Cora Edwards, is reported to be in hospital following a dangerous fall. Ms Edwards, the popular weather girl on New Zealand television, was making her comeback to the stage in a local production of the American musical *Bye Bye Birdie* at Tuapa. During the performance, directed by well known director Ronnie Shore, she fell from the top of a staircase which had been constructed especially for her entrance number. Although Ms Edwards appeared to recover she later suffered a mysterious relapse. She was rushed to Southern Health's regional centre at Tuapa this morning.

The story effectively put up a smoke screen against the real reason for Cora's "mysterious relapse". Bella had driven Skylark and Cora down to the centre earlier that morning. The surgeon on duty, Dr Goodwin, looked into Cora's dilated pupils and immediately diagnosed the reason for her comatose state. His face was grim.

"What has she taken?"

Skylark showed him the almost empty bottle of pills. "A cocktail of speed and alcohol."

"How many? What dosage?"

"I don't know. She also took some before the show. There could have been other stuff she added to the mix. I wasn't there to see."

Dr Goodwin made some additional examinations, and noted the track marks on Cora's arms. "She's an habitual drug user? This has happened before, hasn't it."

"Yes. My mother was in rehab."

Dr Goodwin swung into action. He sent the bottle of pills to the lab for analysis. He telephoned the rehab centre where Cora had been treated and asked them to send her medical details. Skylark started to panic when she saw a television news crew arriving. She put on her best little-daughter face.

"Please, doctor, if the news gets out why Mum's really here, they'll crucify her," she said. "The judge was lenient the last time. He might not be so kind this time around. Won't you help us?"

Dr Goodwin took stock of the situation. "Okay," he nodded. "Let people believe what they've already read, shall we? If they think your mother's condition is due to a concussion arising from a fall, so be it."

By midday Tuapa was a-buzz with talk about Cora Edwards and her sensational accident in *Bye Bye Birdie.* Those who hadn't been at the performance were furious to have missed out on a great event in Tuapa; goodness knows, the last time that anything of note had occurred was when Jackie Fraser had, at fifty-three, given birth to triplets. Those who, like Flora Cornish, had been there told and retold Cora's fall as if it was a replay of a rugby game: the staircase ("It shouldn't have been so high"), the fall ("It's a lesson never to wear high-heeled boots") and the shock as she fell ("We all screamed"). At least Flora's version wasn't as dramatic as Ronnie's. Having initially thought badly of Cora for ruining his production, his unexpected elevation to "well-known director" status gave him a more significant spotlight.

"You know what it's like in the theatre," Ronnie said in a hastily arranged on-the-spot television interview. "Opening nights especially can be very stressful for everybody, cast and crew. But on this occasion there was something I couldn't quite put my finger on. Something about interpolating Madonna into a musical about the 1960s. One should never tamper with the theatre. It only brings misfortune. When I saw Cora at the top of the staircase I just knew she would fall and when she did, right before my eyes, I knew . . ." The television cameras caught moisture in his eyes and trembling lips. "I knew it was all my fault. Because of me, my leading actress is in hospital, the dearest woman I ever knew . . ."

Up in Manu Valley, Hoki watched the interview with relief. The publicity diverted attention not only from Cora's overdose.

"If they only knew," Hoki said.

A bigger and more dramatic event was taking place away from the gaze of Tuapa township, away from the news media, in the ripped sky above Manu Valley.

– 3 –

Boom.

At every loud report of the shotguns the seabirds scattered. Kawanatanga urged them back to the attack. He wheeled like a dark nightmare. Not until all the seabirds were through the ripped sky would he too penetrate it.

Boom, boom. Bella and Skylark had returned from Tuapa Hospital and taken over from Hoki. They were firing the shotguns where the seabirds were blackest.

"How's our ammunition holding out, sister?" Hoki asked.

"We're fine for today but we'll have to get supplies for tomorrow."

"Is this the only way to stop them getting through?" Skylark asked.

"No," Hoki said. She pointed further down Manu Valley. "I called on my hawk earlier this morning to help us. He and his eyrie are doing their best. In the old days the hawk ruled the skies. But today, with the majority of the Great Forest gone, their numbers are small."

"So, really, it's just us," Skylark said. She did not see the look which passed between Bella and Hoki:

We must pray that Skylark divines the pattern and the part she has to play in it.

The seagulls regrouped, diving and cackling and trying to swoop past their guard. Skylark sighted and pressed the trigger of her shotgun.

At that moment, Arnie arrived. He clutched his chest dramatically. "You got me, Skylark!" he groaned.

"What a pity," Skylark sighed. "Just a flesh wound."

"Be like that," he said. He greeted Bella and Hoki, and looked up at the ripped sky. "Bloody hell –"

High above his head something shimmered like a bizarre silver cross. The cross had been created when Cora's match fizzed vertically up the sky and then horizontally to form a short crossbar. If you hadn't known what it was, or known where to look, you'd have thought it was just a strange trick of light. However, every breeze or puff of wind opened the corners of the cross like flaps of a tent. That's when you saw the other side of the sky. Black. Awful. A hole big enough to drive a car through. Whenever that happened, seabirds screamed and plummeted into it, pulled through by some centrifugal force, winking out. One moment there. Next moment gone.

"I guess seeing is believing," Arnie said.

He stepped forward for a closer look and a sense of sickness and vertigo overwhelmed him. He was staring into a dark abyss. Far down was a kaleidoscope of seabirds – those which had managed to get past Bella, Hoki and Skylark – plummeting, stabbing and wheeling back to the beginning of Time.

"Even as I was driving up here and saw the seabirds coming up the valley I didn't want to believe it. I still don't want to believe it," he said.

"You know about all this?" Skylark asked.

"Ever since I was a kid and used to live with Auntie Bella and Auntie Hoki," he answered, as if that explained everything. "I used to think it was a fairytale – until now."

"I should pinch you so that you'll know you're not dreaming," Skylark said. She had meant it to sound like a joke but it came out mean, and Arnie glowered at her. Trying to patch things up, Skylark added lightly: "Come to think of it, you could pinch me too and we'd both know we're wide awake."

But it was too late. "I would be so into that," Arnie said. He turned from her and opened the small backpack he had brought with him. Inside was some cordial and sandwiches.

"Thank you, Nephew," Bella said, tucking in, trying to calm Skylark and Arnie down by acting normal. "This is hot work. What brings you up here?"

"The hospital has been trying to get Skylark all morning. Obviously you three have been too busy up here to hear the phone. I volunteered to come and pick her up."

"Has something happened to Mum?" Skylark asked, her eyes pricking with tears. "Can you take me back with you now?"

"I might think about it," Arnie answered.

Bella put down her sandwich and glared at Arnie. "That's enough, Nephew. Can't you see how worried Skylark is?"

Hoki saw her chance. "I'll take you," she said to Skylark. "We can have a good talk on the way. Can you and Arnie hold the fort, Sister dear?"

Hoki began to make her way down the cliff face. Skylark followed her. All this stuff was getting so hard to take and, halfway down the cliff, her anxieties about Cora made her stop for breath. Would Mum recover? If so, how long would it be before Mum's next relapse? Was Mum involved somehow in all these weird prophecies about the birds? "Oh Mum," Skylark wailed, "What's happening? What's going on?"

When Skylark and Hoki were out of earshot, Bella pulled Arnie's ears.

"Ow! What was that for!"

"No wonder you can't get a girlfriend," Bella said.

"Are you belted in?" Hoki asked.

Skylark would have preferred to take the station-wagon, so that she could be in the driver's seat. However, Hoki assumed they would go in her car, which had been specially configured so that she could drive with her withered leg. Hoki floored the accelerator with her good foot.

"Well, you want to get to Tuapa quick and smart, don't you?"

"Yes, but I've never been driven before by a –" Oops.

"That's the trouble with you and Arnie," Hoki said. "Always shooting from the lip without thinking before you let fly."

They left the homestead behind and drove down Manu Valley. Watching Hoki's hands and feet flicking expertly from gear shift to accelerator pedal and clutch, Skylark marvelled yet again at this old woman who often appeared to be so fragile but was in reality stubborn, strong-minded and resourceful. Hoki seemed to know exactly what Skylark was thinking.

"People have always thought Bella was the stronger sister," Hoki said, "just because she's older than me. They look at me and all they see is that I'm smaller and I have a bad leg. But, you know, when you grow up with a leg like mine it makes you strong, not weak. Even Bella thinks she's the stronger one, and sometimes it's best for me to go along with her. But, you know, my sister cries at the drop of a hat, especially over her birds. They come to her with their broken wings or legs, and by the time she's finished blubbering over them, they can't fly because they're so waterlogged. Bella's the pushover, not me."

Hoki pushed the car around an S-bend. Changed gear. Decelerated. Not even a tap of the brake to do it. Put her foot back on the accelerator. Eased the car back onto the straight.

"I'm really sorry," Skylark began, "for what Mum did, causing that rip in the sky. She didn't mean it."

Hoki slammed on the brakes. They were at a break in the forest, where the trees thinned, and the road curved outwards. Skylark could see Tuapa below and the sparkling sea beyond. Above, like a disturbing dream, seabirds were ascending into the valley.

"You were supposed to stop it," Hoki said to her. "You were supposed to stop the sky from opening. You didn't even need to wave a wand or say abracadabra. All you had to do was stop your mother going up to the ancient tree and smoking a cigarette. Why didn't you?"

Skylark stared at Hoki, angry. "Get out of my face," she said. "Every time I say I'm sorry about something you or Bella take it as an excuse to get at me again."

"I refuse to believe you're not the chick," Hoki said, pressing her attack. Her eyes were glowing, looking into Skylark, slipping into her brain searching for something. The old lady went from one memory to the next, opening one door after another, peering into the darkness of each memory. Trying to find something she could recognise. Skylark closed her eyes, *pushed* – and Hoki found herself being thrown out.

"Don't do that again without asking my permission," she glared. "Don't blame me for what you've failed to do. If you want to stop what's happening, go find a magic needle and sew the sky back together. You and Bella have been coming at me out of left field, throwing one whammy after another at me, and I've made it clear to you to back off."

Hoki was so angry. She was angry at Skylark for talking to her like that. She was also angry with herself for choosing the wrong time and place to bring up the matter of who Skylark was supposed to be. How stupid, when the girl was so concerned about her mother.

"All right, Skylark dear," Hoki said, patting her shoulder. "But I have to say this –"

"Give me a break –"

"You may not have any option, Skylark." Hoki was hardhearted, for Skylark had to be confronted with it. "You may be between a rock and a hard place. We now have a new situation. You're part of it, whether you like it or not."

"You always talk in circles, Hoki."

"The two events – the ripped sky and your mother's hospitalisation – may be connected."

"How!"

"You'll have to figure that one out for yourself."

Half an hour later, Skylark and Hoki arrived at the hospital. Skylark was dreading the worst. Why had Dr Goodwin called her so urgently?

"You go on, Skylark," Hoki said as she parked the car, making a bigger space by pushing the car in front like Mr Bean.

Skylark walked quickly into the hospital, along the passageway to Cora's suite. Cora's bed was empty. Heart beating, Skylark ran back down the passage.

"Where's my mother?" she asked.

The receptionist looked puzzled. She pursed her lips doubtfully at the badge Skylark was wearing: WHY SHOULD I TIDY MY BEDROOM WHEN THE WHOLE WORLD'S A MESS?

"Oh, you mean Miss Edwards? She's been taken to emergency."

The receptionist pointed the way, and even though the signs on the door read KEEP OUT, Skylark barged right on in. She saw Cora and knew something was terribly wrong.

Cora was jerking like a puppet on strings. She was snapping her head backwards and forwards. The doctor and his nurses were holding her down.

"At last you're here," Dr Goodwin said when he saw Skylark. "We've been trying to get you all morning. Do you hold Power of Attorney?"

"Yes," Skylark said. "What's happening to my mother?" She was shivering. Trying not to show she was scared out of her wits.

"She's in a critical condition," Dr Goodwin said. "Her body is in overload. All the drugs she's taken have pushed her to the point where her life signs are spiking. We've taken the temporary measure of stabilising her with sedatives that we hope won't be adding to the problem. But what we really need to do is to induce a coma –"

At that moment, Cora gave a loud groan. Her eyelids flickered open, showing the whites of her eyes. The life systems supporting her went crazy. The whole room transformed itself into a frenzy of movement as the medical team tried to re-stabilise her.

"We're losing her," one of the nurses said.

"Do we have your permission?" Dr Goodwin asked. "We need to act now and put your mother under before she has another attack."

"Isn't that dangerous? No, I won't let you do it."

Doctor Goodwin gave Skylark a firm look. Like Hoki, he was brutal. "It's your mother's only chance. If you want her to live, consent. If you don't . . . Either way, it's your call."

Was this what Hoki had meant about being between a rock and a hard place? Things were moving too quickly. But Skylark had to make a decision fast.

"If I do consent, will you be able to wake her up?"

"With your mother in a controlled sleep we'll have a better chance of sorting out what the drugs she took are doing to her. Right now, they're working on all her life-support systems and putting pressure on her heart."

This wasn't fair. It wasn't fair at all. Skylark closed her eyes, hoped she was doing the right thing and made the call.

"Okay, I give my consent. Do it."

After that, putting Cora into a deep sleep didn't take long. When she saw how peacefully her mother rested, Skylark's distress fell away. She stroked Cora's hair. "In all the world, it's just you and me," she said.

Then it happened. A thought popped into Skylark's head. One minute it was there, next minute it had gone. Her mouth dropped open and she looked across at Hoki.

"You've known all along, haven't you?" she said.

"I don't know what you're talking about," Hoki answered, puzzled.

"The two events – the ripped sky and Cora's coma – *are* related. Saving one will save the other."

Skylark had reached the threshold. She stepped over it.

"Don't you understand? Mum's not going to come out of this. Not unless I go back in Time to ask the landbirds to forgive her for burning down their sacred tree."

[CHAPTER SEVEN]

– 1 –

Kaa. *Kaa.*

The light was waning fast. Kawanatanga exhorted his troops to redouble their efforts. But every time they spilled air and closed wings to dive through the ripped sky, the old hen or the male chick who had arrived to help her let loose with the shotguns – and the formations broke up in terror.

"Kaa-*kaa.* Advance, you cowards."

The sun was beginning to set. The moment it went down, the ripped sky disappeared before Kawanatanga's very eyes.

Thwarted, Kawanatanga screamed his rage at his seabird army. "We will have to return tomorrow." He turned away, flicking a wingtip, and at this signal the seabirds followed him down and out of Manu Valley.

Below him Kawanatanga saw a car returning from Tuapa. It was being driven by the other hen, the one with the withered claw, and in the passenger seat was the chick.

"She is still a threat to us," he said to Karoro and Toroa. "Remain behind and keep watch on her." Then he realised that unlike the two old hens, Skylark was not under the Lord Tane's protection. He placed a bounty on Skylark. "Any gull who brings back her eyes will be richly rewarded."

Kawanatanga could not contain his elation. He swooped down on the car. Flying level with it, he taunted Skylark with a message:

I'd watch my back if I were you.

– 2 –

"You have to do what?" Bella asked, when Skylark outlined her thoughts to her at dinner that evening.

"Don't you see?" Skylark answered. "It makes perfect sense. My mother transgressed a Maori tapu and needs to be forgiven for it."

"And you know tapu," Hoki insisted. "You know how sacred the paepae was. You know that when a tapu is broken it must be put right."

Bella looked darkly at Hoki. She had prepared a meal of bacon bones and puha. She banged the serving bowls down on the table and blessed the food. "We give thanks for the kai we share tonight. We also ask for rescue from the lame-brained ideas of a young girl who doesn't know any better, and from a certain old lady who is egging her on. Amen."

Hoki gave a gasp of anger, but Bella compressed her lips and began to dish out.

"You should be ashamed of yourself, Sister," Bella continued. "Why are you encouraging Skylark to even think of such a thing?"

Stung, Skylark sprang to her own defence. "I've come to this understanding by myself," she said. "And don't think I am doing it for you and Hoki, either. If I don't go, my mother won't revive. The only ones who can give her forgiveness happen to be the Runanga a Manu."

"It's a crackpot idea," Bella said. "It's preposterous, and I won't have a bar of it. Now let's just forget the whole thing and eat. I've been looking forward to my dinner."

Skylark was firm. "If I get there before the seabirds from the present arrive, I can tell the runanga they're coming. That should make up for what Mum did."

"Are you crazy or something!" Bella asked. "Just how do you think you can do that? It's not like flying to Auckland. You're talking about doing the impossible. Where's your time machine! Porangi, that's what you are." Bella looked at Hoki, expecting her to come around and help her out. But all Hoki said was:

"Sister, Skylark has divined the pattern and the part she has to play in it."

Bella reached over the table and rapped Hoki on the head. "Knock, knock, is anybody home? You're unbelievable, Hoki dear. I know we're looking for a solution to our problem but this one is really dopey."

"Oh, get over yourself, Bella," Skylark interjected, not caring whether she was being rude or not. "Whether you like it is of no concern to me. I'll save Mum, and while I'm at it fulfil your prophecy. I could kill two birds with one stone, right?"

Hoki winced. "Skylark, please watch your language."

"All I want you two to do is figure how to get me back there," Skylark persisted.

"I refuse to be a part of this," Bella said, pushing her plate away. "And thank you both so much for spoiling my appetite."

Skylark looked squarely at Hoki. "Looks like it's up to you then," she said.

After dinner Hoki made up the spare bed for Skylark. She was so cross with Bella that she didn't help with the dishes and instead rocked and rocked on the old chair on the verandah. She looked up at the dark sky and into the immensity of the universe. Her mind was open and thoughts were whirling around in it.

"An answer to Skylark's question must be found," Hoki said to herself. "But where?"

All around, she heard the forest whispering, sneezing, seething. There was something so ecstatic about the night world, something slightly dangerous which thrilled her. People were so ignorant to think that everything went to sleep at night; the night forest was as alive as the day world.

Hoki heard Bella grumbling through the house, going from room to room and switching off the lights – including the verandah one. Bella was like that sometimes: grumpy, petty and mean. Sighing to herself, Hoki reached for her walking sticks. Making as much noise as possible, she clattered her way to the bathroom. There, she dropped the soap, scrubbing brush and nail scissors as she washed; then she got into her dressing gown. On the way to her room she stopped at Bella's closed door and opened it. The interior was dark, but she knew that Bella was sitting up in the bed, glaring at her.

"When we were little girls," Bella began, "I put two signs on that door. One was for Mum and Dad, saying KEEP OUT. The other was at little girl height: THIS MEANS YOU, HOKI. The bottom sign's still there but obviously you never learned to read."

"And you never learned that I grew up," Hoki answered. "Isn't it about time you raised the sign so that I can see it?" She felt her way in the darkness and tried to get into bed.

Bella swung a leg over, preventing her. "Oh no you don't," she said. "You've already ruined my dinner, you never even came to help me with the dishes, and since then you've been making enough ruckus to raise a ghost. I will not let you ruin my beauty sleep as well. So go away."

"It's too late," Hoki said as she hopped over Bella's leg. "And I'm not talking about my getting into bed either."

Bella was rigid, her arms crossed. Hoki felt for them and tried to snuggle in under them, but Bella wasn't budging.

Ah well, best to plough on regardless. "I feel so lonely, Sister dear," Hoki said. "I don't know where to turn, where to go, what to do. I feel so hopeless –"

"Oh, what's the use," Bella said. She pulled Hoki over and into her arms. Then, unexpectedly, she said, "You'll find the answer. You always do."

"So you've come around to Skylark's and my way of thinking?" Hoki asked.

"Get real, Sister," Bella growled. "It still sounds like a crazy idea. But the awful thing is that even dumb old me can see the logic and the pattern that is developing from it. Still, it's not going to happen. Even you can't do the impossible."

"Oh can't I?" Hoki said. She never liked it when Bella thought she knew better.

"No you can't," Bella replied. "Now snuggle up and go to sleep, and if I bite you during the night it's only because I'll be dreaming of bacon bones."

The next morning, Bella wasn't at all surprised to find the place in the bed empty beside her. When something was really bothering Hoki she was likely to stay up all night. Bella wandered into the sitting room and yup, there was Hoki flipping over the pages of the Great Book of Birds. Bella went into the kitchen, made a pot of tea and brought a cup back to Hoki.

"Please don't tell me you've found a way of getting Skylark back in Time," she said.

"No, I haven't." Hoki sipped her tea.

"Good," Bella said. "So that's that. Now everybody can wake up."

Hoki gave a sly smile. "But the answer could be in the Apocrypha," she said.

– 3 –

Skylark awoke to the sound of shotguns invading her dreams, but she wasn't dreaming at all. Everything was as real as it had been yesterday and, from the sounds outside, the seabirds had come up the valley with the dawn and were attacking again. Quickly, she got out of bed and went to the window. Bella and Hoki were silhouetted against the sky, shooting into the sun. Gulls and terns squealed and fragmented around them.

Skylark got dressed and hurried down to the kitchen where Bella had left her some breakfast on the table. There was a note: MORENA, SLEEPYHEAD. BRING SOME FRUIT AND DRINK FOR MORNING TEA.

Skylark filled two bottles with water and loaded her backpack with apples and bananas. Then she was out the door and off, walking quickly up the path.

"Why didn't you wake me?" she asked when she arrived at the cliff top. "Tomorrow, wake me."

Bella grinned across at Hoki. "It's the cavalry and I think she's grumpy this morning." She gave Skylark her shotgun while she had a drink of water.

"Hello Skylark," Hoki said. "This might make you happier. Did I ever tell you that as well as the Great Book of Birds there is also an Apocrypha?"

Skylark's mind went into overdrive. Part of her was excited. Part of her was really scared. What was she getting herself into?

"An extra volume? An additional testament?"

"Hoki thinks it will have instructions in it on how to build your time machine, " Bella said with sarcasm.

"Whatever the case, we should consult it," Skylark said. "It sounds like the only chance I've got." She had no option, really. For Cora's sake she had to follow the Mad Hatter down the rabbit hole to Wonderland.

"The problem is," Hoki said, "me and Bella don't have it. If you want to read it, you'll have to go and see Birdy." She looked at Bella. "Did you, by any chance, tell Skylark about Birdy?"

Bella shook her head.

Skylark hesitated. Sighted. *Boom.* "Will this get better or worse?"

"If we tell you," Hoki continued, "we must have your word that you will keep everything you hear to yourself. Will you do that?"

"Yes, I promise."

"Okay," Hoki answered. "Well, the thing is, Bella and I are not the only guardians. There are three other handmaidens of the Lord Tane. Birdy is one of them. Of course there were more in the old days when the Great Forest stretched from one end of the country to the other –"

Skylark sighed. Here we go again.

"To be brief," Hoki said, seeing that look on Skylark's face, "we are descended from the first handmaiden, Hana. Thousands of years ago, she appointed the sisterhood of handmaidens to take upon themselves the task to look after the forest, the birds of the forest and, in particular, the knowledge about the first battle of the birds and the prophecies surrounding it. All this knowledge was written into the Great Book of Birds. It was important to make sure that the story was preserved so that, when the time of the opening of the sky arrived, the handmaidens of this generation would know how to deal with it."

"The sisterhood was the first ahi kaa," Bella added. "The mission of keeping the lore of the Great Book of Birds alive was passed from one generation to the next, from mother to daughter. The First People honoured our roles in the tribe as priestesses of the Lord Tane. They came often to our fires to hear us read from the Great Book and to ask us to mediate on their behalf with Tane. We were respected and loved."

"Then," chimed in Hoki, "the pale Second People arrived in Aotearoa, and they brought a new way of looking at things. They had no use for the handmaidens of the Lord Tane. After all, we opposed everything they stood for. They brought in laws which proclaimed us as being tohunga makutu –"

"Witches," Bella translated.

"Before the handmaidens knew it," Hoki continued, "they found themselves outcasts and hunted down. It's the old, old story. During the Land Wars, only a few of them survived and, therefore, only a few copies of the original Book of Birds as well."

"Our great-great grandmother, Taraipene, was one of the survivors," Bella said. "She fled into the remotest part of the southern forest. She passed down the knowledge to Kararaina, our great-grandmother, who, when the forest began to diminish, migrated to Manu Valley. Why this valley? Because she realised there were only a few generations to go before the prophecies in the Book would come to pass. She intuitively sensed it would happen here, where the ancient tree was."

"Luckily for us, Kararaina also knew how to write," Hoki said. "It was she who transcribed her copy of the original Book of Birds into ledger books. Before she died, she passed her role, and the books, on to Turitumanareti, our grandmother. Grandma married a rich Scotsman, Angus McKay, and he helped her maintain Manu Valley as Maori land before anybody else could chop it down or the Government confiscate it. Turitumanareti passed on the role of handmaiden of the Lord Tane to our mother, Jane, and when we were born Mum anointed us for the task. Basically, I'm the brains —"

"And I'm the brawn," Bella continued.

"So Birdy is one of you?" Skylark said, before the story could make another loop.

"Yes," Hoki answered. "But we haven't seen her for years. Anyhow, Mum told us that the Apocrypha, the extra testament of the Great Book of Birds, is a northern tribal variant to ours. It was written by one of Birdy's ancestresses, and that's why it's kept by her family and by Birdy in our generation."

"She's older than us," Bella said. "But I got a postcard from her last Christmas, so she's still alive. Trouble is, she lives up north at Parengarenga."

"Way up there! That's at the other end of the country."

"Yes," Hoki nodded. "If you want to see what's in the Apocrypha you'll have to go up there yourself."

Skylark paused. "Let's cut to the chase," she said. "I know this is probably a stupid question, but you couldn't text her to fax or email a copy to us?"

Hoki stared at Skylark with a look of horror. "No self-respecting handmaiden of Tane would ever stoop to such modern mumbo-jumbo!"

"I thought as much," Skylark answered, "but one of these days, please put everything onto a floppy." She had a second, suspicious, thought. "You're not sending me on a wild goose chase, are you?"

"Well . . ." Bella pursed her lips. "I wouldn't exactly say that Birdy is a goose."

"The next question," Hoki asked Bella at lunchtime, "is how does Skylark get to Parengarenga? It's a day's drive from here to the Picton ferry, and half a day by ferry to Wellington. She'll be lucky if she can drive from Wellington up to Parengarenga in a day; more likely, it will take her a day and a night."

"You're right," Bella nodded. "And we have another problem." She pointed to Kawanatanga, Karoro and Toroa circling overhead. "I've been wondering why those big brutes are keeping a lookout. Now I know. Kawanatanga's keeping his beady eyes on us. If Skylark leaves, he'll suspect something. He knows she's the one to watch." Bella turned the problem over in her head. "There's nothing else for it," she said at last. "Skylark can't go by herself. Someone will have to go with her." She rolled her eyes and drummed her fingers on the table, waiting for Hoki to take the hint.

"Boy," Hoki said, "you sure go straight to the point."

"You know me, I don't do subtle. It's better that you go."

"Because of my crippled leg you mean?"

"You know as well as I do," Bella said, "that I'm stronger, I know more about shotguns than you do and it will be better if I stay here to stop the birds getting through."

"But I've never set foot outside Tuapa. You and me, we've never spent a night away from each other."

"This is no time to be sentimental," Bella said. She pointed to the seabirds, giant waves coming in and over the top of them. "Their momentum is picking up. You've got to go with Skylark. It'll make it safer and easier if there's two to share the driving."

Hoki bit her lip. "I feel as if I'm being bulldozed into this. Besides, you don't even sound as if you'll miss me."

"I'll miss you," Bella insisted. "Anyhow, this was your own idea, wasn't it? Who knows what problems might crop up on your way to Birdy's. So there's no option." She was talking quickly. "Do you think you two can start tonight? Travelling fast, you could just catch the ferry tomorrow morning."

"Will you really be able to manage?"

"I'll be fine," Bella said. "I'll keep one of the shotguns. If things get worse, Arnie can help me. You'd better take the other shotgun with you. Just in case."

By evening Skylark and Hoki were ready. Skylark was having an attack of the nerves and went around muttering to herself, "I can do this, I really can do this."

As for Hoki, she was still reluctant. She had packed some food, drink and blankets into the car and stashed the shotgun and ammunition in the boot. But what really rankled was hearing Bella ring up Arnie and tell him to come to help her in the morning. "You can't wait to get rid of me, can you," Hoki said.

Just as they were ready to leave, Bella saw that Karoro and Toroa were still on patrol.

"How are you going to get out of Tuapa without being seen?" she asked.

"We've got it all worked out," Skylark answered. "I need to say goodbye to Mum before I go, so the seabirds will think me and Hoki are just visiting her. By the time visiting hours are over, it'll be pitch black. That's when we'll make our getaway. Our main problem will be when morning comes. We'll be on the coast highway. It borders the sea and is in the seabirds' territory. That's when we'll be most at risk. If the seabirds see us –"

"They won't," Bella assured her. "Now go, both of you, before I –" Her face was streaming with tears. She was trying to act tough, trying not to show Hoki that she really would miss her. She kissed Hoki and traced her face as if she would never see her again.

Hoki saw through it all. On the way down the valley, she found herself being troubled by Bella's tears. The further she drove, the more worried she became. "My sister's never been able to survive without me," she muttered to Skylark. "She depends on me to make the breakfast. How's she going to get on without me? I should never have agreed to leave her to deal with the seabirds by herself."

"Then you should stay," Skylark said. "I'll go by myself. I'll be okay."

"With the seabirds trailing you?" Hoki answered. "I doubt it." She pointed to Toroa and Karoro still shadowing them on their way to Tuapa. "Like you, Skylark, I'm also between the rock and the hard place."

But not for nothing was Hoki the brains of the outfit. By the time she and Skylark had reached the town she had an idea:

"You go on in and see your mother. I need to fill up the car and then I have to see somebody. I'll be back for you at closing time."

Skylark followed the scent of roses along the corridor and up the lifts and, sure enough, at the end of the trail was Cora, surrounded by more flowers. Even Daddy darling had managed to remember to send something from him and Rhonda. And Lucas too.

Cora looked like Snow White lying on her funeral bier in the middle of the forest. Zac had given her a toxic apple; she had taken a bite. Now she lay waiting for the handsome prince to kiss her so that she could cough it up.

Skylark felt like crying. "Oh, Mum, why does there always have to be a handsome prince?" Then she heard somebody behind her, and turned to see Dr Goodwin. "How's she doing, doctor?"

"We're just going to have to wait and see. Her body and her mind need time to sort out what they need to do. Sometimes it's better to let nature run its course."

"When will you bring her out of her coma?"

"Once she stabilises and her life signs are out of the red, we'll do it then."

"When will that be?"

"Perhaps next week," Dr Goodwin answered.

"I'm relying on you to do it," Skylark said. "If you don't, I'll put *you* in a coma and, believe me, you won't want to come back, because I'll take that stethoscope around your neck and strangle you with it!"

Dr Goodwin took a step back, startled at Skylark's outburst. Then he steadied himself and accepted Skylark's challenge. "It should be successful. But just in case it isn't, I'd better not wear my stethoscope, right?"

Skylark nodded. Next week. Time enough for her to do what she had to do and get back.

An hour later, a bell began to ring throughout the hospital to announce that visiting time was over. Hoki returned – and with her was Arnie.

"There's been a change of plan," Hoki said. "Arnie's going with you as your sidekick, not me."

"Oh no," Skylark answered. "If you can't come with me, I'll go alone."

"No you won't, "Hoki said. "Arnie's going with you and that's that. As for me, I'll return to Manu Valley to help my sister. It's better this way."

"You think I'm happy?" Arnie asked. He frowned, but Skylark could tell that Hoki had been priming him to expect a great adventure. From the glazed look on his face, Arnie had already entered action movie heaven.

"We're going to deploy the old decoy trick," Arnie said.

"What did I tell you?" Skylark asked Hoki. "We haven't even left yet and already Arnie's testosterone's pumping."

Arnie bristled but decided to let it pass.

"Hoki will go out the front to her car and the seabirds will think you're both going back to the valley. As for you and me, we'll sneak out the back way, hop into my wagon, and we'll be away before they know it."

"I saw that movie," Skylark said. "But there's one thing wrong with your plan."

"There's nothing wrong with my plan!"
"The seabirds will see that I'm not in the car with Hoki."
Arnie coloured. Take that, pimple-brain, Skylark thought. "Arnie's already thought that one through," Hoki said. "For some strange reason, he has one of those life-sized girlie dolls in the garage."
"It belongs to Lucas," Arnie said quickly.
"Skylark, dear," Hoki raised her voice. "You're just going to have to grow up. You're going to have to trust that other people know better than you do about what to do. You're going to have to trust me, and Arnie. And you're going to have to help me out. Just the thought of leaving Bella is making me feel bad. I'm not going to leave her in the lurch. Is that clear?"
"As a bell," Skylark snapped, "but I still don't like it."
Hoki turned to Arnie. "Wait half an hour after I'm gone. When you think the coast is clear, move on out. Don't put on your headlights until you reach the coast road. When you reach Picton, call me. Shall we synchronise our watches? Check our coordinates?" Hoki knew how to push all Arnie's buttons.
"Okay, Auntie. Check."
"One other thing," Hoki added. She rummaged in her flax kit and, when she came up for air, she had a pendant in her hands. Attached to the cord was a bird claw. Hoki placed it around Skylark's neck.
"What is it?" Skylark asked.
"Among all the birds of the land, hawks are the supreme diurnal birds of prey. They are totally fearless. They are also greatly loving of their young. The hen bird offers only the choicest pieces of prey to her young. Each chick is fed in turn. Each gets its share. Arnie already has a claw, and I give this one to you because I have such a claw." Hoki lifted her skirt to show her withered foot. "As the hawk loves its children, I love you both. May this claw protect you in whatever you do. It can open flesh to the bone. Should you be in danger, let all beware of my fury."
Skylark was still fuming about Arnie. "You planned this all along," Skylark accused. "From the very first, you planned that Arnie would come with me. Well, I don't –"
"Oh tough," Hoki answered sharply. "Get over yourself." Ignoring Skylark's open-mouthed look, she grabbed her and kissed her on both cheeks. She would have done the same with Arnie, but he backed away.
"May the force be with you," Hoki said to him as she left out the

front door. "And with you too, Skylark dear."

Skylark watched Hoki leave the hospital and walk to her car. She saw the plastic pumped-up doll on the passenger's side and was disgusted. "It's got blonde hair, mine is brown. And I hardly ever wear lipstick."

"The birds won't know the difference," Arnie argued. "Don't you think it's an improvement on the original?"

"Oh for heaven's sake," Skylark warned. "We haven't even started on our trip."

She watched Hoki drive the car out of the carpark.

Arnie was nervous, raring to go. But it wasn't dark enough – and those strange, sinister seabird shadows were still gliding across the sky.

"We've got to keep to the plan," Skylark answered. "Better to wait for complete darkness, otherwise we're dead before we hit the highway."

"But we've already left it late enough to catch the ferry, "Arnie argued. "Leave it any later and we may as well not go."

Skylark kept a firm grip on the leash. Half an hour later, just as Arnie had reached the limit of his patience, she saw Karoro and Toroa abandon their watch. She gave Arnie the green light.

"Okay, we can go now," she said.

"You just did that to show you're the boss, didn't you."

They left by the back door and had their first argument about who would drive.

"It's my wagon and I will drive," Arnie said.

"And it's my life and you're supposed to ride shotgun."

"Then lets toss a coin," Arnie said.

"Heads," Skylark answered.

Much to her anger, the coin came down tails.

"All that I will say," she hissed as she got in the passenger's side, "is that we the unwilling, led by the unknowing, will try to do the impossible for the ungrateful." She slammed the door.

Meanwhile, Hoki had returned to Manu Valley. She carried Lucas's doll into the spare bedroom and put it to bed. Bella, who had just settled down in her armchair and lined up three vodka shots, watched her agog. "You're supposed to be on your way north," she said.

"Arnie's taken my place," Hoki answered. "I should have known that as soon as my back was turned you'd hit the bottle."

"Arnie's gone with Skylark? You've got to be joking. They'll kill each other."

"No they won't," Hoki answered. "They're only at each other's throats because they don't know each other. It's better this way. They'll be forced to talk, or go out of their minds with boredom. The talking will bring them closer together."

"You hope."

"As well as that," Hoki continued, taking one of Bella's vodka shots and slugging it to the back of her throat, "I just don't have the physical strength and stamina for the journey; it's for younger people to go on, not an old kuia like me. Arnie, he can roll with the punches."

"What happens if there are any big problems?"

"They're just going to have to sort it out themselves," Hoki said. "I'm home, and I'm home to stay. I'm too old to change my habits. And you've become a habit. We've never been apart, Sister dear, never. I'm not about to start now."

However, all that evening, Hoki tossed and turned with worry. She dreamt of skies black with gulls who had not been duped by the decoy routine. In her dreams she watched as the seabirds followed Skylark and Hoki out of Tuapa. They grouped above Arnie's wagon, waiting until it had reached the highest bend of the mountain road.

Now. *Now.*

Horrified, Hoki watched as the seabirds stalled, closed their wings and stooped, uttering their wild hunting cries as they dived.

"No!" Hoki screamed. The seabirds attacked. They smashed themselves into the windows. They covered the entire ute with their wings, as if they were feeding on it. Blinded, Arnie took his foot off the accelerator, but it was too late. The ute smashed through the railing and began to fall over the cliff.

Falling. Falling. Then it hit the rocks and burst into flame.

Hoki woke up, sweating, and saw it was dawn. Dawn? She looked at the clock: five-thirty. The ferry was scheduled to leave at six. She banged on Bella's door, but Bella was already up, washed and ready for the first watch. "I'll go on up to the clifftop. Why don't you wait for Arnie's call? Didn't you say he'd call when they reached Picton?"

Hoki waited by the telephone. Six o'clock came and went. In her mind's eye, she saw the ferry breasting the sea, leaving Picton. She could hear the boom of Bella's shotgun and the squealing cries of the gulls.

Six-thirty. Still no call. I should have gone, Hoki told herself. I shouldn't have left the responsibility to Skylark and Arnie.

Seven o'clock. Seven-thirty. Hoki feared the worst. She had always had the gift of matakite, the second sight, seeing into the future. Perhaps what she had seen last night wasn't a dream at all. Perhaps the police had already been called to investigate a ute, smashed on rocks pounded by the sea. They were already pulling out the bodies of a girl and a boy. Above the scene, Kawanatanga was watching. He turned to Hoki, laughing at her, and she put her hands up to her ears to close him out.

The telephone rang just after eight. For a moment Hoki was too frightened to pick it up, just in case it was the police to tell her the bad news. Just in case it was a doctor at a hospital to say Skylark and Arnie were in critical condition.

"Mother Ship, are you there, Mother Ship? Do you copy? Over."

Hoki gave a cry of relief. "We copy, Arnie. Thank God you're alive. I've been out of my mind with worry. How's Skylark?"

"She's okay. Do you want to speak to her?"

Hoki was so cross that Arnie could be so casual. "In a moment. So, you got out of Tuapa without being seen? How was the trip to Picton? Any problems?"

"No," Arnie answered. "Sweet as. We hit some roadworks on the way, just before Kaikoura, and that slowed us down and –"

"Yes, I know," Hoki said, "you've missed the ferry."

"Missed the ferry?" Arnie sounded puzzled. "I thought we would too. But even when the time went past six Skylark insisted we press on. Nag nag nag."

"Good on her!"

"And guess what, Auntie? The ferry had been delayed. Bad weather apparently. We just made it on time. We're the last vehicle on board. The ferry's leaving right now."

"Now?"

At the other end of the telephone, Hoki heard the blast of the ship's horn, so loud it set up a ringing in her ears. Skylark and Arnie must have been standing right next to it.

"Hoki? Are you there, Hoki? We're on our way," Skylark said.

Then Arnie was back on the line.

"Affirmative, Mother Ship. We have ignition."

[CHAPTER EIGHT]

– 1 –

"Come on, Arnie," Skylark yelled.

Once the wagon had been parked, Skylark raced to the ferry's upper deck. Arnie hung back.

"What's the problem?" Skylark asked.

Arnie was looking ahead at the sea. While the ferry was sheltered within Queen Charlotte Sound there was no problem. Out in the open water, the storm was waiting like a giant fist. "I should have realised," he groaned, "that if the boat was delayed for so long conditions out there must be bad. That storm is really going to hammer the shit out of me."

Sure enough, once the ferry entered Cook Strait the weather slammed it from all sides. It dipped and heaved; Arnie's face turned an interesting shade of green, and he was promptly as sick as a dog. Other passengers were leaning over the rails or hastening below decks for help.

"I think I'll join them," Arnie said to Skylark. "Maybe they've got a nurse who can give me something."

"Do you want me to come with you?" Skylark asked, concerned.

"No," Arnie scowled as he made his way below. "I'd prefer pro-*fession*-al help, thanks."

"See if I care," Skylark called after him. Besides, she couldn't see what the problem was. She had always revelled in stormy weather, wild wind and sea, and was both amused and mystified to find herself almost alone on the upper deck. Only she and an old man tanked to the gills with gin had not fled the elements. The ship dipped, the spray flew up and Skylark and the old man stood at the railing, at ease out here in the open. Out here she was free, she could be herself, and she had space to think clearly about all that had happened to her and Cora. The cold wind and spray from the sea sharpened her understanding of what was important and what wasn't.

"I love you, Mum!" Skylark shouted.

She had always squarely confronted her challenges. No matter what lay before her, she would face the future head on.

Quarter of an hour later the weather turned really nasty. The old man saluted and left, and Skylark was in good humour when she decided it was time to check on Arnie.

"Some hero you turned out to be," she said when she found him, collapsed and ill on a lower deck with other hapless seafarers.

"Do me a favour," Arnie moaned. "Next time you're on deck can you fall overboard?"

"Hear, hear," said another passenger.

"Would you like something from the dining room?" Skylark asked sweetly. "A triple cheese burger perhaps?" She turned to the room at large. "Anybody like a burger with the works followed by an ice cream sundae?"

There was a chorus of moans. Arnie looked at her wanly. "I'd ask you to have mercy, but I know you wouldn't know how to."

"Didn't you know?" Skylark asked. "I'm hard-hearted, and I like myself this way." Even as she said it, Skylark knew it wasn't true. It was simply that she had learnt the art of the caustic rejoinder. Growing up in a society that favoured pretty over plain, and compliant over stroppy, she had honed her skills with the fast put-down; it was the only way to get people to back up, and back off, before they could get a chance to put her down. The big voice and big attitude just seemed to grow with it.

As Arnie's seasickness worsened, however, Skylark's belligerence lessened and she began to feel sorry for him. He might be a pint-sized no-brain jock in overalls, but you should be kind to dumb animals, she mediated with herself. Arnie was half lying back, but he looked uncomfortable. His brow was drenched with sweat, his hair was slicked down with perspiration, and he was breathing in an awful way. When the ferry made a sudden heave and Arnie moaned and joined the rush for the toilets, Skylark took a deep breath and made a decision:

"I will not play at nurse, nor will I be mother, but –"

While their owners were in the toilets, Skylark swiped some of the vacated pillows and made up Arnie a better resting pallet. She ignored the yelps of protests as the previous owners returned – after all, in a situation like this, it was the survival of the fittest – and when Arnie came back she accepted his moan of gratitude as thanks enough. Even so, he almost ruined it.

"How much are you charging me?" he asked.

"Nothing. But I'm driving when we get to Wellington."

"Oh no you won't," Arnie said. "It's my wagon, and it's like your jersey. Anybody else who touches it gets wasted."

Throughout the rest of the crossing Skylark got Arnie to sit up rather than lie down. She held a bowl to his mouth whenever he got sick, and rinsed it out in the loo. She wiped his face with a wet cloth. She urged him to drink water to prevent him from becoming dehydrated. She even made a trip to the dining room to get him some clear soup and, although he protested, held his head up and spooned it into him. But she left the best of her ministrations till last. When, thirty minutes out from Wellington, Arnie asked, "How much longer?" she said, "Only an hour to go." The result was that when the ferry reached the calmer water of Wellington Heads, the earlier arrival made Arnie's face clear with a joyous sense of relief. He smiled his thanks, and Skylark was surprised to see that one of his eyes was green, the other was brown. They gave his face an odd, appealing look.

Wellington was lashed with rain squalls that came up from the south and cracked across the city, stinging every exposed piece of skin. The wind rattled the high-rise buildings, and only a few stupid fools were out, poking vainly at the rain with broken umbrellas. The ferry docked, bumping into its moorings, and Skylark helped Arnie down to the car deck, ready to join the exodus of vehicles. Sheepishly, Arnie handed over the keys.

"I guess you'll have to drive after all," he said. No matter that the ship had docked, he was heaving back and forth just like the sea. He was also feeling drowsy from pills the nurse had given him to take just before landing. She'd handed him four, with the instructions to take one now and three later – but what the heck, he'd taken them all at the same time. After all, if one pill would get you better, four would do the job quicker, right?

"It's four-wheel drive," Arnie said as Skylark started the ute. "Can you manage? You'll need to fill up soon. Ultimate unleaded, I don't like any of the other brands. I think the oil's okay but just watch the pressure. I'm sorry, Skylark, I feel like I'm letting you down."

Skylark had wanted to drive this baby even since she'd seen it. She gave Arnie an evil smile. "You're putting yourself into my hands? Heh heh heh –"

By the time the ferry doors opened, Arnie was out like a light. Skylark looked at her watch. It was just after eleven in the morning. Eight hours to Auckland. Another six to Parengarenga. Add another three or four hours for rest stops, lunch and dinner. If they drove through the night they'd make Parengarenga by the next morning. She gave the ute a touch of juice, took off the handbrake, added some acceleration and the ute leapt onto the dock.

"Kaa. *Kaa.*"

Seagulls swooped low across the windscreen, crying harshly. Skylark gave a gasp of fear. Her heart was racing. Had they seen her? No. Luckily, the windscreen was smattered with rain. She watched as a group of six chased a seventh away from a pie that somebody had thrown onto the ground. Then they returned and began fighting over the pie. Tearing at it with their sharp beaks. Raging at each other.

Skylark followed the exit signs out of the harbour. Not until then did she put the wipers on. The windscreen cleared and she was soon driving away from Wellington on the main highway north.

– 2 –

Hoki stood at the clifftop like a sentinel. All around, the seabirds were wheeling. Whenever they got too close she balanced on her walking sticks and raised the shotgun. "Think you can get past me?" she muttered. "Well think again."

Boom. The force of the shot almost unbalanced her. She blew at the smoke issuing from the barrel. "Yessirree, the sheriff's back in town." She cast a particularly murderous glance at Kawanatanga. He was like a general overlooking the battlefield and marshalling his troops. She'd tried before to pop him off, but he was in a high-flying figure-eight pattern and always out of range.

"Too scared to come down to Momma?" Hoki asked, trying to take a bead on him. "Come closer, you big black brute, come to Auntie Hoki –"

Hoki let off a shot but it fell short. Kawanatanga arched his neck and shouted his mockery down upon her. He soared on the thermals, exhibiting the insolent strength of his scapulars. Watching him, Hoki found herself looking through the ripped sky to the blackness beneath; it was like an eye into the past, and she had to shake her head to clear her vision. She looked at her watch. It was coming on to midday and she was getting hungry.

Bella arrived with a basket containing some sandwiches and drink. She also had a strange piece of equipment with her – a long wooden rod, like a broom handle, with a notch at one end. She spread a blanket on the grass and invited Hoki to join her. If it hadn't been for the screaming seagulls you would have thought that two old ladies were sitting down for a quiet picnic.

"I've just had the fright of my life," Bella said.

Boom. She levelled the shotgun at the sky as some gulls tried to sneak past.

"What from, Sister dear?" Hoki asked.

"You should have told me you had sat that hideous doll in one of the armchairs in the sitting room. I thought we had a visitor."

"I put Skylark's dressing gown on it," Hoki giggled. "Do you think it will fool the seabirds?"

"Let's hope so," Bella answered. "There were a few sitting on our telephone lines, looking in through the window. We've got to give Skylark and Arnie as much of a head start as possible. Once the seabirds find out she isn't here, they may go after her."

After lunch it was Bella's turn on sentry duty, but Hoki decided to stay up on the cliff with her. "Who knows what booze you've got in your flask," she joked.

"That means you're spoiling my surprise," Bella said. She stood, picked up the strange piece of equipment she had brought with her and began banging it into the ground. She placed Hoki's shotgun in the cradle. "Even though you don't deserve this," she said, "given your crack about my flask, this will save you having to balance on your walking sticks. All you need to do is aim and pull the trigger."

"Why, thank you, Sister dear," Hoki answered. She had a practice, swinging the shotgun on its cradle and then: *Boom.*

What was that sound?

One moment Arnie was asleep, the next he was aware of someone singing. At first he thought it was birdsong but then he realised that this was only one voice and it wasn't a bird. Slowly, he opened one eye and peeked out. Skylark was behind the wheel of his ute, earphones on her head, and she was singing along with a portable CD. She had put it on rather than the ute's radio so she wouldn't wake him, but had been carried away with the songs on the disc.

"The hills are alive with the sound of music . . ."

Arnie decided to play possum and just listen and watch for a while. It hadn't occurred to him that Skylark would have such a gorgeous voice – light, bright and, when she opened out the throttle, man, could it soar? Could it what!

"I could have danced all night, I could have danced all night . . ."

The CD was a compilation of Broadway show tunes, which was not Arnie's type of music at all. But for the first time he saw Skylark with her guard down. Sure, she wasn't the slim type that he preferred but she had a really pretty face. Her skin was clear, her eyes sparkled and although her chin was as stubborn as, once you looked past her attitude you found a different girl.

Not for long. Right in the middle of the song Skylark saw that Arnie was awake, staring at her, and she stopped in mid-flight.

"I hate people watching me while I'm driving," she said.

"No, don't stop," Arnie answered. "I didn't realise you had such a terrific voice."

Skylark didn't know whether Arnie was being sarcastic or not. "Yes, well, the CD's not mine. It's Mum's. Would you believe I've brought her music by mistake?"

"Well I think its great," Arnie said. "Did you have lessons?"

"No," Skylark answered, relaxing. "But when I was little and Mum and I used to go on long trips between one gig and another, she loved to have me sing in the car. 'Sing, Skylark, sing,' she used to say. She told me that it stopped her from falling asleep at the wheel." Skylark smiled at the memory. "Mum used to say, 'Skylark O'Shea, a girl should never leave home without a Broadway tune in her purse, just in case she meets an agent and has an audition on the spot! A show tune is just the thing when you're feeling afraid or in a jam. Whenever that happens, sing, Skylark, sing.'"

Skylark gave an incredulous laugh at her own gullibility. Then she realised she had shown too much of herself. She looked ahead.

"We've reached Taihape," she said. "And don't think you can get around me so easily, just by being nice about my singing."

"Already?" Arnie's eyebrows arched with surprise. "Nice driving, Skylark." Then, "I'm hungry," he said. "I could eat a horse and drink a river dry. Let's stop and have lunch when we hit the town."

"You also need a visit to a bathroom," Skylark said. "Your breath is so awful you could turn me to stone – and don't be tempted to do it."

Arnie could have given a smart reply but realised that he had turned the corner with Skylark. After all, she'd been nice to him during the Cook Strait crossing. If he was nice back, maybe they'd get along better. For the first time since they'd started the trip they'd been able to have a conversation – a short one, sure – without getting at each other's throats. It was a start.

Skylark turned into a parking space. Arnie found a restaurant, and left Skylark to order food while he made a visit to the bathroom with a toothbrush, towel and soap. When he came back he was washed, brushed and combed, and Skylark had ordered herself a pie with peas and chips, washed down with coffee.

"What!" Skylark asked. She just knew, just *knew* that Arnie was going to criticise her selection. Well, she needed carbos, wanted carbos and was going to get carbos – and she just felt like a pie, thank you very much.

"I think I'll have the same," Arnie said, deciding to keep the peace, though what he really yearned for was a nice piece of lean steak, some salad and an energy drink to get his electrolyte levels back up. He took a bite out of the pie: "Mmm, good," he lied. Somewhere over the next few days, he vowed, he'd just have to find a gym.

After lunch, Skylark visited the women's room. She scrubbed her face till it shone, put her hair up in butterfly clips, sprayed some perfume in the air and stood under the mist. Arnie, waiting for her by the ute, was pleased she'd made the effort to look like – well, a person of her gender, for a change, but decided on balance not to say anything about it. Why tempt fate?

Skylark handed Arnie the keys. She too had done some thinking about having Arnie tagging along. She'd taken a reality check. They were stuck with each other. May as well try to get on, right?

"Thanks," Arnie said. "Maybe you can take over once we get to Auckland."

They hit the road. For a while they were silent, trying to figure out where to go next.

"Are you related to Hoki and Bella?" Skylark asked at last.

"Why do you ask?" Arnie answered. He was edgy, trying to be careful. If he started to talk, things might fall out that would get them arguing again. After all, it was obvious they were from different planets. She was a spoilt little know-everything girl who used her jersey, badges, mouth and attitude as weapons against the world. Did he want her to know him better?

Arnie decided to take the chance. "No," he began. "I'm not related. I come from Invercargill. My Mum and Dad had nine of us. My Dad was seventeen when he met Mum. She was still at high school. His name's George. Her name's Anna. I suppose they were in love but I wasn't around to see. By the time I arrived, number seven in the family, there wasn't much love left. And both Dad and Mum were on the dole."

"But there must have been something," Skylark answered, trying to keep the small talk going. "After all, another two children came after you."

"Yeah, well," Arnie said, "having sex was a habit they couldn't break."

Small house. Nine kids. Mum and Dad out of work. In the lounge was a photograph of them on their wedding day; when Arnie compared them to the present-day parents he would ask himself: Where did those two bright eyed and handsome young kids go to? Who stole Dad away and substituted the fat, foul-mouthed, violent slob whose only object in life was to go out, get drunk, come back and take it out on the wife and kids? What happened to the shy girl called Anna who became a woman with a scowl, hipping the latest baby from room to room, scattering cigarette ash on the way?

"By the time I was born," Arnie continued, "luckily my oldest sisters, Gina and Sophia, were bringing home a weekly paycheck from their checkout jobs. It was Gina really who brought me up; Mum and Dad were too zonked out to do it. In those days I was the runt of the litter. Dad used to call me Short Arse. At school I got the usual nicknames: Tiny, Squint, Midget, Munchkin. I guess that's why I started to go to the gym. Build up some bulk. I think I was trying to compensate so that if anybody tried to put me down I could bop them one. Then Gina and Sophia got married and left home, so us younger kids started to be farmed out to foster parents."

Some had been good. Some had been bad. One of the foster dads had tried to put his hands down Arnie's pants and Arnie had smashed him.

The foster dad denied it, got off, and Arnie began to receive a reputation as being difficult. Then, the usual story: he joined a gang of delinquents. Before you knew it, he was living under bridges, sniffing glue and breaking into houses and cars.

"That's when Auntie Hoki and Auntie Bella came along," Arnie said. "Social Welfare thought the best thing to do was to get me away from unsavoury influences. They got in contact with Dad's tribe and Auntie Hoki and Auntie Bella said they'd take me in. That's how I ended up in Tuapa. They turned me round. If it hadn't been for them I don't know where I'd be now. Probably in prison. I stayed with them while I finished college. Later, I found the job at Lucas's garage and moved to my own place in town."

Waiouru was ahead. The Army settlement looked like packing crates pushed accidentally out of a military transporter.

"Did Bella and Hoki tell you I joined the Army for a year?" Arnie asked. "We did everything. Running around playing soldiers. Building bridges. Going on route marches. Jumping out of helicopters. Tandem parachuting – wow, you've gotta try that sometime."

"You've got to be kidding."

Arnie shrugged his shoulders, but secretly he was very pleased with himself. He'd been right: once you got past all Skylark's defences – and, boy, was she ever rigged with booby traps, claymore mines and grenades that would go off at any false step – she was okay.

The Desert Road curved through the tussock. On the left side loomed three volcanic cones, their tops dusted with ice and snow. Clouds did conjuring tricks with the mountains, obscuring them one moment, revealing them the next.

Skylark was still curious. "What's all this mother ship business you have going with Hoki?"

"When I was a kid," Arnie answered, "Auntie Hoki took me to *E.T.* I'd never seen anything like it. Do you remember at the end when the mother ship comes to collect E.T.? Well, I started to call Auntie Hoki 'Mother Ship'. It was just a game but it gave me a good feeling when I was young to think that if ever I was in trouble I could just phone home and Auntie Hoki would come to get me. Now I think Hoki and I still do it just to drive Auntie Bella crazy!"

The ute sped onward through the falling afternoon, skirting the bases of the mountains, pushing north.

Skylark and Arnie reached Auckland by nightfall. The Skytower was directly ahead, winking in the twilight sky. Downtown Auckland was buzzing with traffic and action. Arnie eased the ute through the streets.

"Decision time," Arnie said. "We can either stop over and make for Parengarenga in the morning or we can have a dinner break, drive through the night and arrive at dawn."

"We'd better keep to our timetable," Skylark answered. "The sooner we get to Birdy's the better. But do you mind if we detour to Mum's place first? I'd like to pick up the mail and check any messages. We can shower and change there and, after that, I know a place where we can get great Indian food or, if you like, Thai."

"Whatever," Arnie said.

He followed Skylark's directions to a block of high rises in fashionable Parnell. Yes, he thought, just the place for a television star like Cora Edwards.

Skylark brightened as she stepped out of the ute, opened the lobby door and looked in the mailbox. It was filled with cards and letters from well-wishers; Skylark imagined her mother's delighted face when she opened them.

She led the way to the lift. A few seconds later, they were on the top floor. Skylark inserted the key, opened the door, switched on the light. Then she was wide-eyed, and backing away.

"He's been back," she said. "Zac's been back." Arnie pushed past her and charged into the apartment. "What the hell —" The place had been trashed. A psychopath had been on the rampage through it. In all the rooms, the curtains had been ripped. The couches in the sitting room had been slashed and the television set upended. The dining room was a wreck of broken mirrors and crystal. The kitchen was not much better: smashed crockery was strewn all over the floor. In the master bedroom Cora's clothes had been heaped on the carpet. Someone had tried to put a match to them; if the match had taken, the whole place would have gone up in flames.

Arnie heard Skylark sob. She had paused in her bedroom. Her bed was a pincushion of hypodermic needles. The imagery was chilling. Zac had scrawled a message on the wall:

YOU'LL GET YOURS, GIRLY.

Arnie went to comfort Skylark, but she stiffened and pushed him away. When she turned to him, Arnie saw that her mood had shifted.

"No," Skylark said. Her eyes were blazing and she was icy calm. She walked to the telephone and dialled a number. "Hello? Is that the building supervisor?" She reported the condition of the apartment, issued instructions on having it cleaned up, the locks changed, having a police report done, and, under no circumstances, was Zac to be allowed back in. Then she turned and looked at Arnie. Her face was grim. Unblinking.

"I'll get Zac if it's the last thing I do," she said.

Arnie saw that Skylark had again gone beyond his reach. She was so volatile, so reactive. In one second she had switched back on autopilot.

"This is what happens when you trust people," she said. "They trash your lives. Mum and I have always looked after ourselves. We don't need anybody else."

Then Skylark looked straight through him. Her voice was chill. "Hoki had no business forcing you to come with me. What I have to do has absolutely nothing to do with you. You're not involved. This is my business and I'm doing it for my mother. So, Arnie, thank you for bringing me this far, but I'm hiring a car for the rest of the trip. From here I go on alone. You go back to Tuapa where you're needed."

"Oh no you don't," Arnie answered.

"You've got no say in the matter," Skylark screamed. She had learned that sometimes with stubborn people, adding volume to attitude often did the trick. Not today.

"Oh yes I have," Arnie said. He had to think quick . . . Ah well, desperate people had to take desperate measures.

Before Skylark could stop him, he walked over to her backpack and took out her wallet. In it was her driver's licence and credit cards.

"You won't get far without these," Arnie said.

Skylark went through the roof. That was foul play. Out of court.

"How dare you do that! Give them back. They're mine, not yours!"

"No, Skylark. We're sticking together and that's that." Arnie said, keeping his ground.

"You juvenile delinquent!" Skylark yelled. "I suppose you learned that little trick when you were living on the streets, right? Well, I can always get replacements."

"And waste a day when you're in such a hurry? I don't think so." Arnie was dancing out of her reach. Exhausting her. Skylark gave a loud wail and a last lunge and fell to the floor, hoping that Arnie would get close enough for her to grab.

"You're not the only one who can be obstinate," Arnie said. "Auntie Hoki didn't force me. I wanted to come – and whether you like it or not, I'm riding shotgun to the end of the trail. So you have two options. You either come with me – or you come with me. What's it to be?"

It was touch and go. Skylark was simmering; it was just as well she wasn't a volcano. If she called the cops in, that would be the end of Arnie. But she didn't. Phew. Instead, lips compressed, she stalked out of the apartment. Arnie couldn't help but put a jaunty step or two into his walk.

"You think you've got one over me, don't you," Skylark said. "Well, I'm warning you, Arnie, you know zip. So don't follow too close in my footsteps. I could step in something."

– 3 –

Arnie drove all the way from Auckland. Once on the northern highway, the heavy traffic thinned out. By the time they passed Whangarei, where they filled the ute with petrol, they seemed to be the only people on the road.

"Do you want me to drive from here?" Skylark offered. She was still angry, but she could tell Arnie was getting tired. He might get careless and have an accident, and that wouldn't do either of them any good.

"I'm okay, thanks," Arnie said. "If I let you have the wheel, who knows, you might push me out of the ute and take off without me." He wasn't joking either.

"Why, Arnie." Skylark fluttered her eyelashes. "The thought never even crossed my mind."

"Yeah, and butter wouldn't melt in your mouth," Arnie answered.

The consequence was that Skylark stayed awake, fearing Arnie might go to sleep at the wheel. Her alertness saved them when a stray cow came looming out of the darkness. "Watch out!" she cried. Arnie wrenched the wheel to the left, touched the accelerator and zoomed out of the way. The cow's huge eyes filled the windows and then slid to the left.

"I suppose you'll still insist on the imposition of your male testosterone mentality in the matter of safe driving?" Skylark asked. She was seething. As for Arnie, he decided it best not to answer. Things were bad enough already. For the rest of the trip, they hardly spoke. They were like two angry children in a spaceship shooting its way through a galaxy full of stars.

Just before dawn, Skylark and Arnie reached the narrow road that threaded its way up the northernmost extremity of Aotearoa. Not long after that they drove into Te Hapua, home of the last pub, the last petrol pump and the last store in the north. Beyond was Parengarenga Harbour, the sand dunes like spellbinding mountains sloping into the sea. They still weren't speaking to each other when Arnie saw a couple of locals riding horses down the main road and asked directions. "Could you tell us how to get to Birdy's place?"

"Sure. Turn left at the next bend, go two ks on, and follow the road right down to the sea. When you can't go any further, and you see a house, that's Birdy's."

Arnie rapped on the door. There was a shuffling sound from inside. When the door opened, an old woman was standing there, looking at them. She was thin, wiry, with long grey hair tumbling down to her waist.

"You two look like something the cat's dragged in." Her eyes were bright and inquisitive, and she had a way of rocking her head back and forth as if she was looking for something.

Yes, Skylark thought, you're Birdy all right.

"Of course I am," Birdy answered, as if she had read Skylark's mind. "And who are you?"

"My name's Skylark," Skylark said.

"Such a pretty bird. Introduced to Aotearoa in the 1860s, streaked brown and dark brown, eats insects, nests on the ground and has a beautiful song, yes, yes." She turned to Arnie. "And you?"

"My name's Arnie."

"Arnie? Arnie? Are you a Pelecaniformes? Or an Apterygiformes! No, I don't know the bird you're named after. Come in, come in. You haven't come to rob me, have you? There's nothing left in the house anyhow." Birdy ushered Skylark and Arnie in. "So why have you come to see me? Would you like some breakfast? How can I help you?"

"Hoki and Bella sent me," Skylark said.

Birdy gasped. She rushed to a cabinet, opened it, rummaged and found some spectacles, and peered closely at Skylark. "You're the chick! So you have appeared! I'm so happy, so happy." With a sigh, Birdy hugged Skylark.

"But why are you up here at Parengarenga?"

"I don't know what I'm supposed to do," Skylark said.

"Don't you? Don't you? But why don't you know!"

"The Book of Birds only has some of the information. I'm here because you have the Apocrypha."

"Do I?" Birdy cocked her head. "Do I? Of course you do, you silly old hen!" she chastised herself. "But first you two chicks will want to wash up! Have you been travelling all day and all night? Of course you have! There's the bathroom. Here are the towels. Women first. And afterwards, we'll have a breakfast of nice steamed mussels, cockles and seaweed tea! Doesn't that sound scrumptious?"

"Scrumptious," Skylark said, trying to sound enthusiastic.

A shower and change of clothes was just the thing to perk Skylark up. Hair wet, complexion shiny, she joined Birdy in the kitchen while Arnie took his turn to wash. By the time he came back, breakfast was ready.

"Hoe in! Eat the lot! The sea is bountiful!" Skylark didn't think she'd be too keen on the kai Birdy dished up, but man oh man, was it sweet!

"Eat! Eat!" Birdy continued. She dashed backwards and forwards with bread, butter and more tea. "And while you're hoeing in, I'll go and get the Apocrypha." She disappeared into the sitting room. Skylark heard her opening and closing drawers. "Where did you put it, you silly biddy! Not here? Maybe you left it in your bedroom or in the back shed? Maybe it's been stolen! Well, if somebody stole it they better watch out. There's a big hoodoo on the Apocrypha –"

Then there was a cry of joy.

"She's found it," Arnie said.

But when Birdy came to the kitchen she had other news. "I've been a forgetful hen! I haven't got the Apocrypha."

"You haven't?" Skylark asked.

"No. I lent it to Joe."

"Who's Joe?"

"Don't you know?" Birdy asked. "Joe lives near Tauranga."

Halfway back down the island. A day's travel away. Oh no, Skylark thought.

Birdy stared deep into Skylark's eyes. "Don't worry, dear, I can remember the part that involves me." She closed her eyes and began to recite from memory:

"And the Lord Tane said, 'Once the Sky has opened, then shalt the seabirds of that time to come be able to make pilgrimage back to the time that is and, in that time conjoined, the battle of the birds shalt be fought again.' But hearing this, Te Arikinui Kotuku, on behalf of the Runanga a Manu, begged the Lord Tane, 'Forgive us, oh Lord, our arrogance. Just as you have given unto the seabirds a second chance, give the same opportunity unto us also.'

"And the Lord Tane found forgiveness in his heart and said unto her: 'What is done cannot be undone. The promise made to the seabirds is a promise I cannot take back. However, because of my love for you, my children of the Great Forest which bears my name, I will indeed give you what you wish. Hear me: I will send a deliverer, a chick of open heart and innocence, and in her wings she will hold your fate. You should look for her to appear at the same time as the sky opens unto the seabirds. She will be the one. And I will send her out unto the wilderness to be tested and, should she show courage and strength, then she will arrive out of the wilderness bearing claw, wing feather and –'"

Birdy opened her eyes and winked. She saw the necklet that Hoki had given Skylark. "I see you've got the claw. That's a good start. You've come at just the right time to get the feather."

Birdy was off, stepping quickly out of the house. With a laugh, Skylark and Arnie hastened after her. The sun had come up and the sky was a bright blue bowl. Birdy was already climbing the first sand dune.

"Come along! Come along! Don't lag behind!"

The view from the sand dune took Skylark's breath away. For as far as she could see, more dunes. The sun turned them all into dazzling walls of glass.

Birdy reached the edge of an area where strands of blue sea had made a system of intricate sand bars. "Come along, slow coaches!" she yelled. "Can't keep up with an old cluck like me?"

Arnie held out his hand to Skylark – and she took it. Birdy was not far ahead of them now, wading across an estuarine stream.

That's when Skylark saw the seabirds. Thousands and thousands of them dotted upon every patch of sand. Waiting.

Birdy stepped into their midst and some of them took wing. Skylark pushed Arnie's hand away. Heart pounding, she began to run.

"No, Birdy, no." The seabirds were hovering across the old woman. She was unaware of the danger, letting them come to rest on her outstretched arms. But as Skylark splashed across the estuary, Birdy called to her.

"Meet the Scolopacidae –"

What was this? The seabirds weren't attacking Birdy at all. They were still sitting calmly on the sand bars or resting on her arm where she could stroke them.

"I thought they would kill you," Skylark said, awed.

"These?" Birdy smiled. "Oh no, not these, not my godwits."

"Godwits?" Arnie asked. "But aren't they seabirds too?"

"Yes, yes," Birdy nodded. Then: "Oh, *I* understand." Her voice trilled with amusement. "In the time before Man, the Lord Tane gave the godwits special dispensation to be shorebirds rather than seabirds. They are Arctic waders who breed in the Northern Hemisphere but migrate south to Aotearoa to get away from the Arctic winter. It was Chief Kuaka, whose Maori name I carry, who obtained the permission. He said, 'Because my species lives in Aotearoa for six months will you grant me the lease of special places where we might find safety and shelter?' The Lord Tane said, 'Yes,' and leased them Rangaunu Harbour at the neck of Aupouri Peninsula and here, at Parengarenga Harbour."

Skylark felt her body flood with relief. She watched as Birdy moved among the godwits, mottled grey and brown, patting and stroking their heads as she passed each one. Some were feeding at the edge of the tide, keeping up a continuous musical chatter. Many were in pairs, and Birdy looked at Skylark teasingly.

"I'm glad you've got a boyfriend too," Birdy said.

Oo er. Arnie blushed and turned away.

"He's not my boyfriend," Skylark said. "Apart from that he's basically normal."

"Well, whoever he is," Birdy said, "both of you have arrived on a very special day. Around 10,000 godwits come to Aotearoa every year. One-tenth of them actually land here at Parengarenga. But leaving will be the kindest thing to happen to my darlings. It's been a mean summer. The godwits are legally protected, but Parengarenga has become a killing field. People come to net and shoot the birds for food. A one-kilogram godwit primed to fly a long distance is the kind of bird most sought for the pot. There's a black market in them; some birds are sold as far south as Auckland. Many of those who escape the poachers are inflicted with internal injuries and maimed wings and legs. Some are likely to ditch into the ocean on their way back to Siberia and Alaska, or not go at all. But they must get back to breed. They've had ideal conditions in the past couple of weeks. I've been trying to protect them so they can gain strength to begin their marathon journey. South-east winds will carry them up on the first leg into the western Pacific.

"I love my darlings. They are like a huge tribe. They travel together, they come together, they leave together. There is no other tribe quite like them. They have been massing to leave for days. And –" There was an excitement in the air. "Here comes the south-east wind."

As if on some invisible command, the godwits lifted into the air. For a moment the whole world was filled with a mighty fluttering and whirring, and Skylark put her hands to her ears to minimise the sound. Powerful wings beat the air into a whirlwind.

Birdy began to sing a song of farewell. "Haere atu koutou nga kuaka, haere atu ki runga i te reo aroha –"

She almost disappeared in the snowstorm of feathers. "Farewell, godwits, go to your other home on the other side of the world. In the summer, return to me where I await your arrival again."

The godwits flew in a compact flock, twisting and turning in unison, pouring out of the harbour. Beneath them, the old woman fell to the sand, weeping.

"Ah well," Birdy said, "I've done my job for another year." She picked up a feather left by one of the departing birds. "Oh yes, and you had better take this."

She put the feather in Skylark's hands. The godwits were a stain in the sky, disappearing over the horizon. "The feather comes from a strong bird, renowned for covering huge distances. It will hold you up even when you're so tired you can't go any further."

Arnie watched Birdy give Skylark the feather. The whole scene of the godwits' departure had affected him. Coming as he did from a broken family, he was particularly taken by Birdy's remark that they were a huge tribe. They belonged. They paired. They had someone. He saw another feather on the ground, inspected it, and decided that if Skylark could have one he could too. He put it in his pocket.

"Now you'd better get on the road," Birdy said. "When you get to Joe's town, just ask at the hotel. Everybody knows Joe."

Skylark was first back to the ute. What do you know – the keys were in the ignition and Arnie had put her wallet back into her backpack. Now why did he do that?

"You're taking a big chance, aren't you?" she said as he joined her.

"No," he answered. "I'm counting on you to have enough common sense to realise that we need each other to get safely back to Manu Valley. For one thing, you can't drive all the way by yourself."

"Okay," Skylark agreed. "But I wouldn't be too cocky about it." She jumped into the driver's seat and started the engine.

"Good," said Arnie. His gamble had paid off. "But no funny business, right? I'm with you right up to the end credits, got it?"

"Right up to the moment when the hero rides off into the sunset with the girl?" Skylark tried not to sound too sarcastic.

"Something like that,"

"Well, you've just missed out on being stranded up here by that much," Skylark said, eyeballing him, "so if you shut up now you may even escape with your life."

Arnie nodded okay, but then remembered something. "I'd better tell Hoki and Bella not to expect us back so soon. They'll want to know we're making a detour." He took out his cellphone and dialled Tuapa. "Hello? Is that you, Mother Ship? Do you copy? We're just leaving Parengarenga. Birdy hasn't got the Apocrypha. For some reason, she's given Skylark a feather to go with your claw."

"A feather? Why would Birdy want to do that? To go with my claw? Was I supposed to give Skylark the claw?" Hoki was bewildered and very worried. "So are you two coming home now?"

"No, we're on our way to –"

Hoki felt a shiver of apprehension. She glanced out the window and saw Karoro and Toroa hunched on the telephone wires. The hairs on her neck began to prickle. The seabirds were listening in.

"Arnie, listen, I'm cutting the connection. Do you hear me?"

"What did you say, Auntie? Are you still there? We're on our way to Tauranga. Apparently Joe has the Apocrypha and –"

Hoki slammed the telephone down. With a sick feeling, she saw Karoro and Toroa leaving the telephone line. As they did so, they flew past the window where Lucas's doll was, seated and screeched with anger.

Foolish woman to think your deception would work.

Back in Parengarenga, Arnie stared at the cellphone, puzzled. Maybe his batteries were running low. He shrugged his shoulders and nodded at Skylark. Time to go.

"Goodbye, Birdy," Skylark said.

"Goodbye to you," Birdy answered. "Don't be put off by Joe's temper and grumpiness," she said. "The bark is worse than the bite." Skylark and Arnie pulled out, and Birdy waved. Then her face opened with joy and she cupped her hands and shouted: "Skylark! Skylark! Do you know what people call a whole lot of skylarks circling in the air? They call it an exaltation, dear, an exaltation!"

Skylark watched Birdy in the rear-vision mirror. The old woman waved and laughed and danced in the sun.

[CHAPTER NINE]

– 1 –

Kaa. *Kaa.*

Kawanatanga was on the rampage. On his way to the ripped sky, his squad had been attacked by the hawk clan and he had lost two of his best men. Then, as he was encouraging the seabirds to go through the opening he had inadvertently descended to the point where one of the old hens had almost shot him down. Now, Karoro and Toroa, charged with keeping the house of the two old hens under surveillance, had arrived with their intelligence.

"Sir," Karoro said, "the young chick is not there. She is not in Manu Valley at all."

Kawanatanga's tail lifted with anger. His wings trembled as he raised each white plume at right angles. He threw back his head in a malevolent hiss. "Then what is that thing in the nestroom that you have been watching with such commitment and devotion?"

"My Lord, it is a scarecrow made of plastic."

With a quick movement, Kawanatanga advanced on Karoro, extended his neck and caught the hapless bird by the throat. "So where is the chick then? Where is she?"

Toroa backed away, nervous. He tried to bluff his way through Kawanatanga's anger. "My Lord, all is not lost. The good news is that while we were sitting on the telephone wires we overheard the old hen in conversation. The female chick has just left Parengarenga with a male chick companion. They are on their way to the one called Joe. The bad news is that the female chick has the claw and the feather —"

"The claw and the feather?" Kawanatanga shrilled. "But how can that be? All they need now is what Joe will give them and –"

The chick knew about the Apocrypha. If she had got that far, she could get further. "Our future is at risk," Kawanatanga screamed. "As long as the slightest possibility exists that the chick might find a way to overturn what was promised us, she remains our greatest threat." Kawanatanga arched his throat and flapped his wings, calling for his lieutenants to come to him. When they were assembled, he gave his commands. "You albatrosses, mollymawks, fulmars, petrels, prions, shearwaters, pelicans, gannets, boobies, skuas, gulls, terns and noddies all! Urge your troops through the ripped sky! Meanwhile, I must take my pursuit squad of seashags, fifty in all, northward, for we are in great danger from the chick. She must be stopped. Kill, kill, kill."

Karoro and Toroa echoed Kawanatanga's exhortations across the sky. Satisfied, Kawanatanga gathered his pursuit squad around him. "We fly northward on the next wind," he said. "But first I want to leave a little message at the nest of the two old hens."

– 2 –

Long after leaving Parengarenga, Skylark could still see Birdy dancing like a mote of sunlight. What did the old woman say a group of skylarks was? An exaltation, that was it.

Skylark liked that. It made her feel empowered. Humming to herself, she looked in her backpack for one of her badges: WE ARE ALL CLARK KENT.

Arnie was still sleeping when they passed through Auckland. However, at the bottom of the Bombay Hills where the highway forked, he woke up, scratched his armpits and asked: "Do you feel like a break?"

Skylark eased the ute to a halt. She and Arnie swapped sides, and immediately she sensed his relief at being back behind the wheel. She couldn't resist needling him. "I should have realised," she said. "You're a boy racer. You've never been driven by a girl before, have you."

"Well . . ." Arnie shifted uneasily in his seat. "Actually, I've never let anybody drive Annabelle before."

"Annabelle?"

"The name of my ute," Arnie explained. "And before you accuse me of being sexist, Annabelle's the full name of my mother."

"You've made that up," Skylark said, folding her arms.

"Why would I do that! If I'd known you wouldn't believe me I would have brought along Mum's birth certificate."

It was happening again. When would Skylark get past all of her stuff. Arnie remembered how, when he was a boy and some other guy had you in an arm lock, you yelled "Pax" and you were released. Maybe it would also work with a girl. He slowed the ute down to a halt. "Look, we've already had enough fights getting this far. Are we going to fight the whole trip?"

Skylark stared out the window. What was it about Arnie that kept snapping her elastic? How could she even begin to tell him about why she kept pushing him – anybody – away? But she had to try, so that once and for all he would understand.

"Nobody knows what it was like for me when I was growing up," she said. "I was an accident which wasn't supposed to happen. Mum and Brad had fallen in love with the idea of having a baby, especially a little girl, but when I arrived I wasn't exactly what they had in mind. What they wanted was some pretty little doll with a cute button nose that they could dress up and show off. But Mum grew to love me and I loved her back. Then Brad left her and I've been the head of the household ever since. I've had to look after my mother, stand her back up when she's been let down by the series of himbos she's had trashing her life."

Arnie tried to calm her, but Skylark wouldn't be stopped. "I was the little girl who, whenever we had games at school, would say, 'Pick me! Pick me!', but I was always the last chosen. So excuse me if I don't like the world I live in, but I've always had to face it myself – and in my own way. For instance, I must have been around eight, I was walking home from school and I saw a man beating his dog. He was trying to make the dog jump up onto the back of a truck –"

The memory was as vivid as yesterday. The dog was a big, yellow mangy brute. No matter how hard the man pulled on its lead and yelled at it to jump, it dug in its heels. The man had a red face and fierce eyes, and he wrapped a belt around his fist and began to whip the dog with the buckle end. The dog yelped at the pain. Men and women passing by steered a wide berth. None came to the rescue. It was none of their business. And the man looked mean. But Skylark knew that what he was doing was wrong.

"After a while, I pulled at the man's trousers for his attention and I said to him, 'You're not allowed to beat dogs.' The words just came out of me. Well, he swore at me and continued to beat the dog, and it was whining and trying to get away from him by crawling underneath the truck –"

Why hadn't anybody stopped the man? Skylark wondered. He was reaching underneath the truck, trying to pull the dog back out. And all the time he was swearing, "Come out, you bloody brute. You'd better come out or it will be the worse for you." He yanked really hard, the dog squealed, and when it poked its head into the light, the man laid into it again.

"I said to the man, 'If you continue to beat the dog I'll report you to the SPCA.' He got really angry at me for saying that but he didn't take any notice. So I got my school pad out of my satchel –"

Skylark had walked around to the front of the truck and started to write its number plate in her pad. The man saw her. "Just what do you think you're doing, you little bitch?" He started to walk towards her, his fist raised in the air. Skylark stood her ground.

"I said to him, 'And you're not allowed to hit little children either. So if you hit *me*, I'll report you to the police.'"

By that time, a crowd had gathered. When the man saw it he left the dog in the street, jumped into his truck and drove away. Skylark took the dog home, cleaned it up and, when Cora arrived, demanded that they keep it. But its wounds were so grievous that it died within the week.

"Why are you telling me this?" Arnie asked.

"If you want to know what I'm like, this is what I'm like. I've always had to make up my own mind about what to do because I can't trust other people to do what they should. I've always relied on myself, and I can get myself out of any problems that come my way. If I don't, tough, I'm the only one who gets hurt. I do what I do and I don't need anybody to help me, so the sooner you bail out the better because I don't need you. I'm perfectly capable of handling things myself."

Arnie was stumped. How could he get through or around Skylark's defences? "I don't get you, Skylark," he began. "You think you're on one side and you put everybody else on the opposite side. You seem to forget that I'm here, with you, in this ute, and we're on this journey together. If I'd been there when that man was beating the dog, I would have stood up for you. I wouldn't have let you face that man alone."

"It's a matter of trust," Skylark answered.

"You don't trust me?"

"I don't know."

Arnie started the engine. "Skylark, you're so walled up you're like a fortress. One of these days you're going to have to let somebody, anybody, in."

– 3 –

That same afternoon it was Bella's turn to keep her and Hoki's promise to Skylark that they would visit Cora every day. Just before she left Hoki on guard, she saw that their ammunition was running low. "While I'm down in Tuapa I'll stock up," she said to Hoki. "Are you sure you'll be able to manage while I'm away?"

"Of course," Hoki answered. "I may be hopeless but I'm not entirely useless."

"I'll only be a few hours," Bella said.

She walked quickly down the cliff path. She grabbed her purse and flax kit from the house, pulled a comb through her thick hair, and went out to her car. A few moments later, she was roaring down Manu Valley towards Tuapa. The seabirds climbed past her, flying on the rising thermals in the opposite direction.

In that moment of vulnerability, Bella thought of her eldest sister, Agnes, six years older than Bella, eight years older than Hoki. She was as clear as day: Agnes, the beauty of the family, laughing, full of life.

From the beginning, Agnes had the world in her pocket. Mum and Dad adored her, she excelled at hockey and tennis, and had been dux of Tuapa College. "Is Agnes really your sister?" people asked the younger girls. Then, everything changed. Agnes fell in love with Darren, a Pakeha boy. "He's just heavenly," Agnes had told Bella and Hoki. "When we're together my heart goes flip flop and I can't help myself." She used to make Bella and Hoki laugh as she pulled all the pillows off the bed and hugged them. The trouble was that although Darren may have made Agnes's heart do gymnastics, he made no impression on Mum and Dad.

As she drove, Bella tried to recall Darren in her memory. All she could remember was that he had been a high school rugby player with a disarming grin and an easy smile, tucking Agnes under his arm as easily as if she had been a rugby ball. What she recalled most was Agnes' insistence: "I love Darren and we want to be together and we don't care what anybody else says." They had been so young, so awfully young.

One night, Bella and Hoki were woken up by Agnes. "Sshhhh," she said. "I don't want to wake Mum and Dad up. Darren is waiting in the car. We're running away together." Agnes' face was lit with love, so much love that it seemed to be giving her pain. "Isn't that romantic? I'm sorry you won't be able to be bridesmaids. Will you forgive me? I've come to say goodbye. I love you both. Don't worry, though. One day I'll be back.'

The next day, Dad had set out after the runaways. He found them in Christchurch, but Agnes refused to come back with him. The months drifted by. Rumours came back to Tuapa that Agnes was "in the family way", then that Darren had taken off before the baby was born, and then that the baby had died at birth. "Come back to Tuapa, Agnes," Mum had pleaded. But Agnes had said, "No." Maybe she had been ashamed to come back. Or perhaps she had grown used to Christchurch. But whenever she spoke on the telephone to Bella and Hoki she would always say, "One day, my sisters, one day I'll be back."

It never happened. A year later, lovely, smiling Agnes had been killed in a car accident.

"Oh Agnes," Bella said to herself. "If only you were home now. We really need you."

In Tuapa, Bella bought two cases of ammunition from Harry Summers at the farming supplies store.

"Planning a war?" Harry quipped.

Bella looked at her watch. She was running late, but a promise was a promise. She swerved into the carpark, parked in a "Doctors Only" space and hurried into the hospital. When she reached Cora's room she was surprised to find Lucas sitting by the bed, holding Cora's hand. He looked up as Bella arrived.

"Do you think she'll wake up?"

Bella didn't know what to say. Cora was lying as still as death. Her face was waxen. She had an oxygen mask over her nose and mouth, and tubes coming out of the sleeve of her left arm.

"Of course she will," Bella answered finally. She didn't know why Lucas cared so much – or what his girlfriend Melissa would think. But that was really none of her business.

"Ah well," Lucas said. "I'd better go. I'm on my lunch break. You wouldn't happen to know where Arnie is, would you? He's done a runner on me."

"He didn't tell you?" Bella answered. "He's had to go up north. On family business."

"Oh, so he'll be coming back? Good."

Lucas went out the door, Bella sat down in a chair and stroked Cora's face. Cora's skin was so cold, so alabaster. The only perceptive movements were the slight rise and fall of her chest as she breathed and, every now and then, the flicker of her eyelids as if she was dreaming. If she was, she was trapped there, searching for a door, a way out.

"Cora?" Bella began. "I know you can't hear me, but don't be afraid, dear. You must be patient and hold on. You have a lovely daughter in Skylark. She's doing the best she can."

It was time to go. Quickly, Bella stood up and kissed Cora on the forehead. On the way out she happened to glance at Cora's chart at the foot of the bed:

Cora Agnes Edwards nee Wipani
Born Christchurch 1960

Bella closed the door behind her.

She left the hospital and headed back to Manu Valley at speed.

"I've stayed away too long," she said to herself. The forest blurred around her, the sunlight slashing at the windscreen like a whip. She pushed the accelerator to the floor. In no time flat she reached the homestead, stepped out of the station-wagon and slammed the door. The silence became physical and hit her in the stomach.

Bella looked up to the clifftop. She couldn't hear Hoki's shotgun. She couldn't see Hoki at all. Instead, at the summit, a cloud of seabirds was swooping and diving, raining like arrows through the rip in the sky.

"Oh no."

Bella pulled the ammunition out of the wagon and yanked the top off one of the cases. She grabbed some boxes of shells and stuffed them in her jacket. Then she was on the run into the homestead to get her shotgun. Along the verandah she hurried, banging the door open with her shoulder.

She was surrounded with the sound of hissing.

Bella stepped back. Her blood ran cold with fear. The room was filled with black sea shags. They had smashed their way in through the windows. They were perched everywhere. On the sofas. On the table and chairs and the sideboard. The remains of Lucas's doll, shredded, punctured, totally savaged, were scattered throughout the room. Standing on the doll's head, claws dug deeply into its face was the black shag, Kawanatanga. The sight of him brought Bella to her senses and she pointed a finger at him.

"You are trespassing here," Bella called. "The land to the landbirds, the sea to the seabirds. How dare you transgress my personal domain and soil my undefended nest. Go or face the wrath of the Lord Tane."

Kawanatanga's wings unfolded like a nightmare. He filled the room with his mocking sibilants:

The Lord Tane is on our side now. He has granted us dispensation to change the order of things if we can. Once we have the power, old hen, it will be only by our leave that you will live here.

Bella picked up a jug and threw it at Kawanatanga. It smashed, raining him with jagged pieces. His eyes widened and he stretched out his neck.

The threatening movement did not frighten Bella. "That may be," she said, "but it has not yet come to pass. Until then the old order stands. Now get out, and take your dark minions from Hell with you."

Kawanatanga stabbed at the air with his beak. There was a flurry of black wings as the seashags hopped up onto the window sills and out. The sun gleamed on their feathers as they ascended the currents.

Kawanatanga remained behind:

Enjoy your freedom while you have it.

Kawanatanga lifted and, as he beat past Bella, she felt his wingtips like sinister fingers caressing her face. She ran to the verandah to watch the squad of seashags, fifty in all, that were heading north.

"They know about Skylark," Bella realised.

She heard Hoki's scream curling down from the clifftop. Bella grabbed her shotgun and was on the run again. As she climbed the cliff path she was already loading and firing the weapon at random into the air. Bang. Reload. Bang. Reload. Bang. "Hoki, Sister, I'm coming —"

Hoki was lying on the grass. Seabirds were diving at her. She was fending them off with her walking sticks.

"Get away from her," Bella yelled. She reloaded her shotgun. *Bang.* The seabirds scattered, turning away from the ripped sky. Just to make sure that they knew the boss had returned, Bella let off another shot. *Bang.* The sound reverberated across the sky like distant thunder.

"I'm sorry, Sister," Hoki said. "The shotgun stopped working. I didn't know what to do. I tried to fix it myself." Her face was streaming with sweat.

"That doesn't matter. At least you're alive."

Quickly, Bella picked up the shotgun. She inspected it, worked the bolt a couple of times and ejected the shellcase that had jammed inside the barrel. It was just a simple jam, easy to fix; she had shown Hoki hundreds of times. Hoki saw her sister's look of frustration. "I'm sorry, Sister," she wept. "I can't even shoot straight. The sweat pours into my eyes, I can't see anything and –"

"Don't worry. No use crying over spilt milk. It's all over now."

But Bella remained worried. "We've got to get more help," she said. "We can't manage this by ourselves."

With the darkness, the seabirds retreated and the sisters returned to the homestead. Bella had told Hoki about Kawanatanga's visit but she was surprised by the depth of Hoki's reaction.

With tears streaming down her cheeks, Hoki moved through the room on her walking sticks, uncovering the memorabilia of their lives: the smashed photographs, glassware, family mementoes, woven rugs and cushions. Watching her, Bella thought about how Hoki had always been so sentimental, how small personal treasures had always mattered to her.

"Look what they did to your jug," Hoki continued, picking up the pieces. "You always loved that jug!"

Oops, Bella thought. Did I? Ah well, let the seabirds take the blame.

"What are we going to do about that doll?" Bella asked.

Hoki poked at it with distaste. "Lucas can buy another one next time he goes to the sex shop," she said.

They began to clear up the mess. They swept up the broken glass, removed the soiled covers from the sofas, took the carpets out onto the verandah and scrubbed the floor of bird dung.

"I'll go and prepare dinner now," Hoki said.

"While you're doing that," Bella answered, "I'll make a list of the repairs. We'll need a glazier to fix the windows. But there's something more important to discuss."

"I know I'm hopeless," Hoki said, feeling sorry for herself.

"It's not that. But we can't carry on alone. We've managed all right so far, but –"

"But?" Hoki flared. Tears of humiliation stained her cheeks.

"Sister dear, we have to swallow our pride. Either you call Mitch, or I will."

"Are you telling me how to do my job again?" Hoki asked.

Nevertheless she went to the phone and dialled a number.

"Hello? Is that you, Mitch? Good. How's the fishing? Not too good? I'm sorry to hear that. Then maybe, if you and Francis don't have anything on, could you come up to the valley and spare me and Bella some time? Thanks, Mitch. Yes, it's about the seabirds. It's really serious."

Hoki put the phone down. "There," she said to Bella. "Satisfied?" In a temper, she began to hit at her bad leg with a walking stick. Bella restrained her.

"All this is my fault," Hoki wept. "Everything. And now Kawanatanga also knows where Skylark and Arnie are. I should have realised his spies were listening in. Sitting there, on the telephone lines. We'd better warn Arnie that the shags are coming."

"I've already tried," Bella answered. "I can't get through. Arnie's cellphone must be switched off or else they're travelling in an area where it doesn't work."

"In that case," Hoki said, "we must get a message to them through Joe. I'll telephone in the morning."

Dinner was a silent affair. Bella could see her sister was still hurting. Afterwards, Hoki cleared the dishes. She went to the bathroom, washed and got into her dressing gown. She was brushing her hair at the dresser when Bella came in.

"Here, let me do that," Bella said.

"No, it's all right," Hoki answered. She was still feeling sorry for herself.

"I've always loved brushing your hair," Bella said.

"Don't tell lies. You were always so impatient. You used to pull the brush so hard it's a wonder I have any hair left. I used to hate it when you –"

"Oh, shush," Bella said. She took the brush and began to apply long strokes, watching Hoki's long silver hair run through it like a river. How had she and Hoki grown so old so quickly? Here they were, still together, like lovers. "Mitch and Francis aren't coming just because of you," Bella said.

"You're just saying that to make me feel better."

"It's the truth. I need their help too."

"No," Hoki said, biting her bottom lip. "It's because I'm a cripple and I'm hopeless."

Bella sighed with resignation. When Hoki was like this, it was better to let her sulk and get over it in her own time and in her own way.

– 4 –

Skylark and Arnie arrived at Whakatane. The town was chocka with boy racers dragging each other, burning rubber and doing wheelies down the main street.

"Can't be much on television," Arnie said.

"*Coronation Street.* Don't you feel the call of the wild? Wouldn't you like to show the locals what Annabelle is made of?"

"Sure," Arnie said, "but we haven't got the time."

However, just to make sure that everybody knew they'd been paid a visit by the Black Knight, he gunned the motor and made smoke that gobsmacked even the locals. Satisfied, Arnie sashayed out of town and took the coast road to Joe's small seaside settlement.

"So what now?" Skylark asked.

"Look for the hotel. Birdy said everybody knows Joe there."

Skylark peered ahead. They passed a garage, a hardware store and a derelict movie theatre. The road took a fork down to a jetty poking out into the sea. At its end was the hotel, lights blazing.

"Maybe they'll have rooms for the night," Arnie said as they pulled up outside.

"If we find Joe, I'll do the talking," Skylark answered, putting on her jacket. "Got it?"

Arnie tried to think up a smart reply but thought better of it. "Okay, Skylark," he said. "You're coming across loud and clear. No static whatsoever."

Skylark led the way. But as soon as they were through the door she knew she was in unfamiliar territory – and Arnie knew it too. The bar was crowded with locals, some women, mostly men.

"Which one do you think is Joe?" Skylark asked.

"You're the boss," Arnie answered, and he had the gall to look smug.

Skylark had a sinking feeling. Joe could be any one of the grizzled old-timers standing at the bar. Or he could be one of the blokes eating greasy food at tables scattered throughout the room. Off to one side, younger patrons were playing the pokie machines. In another room, Skylark could hear the click of billiard balls. Over everything came the sound of a rugby commentary from a massive television set installed above the bar. Obviously, the hotel was the only place of entertainment in town.

Strangers weren't all that common in these parts. Skylark and Arnie's appearance stopped all conversation, and all eyes swivelled to watch them as they paused in the doorway. Skylark wished she had worn one of her other badges: ARE THESE YOUR EYEBALLS? I FOUND THEM IN MY CLEAVAGE.

She pushed Arnie in front of her. "Ask about Joe," she said.

"Huh? I'm the sidekick, remember?"

"I am the boss," Skylark said, "and I'm giving you an order. Just do it. And while you're about it order me a pie and chips and a Coke. I'm famished."

Mumbling to himself, Arnie approached the bar. An elderly barman with a bad toupee eyed him up and down. "So what can I do for you, my little man?"

Arnie gritted his teeth. He never let anybody make cracks about his height. "Well, how about a lager for me and a Coke for my girl to start with, eh baldy?"

A collective gasp went up in the room. Obviously the matter of the barman's head warmer was as sensitive an issue to him as height was to Arnie.

The man froze, gave Arnie the stare, and came back fast. "Coming up, Short Arse, and count yourself lucky you're a stranger in this town and don't know any better." He poured the drinks.

So it was Short Arse now? Arnie smiled dangerously – and let the barman have it. "So, Bum Head," he asked, "do you know where we can find Joe?"

The barman looked ready to jump across the bar and take Arnie on. Instead he gave an evil smile. "Joe? Now you're really asking for trouble."

He turned and shouted through the swing doors behind the bar. "Joe? Hey Joe! There's a boy out here asking for you. About your size, but he's got more muscles than you and a mouth to go with it."

"Is that so?" a voice answered. "This I gotta see."

The swing doors burst open and Joe appeared.

"You're Joe?" Skylark asked. She was big, butch and built like a brick shithouse. Her hair was cut in a crewcut and there was no doubting that her pecs, underneath her T-shirt, were just as spectacular as Arnie's. She took one look at Skylark, her eyes swivelled to Arnie and, bullseye, she had his number.

"There's only one place where you get a build like yours, boy," Joe said, "and that's the Army. A Company, B or C?"

"C for Charlie."

"Bad answer," Joe answered, flexing her biceps. "When I did my service, C didn't stand for Charlie. It stood for a part of the female anatomy which, in deference to my sex and because there are ladies present, I shall not mention. Did you make corporal?"

"Yes."

"Another bad answer," Joe said. "I made sergeant, so next time you speak to me you'll add a 'sir' to that as in 'Yes *sir*!' Got it?" She began to walk backwards and forwards in front of Arnie, cracking her knuckles. "Man, if there's one thing I can't stand it's corporals of any shape, size or colour. Especially when they come into my bar and badmouth my staff. But I'll give you a break." Joe planted her elbow on the bar and motioned to Arnie.

"Come on then, Corporal, make my day."

"Sorry, I never arm wrestle with a woman," Arnie said. But hell, how much aggro was a guy supposed to take? "However, in your case –" He began to pump his biceps.

Immediately there was a rush to watch – and the barman, always one to make an extra buck, called, "Come on, ladies and gentlemen, place your bets!" Dollar notes came flying from all over the place. Even Skylark put a couple of bucks down.

"Is that all you've got to show me?" Joe sneered, one eye on Arnie's bulging muscles. She gave a few pumps herself and the sleeves of her T-shirt rippled with the strain.

It was a battle of Titans. It was a battle of wills. Arnie kept a grim face and Joe bared her teeth. She forced his arm down to the bar but, at the last moment, Arnie forced her back. She pretended to be surprised and winked at him – and then spat him straight in the eye.

"Hey, ref!" one of the patrons called. "Foul play!"

"And here I was thinking you were a lady," Arnie said.

Amid whistles, Arnie recovered. He forced Joe's arm down to the bar. Closer. Closer. Almost there. He could see the sweat popping on Joe's forehead as she tried to force his arm back.

"You may be strong for a woman," Arnie said, "but you're still just a pussy."

That's when Skylark kicked him. Hard.

"What the heck!" Startled, Arnie lost his concentration – and Joe took the advantage. With a loud grunt, she flipped Arnie's arm down and won the bout. Immediately, there were cheers and the pounding of fists on the bar as the lucky punters jostled for their winnings.

Arnie glared at Skylark. "What did you do that for?"

"Two reasons," Skylark answered. "The first is that you are a chauvinist pig. The second is –" she showed him her dollars – "I had a lot riding on you to lose, and I wanted to win my bet."

"Thank you, Skylark, for your vote of confidence."

"But the real reason is that we needed Joe to win so that she would be okay about helping us."

"Helping you?" Joe asked, looking at Arnie. "Nobody's helping anybody until they apologise to my barman."

That's when Skylark stepped in. "He'll apologise," she said to Joe. "Then you can tell me what's in the Apocrypha."

It was as easy as that. Joe's eyes searched Skylark's face and then probed into her.

"Apology accepted," Joe said. She shook Arnie's hand, and the bar patrons gave good-natured cheers. Then she turned back to Skylark. "You'll both have to come home with me, which means you'll have to stay the night. Meantime, you look like you could do with some food. How about some steak and eggs with a side salad. It's on the house." She slapped Arnie on the back. "That okay with you, Corporal?"

To be truthful, it was great to get some hot food. Afterwards, Skylark found herself ambushed by some raucous Maori women who rushed her off to the poker machines. From the corner of her eye she saw Arnie heading off with some of the younger blokes for a game of pool. He came over to her:

"Is that okay with you?" he asked.

"Sure," Skylark nodded, "Go ahead."

When closing time came, Baldy threw everybody out. Skylark and Arnie waited outside for Joe.

"Shall we follow you in our ute?" Arnie asked when she arrived.

Joe laughed. "Not unless it floats." She pointed across the sea. Far in the distance, they could just make out the dark shape of an island. Above it, the Southern Cross. "That's my home," Joe continued. "Let's vamoose." She led the way along the jetty, and soon they were sliding across the dark ocean in Joe's dinghy, aiming for the pointer star in the Cross's constellation. The outboard motor churned a phosphorescent wake, put-putting a regular rhythm.

Joe ran the dinghy up a sheltered beach. She led Skylark and Arnie along a path, past a barn to a small house. Skylark was almost dead on her feet.

"Let's get some shut-eye, shall we?" Joe said. "Leave the talk for the morning." Her eyes twinkled. "But what's the sleeping arrangements? I've got two spare bedrooms, but if you two are together you could have my double bed –"

Skylark cut her short. "That won't be necessary, and I hope you don't need me to elucidate."

"Oops," Joe said. "My mistake."

Arnie blushed a deep and interesting shade of red.

The next morning, the sound of the telephone invaded Skylark's dreams. It rang and rang, and Joe didn't answer, so Skylark got out of bed, found the phone in the sitting room, and picked up the receiver.

"Hello?"

It was too late. The caller – Hoki – put the telephone down. Kawanatanga and his cohorts, she knew, must be well on their way by now. They would have stopped over for the night at some cliff-face eyrie near Kaikoura. In the morning, with the whales spouting out to sea, they would have woken, fed and continued their mission. Already they were crossing Cook Strait, skimming the waves, their eyes flaring red with the dawn. Kaa. *Kaa.*

"How can I alert Skylark to the danger?" Hoki wailed.

Meantime, Skylark wandered into Joe's empty kitchen. She opened the refrigerator. "Yecch," she groaned. As she suspected, stock full with rabbit food, bunches of carrots, muscle-building stuff, energy drinks and not a carbohydrate or chocolate bar in sight.

Skylark helped herself to orange juice, looked out the kitchen window and saw Joe returning from the barn. Joe wore a T-shirt and track pants and was wiping her face with a towel. She smiled and waved. "Good morning," she said. "Feel like breakfast?"

"Yes, thanks. Do you know where Arnie is?"

"Missing him already?" Joe winked. "We've been working out together. But he wanted to do some extra crunches and work on his abs, so I left him in the barn. It's set up as my personal gym."

Joe began to busy herself in the kitchen, preparing bacon and eggs. "So you're the one we've all been waiting for."

"I wish people wouldn't keep saying that," Skylark said. "When they do it's like the music from *2001: A Space Odyssey* comes booming out of stereo loudspeakers. I don't know if I am or not."

"You'd better be!" Joe smiled. "Or maybe you're an egg a cuckoo has sneaked into the nest? Though I can see that Hoki gave you the claw. Did Birdy give you the feather?"

"This sounds like a shopping list," Skylark groaned.

"Well," Joe answered, "let's see what is here to give you." She went into the sitting room and opened the glass cabinet. Inside was a box, from which she took out a leather-bound book. "This is the Apocrypha," she said. Her voice was hushed and awed. "I asked Birdy if I could borrow it because, as you know, all of us were waiting for you to appear, and I'm just new at this game and didn't know how to prepare for it."

"New?"

"It was my Auntie Ruth who was really the guardian of the birds in this area. This was her island."

"That explains it," Skylark answered. "I was wondering why you were so young and, well, different from Hoki, Bella and Birdy."

Joe leafed through the Apocrypha. "Let's see . . . you've got the claw and the feather and now . . . Ah! Here we are." She traced some lines with her finger:

And the Lord Tane said unto Te Arikinui Kotuku:

"And the chick shall seek and be given claw, feather and beak, and these shall be given unto her by wise guardians of that time to come that I have earlier spoken of . . ."

Skylark tried not to sound grumpy. "You mean I've come all this way just to pick up a claw, feather and a beak?"

"You should be ashamed of yourself," Joe said, wagging a finger. "A claw is not just a claw. A feather is not just a feather. A beak is not just a beak. You diminish a thing's mana, its prestige, when you consider it as such. It is connected to other things and, of itself, it represents a larger thing. Take a leaf of a tree, for instance: it represents the tree. Take a scale of a fish: it represents the fish. So too with a claw, feather and beak; they represent the birds that these things come from. But that is not where it stops. The bird represents a colony. It has a history and a place where it has been born, and where it lives and will die. It is connected to all that exists on the earth and in the universe. In the small thing is the genetic imprint of the larger thing. From it can be made a whole bird. You must revere the small things as well as the larger things. You must learn to see not just with your eyes but with your heart and intelligence."

That's telling me, Skylark thought.

At that moment, Arnie returned from his workout. "You should see some of the weightlifting gear Joe's got in her barn!" Having got rid of the toxins of the past few days, he was feeling a very happy chappy indeed.

"You'd better hear all this too," Joe said as she returned to the Apocrypha:

"Then shalt the chick have in her possession the three keys, beak, feather and claw, that wilt open the Time Portal for her own pilgrimage back to the time that is. But the portal will be opened for the space of seven moons only, counting from the first hour that the sky has opened, so should the chick not appear in time, then will the opportunity be lost. But if the chick goes through the portal, I, the Lord Tane, will grant her safe passage back to that time conjoined. And she will determine the outcome of the second battle of the birds —"

And the Runanga a Manu praised the Lord Tane for his mercy and they carried his words down from one beak to the next. Then came the arrival of Tane's next great creation, Humankind, and Tane's words were passed, in particular, to Hana, the first handmaiden of the Lord Tane, who could speak to the birds. It was Hana who set up the sisterhood of the handmaidens of Tane and bade that the Lord Tane's words be placed in an apocrypha to be passed from handmaiden to successor. All were entreated to keep watch for the chick who would appear in the third year of the second millennium and to give her the keys to open the Time Portal.

Woe of woes, it is written that in the seventh generation a copy of the Apocrypha fell into the wings of the seashags so that they knew also of the chick's predicted coming. They too passed the prediction down from one generation to the next so that they would be prepared for her, to kill her in order to confound the prophecy and opportunity the Lord Tane had given unto the Runanga a Manu.

And these are the words which have been passed down from generation to generation and even unto and throughout the times which have seen the coming of Tane's other great creation: the wingless, beakless and clawless inferior being known as man.

Thus we continue to praise Tane at dawn and dusk unto the world's end, and again we bow down to his holy name, Amen.

Joe closed the book. Skylark began to shiver. "Hey, Arnie, I've got a bounty on my head," she said, trying to joke. She thought Arnie might make a smart crack but he didn't. Instead, he put a reassuring hand on hers – and kept it there.

"Okay," Joe said when breakfast was over, "two moons are already gone and the Time Portal is only open for another five days. Let's go and get Skylark's beak." She strapped a Bowie knife to her left thigh and led the way out of the house and along the beach until they hit a track around the coast. Skylark saw a huge signpost, facing out to sea:

KEEP OUT. PRIVATE PROPERTY. TRESPASSERS WILL
BE PROSECUTED. ALL ANIMALS WILL BE SHOT
ON SIGHT.

"I give everybody due warning," Joe said, "but do you think yachties and rich pleasure-boat owners take any notice? They're a law unto themselves. Before you know it they're anchoring off the island and darting over here on their zodiacs with their cat or pet dog, champagne and dinner. They have a great time littering my beach, and then they return to their boats – but, dear oh dear, did we leave our darling Moggie or Fido behind? Before you know it, Fido or dear little kitty has turned into a bird killer. And if it's not a cat or a dog, it's a rat that has snuck on board and then, when the boat's at anchor, swum ashore. Once here, anything on four legs – actually, on two legs as well – can play havoc with the birds, especially ground birds."

Joe took a track leading away from the coast. The island's forest opened, allowing them to enter, and then closed behind them. They were surrounded by giant tree trunks, like the palisades of some forest fortress. Some of the trunks had flying buttresses. Others were wrapped around with vines and flowering supplejack in brilliant profusion. Between them grew huge tree ferns. Above, the sun filtered golden through the canopy, filling the dark spaces below with veiled light. Wherever the light fell it dazzled and glowed.

How had Hoki described the Great Forest? Like the Garden of Eden. The wonder of the southern world. The lungs of the earth. Even to stand in a remnant of that whole, on this island guarded by Joe, was to evoke the power of how the Great Forest must have been.

And truly, it was the kingdom of the birds. The canopy was alive, positively seething with kakariki, tui and other pigeon species. They set up a cacophony of musical whistles and high piping welcomes.

Kita-kita-kita-kita. Chichichi. Zweet zweet zwee.

Joe put her fingers to her lips and whistled and warbled back. The pigeons redoubled their efforts, and a competition ensued – at least that's how it sounded to Skylark. Joe gave up with a laugh. "You guys are ganging up on me again." The pigeons warbled and chortled and cooed.

Try-again, try-again, u-may be-be-be luck-ee ee ee.

"Would you believe," Joe said, "that once upon a time I used to shoot pigeons? When I came out of the Army I lived on the mainland with my uncle. I was a crack shot, and he used to ask me to sneak over here to the island and pot him some pigeons: twelve bullets for twelve birds. He knew Auntie Ruth owned the island and was a guardian of Tane, but there was bad blood between them. I thought it was a huge joke, banging away at the birds and then getting away before she was able to catch me. When I got home I loved watching my uncle's face as he counted the pigeons. 'One, two, three, ten, eleven twelve . . . thirteen, fourteen, fifteen, sixteen. Hey, girl, I only gave you twelve bullets! Where did you get the extra bullets from?' Then I would tell him how I waited for two birds to come together and kiss – and that's when I would pull the trigger."

Joe's smile turned to regret. "You know what stopped me in the end? Auntie Ruth set an old Maori ground trap for me. I put my foot in it and, next minute, I was dangling upside down from a tree. You know, when she saw it was me, she didn't give me a growling or thrash me. Instead, she cried. She freed me, kissed me and let me go. But when she died, she took her revenge on me – she left me the island and the birds to look after. I've been paying penance for my pigeon-shooting days ever since."

Joe struck inland. She came across a trap. Inspected it. The trap had not been sprung. Cleaned it with her Bowie knife. Set it again.

"How often do you check the traps?" Skylark asked.

"Once a week," Joe said. "But actually, I can always tell if there is a predator around. The birds go into hiding. The forest becomes silent. Beware the forest where the birds do not sing."

The track began to climb, but Joe took it at an easy clip.

"How are you doing?" Arnie asked Skylark. "It's not too tiring for you, is it? All this climbing?"

"Too tiring?" Presumably Arnie was referring to her physical condition. Skylark was just about to cut him down – but instead bit back on herself. "No," she answered. "But thanks for asking."

They reached the very heart of the island. The forest was filled with flashes of red, like feathered lightning.

"We're here," Joe said. "Welcome to my kaka colony."

The air was alive with birdsong:

Hail, guardian! You come with strangers! Welcome, waewae tapu! Welcome to the marae of nga kaka iwi.

The parrots filled the air with their glorious chattering. They were large, olive brown and green with red rump and abdomen. Their heads were topped with grey crowns. They seemed to have an enormous repertoire of conversational liquid songs, whistles and gliding soprano runs. In flight they flashed scarlet underwings, setting the forest on fire.

Skylark was entranced. She didn't know what the kaka were doing, but they were either at very aggressive play or very subdued war. She gave a small scream as one of them flew down and landed on her shoulder. The weight surprised her.

Kra! Kra! Ka! And who is this? Pretty polly, pretty polly, polly wolly doodle.

"Meet Flash Harry," Joe laughed. "He's the most gregarious of the colony. Say hello to Skylark, Harry."

Flash Harry hopped closer up Skylark's shoulder. She gave a small squeal as he started to nip at her with his beak.

Hello darling. What brings a sweetie like you to this neck of the woods?

"He's giving you love bites. Harry loves women."

Flash Harry gave an appreciative whistle and wink.

"That was a wolf whistle!" Skylark gasped.

"Only a bird would get away with it," Arnie whispered to Joe.

Suddenly another kaka came flying down from the trees. This one landed on Arnie's shoulder. "Hey –"

"That's Carmen," Joe said. "She's Flash Harry's mate and she's just reminding him that she can play the flirting game too."

Skylark laughed. Carmen gave a delicious sigh as she nestled close in to Arnie's shoulder, and that set Flash Harry off. He bristled with jealousy, and with a screech, pounced on Carmen. With a haughty flip she moved out of his reach. A flutter of wings and she was away, leading Flash Harry on a merry dance through the forest and delighting other kaka. They joined in the chase, chuckling, whistling, and sometimes breaking off from steady flight to tumble about in the air, looping the loop around each other.

"They're so wonderful," Skylark said.

"Well, if you lived with them all the time you mightn't think so," Joe answered. "Always carrying on and calling day and night. But they're the very reason why Auntie Ruth set up this bird sanctuary in the first place. Did Hoki or Bella tell you how Man interrupted the Great Circle of life, death and renewal? How he chopped down the Great Forest or set fire to it so that he could create pastureland for his sheep and cattle, or create towns and cities to live in, or the highways between? How he brought with him the dog, feral cat, rat and other bird destroyers like the stoat and even the honey bee? The possum and the deer came with Man too, raking the barks of the trees with their claws and antlers. Sometimes Man introduced a new species to control an earlier species he had let loose in the wild. He totally ravaged the forest and changed forever the ecology for all the bird species. What is worse is that Man also shifted the balance in favour of the seabirds. Where he went he created the environment for seabirds to feed upon. Food dumps, rubbish pits, offal: there you will find the great gull scavengers. Because of Man they have increased in numbers, size and cruelty. And, you know, Man was so stupid when he tried to replace the great forest. He planted beech forest, which did not have the same vital food supplies for the landbirds. No wonder they declined so drastically."

Joe's voice was passionate. "This is why *I* live on this offshore island, Skylark. The forest on the island must be preserved because it is the only kind in which the kaka, as a colony, can survive. It provides them with the holes in the trunks where they can build their nests. The big trees also provide the kaka with an all-year-round variety of food – berries, shoots, nectar and the larvae of insects. When the giant trees decay and die, even in their death they attract the grubs of woodboring insects that sustain the kaka colony. The kaka love the wood-boring beetles. Only here has the Great Circle of Life been reinstated – life, death, renewal for the benefit of all. I must continue Auntie Ruth's work and maintain the island's ecology for as long as I can."

Skylark pressed Joe's hands. "You'll do it," she said.

Joe looked away, embarrassed. She began to scrape in the dirt.

"Whenever I find a dead kaka, I always bury the parrot. Somewhere here is Flash Harry's father. Now he was a real Casanova. Ah, here we are."

Joe picked up a skeletal frame. With delicate fingers, she detached its beak and intoned to its owner: "Your beak, old one, goes on a journey of its own now. Give to her who possesses it the power to split any branch, crush any seed, break any rock. Be proud that through it you will live again."

Joe turned to Skylark. "Remember, Skylark, a beak is not just a –"

"Beak," Skylark said. "Yes, I know."

"It comes from a powerful bird with a double-jointed jaw. With a beak like this you will truly have the voice of leadership. It is also through the beak that a bird is able to breathe. A beak allows the bird to eat and drink. To sing, call, cry, warn in the night. And it is also strong enough to kill. All these things a claw and a feather cannot do."

Joe looked at Arnie but winked at Skylark. "I suppose I'd better give your boyfriend one too. You never know."

"He's not my boyfriend!"

"What's wrong with you, boy?" Joe scolded. "Haven't you heard of old Chinese proverb: 'Bird in hand worth two in bush'?"

Joe gave a raucous laugh. The kaka colony caught her laughter in their wings and played a game of netball with it. Thrown like a ball, its sound ricocheted among them as they twisted, looped, chuckled and tumbled in the air.

He's not her boyfriend! She's not his girlfriend! Ha-ha-ha!

Led by Joe, Skylark and Arnie walked back towards the beach.

"This might sound like a dumb question," Skylark asked Joe, "but after we leave you, do you know where we're suppose to go?"

The sun skipped through the thinning canopy. "Why, you have to go to see Deedee," Joe said, as if Skylark should know. "She's the one who knows about the Time Portal. I only know about the beak."

Through a gap in the trees Skylark saw a blaze of yellow sand. Further out, was the blinding blue of the sea. "And where does this Deedee live?"

"She's down in Nelson. When you get there, ask for her at the Maori Language Centre right in the middle of the city. She teaches young Maori children the reo."

Arnie groaned. "Another ferry crossing. Oh no,"

"And I suppose she'll have the magic potion or spell or, hey, maybe she can dial up the Time Portal and ask the pizza boy to deliver it," Skylark said. Joe led the way out of the forest, scrambling among the rocks down to the sand. Skylark was busy looking at her feet, trying not to trip. Arnie was behind.

"Skylark, do you always mock everything? I know you're resistant to being told what to do and I can see that in you patience is not a virtue. But you're just going to have to learn to hold your temper. Don't be so reactive, and don't bad-mouth everything just because you can't understand it. The Apocrypha doesn't tell how these things are done. Sometimes we have to work it out, try to solve the enigmas, find the answers to the puzzle."

"My mother's in a coma. I'm in a hurry."

Joe wasn't listening. Already she had reached the sand. "Nothing of importance ever comes quickly or easily. You're not going to help your mother at all if you don't do everything in the proper order. Hoki's given you the claw, Birdy's given you the feather, you've got the beak from me. With these you can go to the next level. But only Deedee can tell you how to get there."

Just then Skylark felt something thump her hard on the back.

"Ouch," Skylark laughed, assuming Arnie had tripped and put a hand out to steady himself. Then it happened again, hard, this time on her head. She put her arms in front of her, to protect her face, and the world became a crazy kaleidoscope of sky, sand and sea as she fell. But there was something else there too, something solid black in the centre of things, something which kept fragmenting, with pieces falling away –

Kaa. *Kaa.*

"No," Skylark screamed. She remembered the first day at Tuapa when a big black bird had hit her. This time there were fifty seashags in a feathered mass of evil, their wings flaying the sky. Another seashag dived.

There she is, the chick! Attack! Kill her!

Arnie saw Kawanatanga falling on Skylark's body. There had been no time to react. The attack had happened so quickly. He called out: "Joe –"

Joe turned to look. She saw Skylark on the ground, rolling, trying to rid herself of Kawanatanga. She looked up: "Jeez, where the hell did they come from?" She remembered her Army patrol drills. She had scouted too far ahead. In a crouch, she ran back to Arnie who managed to pull Kawanatanga away. But more and more seashags were diving and Joe caught a flash of Kawanatanga as he called out his commands.

Get the chick! She must be stopped! Kill her!

Joe reached for her Bowie knife. "Arnie, here –"

She sent the knife spinning through the air. Arnie caught it and, next moment, was slashing, slashing, slashing out at the seashags. The knife made contact. A seashag squealed and fell to the ground, wing severed from body. Another slash, and blood spouted as Arnie severed the head from another seashag.

"Get them off me! Get me away!" Skylark screamed

Joe hurled herself in, ripping through the birds, trying to disperse them.

"Get out of here, you seabirds," she roared. But she knew that they were all powerless here on the sand. They were in the seabirds' domain.

Vicious beaks were slashing at Skylark's eyes, throat and ears. One lucky strike and they could get into her brain. Joe reached her and threw herself on top, protecting Skylark from the attack.

"When I give the word," Joe yelled to Arnie, "pull Skylark out from under me. Make for the forest. That's the only place she'll be safe."

"What about you?"

"That's an order, Corporal. Do it now."

Joe rolled, Arnie pulled and, with a cry of pain, Skylark was up on her knees and in Arnie's arms. All around her the seabirds were flapping, and Kawanatanga was crying out in deafening anger. Arnie was beating a way through them. Skylark couldn't see. When she went to clear her eyes her hands were red with blood oozing from her hairline. "Hurry Arnie," she moaned. The forest seemed so far away.

They crossed from the sand into the rocks. Still the seashags pursued them. Arnie fell. We're finished, Skylark thought. Arnie picked her up again, carrying her in his arms. Stumbling, almost tripping, he pushed himself up the rocks and fell with Skylark into the shade of the forest.

Kill the hen who guards this island. Kawanatanga's fury knew no bounds as he directed his squad to rip Joe apart.

"You must go back," Skylark said to Arnie. "You can't leave Joe out there."

Arnie bounded into the sunlight, yelling battle cries that he had last used in the Army. He reached Joe, and hoisted her in a fireman's lift. As he clambered from the sand to the rocks, he saw Skylark coming to help him. She had a long branch in her hands and she swung it at the seashags like a baseball bat. "Take that you feathered freaks," Skylark yelled. With her help Arnie and Joe reached the sanctuary of the forest.

"Thanks, Skylark," Joe said. Blood was streaming from her wounds.

But what was this? The seashags had not stopped their attack.

Disobey the law! Cross over into the territory of the forest birds! Kill the chick! Kill her protectors too!

"We're done for," Arnie said as he turned to make a last-ditch stand.

However, behind him the forest ever so softly began to rustle. A wind seemed to be blowing through it. The wind became a veritable storm. It buffeted with battle cries, loud, strong and harsh. From out of the canopy came hundreds of brightly coloured birds. They had grey crowns and, as they glided down to join in the battle, their underwings flashed red.

"It's the cavalry," Skylark said.

The kaka colony, led by Flash Harry, came flying to the rescue.

Kra. Kra. Ka! Return to your domain, seashags. Tarry here at your own peril, for you are in the forest of the kaka, warriors of Tane.

Beaks ready, the kaka colony drove a wedge through the marauding seashags. Reluctant to give way, Kawanatanga ordered his birds to stand their ground. But the kaka were relentless in their attack. They entered into mid-air combat, tearing, slashing, showing no quarter.

"Skylark! Joe!" Arnie pulled the two women to safety as Kawanatanga and the seashags turned to combat their new foe.

With the kaka colony taking a rearguard action, Skylark, Arnie and Joe made their way back to the house. Luckily, Skylark's injuries were superficial. She worked on Joe, whose wounds were more serious, then both worked on Arnie. He had two long rips in his shoulder, and Skylark blanched when she saw the makeshift way in which Joe sewed the flaps of skin together. "It isn't pretty," Joe said, surveying her handiwork. "But it does the job."

Skylark went to the window. The seashags were hovering over the sea. "How are we going to be able to leave here?" she asked. "If we cross the sea we'll be at their mercy."

"You've got to complete your task," Joe answered, "no matter what."

"We'll just have to wait for nightfall," Arnie said.

"But we'll lose a third day," Skylark answered.

"It can't be helped. We'll have to drive by night. If we're lucky, we'll be able to make the ferry sailing from Wellington tomorrow morning. Agreed?"

Even though she didn't want to accept it, Skylark nodded. She started to rock and moan, and Joe recognised the symptoms. Delayed shock. "I'm putting you to bed," she said. "You too, Corporal. You've both got to get some sleep, and that's an order. I'll wake you when it's dusk."

Skylark and Arnie put up only token resistance, and when Joe went to check on them ten minutes later, they were both asleep.

At mid-afternoon the telephone rang.

"Is that you, Joe?" Hoki asked. "I've been trying to get you all day. Are Skylark and Arnie with you? They must be warned. Kawanatanga is after them."

"He's already attacked," Joe answered, "don't worry, the kids are safe, but the seashags are still out there. They've got us pinned down. We've decided to wait for nightfall."

"Good," Hoki said. "So Skylark and Arnie will be on their way home?"

"No, they're going to Deedee's."

"Deedee's? What for!"

"Deedee's the only one who knows about the Time Portal."

Hoki became silent. "I didn't realise all this would be so dangerous," she said at last. "Had I known, I would have accompanied Skylark myself."

"Arnie's doing a good job," Joe answered.

"Tell them I love them," Hoki said. "I will pray that they have safe passage to Deedee's."

Joe put the telephone down and began preparing provisions for Skylark and Arnie's journey. For the rest of the afternoon she sat looking out at Kawanatanga and his seashag squad. She thought of his threat to her kaka colony.

"You think I'm scared?" she muttered. "If it comes to a fight, let it be to the death."

The dusk finally fell. With screams of fury, Kawanatanga searched for a place to settle for the night. Clouds broiled from the east, cutting off the light.

Joe woke Skylark and Arnie. "It's time to go," she said.

She led the way to the dinghy and was just about to start the motor when a grey and red shape came fluttering from the trees: Flash Harry. He circled the dinghy and landed on the seat next to Skylark. He pecked at her hands, forcing her to open them.

"What's he doing?" Skylark laughed.

"He's brought you a present," Joe answered.

Flash Harry regurgitated some berries into Skylark's hands.

Go well, Skylark. Fly well.

"You must have really made an impression on him," Joe said. "They're a gift. Some food for your journey." She started the motor. The dinghy headed away from the island.

– 5 –

At the same time as Skylark and Arnie were leaving Joe's island, Mitch Mahana and his son Francis, acting on Hoki's summons, arrived in Manu Valley. The sun was setting when Mitch stepped out of the truck. He looked up at the ripped sky and the seabirds hovering around it, and gaped like a stunned mullet. Francis's reaction was simpler.

"Holy shit," he said.

"That's our problem, our nemesis," Hoki said. "Sunup to sundown the seabirds try to get through to the other side. They only break off their attacks when night comes."

"The other side?" Mitch asked, his face wan with horror. "In God's name, what's on the other side?"

"The past," Bella answered enigmatically, "and the future –"

"I don't think I want to know," Mitch shuddered. "It sounds like one of those movies Arnie likes. I watched *Aliens* with him once and I couldn't sleep for weeks."

"Dad only likes westerns," Francis confided to Bella.

"Well, where do you want us to put our gear?" Mitch continued. "What time do you want me and Francis up there to do our job?" He had always been a straightforward man, preferring to live without knowing of life's complexities.

"Could you move into the bach?" Bella asked. "You brought your rifles? If you two could take the first shift tomorrow that would give me and Hoki a chance to have a break. We're really glad you're here. With you two with us, the task of guarding the sky will be easier."

Bella cooked dinner – a lovely piece of cod which Mitch and Francis had netted that very day. Soon after dinner, both men excused themselves. They had brought a portable television set with them and wanted to watch the All Blacks playing South Africa.

"I'll do the dishes," Hoki told Bella. "Why don't you go with the men? It'll do you good."

When Bella returned a couple of hours later, she was very grumpy. Not only that, but some pretty interesting fumes, somewhere in the vicinity of vodka and whisky, were coming off of her.

"The All Blacks lost," Bella said. "Me and Mitch placed some bets on them, but Francis won and cleaned us out."

"Oh no," Hoki answered. "How much did you lose?"

"Fifty matchsticks. It's put me off my sleep."

"You big spender," Hoki said. "Well, you'll just have to make the fire tomorrow by rubbing two sticks together."

That night, however, Bella wasn't the only one to toss and turn. Hoki knelt by her bed and said her prayers – she thought that her karakia would calm her, but it took a long time for her to get to sleep. Even when sleep finally came, somewhere in the dark morning hours, it brought with it a disturbing dream.

In her dream, Hoki seemed to be way above the earth. She was frightened at first but, when she began to float down, she was relieved. Gradually, she was able to touch the mountain tops with her toes and that made her feel much better. But what was that? Far ahead, two lights were piercing the darkness. She decided to take a closer look. She swooped down and saw that the lights were the headlights of a ute. She looked inside and, with delight, saw Skylark and Arnie.

Hello, you two, Hoki said. She tapped on the windows and then flew around to the windscreen. Arnie was driving. She yelled out a greeting but he didn't seem to hear her, so she poked her tongue at him. Couldn't he see her? She noticed he had bruises and stitches on his face.

Suddenly, Hoki heard the sounds of loud and menacing twittering. She stood on the bonnet of the ute, balancing herself on her walking sticks to see where the noise was coming from. Uh oh, the dawn had come up and, in the distance, she could see black shapes against the sky. They reminded her of the nasty flying monkeys in *The Wizard of Oz*.

I'd better take a look. Hoki braced and launched herself into the air. Over the ute's roof she went, soaring up to the flying monkeys. As she got closer, the monkeys transformed themselves into black seashags. Kawanatanga was leading them, his eyes as red as a devil's. With a scream, she went to attack him, but something strange happened. He didn't seem to know she was there. Instead, Kawanatanga and his fleet flew straight through her as if she were a ghost. It was a weird feeling, and Hoki examined her body, looking for holes in herself.

Hoki turned and saw the night had ended. The sun was burning a line on the horizon, marking the coming of a new day. Arnie was way ahead but the black squad of seashags was closing in.

Oh no, this can't be happening, Hoki thought. She saw that Kawanatanga had been joined by all the seabirds of the world. For as far as she could see, seabirds had come to block the way to Wellington. They had come across the sea, white feathers across blue ocean. They were sitting on the telegraph poles, fences, everywhere.

Gasping with fear, Hoki realised that Skylark and Arnie needed reinforcements. But where from? She concentrated very hard, and the answer came to her.

Come, manu whenua, Hoki called. *Cleave a path for Skylark so that she might fulfil her destiny.*

The wind began to stir. There was a cyclone as birds of the land heeded Hoki's call: pigeons, thrushes, ducks, swans, quails, pheasants, waterfowls, parrots, stilts, kingfishers, cuckoos, doves, rollers all. Above the main body of birds, swifts volleyed across the sky on long scimitar-shaped wings. They were joined in their aerial acrobatics by the high-flying hawks and falcons. But their numbers were so small compared to the seabirds. Hoki's heart went out to them as, with a great shrilling and whistling, they joined in battle with the seabirds. Even the humble sparrow was there, trying in his own way to help. The clamour shook Heaven, and Hoki put her hands up to her ears because of the din and closed her eyes because she was afraid to witness the outcome.

When Hoki opened her eyes, the dream had transformed itself. *Well done, birds of the forest.* The manu whenua had created enough of a diversion to allow Skylark and Arnie to pass through to Wellington. But not for long. As the ute approached Wellington Harbour, Hoki saw that Kawanatanga had resumed his relentless pursuit.

Skylark, beware the outstretched necks of the seashags.

Hoki's dream exploded. She sat up, her heart pumping hard. She was so worried that it took her a long time to calm down. She went to the kitchen to make a cup of tea. The pot was still warm, so Hoki knew Mitch and Bella had already left for the morning shift on the cliff top. There, Mitch was talking to Bella about the seabirds, the ripped sky – and Skylark. Sometimes he had an uncanny knack of asking the right question, of moving a piece of jigsaw puzzle into a place where it might fit.

"There's one thing about Skylark I don't understand," he said to Bella. "How come she's the chick? She doesn't even come from here."

Bella didn't take much notice of Mitch's question at first. She aimed her shotgun at the sky and let off the first shot of the day. *Bang.* And the jigsaw piece clicked into place: Cora's hospital chart.

Middle name Agnes. Born Christchurch 1960.

What was it about 1960 that bothered her? Then she realised: 1960 was the same year that her sister, Agnes, had left Tuapa.

"Arnie? Arnie, are you awake?"

Skylark was sitting in the driver's seat. Arnie was dozing beside her. They'd made good time to Wellington, and through the windscreen they saw vehicles being marshalled to drive onto the ferry. The day was dark, miserable, and bucketing down with rain. Ahead of them lay the prospect of another wild Cook Strait crossing.

"What's up?" Arnie asked, as he stirred.

"We'll be driving onto the ferry soon. I was wondering if you would like a coffee or something. You really need something warm inside you."

"Not if I'm going sailing I don't," Arnie said. "Look at the weather! Won't it ever let up?"

"Maybe you should stay in Wellington," Skylark suggested. "You could wait for tomorrow's sailing."

"And let you go on by yourself? No way."

Secretly, Skylark was glad that Arnie felt that way. She'd grown used to his company. Even though she'd never admit it, it would have been difficult to get this far without him.

"Whether you like it or not, you're still getting something into your stomach before we get on the ferry," she said.

Skylark got out of the ute and ran to the terminal. Inside, all was bedlam. A number of sailings had been cancelled. Passengers were sitting on the floors as well as the seats. Arguing. Playing cards. Sleeping. Waiting. The only sign of liveliness came from a group of Swedish backpackers for whom this kind of weather was second nature.

Skylark picked her way through the crowd to the self-service food bar: pies, oily chips in cardboard canisters, sandwiches masquerading as BLTs and, aha, soup with toast.

"I'll have your soup to go," Skylark ordered. "Two black coffees as well. Oh yes, and three of those milk chocolate bars, thanks."

The waitperson, who seemed to think she was working at some upmarket establishment, took Skylark's money and began to service the order . . . and that's when it happened. Something clicked and popped inside her head, as if someone was dialling long distance. The connection was made – and Skylark's first thought was: Oh no, maybe I am the one after all.

As clear as day she saw Kawanatanga and his seashag squad, and they were closing in on Wellington Harbour. Then she heard Hoki's voice:

Skylark, beware the outstretched necks of the seashags.

The warning sent Skylark staggering out of the terminal. She pushed past the people in the waiting line, almost tripped.

"But Miss, your order," the waitperson called.

Skylark was already running fast. Out of the humid interior she went, into the rain. For a moment all was confusion. The noise, the traffic, the bustling port. Where was the ute?

Skylark heard the giant rear doors of the ferry open. A marshall came forward and began to wave the cars in. Skylark kept looking at the sky. So far it was clear. She reached the ute, swung herself in and started the engine.

"I thought you were getting us some food," Arnie said.

"There was a queue," Skylark answered. "I realised we'd be boarding soon. See? We're moving."

But why was it taking so long? Skylark had never been patient. Not only that, but her mind was ticking over all the variables. Arnie and ferries didn't mix, check. Out here they were sitting ducks, check. But even when they boarded the seashags would know they were on the ferry, checkmate. She compressed her lips, nodded to herself and made a decision.

"Hold on tight, Arnie, we're going to Plan B."

"Get a grip, Skylark, there isn't a Plan B. We have to get on the ferry."

Skylark reversed. The truck behind her blared its horn as she bumped it. Arnie watched wide-eyed.

"Rubbish," Skylark said. "There's always a Plan B. Harrison Ford had one in *Star Wars*. Bruce Willis had one in *The Fifth Element*. How are we going to save the world from the Evil Empire without a Plan B? Let me think. Wasn't Carrie Fisher in this same situation in *Star Wars*? When the Imperial Troops boarded her spaceship and they had her trapped at both ends of the corridor, what did she do?"

"She blasted a hole through the wall."

"Why, Arnie." Skylark smiled sweetly. "Why didn't *I* think of that?"

Next moment, Skylark had wrenched the steering wheel, this time bumping the car in front. She pulled out of the queue, made an illegal right turn and sped past the marshall. He waved desperately at her to stop. She saw a railway shunter coming towards her.

"Back up, Skylark! Back up," Arnie yelled.

"Trust in the force," Skylark answered. After all, there was plenty of room for her to squeeze through on the right of the train and – wasn't that an exit coming up? Sure it was a one-way on-ramp, but beggars couldn't be choosers. Skylark touched the accelerator and roared up the on-ramp to the motorway. Now the problem was how to get into the correct citybound lane. No sweat. A couple of big bumps later, and Skylark had taken the ute across the median and pulled it into the line of traffic streaming into Wellington.

"Stop the ute," Arnie roared. "Stop it right now. Now get out of the driver's seat. Don't even think of saying no. Just do it." He was really angry, not to mention worried about his paintwork. "Now just tell me, Skylark, what is this all about?"

"I've already told you," Skylark answered. "This is Plan B."

Half an hour later, the ferry was ready for sailing. The marshall signalled the rear doors closed. All the vehicles were aboard. The ferry weighed anchor and headed out of the harbour. As it approached the heads, it began to pitch and yaw in the currents coming from the Straits. The captain, looking ahead, saw the white-tipped waves just waiting to have fun with his ship. "Tell the crew to prepare for a rough-weather running," he said. "Better let the passengers know it's not going to be an easy crossing."

The open sea was a fist which hit the ferry hard. The ship shuddered, dipped, and mountainous waves sprayed across its bow. For a second it wallowed in a trough, until the next fist hit it again. Behind, the captain saw a huge black storm cloud approaching from the rear, broiling over the sea.

Approaching from the rear?

The storm cloud splintered, separated and fragmented. When the captain looked again he saw black seashags diving down upon his ship. As they hurtled lower, their leader, Kawanatanga, uttered his hunting cry.

Find the chick. Kill her. Do it now. Now.

The seashag squad entered the companionways, flying into the staterooms, along corridors and down stairways. There was pandemonium as passengers and seashags confronted each other. News broadcasts would later report that the incident was a freak occurrence to do with seabirds confused by the weather and trying to find shelter.

Where is she! She must be here. Find her.

Meantime, at Wellington Airport, the morning flight to Nelson took to the air. Arnie looked out of the window and saw the ferry ploughing its way through the waves below. He thanked his lucky stars for Skylark's credit card.

"This is a great Plan B," he said. "Thank you. Are you sure you don't want the window seat?"

Skylark's face was white and she was clutching the arms of her seat as if her life depended on it. "Please don't make this any more difficult than it is," she said. "Did I tell you that I hate flying?"

"So I guess," Arnie said, "you wouldn't want a triple cheeseburger followed by a chocolate ice cream sundae, would you?"

Skylark glared at him.

"Look, mate," she hissed, "I'd quit while I was ahead if I was you."

[CHAPTER TEN]

— 1 —

"You mean Deedee is dead?"

Skylark looked into the face of the kaumatua who greeted her at the Maori Language Centre where Joe had said they'd find Deedee. Behind him she could see a young teacher taking children in Maori language lessons.

"Ae, kua mate te koka," the old man confirmed. "She died three weeks ago. We had a big tangi for her. She was well loved."

"But she can't be dead," Skylark protested. She looked back at the street, where Arnie was waiting for her.

"The children, particularly, will miss her," the kaumatua continued. "Although Deedee lived way up on the mountain tops, she never missed a day's work teaching them to look after the forest and the birds she loved." He gestured in the direction of Deedee's mountains. The peaks were like arrows pointing at Heaven. "All that you see up there belonged to her," he said. "The tribe is taking it over. After all these years of complaining about her sitting up there protecting the land, they've now realised that Deedee saved a valuable resource for us."

"I've come so far," Skylark said. "I've come all this way just to see her." She felt as if a wall had arisen between her and where she should be going. There was no way around it, over it or under it. Nothing.

The old man tried to be sympathetic. "Were you a mokopuna of Deedee?" he asked.

"No," Skylark answered. She saw the look of puzzlement in his face, but she didn't want to explain. "Thank you for letting me know," she said. She turned to leave, and as she did so the young teacher gave her a curious glance, her eyes widening.

Skylark went down to the taxi to tell Arnie the news. "Could you ring Hoki?" she asked.

Mitch answered the telephone. "Are you there, Mother Ship? Do you copy?" Mitch thought it was a kid playing jokes, and was about to hang up when Hoki walked in. She snatched the receiver from him.

"I copy, Arnie. What's the matter?"

"Deedee is dead. She died three weeks ago."

"Aue, te koka kua ngaro ki te Po," Hoki wailed.

Now it was Skylark's turn to grab the phone. "Hoki? Are you there?" she said. "I'm really sorry about Deedee, but Arnie and I have to keep going. Do you have any idea where we should go now, where we should look? I've got to find the Time Portal."

Hoki calmed down. "Deedee may have left a message for you in her house up in the mountains," she said. "Go up there and see if you can find it. If you can't, search for the Time Portal itself."

"What does it look like?" Skylark asked.

"How would I know!" Hoki answered. "A doorway, I suppose."

Arnie shrugged his shoulders. "A doorway? What kind of doorway?"

Skylark was in no mood for questions. "Let's just do it," she answered.

She was halfway into the taxi when she heard a voice calling to her.

"Were you looking for Deedee?" The young teacher was standing on the steps with the kaumatua, who was looking somewhat abashed. "The kaumatua is getting forgetful in his old age," the teacher said. "He was supposed to give you an urgent message from Lottie."

"Lottie?"

"She's Deedee's granddaughter. She told us that a strange girl would come looking for the koka. That's you, isn't it! Lottie works at The Warehouse on the checkout. You're to go there. She said to tell you to hurry. There's not much time left."

–2–

The Warehouse was really hopping. All end-of-season lines had been discounted up to 50 per cent, and the locals had come in searching for bargains in clothes, shoes, garden furniture and kitchenware. Six checkout lanes were operating.

"Which one do you think is Lottie?" Skylark asked.

"The one chewing the gum," Arnie answered. He pointed to a big, boisterous girl with blonde highlights in her hair (and she had lots of hair), greasy lipsticked lips, and cleavage – and there was lots of that too.

Skylark's eyes connected with Lottie's and, from the girl's reaction, she knew that Arnie was dead on target. Lottie put up her "Position Closed" sign, took off her smock and yelled out in a loud voice: "Jack? I'm taking my lunch break now." No asking. Just an announcement. Take it or leave it.

"How did you know she was Lottie?" Skylark asked as Lottie shoved her way through the shoppers.

"Easy," Arnie said. "Just look for the bossiest girl on the block and she's bound to be one of you."

Lottie was fumbling in her purse for her car keys. When she reached Skylark she introduced herself. "Hello, I'm Charlotte. People call me Lottie, but my enemies call me Charlie. I'm Nani Deedee's mokopuna. I know who you are. I was expecting you three days ago. I must say you're cutting it really fine." She swept on past, and Skylark and Arnie followed her out to the car park. She fumbled in her purse again and brought out a cellphone. "So what's your name?"

"Oh, I'm Skylark," Skylark said.

"Cool," Lottie said. She was walking a fast clip, noticed Arnie, punched in a number and waited for the connection. "And is he your –?"

Skylark wished people would stop asking about Arnie or assuming he was her boyfriend.

"No, he's just a friend."

"Is he going with you?"

Gosh, Lottie sure asked a heap of questions. "Um, I don't know."

Lottie aimed her key ring at her car and automatically unlocked it. "No," she said as Arnie went to get in the front. "Back seat for you. Us girls in front."

"What did I tell you?" Arnie said. "Bossy."

Lottie's call was connected. "Hello? Is that you Quentin? The girl's arrived. She's got a boyfriend with her. No, I didn't know there would be two of them either. You'd better prepare two parachutes –"

Parachutes?

"We'll be there in twenty minutes. See ya, babe." Lottie flipped her cellphone off and stepped into her car. She reversed without looking in the rear-vision mirror and drove at speed out of the carpark. An outraged skateboarder managed to get out of the way just in time. "If you don't like the way I drive, get off the pavement," Lottie yelled.

Apparently Lottie only used the mirror to put on lipstick or to primp her hair. Once she had done that, however, she seemed to relax. "Ever since I took over as guardian from Nani Deedee," she began, "my whole life has been like this! Rushing here. Rushing there. I didn't want it and certainly wasn't looking for it. Once upon a time I used to go clubbing on Mondays. What do I do now? I go up to Nani's mountains and check up on her birds. I used to have a girls' night out on Wednesdays – and last Wednesday we had some male strippers in town. But where was I? Working on a brief with my tribal elders to put a case to the courts on Nani's land. Then last Saturday I had a hot date, but what happened? I was back up on Nani's mountain again, playing nursemaid to some kiwi chicks. I tell you, my entire social life has been ruined. Ah well, I guess there are things you just have to do. It's not anything I have any choice about. At least you've finally arrived and that's the main thing."

Lottie drove through a red light. "Why all the rush?"Skylark asked. She was feeling very nervous of this girl who, like Hoki, seemed to think she would do what they wanted her to do.

"You know about the Time Portal, don't you? Well, the way it operates is not all that straightforward. In particular, there's only certain times during the period when it's open that you can actually go through. You can go through right now but I haven't a clue how long it will stay that way! So my cousin Quentin has been on call to fly us to the portal as soon as you got here.

"Fly? But I hate flying. I've just got off one plane and I am not getting on another!"

"Nani Deedee made me swear on the Book of Birds that I would get you there so that you could go through –"

"Go through to where!" Skylark asked angrily.

Lottie rolled her eyes. "To the other side, of course! Haven't you been properly briefed? Don't you know anything?"

Lottie zoomed into the airport carpark. Immediately she was out of the car and walking fast.

Arnie took one look at Skylark's face and tried not to laugh. She had finally met someone as stroppy as she was – and she didn't like it one bit.

"Don't just stand there," Lottie yelled. She motioned to Skylark and Arnie to keep up. They crossed the carpark, went around the terminal and towards a small hangar: NELSON AIR CHARTERS. Inside were a helicopter and two small aeroplanes. A young man was waiting nervously beside one of them: a six-seater Piper Cherokee belonging to the local parachuting club with a cartoon character – Betty Boop – painted on the fuselage.

"Okay Quentin, rev her up!" Lottie called.

Quentin nodded at Skylark and shook Arnie's hand. "Do you want me to s-suit them up f-first?" he stuttered.

"We'll have to do it when we're in the air."

"Stop right there," Skylark ordered. "I am not getting on that plane."

"Of course you are, dear," Lottie said. Before Skylark knew it, she had been pushed through a door and Lottie was buckling her in.

"Arnie? Arnie!" Skylark called. But he was too busy talking to Quentin and throwing equipment through the same door that Skylark had been pushed through, preventing her from getting out.

Then Arnie himself jumped in and closed the door. Next moment Lottie and Quentin had climbed into the pilot and co-pilot's seats.

"You're not going to fly this thing are you?" Skylark asked.

Lottie was too busy doing her pre-flight check to answer. Arnie was grinning like a cheshire cat. "Skylark," he said, "you're going to love this."

"Get me out of here immediately."

But it was too late. Lottie switched on the ignition. She had a brief conversation with Quentin and was very cross with him. "You did what!"

"Have a h-heart," Quentin moaned. "You know what the p-procedures are. There was n-no w-way I could g-get out of filing a f-flight p-plan."

"Why do you always have to d-do things by the b-book, Quentin?" Lottie asked. "What a pain in the butt. I told you to tell the tower that we were just going on a sightseeing flight."

"Y-yeah, and they b-believed that the l-last time."

The starter motor whined, the propellers began to turn, there was a small concussive sound, and the engine roared into action. Lottie eased the throttle, and the plane taxied forward, out of the hangar and into the daylight.

"Are you two belted in?" she asked. "Good." She had her earphones on. "Tower? This is Betty Boop, over. Request permission for takeoff, over."

The tower came back. "Betty Boop, grateful you confirm your flight plan, over."

"Tower, I have two American millionaires on board for sightseeing flight of Nelson City and surrounding environment, over. Request clearance for take off, over."

"Betty Boop, the Department of Conservation has requested you be denied permission to take off until satisfaction of your intentions, over."

Lottie sighed, rolled her eyes and elbowed Quentin in the ribs. "This is all your f-fault," she said, as she headed the plane out onto the runway.

"Betty Boop! You have not been given permission for take off, over."

"Thank you, Tower," Lottie answered blissfully, as if she was just taking a walk in the park.

"Betty Boop! Return to the airport. Your take off has not, repeat not, been authorised, over."

"Tower? Say again? Oh damn this radio, Quentin, I told you to fix it! Sorry, Tower, you're breaking up, over."

"Betty Boop! This will be your second violation in one month. Return immediately as requested to the airport, over."

Lottie just kept on heading out to the runway. When she arrived she positioned the plane into the wind.

"Betty Boop, you are in violation of instructions, over. You run the risk of being grounded, over."

"Tower? Tower? Proceeding to take off –"

Lottie revved the engine. The plane roared down the runway. As it took off, Lottie waved at the controllers in the tower. "And do have a nice day," she said.

The plane leapt higher into the air. The earth receded, the clouds came closer. The plane reached cruising altitude. Lottie motioned to Quentin that he should take over piloting the plane. She clambered back to Skylark and Arnie.

"Right," Lottie said. "Time to get you both suited up. Have you done any parachuting before?"

"Absolutely, positively, never," Skylark said, "and I'm not about to start, so just get me back on the ground now."

"You lucky girl, you," Lottie said. "We're offering you a free jump today. What about you, Arnie?"

"Yes, I got my certificate in the Army. For solo as well as tandem."

Lottie's eyes lit up. "Great, then you can do the jump with Skylark?"

"Well . . . yes."

"Primo," Lottie answered. "Here was I thinking I would have to take you both down myself. This really solves my problem – I'm expected back this afternoon to do our stocktake. Not to mention that I only got my hair done yesterday and helmets play havoc with the styling."

"Haven't you heard anything I've said?" Skylark yelled. "I know I've come all this way to go through the Time Portal but jumping out of a plane is not on the agenda and I'm not going to do it."

"Of course you are," Lottie answered.

"Oh no I'm not."

"Oh yes you are."

Skylark started to push Lottie away, but every time she pushed, Lottie pulled. Before Skylark knew it, one arm was in one sleeve, the other arm was in the second.

"What are you doing!" Skylark screamed. She kicked at Lottie, and one leg went into the jumpsuit. She kicked again and, oh, clever Lottie twisted, zipped and voilà!

"Done," Lottie said. By magic, Skylark had been trussed up like a turkey.

Meanwhile, Arnie was really sparking, gung ho, loving every minute – and Skylark hated him for it. "I think you've met your match, Skylark," he said.

"And I th-think you're about to m-meet yours!" Quentin said to Lottie. "The tower has c-contacted the Department of C-Conservation. They've got a plane on the r-runway right n-now. They're coming after us."

– 3 –

Lottie clambered back into the pilot's seat. "This is all your fault, Quentin." she said.

Quentin let it pass. "The pursuit p-plane is in radio c-contact with us, Lottie. What do you want me to do?"

"Ignore them. Keep pretending that our radio is broken – and don't forget to break it before we land! Otherwise we'll really be in the proverbial."

Skylark cast her eyes upward: If there is a God in Heaven . . .

"So what's with the Department of Conservation?" Arnie asked.

"Why would they try to stop this plane?"

"Well," Lottie began, "what we're planning to do is not exactly wrong, but it's not exactly right either."

"I gathered as much," Arnie said.

"The fact is that where we're going was once part of Nani Deedee's land. But it was taken by DOC when some fool tribal elder blabbed about what was on it. They came to take a look and, next minute, Nani was slapped with a forced sale of the land when DOC brought in a new Act of Parliament which allowed them to do it. Some Act to do with historic places or antiquities, blah blah blah. Anyhow our lawyers are on to it, so the point of view *I* take is that the land is still ours, though DOC says it isn't. Meantime, the police have put the land off limits until the matter is settled in the courts. No trespassers are allowed there. But I don't consider myself a trespasser."

"So what exactly *is* there?" Skylark asked.

"Why, the Cathedral of the Birds of course," Lottie said. "I thought you knew. You don't? Well, in the days when the manu whenua ruled the world, they were born, lived their lives and died in the Great Forest. At old age, when they felt Death approaching them, many of the birds would actually fly to particular places in the Great Forest to wait for His coming." Lottie unrolled a topographical map and pointed out the location. "One such a spot is here. See how it's adjacent to Nani Deedee's land?

"Now, the place that I'm referring to is over 150,000 years old. It's a secret location. The ground is porous limestone and, over the years, rain has carved out channels that lead to potholes and subterranean caverns. No wonder DOC went gaga when they saw it. Well, when the birds said their farewells to the world above and died, their bodies lay on the ground. When the rains came, they washed the bones down the limestone channels and into the labyrinth below. You must remember that we are talking about thousands of birds and millions of beautiful fragile bones. Eventually, all the bones piled higher and higher and collected in one giant amphitheatre. Nani Deedee described it to me once. When she shone her torchlight in that place the light shimmered on all those tiny bird skeletons and made it look like a giant cathedral. She thought it was a holy place. She told me that she was able to walk through it to a small circle at the very centre of the cathedral."

Lottie's eyes gleamed with awe. "That is where the Time Portal is."

"Couldn't I have walked there?" Skylark wailed.

"Not an option, sweetheart. You left no time for yourself. You're jumping, and I'm sorry if you don't like it, but you'll just have to be very brave and suck on it."

At that moment, the plane lurched. Lottie grabbed at the webbing that covered the interior fuselage to prevent her from falling. "Jeez, Quentin, can't you keep the plane level?"

"Sorry c-cuz, but I've just had v-visual contact with the pursuit plane. From the l-look of it, I think W-Wayne's on our case."

"Get out of here," Lottie yelled. "Dive, dive, dive!"

"Great," Skylark muttered. "Now we're turning into a submarine."

The plane went into an almost vertical descent. The engines whined, and boxes, equipment, anything that wasn't strapped down, came flying through the air. Down the plane went, through the clouds to the clear air below. Quentin levelled out.

"Do you think they saw us?" Arnie asked Lottie.

"I don't think so," Lottie answered.

Next moment there was another whining sound, and through the clouds came the pursuit aircraft. It drew level and the pilot looked across at Lottie and shook his finger at her. His voice came over Lottie's headphones: "Betty Boop, you naughty, naughty girl, over."

"Bloody Wayne," Lottie said. She clambered back into the pilot's seat.

"Turn back, Betty Boop, there's a good little girl, over."

Lottie blew Wayne a kiss – and made a rude gesture with her fingers.

"Like it or loathe it," she said to herself. She banked the plane in a 30-degree turn away from the other aircraft.

"Wayne's one of the conservation rangers. He likes to make my life a misery," she explained. "He's so into control and his ass is so tight he could crack walnuts with it. But he's not getting me today. We're heading for the clouds. Let's try to lose him there."

Skylark saw red. "Look, I'm perfectly willing to go through the Time Portal for Mum, but not this way. Arnie, call Hoki right now and tell her to get me there by some other route."

But nobody was listening. Wayne had imitated Lottie's strategem and was fast catching up. "Oh, Betty Boop," he chortled. "You'll have to do better than that."

Ahead were tall cirrus clouds. "He's figured out your plan," Arnie said to Lottie. "He's trying to cut you off before you get there."

"Not if I can help it," Lottie answered. "When it comes to flying, Wayne's just a wannabe."

She pushed the plane to greater speed and they were in among the tall towering clouds, engaged in a hair-raising game of hide and seek. When the clouds thinned, sometimes Wayne would be there. Sometimes he would be flying parallel with them; sometimes he would be above them. He seemed to be teasing: Now you see me, now you don't. Little did Wayne know that Lottie was playing for time.

"Come on, Betty Boop, stop shaking your booty and come out with your hands up in the air, over."

Lottie had Wayne so caught up in the chase he did not realise that both planes had reached the area of the Cathedral of the Birds. Below, the landscape was filled with the Giant Forest. Right in the middle of it, a huge escarpment reared into the sky.

Quentin tapped Arnie's shoulder and pointed out the plane's window. "There it is!"

"We're almost at the drop zone," Lottie yelled. "See that river valley below? There's a sandy spit at the river bend. See it, Arnie? That's where I'll be dropping both of you, okay? As soon as you're on the ground, head for that white escarpment over there. Can you see it? The white cliff face?"

"Roger," Arnie answered.

"What do you mean, *Roger*!" Skylark hissed. "I'm not jumping and that's that!"

"The entrance to the Cathedral of the Birds is to the extreme right," Lottie continued. "It's a quarter of an hour climb." She turned to Quentin. "Get Skylark and Arnie into their harness."

Quentin started to fit Arnie's harness and parachute to him; he also gave him a map, two torches, a compass and a pair of binoculars. Arnie, meanwhile, was helping Skylark put on her helmet. To continue distracting Skylark, Lottie asked, "Have you got your karanga ready?"

"My what?"

"You mean you haven't been taught the karanga you'll need when you meet the Runanga a Manu? You'd better be a fast learner. The karanga is the call you make as a sign that you come in peace. When you get to the other side, head for the brightest rainbow in the sky. It will show you the way to the twin mountains. Beneath the rainbow will be the sacred tree, the paepae. That's where the Runanga a Manu will be waiting. When you see them that's when you should begin your karanga. You must do this so that the manu whenua know you come in peace. Those birds have always been very territorial and their sentries will be on guard. If you don't karanga to them, they'll think you're an enemy. Listen to me:

"Karanga mai ki o tatou te manu whenua e, karanga mai, karanga mai, karanga mai! Easy! Now you repeat after me –"

Lottie was diplomatic. "Well, those birds won't understand your dialect, and your pronunciation is atrocious, but seeing as you'll be coming from the future, it'll all sound like double dutch to them anyway."

Lottie had been flying the plane in slow figure eights. Now the pattern was getting tighter, more focused, moving closer and closer to the drop zone.

"One last thing," Lottie said. "Whatever you do, when you go over to the other side, do not fly too high. Do not let the winds of the Heavens take you up into the uppermost reaches of the sky."

"Why is that?" Skylark asked.

"It's very simple," Lottie explained. "When the Lord Tane pushed up the sky, he opened the gates of the Heavens so that the birds, the manu whenua and manu moana, could claim the world he had created for them –"

"Yes. The lords Punaweko and Hurumanu were made guardians."

"Well –" Lottie shifted uneasily. "Some of the birds didn't leave the sky. They stayed up there, in the uppermost reaches. They were manu Atua."

"Manu Atua?"

"God birds," Lottie said. She tried to say the words lightly, but her entire body language was squirming and wriggling in a very strange manner.

"Do I really want to hear this?" Skylark asked.

"The God birds were spirit birds. Their guardians were the lords Rakamaomao and Hurutearangi. They were mythical birds with marvellous powers and thus were exalted far above the ranks of the ordinary manu whenua and manu moana. Some were giant birds, like the poua or pouakai, able to circumnavigate the world and having the awesome power to devastate entire territories if they were hungry or if you made them really mad. Others were supernatural birds, like the manaia, and some were man-destroying birds."

"You're giving me nightmares," Skylark answered.

"Then there was the Hokioi, Spirit Messenger of the Gods and of Immortal Life. The old-time Maori often heard this bird but never saw it.

Whenever they heard its cry, 'Hokiii-oiii! Hokiii-oiii!', they knew it was a portent that something was going to happen. That the gods were going to intervene and change destiny."

"So what's the catch?" Skylark asked.

"Just don't stray into their kingdom, that's all. Just make sure the winds don't take you up there and you'll be all right. But if they do, pray hard."

"*Very* hard," Quentin added.

"You don't have to frighten the life out of Skylark," Arnie reproved.

"Above all, don't go anywhere near the volcanic island where the giant pouakai lives. Otherwise, gotcha!"

"And if all else fails? "Skylark asked.

"Don't look back, fly like hell and get the blazes out of there!"

Everything happened very quickly after that. First, Wayne finally realised he'd been duped. "Betty Boop! Betty Boop!" he called. "You are flying over government land and have no authorisation to enter this airspace, over. Leave the area immediately, over." He broke into the vernacular. "What the bloody hell do you hope to achieve, anyway, Lottie? If you're planning yet another unauthorised parachute jump into the area, I warn you we have two rangers posted on the ground and they have been ordered to go directly to the Cathedral of the Birds to prevent contamination."

Lottie grabbed the microphone. "Oh, go bite your bum, Wayne," she said. She turned to Skylark and Arnie. "You've got to get out now. You'll find the entrance to the Cathedral of the Birds at the base of the escarpment."

Skylark was still trying to evade the inevitable. She struggled with Arnie and Quentin as they tried to get the parachute harness around her. "No way. I am not going to be strapped to somebody as if I was a backpack and then jump out of this plane."

"It's not the b-back. It's the f-front," Quentin answered. He continued to clip Skylark to Arnie.

"Look at it this way, Skylark," Lottie said. "It will be good practice for when you go through the portal."

"What do you mean by that? Do you know something I don't know? Are you in on it, Arnie?"

"In on what!" Arnie answered. "I'm just the sidekick remember?"

Then it was done. Skylark was harnessed to Arnie whether she liked it or not. Quentin pulled the exit door open. The wind rushed in. Cold. Frightening. Outside were all those clouds, all that empty sky – and the ground was sure a long way down.

"Betty Boop! Betty Boop! Do not attempt to land anybody on the ground!"

But Lottie wasn't listening. "I forgot one other thing," she said.

"I hate it when people say that," Skylark answered.

Her heart was pounding with fear. Her mouth was dry. Arnie was pushing her ever so gently towards the centre of the open doorway. She was trying to get back into the plane.

"Don't forget you've only got four days. You have to get through the Time Portal and come back before your time's up, otherwise –"

"Otherwise?"

That's when Arnie ever so gently butted Skylark. "Snuggle up and hold on tight," he said. "It's time to go."

Next moment, Skylark was falling out of the plane, screaming.

– 4 –

All the way down Arnie was stoked, whooping with joy.

"Didn't I tell you you'd love this?" he yelled.

Love this? Skylark was still screaming, and she was frightened to death because the ground was still a long way off. She hated Arnie as he guided them down to the landing zone, because being trussed up like this was like . . . like having . . . simulated sex. And even if Arnie was kind enough to take the brunt of the landing upon himself, rolling so that Skylark wouldn't get hurt, she wasn't in any mood to thank him for his kindness. She went ballistic.

"You did that on purpose, you terrorist," Skylark screamed. "You pushed me out."

"No I didn't," Arnie answered. He was standing, trying to unclip the parachute. He was in a self-congratulatory mood: he had managed to land the parachute smack dead centre of the sandy spit at the bend of the river. He unzipped his suit. He turned to Skylark and freed her of the harness.

Was she grateful? She rounded on him, made an almighty swing, and socked him one in the mouth.

"And what's worse," Skylark screamed, "you enjoyed every minute of it, didn't you. You enjoyed humiliating me and having me close up and personal. Don't try to say you didn't. Well that's as close as you'll ever get, mister, so wipe that smirk off your face."

Skylark was trying to stamp her feet out of the suit. She fell in a tangle. "Well, don't just stand there, you ape! Make yourself useful and get me untangled."

Nursing his jaw, Arnie played the gentleman. Skylark was still yelling at him and, when she was freed, stomped off down to the river's edge to splash some water on her face.

"Skylark, we're here," Arnie said. "It was the only way to get here. You can scream all you like, but on a scale of one to ten you don't even register on my radar." He was already thinking ahead. He took the binoculars out of their pouch and swept the surrounding landscape. On their side of the river, everything was okay. But on the other? He swept the opposite terrain and saw the flash of the sun on something metallic. He focused. Coming down through the bush were the two rangers Wayne had mentioned.

By Arnie's calculations, the rangers were ten minutes away from crossing the river – so he and Skylark were ten minutes ahead. Not much of a margin.

Arnie gave the binoculars to Skylark so that she could take a look. "We'd better get moving," Arnie said.

It wasn't all that difficult to find a way up the escarpment. Despite Skylark's gloomy assumption that she would be pulling herself hand and foot up a steep cliff and hanging from a rope like in *Vertical Limit,* the opposite proved to be the case. Arnie scouted the area and found a path leading from the sandy spit up the face of the escarpment.

"The path is probably the original track to the cave," he said. "Lottie's Maori forebears must have used it when the land was owned by them. Then, when DOC took the land, this –" Arnie indicated the sandy spit – "was probably where they helicoptered in personnel and equipment. It's the closest you can get to the cave. See? They've made an effort to widen the path."

Skylark got over her temper tantrum. She followed Arnie as he led the way. The track ascended through scrubby bush. The river fell away to the left. Then the path made an abrupt turn up a spur, taking them at right angles away from the river. Five minutes later, the scenery transformed itself: breathtaking native forest shafted by dazzling sun surrounded them in an emerald world entirely made up of ferns. Tree ferns formed the canopy overhead. Smaller ferns were interlaced below them, glowing soft green. The grass beneath their feet was moss of the most delicate texture. Truly a lost world, a world that dreams were made of.

And there were birds everywhere. Piping in the ferns. Flitting through the sunlit interior. Singing, always singing.

Ke-*eet,* ke-*eet. Kraak kraak kraak.* Stit stit *stit.* Tweep, tw-*eep,* tw-*eep, too too too! And who are you, too too too!*

The path ascended to a ridge. When Skylark and Arnie reached the top, they took their bearings. Arnie noted that the land slipped away in a natural gradient towards a V-shaped trap below.

When it rained, Skylark remembered, the water must have washed all the bones of the birds down there.

Arnie was already descending into the trap. "We should strike the entrance of the cave soon," he said.

Ye-es, too too too. Not far, not far. Hurry, hurry hurry twee twee twee.

Sure enough, five minutes later, Skylark and Arnie came across a barrier on the path: ENTRANCE PROHIBITED. AUTHORISED PERSONNEL ONLY BEYOND THIS POINT. Arnie stepped over the barrier. Skylark followed him. They came to another sign: DON'T EVEN THINK OF GOING ANY FURTHER. They ignored it and rounded a bend.

"There it is," Arnie said.

For a moment, Skylark didn't know what to think. The entrance was to the left of the path. One slab of rock was cantilevered on top of another. The entrance was the gap between.

"Ah well," Arnie said. "Here goes." Before Skylark could stop him, he was on his back, edging his way into the gap, and letting out an ear-splitting scream.

"Arnie. *Arnie!*" Skylark yelled.

She scrabbled after him, pressing herself through the gap. Arnie was lying motionless on the floor of the cave.

"Oh, Arnie! Wake up. Please."

Then Arnie began to shake. At first, Skylark thought he was in some sort of delirium. But Arnie couldn't contain his laughter. "That was a dirty trick," Skylark seethed.

"You must admit it worked. If I hadn't done it, you'd still be outside deciding whether or not to follow me."

Arnie dusted himself off, switched on his torch, and indicated to Skylark that she should switch on hers. Steps led down into the underground. "Let's get going on our journey to the centre of the earth," he said.

Arnie led the way down into the underworld. "I think we're in the main channel," he said. He had expected complete darkness. Instead, the entire descent was bathed in a bluish light. "Can you see, Skylark? Smaller channels are draining down into the channel from all sides. They must lead to potholes on the surface. The light is coming from them."

"There's glow worms down here too," Skylark whispered, pointing to where the darkness was dotted with light like sparkling diamonds.

They continued the descent deep into the earth. Ahead, Skylark could see more light. But how could that be? Where would light come from at this depth? It was so powerful that Arnie's profile was lit by it. Then Skylark felt a draught on her face, and knew that something wonderful was about to happen.

Arnie was caught in the same emotion. He grinned at her, and she grinned back. They took two more steps forward. Ahead, the channel opened up on both sides of them like a curtain. A rock jutted out.

"There it is, Skylark," Arnie said, his voice hushed with awe. "The Cathedral of the Birds."

Nani Deedee described it to me once, Lottie had said. *The light shimmering on all those millions of fragile bones. She thought she was in some holy place –*

Skylark was overcome by what she saw before her. She and Arnie were in a huge underground amphitheatre that in darkness seemed to stretch on forever and ever. Right in the middle of it was a slender glittering tower. The tower was made entirely of delicate bones which, at the ceiling, twisted, curled, interlocked and splayed across the dome like thousands of angel wings. Each wing had begun its formation from one of the thousands of potholes feeding into the dome. The light, coming through the holes in the ceiling, glowed on the bones. Where the bones were moist with water seepage they sparkled, sending glittering flashes from bone to bone in a fascinating and ever-changing interplay of beauty.

That wasn't all. Around the tower were smaller sculptures of extraordinary and unearthly beauty. They had been constructed from other bones that had either fallen from the central tower or, perhaps, from other potholes in the ceiling. Some seemed to be kneeling angels in prayer in that place. Others seemed to be flying figures reaching up to the light.

"Come on," Arnie said. He took Skylark's hand and they descended to the amphitheatre floor. Treading carefully, they made their way toward the central tower. The closer they got, the higher and larger it became. The light played and shimmered around it, on it and through it.

Suddenly the tower blazed and, in a chiaroscuro of brilliance, Skylark saw that at its base was a carving in the shape of a giant bird with wings outstretched, beak open in challenge and claws splayed ready for attack. It was as tall as she was.

As soon as she saw the symbol, Skylark knew what she had to do. For a moment she hesitated, both scared and shocked to know that she'd actually made it this far – and that this was only the beginning of her journey. "Oh Mum," she whimpered. Then she took a deep breath, said a silent prayer and placed the feather which Birdy had given her on the left wing of the symbol. The beak from Joe, she put on the beak of the carved bird. She decided to leave the claw given to her by Hoki around her neck.

There was just one task left to do. Gently Skylark pushed Arnie away from the carving. "I think this is where I go on alone," Skylark said.

"What?" Arnie asked. "No. I won't let you." He took a few steps back towards the carving.

"No, Arnie," Skylark said. "There's only room for one of us. Can't you see?"

"Give a guy a break! How can you do what you have to do without me? We've come all this way together. I've grown used to you, can't you see that? We're a good team." Arnie's face was pale with anxiety. "I don't care what you say," he continued, compressing his lips. "I'm coming along as your co-pilot and that's that. Just let anybody try to stop me."

He came towards her but she pushed him hard and he fell back on the floor. "No, Arnie. Thank you for bringing me this far. But from here I'm flying solo."

With that, Skylark stepped into the shape of the bird. At that moment torchlight flashed through the amphitheatre. "You aren't going anywhere, Missy," a voice said.

Up on the rock jutting out and overlooking the amphitheatre were the two rangers. They began to clamber down the stairway, making their way towards the base of the tower.

"That settles it," Arnie said. He jumped into the bird shape, put *his* feather and beak alongside Skylark's, stepped behind her and put his arms around her.

"What are you doing!" Skylark yelled. "Let me go!"

"I've got two choices. Either I stay here and get arrested or I go with you and take my chances wherever we end up. We've been tandem once. It can work again."

"Oh no you don't," Skylark roared. "Once is enough." She was trying everything to wriggle out of Arnie's arms. Every time she wriggled his grip got tighter. "Wait up, Arnie, hang on a minute, let go of me –"

It was too late. Skylark felt dizzy. Her eyesight blurred. Her voice caught in her throat. For some strange reason the room seemed to be growing larger. And what was this? She seemed to be growing smaller. She tried to protest again but all that came out was a slight chirrup and flutter. The air shifted and next moment, Skylark found herself looking out of the rim of her right shoe. She let out a guffaw of laughter.

"Is that you, Arnie?"

Arnie's overalls lay in a crumpled heap. There was a pecking movement from within. Then a face appeared – the face of a falcon. One eye was green, the other brown. Payback time.

"You should laugh," Arnie said. "Look in a mirror."

Skylark had a short crest and her coat was streaked brown and dark brown. Her underparts were buffy white, her breast was streaked brown, and her outer feathers were conspicuously white. She gave a short scream and discovered that her voice had changed into continuous liquid trills and runs. She had turned into a – well, a skylark.

The transformation had Arnie in fits of hysteria. He hopped out of his clothes and he just loved the way he looked. Hooked bill and grasping talons. Long and narrow wings. Overall plumage brown. He flexed his muscles and was thrilled to feel the *powah*. "Uh oh, trouble," Arnie whistled.

The two rangers had arrived at the tower. When they spoke, their voices sounded huge. "Where the hell did they go?"

And there were other sounds too. New ones. Skylark's new perceptions caught another presence coming into the caverns. Kawanatanga had finally caught up, and he was leading his seashag squad thundering into the amphitheatre.

"Arnie, quick, do something!" Skylark trilled.

Kawanatanga glided through the amphitheatre flicking at the fragile bones with contempt. The rangers watched, stunned. Kawanatanga saw Skylark and Arnie. He stalled and stretched out his neck.

Stop them! Kill the chick! Kill them both before they go through the Time Portal.

As for Arnie, what was he doing? He saw his cellphone, flew to it, and hopped out the number for Hoki and Bella.

"Mother Ship, I think we have lift-off."

With a scream, Kawanatanga dived.

"Arnie!" Skylark yelled.

Arnie flapped his wings and enfolded Skylark in them. Just as Kawanatanga opened his beak to strike, the cathedral opened like a door. Something big and black, made up of trillions of whirling bones, came at Skylark and Arnie like a huge mouth, and swallowed them.

Kawanatanga howled his rage to the universe.

No. No. *No.*

In Manu Valley, Hoki ran to answer the telephone.

"Hello? Hello?"

All she could hear was a series of harsh squawks and whistles.

"Is anybody there?"

The telephone went dead. For a while, Hoki stood there, puzzled. Then she gasped, put the receiver down and took herself up to Bella, Mitch and Francis as fast as her walking sticks would let her.

"Bella! Arnie's just called. I think he's gone with Skylark."

"How can Arnie go with her!"

"I don't know," Hoki answered. She gave an incredulous laugh. "But I think they've both gone through the Time Portal."

Hoki stayed on the clifftop. She knew she was right about Arnie calling her. Just before dusk, she looked west and saw a black convoy coming across the twin mountains. It brought thoughts to her of Armageddon, of something apocalyptic, of a world that was about to descend into chaos. Hoki stepped forward:

"So, Kawanatanga, you're back."

With an angry scream, Kawanatanga circled the ripped sky.

We may not have been able to stop the chick on this side of the sky. But we will meet her on the other side. When we do, we promise you we shall spear her like a fish and shred her to pieces.

Hoki grabbed her shotgun and aimed for Kawanatanga. With contemptuous ease he twisted, stilled, dived and was in.

The sun fell into the sea. There was a sudden silver flash along the line where sky met ocean.

Part Three

[CHAPTER ELEVEN]

– 1 –

The next morning, Bella left Hoki, Mitch and Francis guarding the ripped sky and went into Tuapa to stock up on food and drink from the local supermarket. With Mitch as a drinking partner, Bella's booze cupboard was already low, and that boy of his could sure eat.

Bella's second call was to Harry Summers at the farming supplies store for another two cases of ammunition.

"Out already?" Harry asked.

"I'm teaching Hoki how to fire a shotgun," Bella said. "Now I can't stop her from taking potshots at anything."

"In that case, I'm staying clear of Manu Valley," Harry quipped.

The next stop was to see Lucas at the garage and return his doll. "What happened to Maisie?" he asked, gaping at the shredded pile of plastic in Bella's arms.

"Sorry, Lucas, Hoki was mowing the lawn and ran over it. Would you like another one? I notice the massage parlour has a sale on some of its products. They have one of these dolls in the window and –"

"No," Lucas said, blushing. "Let Arnie buy his own when he gets back."

"That's the other thing I want to tell you," Bella said. "Hoki asked him to take Skylark to Auckland to get some clothes and other personal things that Cora needs. He'll be gone for a week."

"A week?" Lucas yelped. "Why so long? You could go round the world in a week."

"You don't know the half of it," Bella clucked sympathetically. "But look on the bright side, Lucas. Just think how grateful Cora will be that you did this for her."

"You think so?" Lucas asked hopefully. "You really think so?"

Bella nodded and patted him on the shoulder. "You're a good man, Lucas," she said as, finally, she was able to leave him and go to visit Cora at the hospital.

There, Bella's heart went out to this woman who had come to mean so much to so many different people.

"Cora? Can you hear me?" Bella asked, as she sat down beside her and held her hand. "Hold on, dear. Skylark's on the way to save you. She'll be back soon."

Cora seemed to hear her, gave a sigh and turned her head away. In profile, Bella saw the look of her dear sister Agnes, and her thoughts turned to the possibility of some connection.

"No, it's a crazy idea," Bella muttered. But the idea kept nagging at her and soon she was making two and two out of so many flimsy possibilities. Cora was born in Christchurch in the same year that Agnes ran away from home. Cora had Maori ancestry on her mother's side, so could that mother have been Agnes? Looked at from another angle, if Skylark was the chick, it made sense that she should have some kinship relationship with Manu Valley, didn't it?

Yes, and pigs could fly.

"Get a grip," Bella scolded herself. She looked for some way of diverting her attention. A bouquet of beautiful long-stemmed roses had been delivered to Cora. Bella found a vase, filled it with water, took the roses out of their cellophane wrapping and began to arrange them. Fantasising that they had been sent by Tom Cruise or Brad Pitt, she couldn't resist looking at the card: TO MY DARLING GODDAUGHTER, CORA. GET WELL SOON. LOVE FLORENCE.

"Florence?" Bella mused. "Who the hell's Florence?"

Her curiousity piqued, she walked out to the hospital receptionist. "Can you tell me who sent the roses?" she asked.

"They arrived this morning," the receptionist answered. "Beautiful, aren't they? I had to sign for them." She rummaged through the filing cabinet for the receipt. "Here we are," she continued. "They came from Mrs Florence Wipani of Christchurch."

"I know that name," Bella said, and her eyes widened with recognition. "You wouldn't have a phone number there would you?"

"You can use the telephone in Dr Goodwin's room if you wish," the receptionist said, giving the number to Bella.

Bella went to the room and closed the door behind her. She sat down feeling a bit weak at the knees. Things were getting curiouser and curiouser. It had been years since she had even thought of Florence; after all, Florence had been more Agnes's friend than hers or Hoki's.

"Nothing ventured, nothing gained," Bella said as she picked up the telephone and dialled the number.

"Hello?" a voice answered. Cultured. Upper class.

"Is this Florence Wipani?" Bella asked.

"This is she," the voice answered. "To whom am I speaking?"

No doubt about it, Bella thought. She was talking to Florence all right, her sister Agnes's best friend; when Agnes had left Tuapa, Florence had joined her in Christchurch. Florence had always had a slight lisp – Thith ith thee – and no amount of cultivation could hide it. She'd come up in the world since the days when she had been plain old Flo, Fred the butcher's daughter.

Bella decided that the best strategy was to cut the crap and go straight for the jugular. "I know it's you, Flo, so don't try to hide it. This is Bella here, Agnes's sister. I want the truth about Cora. What are you hiding? What's this all about?"

– 2 –

It seemed to Skylark that thousands of small bones were flying all around her, twisting, whirling and wheeling. At first she thought they might hit her, but they seemed to know she was there and whizzed, sizzled and spat past her with centimetres to spare. The bones trailed light like after-images and, as she watched, Skylark saw they were moving in a particular sequence. They were building a circle. One by one, they spun, hovered, edged in with each other and clicked into place until –

Interlock.

The bones became stationary. Time was in stasis. But for how long? What had Lottie said?

She had four days.

The circle began to hum. Skylark flew closer to it. She saw that a dark indigo tunnel had formed inside the circle. "The Time Portal," Skylark whispered to herself. It looked as if it went on for years and years. It was so dark in there. Dark. Windy. Scary.

"Where are you, Arnie?" Skylark called.

"Right behind you," he whistled. "Feel like doing another tandem jump?"

Before she could say no, Arnie pushed her through.

"You boofhead!" Skylark screamed. "I really hate you."

"Oh Skylark," Arnie laughed. "Can't you just switch off your brain and enjoy the ride? Just pretend you're in a hydroslide at the swimming pool."

"I avoid those slides like the plague," Skylark answered.

She looked for something to hold onto – but what? There was nothing there but air.

"Just think of all those sci-fi movies where the hero has to go back in time or through a stargate or wormholes into an alternative universe."

"Hero? Excuse me?" Skylark asked. She hated this sensation of falling and of having no control over it.

Arnie, of course, was loving it, revelling in his new abilities: "Oh man! Oh wow! Oh awe-*some*!" Skylark got so tired of his darting over, under and around her, not to mention his persistent male chauvinism, that she accidentally on purpose tipped one of his wings with hers. Arnie gave a yell as he tumbled off to the left.

"Oops," Skylark said. "Heh heh heh."

"You meant to do that," Arnie accused as he righted himself and sped back. But he was so revved up, he couldn't stay cross for long. Everything excited him, and when he looked ahead, the pupils of his eyes dilated. "Oh man, I've got telescopic vision!" he yelled. "I can see light down there."

"Down there? Where?"

"Can't you see it?" Arnie asked. "Oh, I forgot," he added slyly, "you're a skylark and you have limited vision."

"Don't push your luck," Skylark answered. "But yes, I can see it!"

Sure enough, far down in the distance was a pinhole of brightness. Then the pinhole began to widen. "Uh oh," Skylark said. The pinhole had now become like the plughole of a bath. She felt centrifugal forces sucking her down, buffeting her around, and she had the sudden urge to fight against them. Just because she had agreed to go back in time didn't mean she had to like it. Nor did she have any experience of being a bird, and it was difficult learning about the controls. "Where are the bloody brakes?"

she yelled. "How do I get this thing into reverse?"As for Arnie, he was totally into it.

"Don't fight it! Go with the flow!" Arnie folded his wings and dropped like a stone through the middle of the light.

"But I hate flying," Skylark moaned. The brightness became so intense she had to close her eyes. She felt giddy from fighting against the descent, and she felt as if she was spiralling out of control. As much as she hated to follow Arnie's example, she realised that pretending to be a sky diver was the only way to get out of this mess. And because Arnie wasn't around, she let out a most unladylike scream of terror.

"Eeaarggh!"

The tunnel spat Skylark out. She had the sensation that she was falling through a huge sky. She felt coldness. She felt currents of air . . .

Then something nudged her.

"You can put on your brakes now," Arnie said. "And you can open your eyes."

"I don't want to look," Skylark said. Even so, she peeked out of her left eye and saw the Southern Cross directly above. She would have to remember that when she and Arnie needed to find their way back. The Time Portal was between the two pointer stars.

Skylark took a deep breath and looked down. Big mistake. For a moment vertigo overwhelmed her, and she screamed again. Who would catch her if she fell?

"You can use your wings now." Arnie said as he flew alongside her. He saw that she was frightened, and tried to calm her fears.

Skylark remembered what she was, spread her wings and stabilised. Her heart stopped beating so fast. Her breathing became normal. She would have thanked Arnie for his solicitude, but he spoilt it by smiling like an idiot.

"*What!*" Skylark asked him.

"I heard you as you came out of the Time tunnel," he kidded her. "What's with the 'Eeaarggh'?"

"I was practising my karanga," Skylark sniffed.

"Your karanga? Do you want to frighten the birds away? Come on, Skylark, admit it. You were scared, weren't you! You were out of your tree!"

"A Masters in avian aeronautics is not part of my CV," she answered. "Nor is finding my way without a map."

Arnie laughed, then quickly became more sober. The Southern Cross had winked out and, in its place, was a primaeval sky. Planets whirled around like pinballs. Comets trailed fiery tails from north to south. Strange shapes like winged snakes were gathering above them.

"I'm getting a bad feeling about this," he said. "I think we're in the highest Heavens, the uppermost reaches of the sky, where the giant pouakai lives."

Don't look back, Lottie had said. *Fly like hell and get the blazes out of there.*

"I was hoping you wouldn't say that," Skylark said. "We'd better not stick around."

This time it was she who folded her wings and dived. Arnie zoomed after her. All the way his feathers were prickling, and he had the sense that he and Skylark were being followed.

"Hurry, Skylark!" he urged.

Down, down, down they went, dropping from one Heaven to the next. Not until he felt they were safe did Arnie call out to Skylark that she could rest.

"Well, wherever we are," Skylark said when he caught up with her, "one thing's for sure. You're not in Guatemala now, Dr Ropata."

Below, the sky became dark with thickening clouds. A distant blue star was trying to break through the cover. Everything was rippling, faster and faster, and all around them the sky was transforming from one shape into another. From far off came a glow.

"That's *it,*" Arnie said "We're in a time warp. It's not just a question of where we are but also of how far back we've come –"

The clouds shimmered with the shifting pastels of the dawn horizon. As the glow brightened, they rippled with blues, ochres, vermilions and crimsons. Right at the centre of the glow emerged an orange core.

"The sun is rising," Arnie said.

"But look at it! It's so huge, so bright, and the sky, Arnie, it looks so new as if, as if –"

Shades of pink began to spiral out from the core of the sun. They were followed by shades of crimson which, as they reached the earth's atmosphere, filled the air with auroras that bathed the sky with shimmering beauty. Blessing it, purifying it, sanctifying it. Benediction after benediction.

Skylark turned to Arnie. "You're right," she said. "We've done it. We're back at the beginning of Time when the Lord Tane made the world. This is the First Sky, and –" She looked up. Remembered the Great Book of Birds. The clouds were opening like a huge gate. From the other side of it came swathes of glorious excited song. Then there was a boom as the gates opened, and the sound of a laughing voice: "Go then, my impatient ones!"

Skylark took one look at Arnie. "Clear the way!" she yelled.

Brightly coloured ribbons were falling from the sky above them. As they dropped closer, Arnie saw that they weren't ribbons at all. They were feathers. They were –

"Holy cow!" Arnie said.

Skylark was already streaking clear and away to the perimeters of the sky. Arnie sped after her, spearing into the orbiting sun, and hovered. Currents of disturbed air chased after him.

"It's the great exodus," Skylark said with awe. "The Time of the Falling Feathers."

Great fleets of birds were corkscrewing down through the sky. Dancing, twisting and turning, whirring and jostling, they filled the air with grandeur. As they descended, they sang their songs of liberation, melodies such as the world has never since heard. "The world is ours, sing praises to Tane for his bounty –"

"Let's follow them," Skylark said.

She dived after the birds. When she had penetrated the clouds she saw that the world below was filled with light, and thousands of birds – grebes, dabchicks, pigeons, tui, pelicans, herons, egrets, shovelers, cranes, bellbirds, crakes, dotterels, plovers, sandsnipes, curlews, whimbrels, godwits, huia, greenshanks, turnstones, knots, dunlins, sanderlings, kea, parakeets, cuckoos, kingfishers – were making their way across a brilliant azure sea. Way out on point were albatrosses. Guarding the upper air was a flight of hawks.

"Hey, there's some of my cousins!" Arnie said. Skylark watched as he joined the hawks. One in particular was very playful, and Skylark knew intuitively that she was a female. But there was no time to protest. All of a sudden she felt the buffeting of the wind.

Shadows were cast in the sky. Skylark found herself in the slipstream of some hard-pressed swans and heard them chanting: "Hii haa! Hii haa!" What were they doing? Skylark moved out of the shadows and saw that the sky was filled with hundreds of giant canoes. Each canoe was made up of groups of swans flying in close formation.

"Neke neke! Neke neke! Keep your ranks!" The giant sky-going waka cruised above and around her, making a slow descent. Across their backs, hanging on for dear life, were moa, kiwi, weka, moorhens, kakapo, penguins and other flightless birds being carried down to the Earth. Flycatchers, finches and starlings twitted and twirled among the swans, soothing their fears. Authoritative kaka, like canoe captains, shrilled their orders, encouraging the swans onward. "Toia mai, nga moa! Ki te urunga, nga kiwi –"

Skylark felt her breath catch with wonder. She even failed to notice Arnie's return until he nudged her. "My cuzzies wanted me to stay with them," he said, irritated she hadn't missed him. "One of them was a cute terciel," he hinted.

"What's that?"

"A female," he said nonchalantly. "But I told her I was with you."

"You can go if you want. I can always ask for help from some of my kind," she said. Two could play that game.

To prove her point, Skylark flew off to join some bush wrens. She assumed they would welcome her with open wings. But some of them started to jostle her and she was soon surrounded by a small group of males who were getting too close for comfort. She slapped one of the bush wrens with a wing and hurried back to Arnie.

"So what happened," Arnie asked, pleased to see her back. "Didn't you want to stay with your kind?"

"Hmph," Skylark glared at him. "Men! You're all the same."

By this time, all the birds that had been waiting in the upper sky had been released, trillions of glittering feathers falling through the air. Some began to wheel away from the main exodus: mollymawks, fulmars, petrels, prions, shearwaters, frigate birds.

"The seabirds are claiming their dominion," Skylark said.

Dizzy with delight, the seabirds were diving into the teeming sea, bountiful with darting fish. The albatrosses among them ceased their point duty and began to wheel away into the distance.

For the landbirds, however, the exodus was not yet over. On they flew – fantails with owls, robins with quails – towards the horizon. The smaller birds, tiring of the long flight, took respite by resting on the giant swan canoes as they continued to strain across the sea.

"Neke neke! Keep your ranks! Neke neke!"

Suddenly the swallows, which had been scouting far ahead, came streaking back from the horizon. Something was there, awaiting the exodus. The birds redoubled their efforts.

"Hii haa! Hii haa!"

Gradually, something began to appear. Something bright. Something wondrous. On the horizon something was lying like a huge smooth piece of pounamu washed by the sea. The greenstone was glowing, glorious.

"It's Aotearoa," Skylark said.

The sky began to sing. A great trilling filled the air, a karanga to the land. "Receive us, welcome us, open to us." The birds announced they were coming.

"We're almost there," Skylark cried.

The wind came up from the south, buffeting the birds. Some were blown high and some were blown low.

The wind was cold and strong, and Skylark began to shiver

"Hang in there, Skylark," Arnie said.

Skylark and Arnie flew onward, intent on making landfall. As they approached, the land fragmented into two main islands – Te Waka a Maui and Te Wai Pounamu. The wind increased, funnelling through the strait between the two islands. The ocean stormed through the break and, on its front, dolphins were leaping.

"Aren't you glad we're not on a ferry?" Skylark asked Arnie with an impish look.

A mood of anticipation came over the landbirds. They began to circle and circle in that midway place, calling their farewells to each other. Some split away, parrots and other birds, twirling like brightly ribboned cyclones, heading upward to the warmer climate of the north. The swans, however, flew their giant waka bearing the moa southward where there were grazing grounds. "Neke neke! Hii haa!"

The blue sky was a maelstrom of feathers as the birds chittered and chattered and wheeled in all directions. "Which way should we go?" Arnie asked Skylark.

Skylark hovered, unsure. She remembered Lottie's instructions: *Just head for the rainbow*. But where was it?

"There!" Arnie cried. "To the south."

Even as he pointed Skylark saw it – the First Rainbow in the World being born out of the cradle of the sea. Where it began, the water bubbled and hissed, creating myriad water spouts. Up the rainbow came, woven by those water spouts, taking colour and strength from them, vaulting the dome of the sky from east to west like a blessing.

The rainbow created a current in the air. Sensing an upward thermal, a convection current heading towards the Antarctic, Arnie sidled up, made some fancy rolls into its jet stream, and stabilised when he reached the centre.

What a show-off, Skylark thought. She wasn't about to let Arnie think he was king of the air, so she copied what he had done and came in behind him, riding his slipstream.

"You're learning fast," Arnie said, and winked. He was really proud of her.

"It's easy once you get used to it," Skylark sniffed.

Arnie grinned at her answer. He must be getting through to her. She had accepted his compliment without biting his head off.

They were over the South Island, and down below was the Great Forest of Tane. Nothing had prepared Skylark for that first sight.

"It's even more stunning than Hoki described," she said.

Close up, the Great Forest was luminous, an emerald sparkling and glittering in the sun. Like Eden, the lush growing trees, palms and shrubs flowered underneath. The titan kauri were tall, triumphant. No less grand, other trees like totara, karaka and kahikatea added their majesty to the mosaic. Stitched among them were the flowering trees, the pohutukawa reds, kowhai yellows and many others, splashing the Great Forest with colours.

It truly was the wonder of the southern world. And it was breathing like a living thing. At every inhalation it rippled with life. When it breathed out, it released its heady fragrances upon the air.

Sensing they had finally arrived at their destination, the birds began to spin away in their thousands down into the Great Forest. As they descended they sang hymnals to Tane, praises to the Lord of Birds. "Thank you, Lord, for your great gift."

Skylark and Arnie continued southward, following in the wake of the swans with their giant moa cargoes. With the thrill of excitement, Skylark saw that straight ahead were snow-capped mountains. They were like the palisades of a pah, wedged there to keep Earth and Sky apart so that there could be space for all living creatures between.

"The sacred mountains," Skylark whispered. She would have recognised those southern alps anywhere. Excited, she flipped down, and Arnie followed her. Soon they were skimming the snow and following the contours of the mountains. "Catch me if you can," Skylark called.

Laughing, Arnie played tag with Skylark over the alpine peaks. They rode elevator winds and skimmed the downward escalator currents. He could have caught up with her any time, and maybe given her a playful nip, but wiser counsel prevailed. Skylark was having fun and thought she was still the leader, and while she was happy there was peace on the planet.

Skylark saw a river valley cutting a pathway through the mountains.

"This is where I can give Arnie the slip," she said to herself.

She caught a swift current pouring through it. The river ended at the lip of a giant waterfall and, all of a sudden, the ground dropped away.

"Arnie we're here," Skylark yelled. Her voice echoed through the well of the sky. Behind her were the twin mountains themselves, the closest point between the Earth and the moon. Below was Manu Valley. Thousands of years later, a small town called Tuapa would be built in its shadows. Ahead was the glistening sea. Somewhere to the left would be the ancestral paepae for the landbirds, the first tree that Tane had planted in his Great Forest. When Arnie stilled beside her, he pointed it out.

There it was, like a huge candelabra. And above, the rainbow.

Then something shifted, changed. It was as if the defensive system of the world, the shield that had kept everything in place, had come down. The forcefield that had been this world's protection flickered and died. Skylark thought of the Garden of Eden: the Angel guarding the garden had walked away and left it defenceless.

Something physical slammed into Skylark and Arnie. Flailing, their heads spinning, they found themselves falling out of control. For a moment Skylark blacked out completely. Quickly, Arnie flew beneath her and managed to stabilise her until she regained consciousness.

"What the heck was that?" Arnie asked.

"I'm sorry, Arnie, I don't know. I —" She looked up. The rainbow was on fire. The ash flaking from it, was falling from the sky. The rainbow turned ghastly white, like an after-image, and warped out of existence. In the blink of an eye, everything had altered. A sick feeling punched Skylark in the chest.

"Time has finally caught up on us," Skylark said. "It has accelerated and passed us. Although we've arrived before the invasion of the seabirds, very soon the time will come when the sacred tree will catch on fire, the sky rip apart and the seabirds from the future come through the ripped sky. We must warn the Runanga a Manu."

Arnie caught the panic in Skylark's voice. She had spilled the air from her wings and was gliding down towards Manu Valley. They had reached the Runanga a Manu, the Parliament of Birds. Far ahead she could see the sacred tree and, yes, on every branch were the bird elders of the Great Forest. More forest birds were gathered at the base of the trunk.

Well here goes nothing, Skylark thought. She took a deep breath, hoped she could remember all the words that Lottie had taught her, and began her karanga.

"E nga manu whenua, karanga mai, karanga mai, karanga mai . . ."

[CHAPTER TWELVE]

– 1 –

As soon as she returned to Manu Valley, Bella made morning smoko for Hoki, Mitch and Francis, and took it up to the cliff face. She was late with it, so when Francis saw her coming he breathed an audible sigh of relief. "You've arrived just in time, Auntie! If I was in town I'd have had two KFCs by now."

"Please, Francis," Hoki shuddered, "don't mention fried chicken in Manu Valley." She unpacked the food, and Francis was soon hoeing into the sausages, corned beef and tomato sandwiches, salad, cordial and, to wash it all down, plenty of tea. Hoki and Mitch, a few metres away, maintained shotgun duty, pulling the trigger every now and then. The seabirds wheeled away, enraged.

Bella gave Hoki a drink of cordial. "Thank you, Sister," Hoki said. "It's hot, standing out here in the sun. Did you get more ammunition?"

"Yes," Bella answered. "I also went to see Cora in hospital. There's something I have to tell you –"

"Oh no. Has she? Is she –"

"Nothing like that," Bella answered. "She's okay. But I've discovered something."

"Why do I always want to duck for cover when you say that?" Hoki asked.

Bella ignored Hoki's scepticism. "A few visits ago," she went on, "I noticed from Cora's medical chart that her middle name was Agnes."

Hoki frowned, trying to make the connection. Sometimes Bella could be so difficult to follow.

"Her full name is Cora Agnes Wipani and she was born in Christchurch in 1960," Bella continued impatiently. "Oh come on, Sister, I know you're slow but not that slow. Our eldest sister Agnes, she was in Christchurch at the same time –"

"So?"Hoki asked.

"Agnes was pregnant from her boyfriend Darren. Remember?"

She watched Hoki's face. What do you know, a light went on in her brain as Sister dear made the connection.

"But we were told that the baby died," Hoki gasped. Sometimes she doubted Bella's cognitive faculties, but this time she didn't need Polyfilla to fill in the gaps.

"I know, but the coincidence of Cora being born in 1960, and having the same middle name as our sister – it's not a common one, you know. It nagged at me, and I couldn't let it go. Today, when I was at the hospital, I saw some roses that had been delivered to Cora. They had been sent from Christchurch by somebody called Florence Wipani, Cora's godmother. So I telephoned her."

Hoki's eyes were as wide as saucers.

"When I talked to Florence, I knew immediately who she was. She's done very well for herself, has our Flo. Married three times and now sits in a palatial two-storey house in Sumner. She always had a lisp –"

Hoki gasped in recognition.

"And she tried to lie her way out –"

"I'm thorry, you have the wrong perthon and the wrong telephone number," Florence Wipani said. "Good day to you."

"Don't you dare hang up on me, Flo," Bella warned. "I want some answers and I want to know them now."

She decided to bluff. She was always good at cards, pretending she had an ace when she didn't. "Cora needs an emergency blood transfusion."

"The doctorth haven't told me that –"

"It's only just arisen this minute," Bella said. "Why else do you think they've given me your number?"

"They gave you thith number? They had expreth orderth not to."

"Cora's at death's door."

"Put Dr Goodwin on the telephone immediately. I want to hear thith from hith own lipth."

"Oh my God, she's going into cardiac arrest," Bella said. "Tell me, quickly, Flo. Cora's life depends on it. Would my blood type be okay for Cora?"

Would that bring Flo out into the sunlight? Come on Flo, show me what's in your hand.

Florence Wipani began to sob. "Yeth."

Hoki's eyes were brimming with tears. She was thinking of her beautiful eldest sister. *Sshhh, I don't want to wake Mum and Dad up. Darren is waiting in the car. We're running away together*. Hoki had always been sentimental. Cried over the smallest thing.

"At first," Bella continued, "Flo was very angry at being tricked –" *You and your little thithter were alwayth nathty manipulating little girlth.* – "but in the end she confessed everything. How Darren had left Agnes in the lurch when she was just about ready to have the baby. How, when the baby was born, Flo and her first husband adopted her. When Agnes died, they continued to keep the secret to themselves. Over the years it just seemed easier to do this. Cora has never known. Cora's our niece, Sister. And Skylark is the one. She's our mokopuna."

Hoki gave a cry of pain. She had loved Agnes so much. Then she realised what she had done to Skylark.

"Look where I've sent our granddaughter," Hoki moaned. "Through the portal and back into the past!"

Hoki was shivering. She clasped Bella, her eyes wide with horror. "What happens if she can't get back?"

– 2 –

"Karanga mai, karanga mai, karanga mai . . ."

It was Te Arikinui Kotuku who first heard the strange, unearthly, beautiful sound coming down from the sky. She and Huia had been giggling at the antics of the males, who were still celebrating their great victory in the battle of the birds. Having drunk fermented berries and gorged themselves during the victory feast, the chieftains rolled, farted, burped, bumped, fell down, snored, and sang roistering ditties about their heroic acts of valour.

"It was our leader, Tui's, role
To lead us into battle
He called out, 'Forward all'
And off we flew, our score to settle!"

A glazed-looking Chieftain Koekoea was wandering about, with a wing around Chieftain Teraweke. Who was holding up whom was difficult to fathom.

"Teraweke, matey, you're the man. My goose would have been cooked if you hadn't taken that tern off my tail –"

Across the way, Kawau was declaring eternal friendship to Chieftain Kokako when, in the real light of day, they avoided each other like the plague. As usual, Kaka was holding forth with boasts about his fighting prowess. "Did you see me make mincemeat out of those mollymawks? I felled three with one blow, three in one go –"

Chieftain Pekapeka of bats had become so intoxicated that instead of hanging upside down he was hanging downside up. As for Tui, who should have known better, he was creating a scandal with his public and very amorous display towards a young and flirtatious bellbird who came – where else? – from Te Arawa.

"Come into the trees, e hine, and let me preen you."

Another ditty started up. This time, Chieftain Grey Warbler led the roistering crowd:

"O, then it was Piwaka's turn
He mooned the skuas with his bum
Their faces did with embarrassment burn
Piwaka had them on the run!"

Te Arikinui Kotuku and Huia watched it all with growing disdain. "You'd think," Huia said, "that a certain timely intervention by certain female birds had not played a crucial part in the outcome."

"Kia whakatane au i ahau?" Kotuku trilled. "Such is the way of man only to record the achievements of man. Man's world, man's history." She tossed her gorgeous head in laughter – and that's when she heard the outpouring of continuous liquid trills spilling through the air. "Huia, can you hear that? Girls?" she asked Te Arikinui Parera, Te Arikinui Korimako and Te Arikinui Karuwae. "Can you hear what I hear?"

The women bobbed their heads, mystified. Karuwae raised a wing at the sky. "There!" she pointed.

Coming out of the sun was a strange chieftainess, a small streaked brown bird with white tail feathers. The bird was still high in the heavens but her song was like crystal, every note threaded together in a strange bell-like karanga.

"Do you recognise her?" Korimako asked Parera.

"No. I've never seen such a bird before. However, that karanga is in Maori, though I must admit it's delivered with an atrocious accent. There must be long-lost tribes beyond the Great Forest."

"Not only that," Kotuku said, "but for a chieftainess she looks such an ordinary bird! How can such a bird make such extraordinary music? She brings Heaven down to us. Who is she? Where does she come from?"

"She might be a spy sent by the manu moana," Parera shivered.

Kotuku cocked her head, thinking this through. "Better to be safe than sorry," she decided.

She stood up, lifted her throat and called to the assembly. "Kra-*aak*. Kra-*aak*. Hey, Tui, e moe ana te mata hi tuna, e ara ana te mata hi aua. When the eyes of those who fish for eels are sleeping, it is lucky for all that the eyes of those who catch mullet are open. Look, strangers are approaching."

Taken aback, Chieftain Tui turned his gaze to the sky. He saw the two strangers. What bad luck that they had appeared right when he almost had that pretty bellbird in his feathery pocket. He heard the beautiful karanga.

"Karanga mai tatou e te manu whenua e . . ." Like Te Arikinui Kotuku, Tui had never heard such a karanga. It carolled away in a continuous cantilena of extraordinary simplicity and honesty. It existed beyond the ordinary compass of birdsong, even defying the normal rules of requiring breath. The song was sung with such sweetness that it pierced Tui's heart with joy and he did not want it to stop.

Kotuku caught the flash of another bird in the sky. "The strange chieftainess does not come alone," she said. "She has a warrior – and he, like her, is of an equally unknown appearance." She turned to Chieftain Kahu. "Do you recognise the warrior, Kahu?"

"If he was as large as I am, I would say he was a hawk," Kahu mused, "but he is only half my size and his wings are pointed."

He scanned the sky for the rest of the travelling ope but, no, the two birds had come unaccompanied.

"They are either foolhardy or very brave," Tui said, "or else the warrior must be of considerable prowess. We shall see." He called out to Chieftain Popokotea of whiteheads and Chieftain Koekoea of long-tailed cuckoos.

"Kia hiwa ra! Kia hiwa ra! Kia hiwa ra i tenei tuku! Kia hiwa ra i tera tuku! Be alert! Beware! Strangers are coming! Send out your sentries to challenge them."

In a trice, the first warrior, a perky whitehead by the name of Hore, flew into the air. Typically inquisitive, territorially alert, Hore rushed up to the strange warrior and stilled just above his head.

"Swee swee swee *chir chir!* Advance no further unless you can justify your credentials!"

Hore turned and spiralled, winning admiring glances from the Runanga a Manu for his fancy wingwork. But what the runanga was really curious about was how the strange warrior would respond.

"I am Arnie, Chief of Falcons," the warrior answered. "I come with my Lady Skylark to address the Parliament of Birds, here, in the Great Forest of Tane. Let us pass, little one." Gently, but firmly, the strange warrior made a quick jab at the capering Hore and plucked some of his bum fluff.

With a slight yelp, his breast burning red with embarrassment, Hore turned away and retreated to the sacred tree with as much dignity as he could muster. Feathers ruffled, the chieftains set up a raucous cry of anger. To treat a sentry like that, when all around him the strange warrior was outnumbered, was foolhardy indeed. Who were the interlopers? Why had they come?

"Go," Tui ordered the second challenger, Kawe, one of the best warriors of the long-tailed cuckoo clan.

Kawe had psyched himself up to the job. Hissing, wheezing and blowing he launched himself from the sacred tree and, as he came, called out to the strange chieftainess and her warrior. "*Shweesht!* State your business! Name your tribe! Why do you seek to korero with the Runanga a Manu –"

Kawe planed back and forth in front of the warrior. His baleful yellow eyes glared at Arnie in anger at the arrogant manner in which his mate, Hore, had been so summarily dispatched.

"I have already stated our names," the strange warrior responded. "As to our tribe, my lady and I come from the future."

The future? The Runanga a Manu tried to puzzle that one out. "Have you ever heard of that tribe?" Kotuku asked Chieftain Ruru of owls.

"Noooo," Ruru intoned. "But I would think that it was a lo-ong way away from here."

"State your business, state your business!" Kawe screeched again.

"Our business is the business of chiefs," the strange warrior said, "to be discussed only with chiefs of the Runanga a Manu. Be on your way." With that, the strange warrior made a deceptive pass then turned on his back and struck at Kawe's rump. Before Kawe knew what had happened, he was falling, destabilised because he now lacked his tail feathers.

Again, the birds of the sacred tree set up an outraged commotion. "Did you see that? That was below the belt!" Scandalised, they flew among the branches, their feathers displayed in protest. "The stranger is asking for trouble," Chieftain Kaka screeched. "Tui, dispatch a squad of warriors to teach the arrogant cock a lesson he thoroughly deserves."

"Yes," other birds called. "Teach the upstart a lesson! Rid him and his mistress from our territory!"

Chieftain Kahu intervened. "No," he said to Tui. "The strange warrior is to be admired for his valour. His business, he says, is the business of chiefs? Then let the third challenge come from such a chief."

Ignoring the gasps of astonishment, Kahu flew up to confront the strange warrior. His flight was so quick and strong that the newcomer, taken by surprise, backed away.

"That's the way," Chieftain Kawau yelled. "Show him who really rules the roost, Kahu!"

Kahu smiled at the strange warrior. He made a quick feint and jabbed at him with his long legs and their clawed extensions. The strange warrior did not retreat but, instead, deflected with his raking claw. Kahu felt the thrill of admiration.

"There are not many birds who would wish to engage me," he said. "I am bigger than you, boy, and I could quarter you so fast you wouldn't know until you hit the ground – all four pieces of you."

The strange warrior bent his head in salute. "I acknowledge your mana, Chieftain Kahu of Harrier Hawks, for, although you do not know me, I am cousin to all hawks and eagles. I am Arnie of the falcon iwi, knight to the Lady Skylark, who comes from the future –"

"Knight? Future? Your language is strange, sir."

"I am my lady's protector and although you and I are close relatives, my job is to provide safe passage for her so that she may address your Parliament of Birds. Our time is limited and brooks no delay. If you value your life, let us pass, for although you are bigger than I am, I am known as the most aggressive bird of the forest. Nor do I ever retreat from battle."

With that, the strange warrior opened his wings and gave a cry, such as had never been heard before. *"Kik-kik-kik-kik! Kik-kik-kik-kik!"*

He flew directly at Kahu and, this time, it was Kahu who backed away. Watching from the sacred tree, the Runanga a Manu was stunned into silence. Nobody before had initiated a duel with Kahu. Was not the harrier hawk, with his long-winged, long-tailed, high-soaring abilities, Lord of the Skies?

"Teach the stranger a lesson! Show him who's boss, Kahu! Send him on his way with his tail feathers between his claws!" The runanga sent their loud voices up to Kahu as he duelled with the stranger. The two birds, chieftain and warrior, darted at one another, displaying their feathers, gesticulating and uttering harsh battle cries. Kahu's admiration grew as he realised that the strange warrior had an impressive repertoire of military responses. He met every one of Kahu's attacks with counter-attacks of his own. He swooped, stalled, circled and raked at Kahu and, often, more by luck than by technique, Kahu found himself dancing out of the way.

It was Te Arikinui Kotuku who began to turn the tide of opinion among the runanga. "Oh, strange warrior," she called. "Who cannot but admire such foolhardiness! Fight well, fight bravely. Kia kaha! Kia manawanui!"

Very soon, chieftains were barracking for both Kahu and the strange warrior. They loved nothing more than to see a good fight. A good challenger. A good defender. Kahu would eventually win, they were certain, but there was nothing like acknowledging the bravery of a young warrior against a battle-hardened veteran.

At that very moment, Kahu slashed at the strange warrior's left wing and drew blood.

"Arnie!" Skylark called. Terrified, she came rushing between him and Chieftain Kahu, and the harrier hawk backed away. Blood was streaking through Arnie's wing feathers and dripping like rubies in the air. "Arnie, are you all right?"

Arnie nodded his head. "No matter what happens to me, Skylark, you must carry on and do your job." He turned to Chieftain Kahu: "Come on then, you bastard, if you must kill me, make it quick."

But Skylark flew in front of Chieftain Kahu. "No way," she bristled. "If you want to get at Arnie, you have to get past me first, you fowl piece of flying feathers!"

Kahu watched, amused. He was enjoying what was happening. He turned and lazily circled down to the sacred tree. "What do you want me to do, boys?" he asked. "Do you want me to dispatch the strange warrior?"

"Finish them both," Chieftain Koekoea called. "Look what they did to my warrior."

Kahu nodded. He flew back to the strange warrior and the silly brown chieftainess who was trying to protect him. He prepared to give the *coup de grâce* – and made a quick jab. But Skylark flew at him again.

"Oh no you don't," she said.

Kahu laughed and went to peck at her jugular. But at the last moment he saw the flash of something around her neck. The binocular lenses of his eyes located what it was. A claw on a silver chain.

"Who gave you the sign of the hawk?" Kahu asked, his eyes wide with shock.

For a moment, Skylark didn't know what he was talking about.

"Of course!" Arnie yelled. "You're still wearing Auntie Hoki's pendant."

May this claw protect you in whatever you do, Hoki said. *Should you ever be in danger, let all feel my fury.*

Yes, Skylark thought. She looked straight at Kahu. "The sign was given to us by Auntie Hoki and she'll be really cross if you harm one feather of Arnie's head. She gives protection to the hawk clan. I ask, in her name, that you grant us yours."

Bewildered, Kahu backed off. He flew down to Tui, waiting on the papepae of the sacred tree. "Sir, I honour you as my leader but I am bound by the code of all hawks to honour those who bear the sign of the hawk. Ask me anything, but do not ask me to kill the strangers, because I cannot."

"Should I send up another warrior to carry out the death sentence?" Tui asked the Runanga a Manu. "What say you?"

"If you do," Kahu said, "I am bound by my code to fight on behalf of the strangers – and to the death."

Tui's beak fell open with astonishment. He looked at Te Arikinui Kotuku.

"Oh, why do men always turn to women when they can't figure anything out for themselves?" Kotuku sighed. She stood on her beautiful long legs, struck a pose, and then plucked a green twig from the sacred tree.

"Take this leaf up to the strange chieftainess and her warrior," she said.

Immediately there was a clamour from the Runanga a Manu. Thunderous cheers followed Chieftain Kahu as he mounted the sky.

"Do you come in peace?" Kahu asked the strangers.

Skylark looked at Arnie and nodded. "Yes," he said.

"Then accept the token of peace," Kahu answered.

He let the green twig fall from his claws. Despite his wounded wing, Arnie spilled, zoomed down, rolled under and, putting on a show, used his hind claw to snatch the twig a few centimetres from the ground.

The Runanga a Manu burst into thunderous applause and began a haka powhiri, a dance of welcome. "Toia mai," they called, "te manu! Ki te urunga, te manu!" They watched as the strange chieftainess and her warrior, led in by Kahu, flew down to the sacred tree and took the branch reserved for visitors.

"Who taught you how to do all that warrior stuff?"

Skylark fluttered down to the paepae and Arnie followed her.

"I was the leader of the kapa haka group at Tuapa College," Arnie answered. "We won the South Island secondary school championships. I've even got a trophy at home for being best haka captain."

"And what was all that 'I am knight to the Lady Skylark' business?" Skylark regurgitated a seed and spat it at him. "Yeecch!"

"I had a teacher who believed that the world of birds was a world of chivalry. He showed me the formal ways the birds conducted their relationships. The way they do battle is long, elaborate and characterised by a great deal of knightly interplay. Their codes of honour are similar to the Knights of the Round Table at the court of King Arthur. When they mate, it's like watching a courtly dance."

"Don't get carried away now," Skylark interrupted. "What's your point?"

"When in birdland –" Arnie shrugged – "do as the birds do."

He noticed that the Runanga a Manu was quietening, settling down. In every branch, every chieftain and arikinui with the gift of flight was waiting, expectant. Down on the ground, the wingless birds settled themselves in the grass.

"So how are you going to do this, Skylark?" Arnie asked.

Skylark's heart was beating fast. She should have been prepared for this, but now that the time had come for her to do what she'd come to do, all she wanted was get the blazes out of there. But that wouldn't do her mother any good. She'd have to make her mind up – and fast. Already, Chieftain Tui had taken the branch reserved for speechmaking.

"Ki a korua, nga manuhiri," Tui began. "Welcome, our visitors from afar.

You say you have come to deliver us a message? Korero, korero, korero."

"Yes," the assembly chorused. "Speak, speak, speak."

Tui flew back to his branch. With discomfort, Arnie realised that all the chieftains and arikinui were looking at him to respond. Would Skylark understand why?

"Do you want me to do the talking for you?" he asked Skylark. "It would be better if I did."

But protocol was the least of Skylark's concerns. She was in the spotlight, and it was time to act. She took a deep breath and opened her wings. "Here goes nothing," she said. She looked at Arnie. "I'll just have to wing it."

With that, Skylark flew down and took her place, alone, on the branch reserved for speechmaking.

"E nga reo, nga manu, nga rangatira, tena koutou katoa," she began.

Immediately there was a storm, a commotion. "Oh no," Arnie groaned. "Out of the frying pan and into the fire."

"A woman standing to speak?" Chieftain Kea screamed, attacking the bark with his beak. "The stranger tramples on the kawa, the customary practices of the manu whenua."

"Ae! Ae!" agreed Chieftain Kakapo. "Wring her neck! She tries to be a cock when she is only a hen!"

Skylark staggered under the weight of the tumult. Chieftain Kawau left his perch to attack her. "Our protocol is sacred! How dare you demean it."

"Don't shoot me, I'm just the messenger, "Skylark cried.

Seeing her so defenceless, Arnie flew down beside her, glaring, displaying his wings and strength, fighting Kawau off.

"*Kik-kik-kik-kik!* Keep away. *Kik-kik-kik-kik!*"

"I'm sorry, Arnie," Skylark called. "I should have remembered –"

"That's okay," he replied. "But I'm afraid our credit rating just went down and our card is out of funds."

A dark shadow cast itself across Arnie's right shoulder. He was busy defending Skylark from Kawau but even so he tried to do a backward-kick boxing move he had learnt at the gym. Too late – a huge white kotuku landed on the branch. Her beak flashed like a razor. But what was this?

"Kra-*aak*! Kra-*aak*!" Te Arikinui Kotuku screamed. "I give this child the cloak of aroha, the protection of my rank. She is waewae tapu. Her claws, while she is among us, are sacred. If any of you want to take issue with her, face me first and do so at your peril."

Then another bird settled beside Skylark and Arnie. "Is Trouble your first name, boy?" Chieftain Kahu shouted.

He flapped for attention. "The child and her warrior are under my wing also. It was I who brought them in, and like Kotuku I give the child the dispensation to stand to speak."

Neither Kotuku nor Kahu could stop the full fury of the Runanga a Manu. "The strange chieftainess must pay for her wilful transgression," they cried. From all branches came whirring wings, fierce beaks, outstretched claws, all intent on punishing the interloper.

"No," Kotuku repeated. "I tell you she is waewae tapu –"

Then it happened. Something shifted. Something changed. Skylark felt giddy, sick, as she was struck by the same overwhelming sense of physical assault she had experienced when the rainbow had turned to ashes. Her head was whirling with vertigo and she would have blacked out again, except that Arnie pulled her back from the brink of unconsciousness.

"Time has accelerated again, hasn't it, Skylark?" he asked.

Skylark nodded, trying to recover.

"Yes, but this time it's worse –"

She heard cries of alarm coming from the wingless chieftains at the base of the paepae. They were pointing at something moving up the cliff face toward the sacred tree. It was a strange creature such as none had ever seen before, neither real nor unreal, walking as if in a dream.

"What is this giant demon?" Tui asked. "Is it a pouakai come down to haunt us from the uppermost Heavens?"

"Where are its wings?" Kawau cried. "Where are its claws? Look, it has no face, no beak, no crest –"

Skylark cleared her head. She looked at the apparition and gave a gasp.

"Do you know what the demon is?" Te Arikinui Kotuku asked.

"Yes," Skylark nodded. "It's Mummy."

Coming towards the tree was Cora. But something was wrong with her. She looked like a sleep walker. She was wearing the Madonna outfit she had worn for the production.

"Skylark, don't you understand?" Arnie said. "It's not really Cora. As Time speeds onwards it creates these strange after-images of what is happening until real Time asserts itself again. It's a hologram of your mother."

Arnie was right. Even as he spoke, Chieftain Ruru flew at Cora, beak open to tear her to pieces. There was no contact. Cora's image wobbled like jelly as he flew straight through her. The Runanga a Manu set up a cry of awe. "What witchery is this?" screamed Chieftain Kawau at Skylark. "What tribe are you from! Who are you! Kill the female sorcerer and stop her witchcraft."

"No," Skylark pleaded. "What happened was not my mother's fault. She didn't know what she was doing –"

Helpless to stop events that had already occurred, Skylark watched as Cora sat down, lit a cigarette and put it to her mouth. To the manu whenua, the action looked like Cora had made fire from a fingernail. Cora threw the match at the sacred tree. It moved in slow motion through the air.

The sacred tree burst into flames.

"Save yourselves!" Tui yelled.

The flames spread quickly among the branches. There was pandemonium as the manu whenua tried to escape. In a trice the tree had become a flaming torch, sending sparks up into the sky. Not one bird had managed to take wing. But something extraordinary was happening. Tui was still alive, looking as if he was bathing in the flames. Te Arikinui Huia, instead of being burnt to a crisp, was turning and dipping, and her wings were going right through the flames.

"How can this be?" Chieftain Kahu asked Arnie.

"The flames aren't real," Arnie answered. "Like the creature, they are a hologram, a simulation. They're like the burning bush that Moses found on Mount Ararat, burning but not really burning. Have no fear. The flames will soon pass."

As he spoke, the flames vanished. Cora's image wavered and then it too disappeared. A hubbub arose among the Parliament of the Birds.

"This is your chance, strange chieftainess," Kotuku said. "Deliver your message quickly before the manu whenua regroup against you."

Skylark stepped forward and cut through the din with her glorious karanga. Even as she was singing, she could feel the sickness overwhelm her as Time accelerated again.

"Watch the sky," Skylark called.

There was a sudden *boom* and *crack*. A seam of the sky caught fire and the sky ripped open. Giant black creatures which looked like spiders began to crawl through. Only, they weren't spiders. They took wing as seabirds, flying out of the burning belly, heading down towards the offshore islands.

"What unholy intervention is this?" Chieftain Tui asked.

The coming of the seabirds from the future looked like a video in fast forward mode. On and on the seabirds came, spilling out in their hundreds. The sky reverberated with their menacing cries of triumph.

"Is there no end to them?" Kotuku turned to Skylark for an answer. Already the seabirds had obscured the sun, casting premature night across the Great Forest. They were spreading out towards the horizon, smothering the light.

Then suddenly Time stopped. Reached the present. Through the ripped sky slid a sinuous figure. Skylark shivered with fear.

"Kawanatanga!"

The wind turned cold and sharp. In an attempt to sober up his chieftains, Tui ordered that they all bathe under the waterfall. The brisk water flowing from the snow-covered mountains certainly had the desired effect, shocking the chieftains into sobriety and to focusing on this new and ominous threat.

Tui called them to order. "I am reconvening a Council of War," he declared. "Chieftain Ruru, we will again need your advisory skills. Chieftain Kawau, the new battle will no doubt be fought again over your inlet, so we will need you to do a ground plan. Chieftain Kuku, Chieftain Kaka, Chieftain Pitoitoi and Chieftain Koekoea, please step forward. You all commanded the front-line troops in the first battle; we will need your leadership skills for the second. And Chieftain Kahu, your long-range surveillance will be invaluable to us."

"May I speak?" a young voice intervened. It was Piwakawaka II, son of the valiant Piwakawaka who had died in the first battle of the birds. "My clan wishes to be involved in the second fight that is to come and to take revenge for the death of our father."

"Of course," Tui said. "Is everybody agreed? Do I have your approval that the son of Piwakawaka should take his father's place among us?"

"Ka tika," the chieftains nodded. "Yes, agreed."

"As usual, not a woman among them," Te Arikinui Huia muttered as the chieftains huddled in conference.

Meantime, other members of the Runanga a Manu had gathered around Skylark and Arnie. They were intrigued by the strangers and wanted to know more about them. "Ko wai koe?" they asked. "No hea koe? What is your genealogy? Where are you from?"

"My species originates from Europe," Skylark answered, "but was also found in Asia. We weren't introduced to Aotearoa until the 1860s."

The young female birds, and especially Kahurangi, Chieftain Kahu's lithesome daughter, found Arnie particularly interesting. Indeed, Kahurangi was becoming quite hormonally distressed. Arnie's bodybuilding physique had made him a strong, tough-looking falcon with spectacular musculature. Not averse to attention, he was striking poses, isolating and flexing the various muscle groups, pumping them up until they popped and sizzled. The young females poked and prodded him.

"What kinds of food does he eat to get a body like that?" Te Arikinui Huia asked.

"Raw steak, eggs, vitamins and energy drinks," Skylark said.

Huia was dumbfounded. "Some of those foods are unfamiliar to me, but he eats eggs?"

"You mustn't worry," Skylark said. "He only has them sunnyside up, so you're perfectly safe."

She could have made a more sarcastic comment but Chieftain Tui called everyone to attention. He flashed his mazarine cloak, lifted his head and, white collar bobbing, trilled:

"Whakarongo ake au ki te tangi a te manu nei, tui! Tui! Tuituia!"

There was a hush. The other councillors of war took their place beside Tui to underline the fact that what he was about to say had arisen out of group consultation. Their demeanour was serious. Tui cleared his throat.

"Oh save the dramatics," Kotuku said, "and get on with it, Tui."

"Friends, nobles, countrymen," Tui began, "we face again the threat of war, and we thank our two strangers, the Chieftainess Skylark and her warrior prince Arnie, for their long journey to warn us of the coming of seabirds from the future. As we have all seen, these reinforcements are of such number as to tip the balance of any second battle in their favour."

The parliament warbled, whistled and chirruped with concern. Chieftain Titi was particularly agitated and took the opportunity to get into a close conference with Chieftain Kaka.

Tui turned to Skylark. "We seek more information from you, Chieftainess, before we come to any decision as to how to respond to the current threat. We have already won the battle at Kawau's inlet. Did not Karoro flee the field? With his departure, did not Karuhiruhi sound the retreat? Why is it that we must fight this battle again? There is no logic to it."

Skylark breathed deeply. She knew what she would say would hurt Tui, but there was no alternative except to tell the truth.

"Sir, the Lord Tane has given the seabirds a second chance."

"But what is the reason?" Tui asked, trying to comprehend. "The Lord Tane has always favoured us."

"I mean no offence to you," Skylark answered, "but following your victory you forgot to make appropriate sacrifice to him, the very Lord Tane, who gave you your win."

Te Arikinui Kotuku gave a gasp. "Of course, that's the matter that has been troubling me –"

Tui blanched. "Stronger chieftains than you have made such accusations about me and lost their lives for it. But your truth is straight and I acknowledge the fault." His face grew grim.

"It is no one individual's fault," Skylark answered. "A chapter of accidents has brought this about. For instance, my mother, in the future, could be said to have been the one to have caused this too. After all, it was she who, by her careless act, set fire to the sacred tree and led to the sky ripping open."

She turned to the councillors of war.

"Sirs, please forgive my mother."

"Yes, yes," the chieftains responded. And that was that. Agreed. Done.

"I can't believe it was so simple," Skylark said, astonished.

"They have more important things on their mind," Te Arikinui Kotuku answered with gentle sarcasm. "Once talk of battle is engaged, the cock is unconscious of anything else."

"But that means I can go home now," Skylark said.

Not quite. The chieftain looked at Skylark and then at Arnie, unsure of how to proceed.

"Chieftainess," Tui coughed, "may I have your leave to discuss with your warrior escort the military disposition of the new seabird reinforcements?"

"You may," Skylark answered with as much dignity as she could muster.

"Thanks, Skylark," Arnie said. "I know more about these matters than you do and –"

"Oh give it a rest," Skylark hissed as she stamped on his feet.

Oblivious to her and Arnie's needling, the relieved chieftains turned to Arnie for intelligence about the new arrivals. "Brave warrior," Chieftain Kahu asked, "what can you tell us about these new seabird reinforcements?"

Arnie stopped hopping around, and pondered his reply. He could have tempered his advice but he didn't. "The birds from the future are like nothing any of you have ever seen before. They are stronger, more ferocious than Karuhiruhi and his iwi. They are bigger birds with sharper beaks –"

"You keep talking about this thing – the future," Chieftain Kawau spat with irritation. "What place is that? Is it further away than China?"

"It is not a place," Arnie explained, "but rather a Time that is still to come. It lies beyond more birdsong mornings than you have ever dreamed of. To get there you would have to fly over a thousand dawns, even more years, and you would still not reach it."

"Beyond a thousand birdsong mornings?" Kawau said. "You speak of things beyond our comprehension."

Chieftain Piwakawaka interrupted him. "And what is in the future that gives the new seabird reinforcements such a size advantage, sir?"

"Well, for one thing, the food is better and more plentiful," Arnie said. "Man has created a rubbish tip of the earth."

"Man? What is that? Who is that?" Chieftain Koekoea said. "All you say sounds very odd to us. None of it makes sense –"

"What does make sense," Kahu chipped in, "is what warrior Arnie has pointed out: the size of these new seabirds. Surely that is the reality of what we are faced with. Already our landbirds are becoming nervous –"

"That was because in the past God was on our side," Ruru hooted, striking a note of doom and gloom. "Now we are being punished."

"Yes, it's all my fault that the Lord Tane is angry with us," Tui said. "I have been too arrogant."

"And because of it," Chieftain Popokotea added, "God has taken the side of the seabirds, and we are lost."

The korero was spiralling downward. Arnie realised it had to be stopped. "No," he said. "This is all defeatist talk. You are thinking about losing the battle before it has begun."

The runanga murmured in fear and indecision. Growing hysterical, Kawau intervened again. "How do we know you are not infiltrators or agents for the enemy? Are you pretending to be on our side when, in truth, you are not?"

“What a ridiculous accusation, Kawau,” Kotuku scoffed. “Look at them! They are not spies. They are landbirds.”

At that moment, Chieftain Titi coughed for attention. Both he and Chieftain Kaka stepped forward. “We have already suggested a treaty once,” Titi said.

“Not that old idea,” Kotuku sighed.

“Might not a treaty work this time?”

Arnie’s look was ferocious. Titi and Kaka backed away, and Arnie softened a little. “Kind sirs, no. The new birds from the future are here with only one purpose in mind. To overturn the Great Division so that their descendants will rule the future and the world. They are determined on your absolute extinction.”

Immediately a loud hubbub arose. Absolute extinction? The overturning of the Great Division? No. *No.* With heavy heart Chieftain Tui pondered Arnie’s words. He took a brief moment to confer with the Council of War, then announced the verdict. “We have decided,” he said. “It shall be war, not because we want it but because we have to defend ourselves.”

A few scattered cheers punctuated the silence.

“Chieftainess Skylark,” Tui confirmed, “thank you for your message. You have given us our warning. Although the Lord Tane has deserted us, let us pray that he will forgive us and return to us the mantle of his protection. Let all birds of the forest rest tonight and prepare for the morrow.”

The meeting broke up. Arnie turned to Skylark.

“Well, we’ve done our job,” he said. “You’ve obtained forgiveness for Cora and we’ve delivered our message about the seabirds. I know you want to go home now.”

But Skylark knew that Arnie’s heart wasn’t in his words. He had a mournful hang-bird look on his face and he kept on kicking at the paepae and glancing back at Kahu and the other chieftains as they planned the following war. Man oh man, how he wanted to be part of it. But he had promised Auntie Hoki he would look after Skylark and, like it or not, his job wouldn’t be over until he delivered her safely back to Tuapa.

Skylark did some quick thinking. Although she really wanted to get back to Cora as soon as, the problem was that Arnie had entered the equation. Without a doubt she would never have been able to make it this far without him, so didn’t she owe him one? Not only that, she also sensed in him some common ground.

There are solitary places in your heart, Arnie, she thought to herself, just as there are in mine. They have kept us both confined in the world of the ordinary. But does that mean we can't dream? Does that mean we can't find some extraordinary challenge in our ordinary lives and prove to ourselves that we can meet them? I've had my chance to do something amazing, something that other people only dream of and –

Skylark made up her mind. It was Arnie's turn now.

"You know, Arnie," she began, "We've actually got three days left before we need to go back through the Time Portal –"

Arnie's eyes grew wide, but he was wary of the thought behind her words. "Don't do this to me," he said. "Don't hold out something to me that you can't follow through on."

"I'm serious, Arnie," Skylark said. "There's a very good reason why we should think of staying for a while."

Arnie's heart began to beat fast. This can't be Skylark speaking, he thought to himself. This is the girl who always wants to be the boss, in control, the one who brooks no argument. What she says, goes.

"Think about it," Skylark said. "You know more about Kawanatanga and his cohorts than anybody here. You're the warrior from the future with the knowledge of advanced technology! And you have army experience too. Can't you see? You've already become their leader. They trust you and they need all the help they can get. You can't leave now and miss all the fun and –"

Arnie gave a cry of joy. Skylark was acknowledging him as a partner, not just the sidekick. She was telling him that she wasn't the only one who mattered; he did too.

"Thank you, Skylark," he said. "Nothing would make me happier than to stay around and help the manu whenua." He grabbed her in his wings and waltzed around the branch with her.

"Puh-*lease,* Arnie, get off me, "Skylark laughed. "Don't make a federal case out of it." Arnie took off after Chieftain Kahu to tell him the news. Watching his excitement, Skylark congratulated herself for having reached right to the centre of his action-movie heart and making his day.

"Yes, Arnie," she said, "this is your chance to become the hero you've always wanted to be. Go forward, follow in the footsteps of your namesake. Fight for truth and justice and save the world. You are indeed the knight who appears at the eleventh hour."

And after all that, it was only logical that Chieftain Kahu would nominate Arnie to the Council of War as chief strategist.

"Chieftain Arnie is the only one among us who knows about these new seabirds from the future," Kahu argued. "He knows how their minds work, their strengths and weaknesses. We can provide the troops, but he can devise the best strategy by which we can win the day."

"I'm not so sure," Chieftain Kawau answered. "We've always fought our own battles. We've never needed strangers to help us."

"Pull your head in," Chieftain Tui interrupted, irritated at Kawau's continuing suspicions. "What Kahu proposes makes sense. Chieftain Arnie's prior knowledge and experience of the new seabird reinforcements will give us the edge. And you, Kawau, should be be the first in line to thank Chieftain Arnie for his offer to stay because tomorrow, if we fail, your inlet will be the first to be pillaged."

The vote was taken and Arnie was in.

"Let's get operational," he said, spitting on his wings and rubbing them together. "I want a squad to go out with me on a surveillance mission tonight. He titi rea ao ki kitea, he titi rere po e kore i kitea. The muttonbird which flies by day is seen, but the muttonbird that flies at night cannot be detected."

"Tonight?" Tui asked. "But we never fly at night –"

Luckily, no muttonbirds were there to hear Tui, but, "Excuse us," said an offended Chieftain Ruru of owls and Chieftain Pekapeka of bats.

"I will need your eyes and your sonar," Arnie said. "Chieftain Kahu, will you also join us with your best warriors?"

"What is the purpose of the mission?" Kawau asked, as argumentative as ever.

"We must ascertain the size of the enemy force," Arnie answered. "Once we know how big the threat is, the better we will be able to mount our defensive networks against it. We will leave under cover of dark, immediately after sunset birdsong."

He left the council meeting and went to see Skylark, who was with Te Arikinui Kotuku. As soon as Skylark saw him approaching, she knew that Arnie was growing into his role.

"I'm taking the boys out on a reconnaissance mission tonight," Arnie said. "Do you mind? I'll be back soon."

Skylark couldn't resist kidding him. "Yeah yeah," she answered, rolling her eyes. "I know this script. This is the scene where the hero says goodbye to the little lady before he gets on his starship and thunders off into space. A boy's gotta do what a boy's gotta do."

Arnie gave her a wide grin. "I should have known you were on to me," he said. "But I wouldn't get too far ahead if I were you." He flew back to talk to Chieftain Kahu, who was speaking to his daughter, Kahurangi.

"You'd better watch out, Skylark," Kotuku said. Kahu was pushing his beautiful daughter, Kahurangi, forward. "You have competition."

"Arnie and I are not together," Skylark said.

"You're not?" Kotuku teased. She watched Skylark's face as Kahurangi placed a small lizard in front of Arnie.

"A small token of my esteem," Kahurangi simpered, batting her eyelids for all they were worth. "Please accept it, strange heroic warrior from the iwi of the future."

"Gee, thanks," Arnie said as he swallowed it.

"Gross," Skylark said.

Now, Kotuku wondered, was Skylark's disgust to do with the lizard or with Kahurangi's obvious advances?

"Time to rock and roll," Arnie said.

All the long afternoon, formations of seabirds had been practising military manoeuvres over the offshore islands. The landbirds' evening birdsong was muted. Now, darkness was falling and, under its cover, Chieftain Pekapeka and his best bat warriors left their underground caverns to rendezvous with Arnie at the neck of Manu Valley. One minute the branches around Arnie, Chieftain Tui, Chieftain Kahu and Chieftain Ruru were empty. Next minute, bat warriors were settling softly like sinister dreams.

"I hate it when they do that," Ruru said, shivering. "Couldn't they knock?"

"What is your command, Chieftain Arnie?" Pekapeka asked, his face twitching with anticipation.

"Your mission, should you decide to accept it," Arnie said, "is to scout the area between here and the offshore islands. If the seabirds see you they won't worry because, after all, are not bats creatures who fly in the night? On your report that the air is clear, I will begin our operation."

With whistles and clicks, Pekapeka ordered his bat scouts to take wing. Soon, they were flapping silently into the air away from Manu Valley.

Pekapeka began to scan the sky with his sonar. He had flown the area many times before and recognised the familiar contours of the valley which bounced back to his receptors: the forest below, the waterfall, the river, the lowland leading to the coast. Ahead should be the sea and the three offshore islands. Two were nesting places for the seabirds where they had established their rookeries and nurseries. The third was topped by Karuhiruhi's fortress. Even as Pekapeka approached he could hear the seabirds at haka, feasting and carousing before the battle to come. "Ka mate, ka mate, ka ora ka ora . . ."

Pekapeka could also smell the smoke of many cooking fires. But where was the sea? It had disappeared, and instead a solid mass presented itself to his sonar. Something was wrong there too: the mass seemed to be moving.

Puzzled, Pekapeka issued an order to his scouts. "We must grid the area. How far out to the horizon does this new mass extend? Find where the sea begins again."

Ten minutes later, whistling through the night, Pekapeka reported back to Arnie. "Chieftain Arnie, the seabirds are celebrating on their offshore islands."

"Karuhiruhi must be overjoyed to see his descendant, Kawanatanga." Arnie said.

"The seabirds are so confident of victory tomorrow," Pekapeka continued, "that they have not posted sentries. The sky is clear. However, I must report that the sea seems to have receded from the land. Where the coastline once existed, there is no coastline, nor could we find the new coastline."

"How can there be land where there was once sea? How can this happen within the space of a day?" Chieftain Ruru asked.

Arnie digested the news, puzzling over it. "All will be made clear when we are airborne," he said. "Timata."

He launched himself and gaining the air, waited for Kahu, Ruru of owls and their warrior scouts – a group eight in all – to join him. Kahu's impetuous warriors were already climbing higher.

"Come back," Arnie called. The moon had come out, a huge wan eye flooding the sky. "Your silhouettes will be seen against the moon. Stay close to the ground, follow the contours of the land and hide against the darkness where we will be invisible. Keep close ranks. Do not engage the enemy. Do not attack unless attacked. Let's get in there, assess the situation, and get out. I want no fancy stuff from any of you, is that clear?"

"Not even one tiny aerial encounter?" a hawk warrior asked.

"Save that for tomorrow," Arnie answered. "Chieftain Ruru, would you lead us? All birds respect the wisdom of the owl clan and know that you, above all others, are experts at low-level flying."

"As you say," Ruru answered.

Soundless, he dipped below foliage level, found a slipstream heading down through the Great Forest and planed into the centre of it. Arnie, Kahu and the hawk warriors followed him, cursing whenever they flew into overhanging branches.

"You boys would wake the dead," Ruru sighed.

Ruru reached the neck of Manu Valley, where the lowland began. Arnie braked and used his binocular vision. "There before us is the reason why the sea has become solid."

By moonlight, an extraordinary and chilling vista presented itself. For as far as the eye could see, seabirds smothered the sea – albatrosses, mollymawks, fulmars, petrels, prions, shearwaters, gannets, boobies, pelicans, shags, tropicbirds, frigate birds and skuas – a presentiment of ominous power.

"What is this unholy vision?" Ruru asked. "It looks like a Sea of White Feathers."

"Aha," Arnie said as he recognised Ruru's imagery. "Auntie Hoki always wondered who was the original author of the Great Book of Birds. You must be the one, and your owl clan the ones to carry the stories of these times down through all the ages –"

"There must be thousands of seabirds," Chieftain Kahu interrupted. "Do they all come from the future, Chieftain Arnie?"

"Yes, and these are but a small number of the seabirds that now ravage our world."

"How can that be?"

"The world of the future has become a rubbish dump. The seabirds are the ones who have most benefited by this. They are the great scavengers of the Earth. Come on, follow me –"

"What do you intend to do?" Kahu asked.

"We must fly across that Sea of White Feathers and make an accurate count of the seabird numbers."

"It will be suicidal," Kahu said. "As soon as the seabirds see us, they will rise up and kill us."

"There's no way out of it," Arnie answered. "Without good intelligence we cannot mount a defence to match. Trust me, Chieftain Kahu, I know what I'm doing. When I was in the Army I learnt a thing or two about camouflage. See the moon? As we fly across the sea, it will light our backs, but all the seabirds will see will be our shadows. Although our configuration does not match that of gulls, they will assume we are seabirds."

Before Kahu could argue, Arnie turned to Ruru. "I will rely on you to do the count. Let's go. Neke neke." His strategy was to keep the surveillance team on the move. If they had the chance to think about what they were doing, they could take fright, make a false move and destroy their cover.

The surveillance team had good reason to be afraid. The seabirds were yelling, jostling, laughing with each other over the battle that would come with the dawn. Their voices rose up to Arnie and his team with chilling clarity:

"Just think, my brothers, tomorrow we shall rule the world."

"We shall divide the spoils amongst us."

"Kawanatanga has promised me and my recruits all the lands to the east."

"For my support, he has told me I can divide the lands to the south amongst my iwi. We are looking forward to feasting on the flesh of the landbirds."

The air was filled with hissing and boasting. Chieftain Kahu was aghast. Until that moment he had been unaware of the seabird's real intent.

"The seabirds from the future are mercenaries," Arnie said. "They are piratical. They are a military nation of great intelligence. It is not to be wondered at that their whole purpose in life is conquest. Thousands of years of living with man has given them an accumulation of greater cunning, greater hunting skills, greater practice in killing. To you they will seem to move faster than any bird should move. They will seem like terminators of supernatural strength. Keep in formation now. Neke neke."

It took nerves of steel to fly back and forth over that unholy sea. Some of the young hawks under Chieftain Kahu's wing were sweating and beginning to break under the pressure. One of them let out a squeal of suppressed fear, drawing the attention of an alert seagull.

"Who goes there?" he called.

"At ease, Corporal," Arnie called back. "We've just been to the celebration at the fortress. Our general drank too much and is a little under the weather."

Arnie was right. The seabirds suspected nothing. After all, who'd have thought that land-bound birds would have the audacity or courage to venture out over the sea? As they continued their journey, one aspect of the survey made Arnie curious. Between one of the offshore islands and the coast there was a small area of sea that was devoid of seagulls.

"What place is that?" he asked Chieftain Kahu.

"No birds ever go there," Kahu said, wrinkling his face.

"Why not?"

"A foul-smelling substance rises to the surface," Kahu explained. "It is black and viscous, and any bird that alights on it is immediately coated with it. Once trapped in the mire, none can escape. Even to inhale the substance can be poisonous: it can make you lose consciousness, fall into the sea and drown."

Curious, Arnie flew over to the area to investigate. As soon as he smelt the toxic fumes, he knew what the substance was: oil, bubbling up from coastal vents. "Hey, hey, hey," Arnie exclaimed. "The folks at Tuapa are not going to believe me when I get back and tell them about this! And Lucas's garage is right in the middle of it."

The survey was completed. Ruru confirmed the tally.

"Now give me the odds," Arnie said.

"The seabirds outnumber us at four to one."

"As high as that?" Kahu asked.

"It could be worse," Arnie said. "But we'd better keep this information to ourselves. Let's not worry our landbirds unduly. Chieftain Ruru, please return with the statistics to Chieftain Tui. We'll have to try to figure ways to chip away at the seabirds and balance the odds more in our favour. In the meantime I'm going to take a look at Karuhiruhi's island fortress."

"I had a feeling you'd say that," Kahu sighed.

"I have to deliver our foes a message," Arnie answered.

"In that case, me and my boys better protect your butt!"

"Keep up if you can," Arnie said. "Neke neke."

He banked and, using the offshore winds to carry him, glided back across the silver sea towards the seabird islands. Very soon he was over the first of them. The mating season had just passed, and the guano-encrusted plateau was dotted with gulls' nests and parent birds protecting their fluffy young. Further on, the second island appeared similar to the first, except that the seabird nurseries were in holes in the cliffs. Territorial roosting seagulls came out to shriek at Arnie and his squad as they wheeled past.

Ahead, on the third island, was Karuhiruhi's pah. The jagged rim of an extinct volcano circled the island, providing an impenetrable wall of foam-smashed cliffs. In the moonlight it was like a bizarre crown of tall crags and eyries. Embedded within the crown was the pah, an astonishing creation of natural parapets, wingways and launching pads. Right in the middle was the marae atea – the courtyard – around which defensive channels had been dug. Military outworks added to the formidable defences. Hundreds of burrows tunnelled away from the courtyard, descending down to the soldiers' barracks at the innermost core of the island.

With a hiss, Arnie landed on one of the outer parapets. He closed his wings and walked stealthily forward to take a look at what was happening below. When Kahu and his hawks joined him, they whistled with wonder at the awesome sight below. Karuhiruhi had invited all his seabird lieutenants to meet Kawanatanga, his heir from the future, and Kawanatanga's captains. There were hundreds of them, all at attention, rank after rank.

A fly-pass parade was taking place. On the ramparts of the fortress, Karuhiruhi was standing with his consort Areta at his side. Next to her was Kawanatanga, who had been given the honour of taking the salute. Karuhiruhi was intoxicated with pride in his ferocious descendant.

"Look at the size of the bastard," Chieftain Kahu said, noting that Kawanatanga was two times bigger than his ancestor.

It was clear that Kawanatanga had already established his powerful presence. The moonlight flashed off his carapace. His movements were mechanical, his head and arms coordinated as if by computer. His voice was huge, as if digitally manipulated.

"No doubt about it," Arnie said to himself. "A series 4 model."

A squadron of seabirds came spiralling down into the fortress. When they landed, Karuhiruhi called for attention.

"This is a happy day," he shrilled. "On this day, the Lord Tane has answered my prayers and given all seabirds the chance to re-litigate the battle of the birds. Not only that, but the incredible has happened. The Lord Tane has sent my descendant, Kawanatanga, to help us and, with him, reinforcements from the future."

Areta tilted her head in acknowledgement and gave Kawanatanga a seductive look. There was no doubting that Kawanatanga had a rampant quality that was lacking in her consort.

The seabird battalions roared and began to chant. "Ka-wana-tang-a! Ka-wana-tang-a!"

Kawanatanga elbowed his way to the front. Although he paid tribute to his ancestor, his words were double-edged, ironic. "Beloved ancestor, Karuhiruhi, I honour you and your consort and pledge to fight alongside you tomorrow. Together, the seabirds will fulfil their ultimate destiny. Tomorrow we will achieve the world's domination."

The seabird army erupted in acclamation, celebrating the occasion in a riotous haka. "Tenei nga manu moana hokowhitu a Tu," they cried. "Upane, kaupane, whiti te ra!"

Arnie saw that a sacrificial feast had been prepared, and that Kawanatanga was preparing to eat a young female chick of his own kind. Flames danced in Kawanatanga's eyeslits. Seabirds had always had a covetous nature, and once it was released its rampant force could easily turn emotions from sense to savagery.

"Bring forth the sacrifice!" Kawanatanga called. The chick screamed and struggled as she was brought to the altar. With a quick jab, Kawanatanga pierced her heart, pulled it out of its ribcage and began to eat it. Blood dripped from his lips.

That's when Arnie launched himself from his hiding place. His appearance was so swift and dramatic that the seabird army was stunned into silence.

"Kik-kik-kik-*kik*," Arnie screamed. "Kik-kik-kik-*kik.*" He looked like an avenging demon, a threatening adversary slicing the full-bellied moon.

"Who is that?" Areta asked Kawanatanga, leaning into him.

Kawanatanga recognised Arnie immediately.

"Another bird from the future," he sneered. "But he is of no consequence to us."

Arnie glared down. Contemptuously, he turned his bum to Kawanatanga and delivered his message.

A long white string of crap arced through the air, splattering Kawanatanga and the sacrificial victim, who still shuddered in her death throes.

With supreme insolence, Arnie retreated, his squad with him, spearing into the moon.

"Neke neke, neke neke –"

When his squad returned to Manu Valley, Arnie reported to Chieftain Tui and the Council of War. Tui received the intelligence with a grave demeanour.

"Let's draw up a battle plan for tomorrow," he said. "We will need to plan it to the last detail."

It was well into the night before Arnie was able to slip away. He was pleased to see that Skylark had waited up for him. She and Te Arikinui Kotuku had been tending to small chicks in the nurseries, trying to soothe their nightmares of bogeybird, ghosts and demons.

"You've only got a couple of hours sleep," Skylark said. "How will you be able to manage?"

"I'll be okay," Arnie said, "though I must say I wouldn't mind an energy boost."

Skylark could tell Arnie was very worried.

"What I really need is a few aces up my sleeve. Something that the seabirds will be unprepared for."

"I can get you a couple," Kotuku said. "Leave it to me."

Arnie smiled, not taking too much serious notice of Kotuku's offer.

"If only I could phone home," he said.

"What would you ask Mother Ship for?"

Arnie shrugged his wings. Then he grinned, lifted his beak and screamed out as loudly as he could: "Mother Ship, are you there, Mother Ship? Heeellllllppp!"

[CHAPTER THIRTEEN]

– 1 –

From the kitchen window, Hoki could see the hawk clan, still keeping up a first line of defence against the seabirds as they ascended into Manu Valley. "Fight hard, my friends," she prayed.

Hoki could also make out Bella and Mitch, at work on top of the cliff where the sky had ripped. Above them the seabirds whirled like demons. Now that Kawanatanga had gone through, they were in a hurry to join him. They divebombed the rip like birds on a suicidal mission. Some were killed or wounded by the gunshots, but many were getting through. It was now or never. The battle on the other side of the sky was imminent.

Hoki and Francis were on the next shift. Francis was still in the bathroom combing his long hair and doing whatever teenage boys do in front of a mirror. "Will you hurry up in there!" Hoki yelled. As if he would meet a girl up here, for goodness sake. She twirled her thumbs as she waited for him to come out and help her carry the morning tea up to Bella and Mitch. Despite her impatience, she and Bella were enjoying male company – it prevented them from pecking at each other – and she would miss Francis when all this was over.

Over? Hoki shivered at the thought of what "over" might mean. Either the landbirds would lose their second battle. Or they would win.

She was jolted out of her reverie by the sound of the telephone.

"Hello? Is this Bella or Hoki?" The voice on the other end was unfamiliar.

"Hoki speaking, and who are you?"

"You don't know me, but my name is Lottie and I'm ringing from Nelson. I haven't got much time because the cops are after me. I just managed to get out of the house in time. I'm on my way to hide out on the West Coast and I'm calling from a telephone box."

No wonder she talked so fast.

"I'm Deedee's granddaughter," Lottie explained. "I'm the one who's taken over the guardianship of the Great Forest of Tane in this region."

"Is Deedee dead?" Hoki felt a rush of tears. "Why didn't anybody tell us?"

"I'm sorry. I don't know why you weren't informed. But perhaps we can talk about that another time."

She was interrupted by a noise in the background. "Hurry up, Lottie," Quentin called. "There's an all-points alert out for us on the police network. We gotta go."

"I thought you should know," Lottie continued, "that Arnie went with Skylark."

"I thought he had," Hoki said. "He wasn't supposed to."

"No? He had the claw, the beak and the feather. Ah well, it's too late to bring him back. Anyhow, just as me and Quentin were leaving the house this morning, I heard Arnie's voice. Don't ask me how these things happen, but I think he was trying to get a message through to somebody. He was saying something that sounded like, 'Mother Ship, are you there, Mother Ship?'"

Hoki gave a gasp of excitement. "What was the message?"

"It sounded like —" Lottie made a guttural cry, imitating a falcon. The sound was so piercing that Hoki had to hold the phone away from her, but she recognised it immediately. It was the call falcons made whenever they needed her.

"Did you get that?" Lottie asked

"Loud and clear," Hoki answered.

She put the telephone down. Francis appeared, spruced up enough to go to a dance.

"Kua reri koe?" Hoki asked. "So you're finally ready." She loaded him down with the backpack of drink and sandwiches and accidentally on purpose, while she was helping his shoulder straps on, mussed his beautifully combed hair. Before he could do a moan about it, she also gave him the shotguns and ammunition.

"What are you carrying?" Francis asked.

"Nephew," Hoki answered, pretended to be hurt. "I'm just a little old weak lady on crutches."

Hoki pushed Francis out of the door and followed him up the cliff path to the plateau. Francis stood guard while Hoki laid out the kai. While they were eating, Hoki told Bella about Lottie's call and her curious claim to have heard Arnie calling for help.

"She must have been dreaming," Bella said. "Anyhow, there's nothing we can do for them. They're on their own. Whatever they're facing, they'll have to face by themselves."

"Yes, I know," Hoki answered. "I feel so helpless, so frustrated about it. There must be something we can do."

Once smoko was over, Bella and Mitch went back down to the house for a break. Bella needed to check her traps, and Mitch thought he might go into Tuapa and see some of his mates on the wharf. Hoki and Francis began their watch on the ripped sky, firing intermittently at the seabirds, but Hoki brooded over Arnie's message. As a young boy, no matter what trouble he was in, he had always relied on her to be there for him.

It was pure frustration that did it.

The day was hot. Hoki glared at the rip in the sky. "Oh, bother, bother, bum," she said. She walked towards the rip, took a deep breath, balanced herself on one walking stick, gave a mighty heave and threw her shotgun up and into it. The shotgun cartwheeled through the air, went through, and there was a flash as it disappeared.

"What did you do that for!" Francis looked flabbergasted. "You could brain somebody doing that."

"If seagulls can go through it," Hoki answered, "so can other things."

Francis shook his head and muttered, "Well, a shotgun's no good without ammunition. Waste of a good shotgun."

In a temper, Hoki grabbed some bandeleros of bullets and gave them to him. "Here," she said. "Biff these through the rip. Don't argue, just do it. And while we're at it –" Before Francis could stop her, Hoki had taken his favourite penknife from his pocket. He had a box of matches there too.

"These are going as well."

Hoki chucked the penknife and matches through the rip.

"Are you nuts?" Francis yelled. "That was my best penknife. I had to send away to America for it. Stupid woman –"

"Stupid, am I?" Hoki glared. "You'd better watch it or you'll be next."

Francis backed away. All Hoki could feel was just the slightest satisfaction that, at the very least, she had made an effort, crazy and futile though it might be, to answer Arnie's call.

"I hope you like your presents, Arnie," Hoki said.

– 2 –

The sun hurled itself into the sky like a fireball, drenching the sea the colour of blood. From the unholy Sea of White Feathers arose a loud screaming, cawing, hissing and squealing as the seabird squadrons greeted the dawn. Beaks open and wings flapping, they turned black eyes to the island fortress. Three figures appeared on the ramparts: Karuhiruhi, chieftain of seashags; Karoro, his co-conspirator and leader of the black-backed gulls; and Kawanatanga, the leader of the seabirds from the future. Immediately, the cry went up. "Kawanatanga! Karuhiruhi! Karoro! Kawanatanga!"

That's when Kawanatanga made a big mistake. Presumptuously he stepped forward in front of his ancestor, Karuhiruhi, to receive the acclaim. "This is a fine day to go hunting," he began, "but not for fish. Rather, it is the flocks of manu whenua that will fill our ovens tonight."

A thunderous cheer arose from the sea. But just as Kawanatanga was about to resume he heard Karuhiruhi hissing angrily at him. "Step back, Kawanatanga, I command you to step back." The old bird was quivering with rage, his eyes red and enormous with anger. "You are usurping my position. You may be chief in your world, but in this world I am the chief. It is I and Karoro who lead this army, not you."

Kawanatanga tried to make light of it. "Our first argument, venerable ancestor?"

Karuhiruhi pushed past him and took the leadership back. "My descendant, Kawanatanga, has forgotten that the youngest born, even though an important person, must be subordinate to his elder." Then he smiled forgivingly. "On one matter, however, he is right: tonight the ovens will be filled and the flesh that we taste will be birds of the land."

The seabirds cheered louder than ever, and it was a balm to Karuhiruhi's wounded vanity. He saw that Areta had come to the dais with his baby son in her arms. He picked up his son and lifted him high above his head. "My brothers, we fight again to overturn the Great Division,"

Karuhiruhi continued. "We fight for the new generation, so that they will grow up enjoying the freedom we will surely win for them this day. This time we have the blessing of the Lord Tane, who has sent my descendant Kawanatanga to ensure our victory –"

Karuhiruhi returned his son to Areta. He motioned Kawanatanga forward. He had a magnanimous smile on his face, but his eyes were still angry.

"Bow down before me, mokopuna," he whispered. "Do it now, so that all can see your allegiance to me. I command you to do it."

Command? For a fleeting moment Kawanatanga felt murderous rage. How dare Karuhiruhi put him in this position of subservience. Then cold reason flooded his mind. It was imperative to show a united front. Success against the landbirds depended on it. Slowly, Kawanatanga sank to his knees, swallowing his pride as the acclamation mounted – not for him but for Karuhiruhi. Triumphant, Karuhiruhi patted Kawanatanga's shoulders.

"Waiho ra kia tu takitahi ana nga whetu o te rangi. Let it be one star alone that stands above the others in the sky," Karuhiruhi said.

Meanwhile, Arnie had been very busy. He had established the frontline of the manu whenua at the seaward end of Manu Valley. The command post, however, was at Chieftain Kawau's lagoon, deep in the heart of the valley. There, he was trying to convince the Council of War that rather than wait for the war to begin they should go out and meet the advancing enemy.

"Our normal strategy," Tui began, "has been to wait until our borders have been crossed before we retaliate. But I like the idea of a pre-emptive strike."

"Ka tika," Ruru hooted. "We have always maintained the defensive. Such a move, however, will take the battle onto the offensive."

Chieftain Kuku of wood pigeons, who happened to overhear, and who never really had an opinion, added his voice to the considerations.

"He kuku ki te kainga," Kotuku sighed, "he kaka ki te haere. A pigeon at home becomes a kaka abroad, loud in his opinions."

"Thank you, my elders of the war council," Arnie said. He turned and gave his instruction to Chieftain Kotare of kingfishers. "Take my command to the landbirds of the open skies, windhovers, harriers, eagles, hawks, swifts, ducks, godwits and curlews, that they are to advance to the front and await my order. All forest birds are to take up positions in a second line of defence to be activated only when the seabirds cross the border into Manu Valley. Make sure that the forest birds control their ardour. The windhovers must have a clear shot. The only way to win this battle is to maintain control and strategy. That's how I was taught in the Army."

"The Army?" Chieftain Kotare asked.

"Oh, it's too difficult to explain," Arnie answered.

"And where would you like us, oh Chieftain?" Skylark interrupted. She motioned to Te Arikinui Kotuku, Te Arikinui Huia and Te Arikinui Karuwai, all of whom were making their mock obeisances to the Council of War.

"We're the third line defences, eh girls!" Kotuku said as she put on her battledress and armour.

"Um, thanks," Arnie said, not knowing what else to say. Then he turned to Skylark. "Have a heart, eh? Don't give me such a hard time. I'm trying to fight a war here, and –"

Suddenly Arnie saw something from the corner of his eye. He looked up, and his binocular vision caught a glimpse of a strange object.

"Oh my god," he yelled. He grabbed Skylark and the three arikinui, and pulled them down to the ground.

Just in time. Hoki's shotgun landed right in the spot where they had been standing.

"E hika!" Huia screamed "What's *that*."

"Keep down," Arnie yelled. "There's more incoming on the way."

This time it was Karuwai who screamed as three more objects came sailing through the sky. For a moment afterwards there was silence. Skylark found herself beak to beak with Arnie and saw his brown and blue eyes staring into hers.

"You can let me up now," she said to him, as Tui and Kahu came to their aid.

"Oh . . . sure . . ."

"We are definitely a crowd," Kotuku said to the other three arikinui as they stood up. Skylark brushed herself down and stared at the objects that had almost brained her. Stuck in the marshy ground was a shotgun, rounds of ammunition, a pocketknife and a box of matches. As recognition dawned she began to hop about, giggling and jumping in the air.

"I just don't believe it! Where did they come from?" she asked. She flipped onto her back, kicking her legs and chirruping with mirth.

As for Arnie, he was gobsmacked, totally speechless.

"You've had a special delivery," Skylark giggled.

"Hoki must have heard me!" Arnie answered. He grabbed Skylark with joy.

"What's all the fuss about?" Chieftain Kawau asked. The commotion had attracted the Council of War.

"We've just been sent a secret weapon," Arnie said. "Those seabirds are in for the shock of their tiny feathered lives."

Hoki's gift had come just in time. As Arnie and Skylark were celebrating, a forward scout came whirring down to the ground.

"Sir, we were looking seaward when something strange occurred. A blanket made of white feathers has just lifted off the sea. What does it mean?"

"The manu moana are on their way," Arnie said.

The seabird army lifted off. From the start Karuhiruhi and Kawanatanga became locked in a dangerous play for power. Much to Kawanatanga's anger, Karuhiruhi ordered that he and his seabird reinforcements should bring up the rear.

"This is my fight, not yours," Karuhiruhi said. "I will lead it with Karoro of black-backed gulls, Parara of prions and Taranui of terns."

Karuhiruhi also wanted to teach his upstart descendant a lesson on who was the leader. It was a risky game, for Kawanatanga was clearly the stronger.

"That makes no sense, ancestor," Kawanatanga said. "Already my seabirds, by virtue of their greater physical power, are overflying your own contingents."

"Then keep them back, keep them back, I say," Karuhiruhi thundered. "It is my prerogative to lead the army and for my lieutenants to avenge themselves for our defeat at the first battle of the birds."

Kawanatanga gave a cynical laugh. "I will bide my time," he said, under his breath. "From being your descendant, I have become your greatest opponent."

Ah yes, uneasy lay the head that wore the crown.

Ignorant of Kawanatanga's ambition, Karuhiruhi gave orders to Toroa. "Go ahead, my albatross friend, and be our eyes on the battle." Then he turned to Karoro, Parara and Taranui. "Order all your gull battalions to the front."

"Thank you, my lord," Karoro answered. His clarion call was echoed by Taranui and Parara. "All black-backed gulls, all black-billed gulls, all red-billed gulls, come forward. Join us, our cousins, all black-fronted terns, Antarctic terns, white-fronted terns, sooty terns, white terns and all prions. We have been given the honour of leading the utu on the landbirds."

Burning with suppressed fury, Kawanatanga wheeled away from Karuhiruhi and took up his position with his seabirds from the future.

"Have your day, old bird," he said to himself. "Tomorrow it will be my turn."

The arrival of Hoki's special delivery caused a slight delay in Arnie's departure to the front.

"Could you go on ahead to marshal the troops?" he asked Chieftain Tui and Chieftain Kahu. "I'll be there as soon as I can."

At the front, all the windhovers, the birds of the open sky, were waiting for the order to attack.

"Look!" Kahu said.

The seabird army was approaching, its frontline stretching from one side of the horizon to the other. The sight filled the manu whenua with dread.

"Their beaks are open," said Tui, "as if they are already preying on shoals of fish!"

"We shall be overrun in the first attack!" said Chieftain Tere of swifts.

But Kahu gave them cause for hope. He noticed that as the seabirds approached, their frontline began to narrow down to a spearhead.

"They persist in their traditional strategy of a single, full-frontal attack on Manu Valley," he pointed out.

"In that case," Tui affirmed, "the balance of power may still be ours."

He raised a wing for silence. His voice carried in the wind to the landbird army. "Let the seabirds know that we are not an opponent to be taken lightly."

The landbirds set up a deafening clamour, a huge, formidable shrilling. The ruse had been Arnie's suggestion, designed to confuse the seabird army into thinking there were more landbirds defending Manu Valley than expected. The rifleman iwi called zipt-zipt-zipt, a high-pitched challenge which jarred the air. The fernbird tribe called u-tick, u-tick.

The paradise shelduck whanau set up a gutteral glink-glink, glink-glink. Overhead, the grey teal tribe had massed in a ferocious squad, adding to the din with their peculiar hoarse quack. Beside them, flanking to the left, the shoveler iwi made took-took noises.

The clamour also arose from the ground. The weka tribe called coo-eet, coo-eet. The marsh crake clan click-clicked. The kiwi whanau set up a shrill ear-splitting ki-wi, ki-wi. The bittern tribe began to boom, one of the most far-carrying of all bird sounds. They set up a competition with the kakapo clan. The kea whanau rattled, cackled, roared and yelled for all they were worth. Higher up the scale, the parakeet tribe screamed and screeched like banshees. The noise rose in a cacophony, a whirlwind wall of sound that went off the decibel range, a psychic fist punching into the approaching seabirds.

Back at the inlet, Arnie heard the distant roar. "The battle's begun," he said. He had set up the shotgun on a rocky promontory overlooking the lagoon and drafted Chieftain Ruru and his owl iwi to lift the shotgun into position. There, he stabilised it on a base of rocks, with the double barrels firmly pointing down Manu Valley.

Meanwhile, Skylark was supervising the females in weaving small cradles and ropes for the pulley and winch system by which the shotgun could be fired.

"I can't stay any longer," Arnie said.

"You can't?" Skylark began to panic. Now that the battle was imminent she was really scared. She didn't want him to go.

Words failed them both. How do you say goodbye when you've gone beyond words? There was only one thing left to do – and Arnie did it. He swept Skylark up in his wings and gave her a hug. It was quite a shock.

"Get the shotgun loaded, and if the seabirds make it past our defences, pull the trigger at my signal. Okay?"

"Okay," Skylark said, trying to recover.

"By the way, did I tell you that I discovered oil when we went on our reconnaissance last night?"

"Oil?"

"Right there between the offshore islands and where Tuapa will be built. The stuff is just oozing out of the ground. Goodbye, Skylark!"

Without thinking, Arnie pecked her on the cheek and took to the sky.

"So you're just friends, right?" Kotuku teased.

Arnie's ruse worked. As the shrilling increased, Karuhiruhi quailed and called a halt on the advancing army.

Kawanatanga flew forward to investigate.

"The landbirds offer strong resistance," Karuhiruhi said.

"No, my ancestor," Kawanatanga answered. He saw Karuhiruhi was jittery, nervous. "Do not do as hens do and take flight at the slightest noise of opposition."

"You were not here for the first battle," Karuhiruhi hissed, offended at the inference that he was a woman. "You know nothing of the landbird forces."

While they were arguing, Arnie reached the front. He took his place with Chieftain Tui, Chieftain Kawau and Chieftain Kahu and scoped the situation. "We have the advantage of the wind," he noted. "It's coming down Manu Valley. The seabirds will have to beat into it. Are our first line of windhovers in position?"

"Yes," Tui nodded.

"Then lets get down and dirty," Arnie said.

With that, Tui stood and called to the manu whenua. "Ka mahi te mea i tohia ki te wai o Tu tawake. All honour to those who have been baptised in the waters of the war god. Tukua mai kia eke ki te paepae! Let the seabirds come to the threshold if they dare! Toi te kupu, toi te mana, toi te whenua! Fight for our right to sing, for our right to hold the land, for our right to our own prestige!"

Ever the showman, Tui let his voice roll out to the horizon, echo following echo. Once that was done, he ordered the battle to begin.

"Go forth, Chieftain Whiorangi of the silver eye clan," he said. "Do your job. Divert the enemy –"

At the command, Whiorangi flitted across that lonely sky, a small speck disappearing into the maw of the seagull army.

Karuhiruhi laughed when he saw him. "What are you doing so far from the forest and over the sea?"

"I come to give you warning," Whiorangi chirruped. "You lost the first battle. You will lose the second. Retreat or face the consequences."

"Ka mahi te ringaringa aroarohaki taua," Tui called. "The wing which quivers in the face of the enemy is to be admired."

Karuhiruhi roared with laughter. "Get out of our way, you little sliver of silver, before you become a toothpick for my beak."

"Oh, is that so?" Whiorangi answered. He folded his wings and dropped like a stone. Only then did Karuhiruhi see that the fork-tailed swift clan, the fastest-flying and most aerial of birds, was plummeting from the highest sky. Led by Chieftain Teretere, the first squad went in, blurred lightning, with wings long and scimitar-shaped. Large and powerful, they whistled down the wind like arrows unleashed from a thousand crossbows.

Karuhiruhi could scarcely believe it. "They come to us, Kawanatanga. Who gives them such bravado?"

"It is the falcon from the future," Kawanatanga realised. "I have misjudged him, but I will not do it again. Front ranks, prepare to engage."

The order was given just in time, for when the swifts closed with the enemy, they used their speed to scythe through the seabirds. Those in their way were speared where they flew. Those who were alert deflected their attackers. The first blood of the battle went to the landbirds.

The second squad was unleashed. This time Karuhiruhi had his wits about himself. "Let them through," he commanded. As the swifts arrowed closer, the front lines of gulls, prions and terns opened up. "Now close and kill," Karuhiruhi screamed.

Trapped in a circle of snapping, ripping beaks, the swift squad succumbed.

"Never mind your losses!" Chieftain Teretere yelled from the middle of the melee. "Press on, press on."

Kawanatanga turned to look in Arnie's direction. "Come on, my little chickadee," he called, "show me the stuff you're made of."

Arnie gave the signal for the second contingent of windhovers to go forward.

"Chieftain Kahu, it's your turn," he said.

Kahu nodded and with a single flap of his powerful wings took to the sky. His hawk squadron followed him, using the thermals to gain cruise altitude. Aware of the danger, Karuhiruhi ordered Karoro's battalion to pursue the hawks and form a buffer between them and the seabird army. As the battalion did so, Karoro realised with alarm that he was being blinded by the light. He cursed that his gulls were so vulnerable. "Watch for hawks coming out of the sun," he cried.

Too late. Kahu levelled and screamed his harsh hunting cry to his warriors. "At my command, pick your own targets and dive, dive, dive –"

One by one, the hawks banked, closed their wings, approached attack velocity and struck with hooked bill and powerful grasping talons. Flying with the sun at their backs, they swept a bloodied swathe through

Karoro's blinded seagull troops. Many were the gulls who went to meet their Maker that day.

The battle was not all one way, however. Kahu let out a cry of sorrow when he saw that two of his favorite nephews had been engaged, lost the fight and were falling headless to the earth. To his left flank, another of his lieutenants was wounded, and fighting wing to wing against four opponents.

Then Toroa and his albatross squad came whistling down from the upper Heavens – and the hawks were fighting for their lives.

Watching from the forest, Chieftain Tui turned to Arnie. "We are outnumbered. The odds are against us," he said.

"Send in all our birds," Kawau yelled. "Throw everything at them."

"Yes," Chieftain Kaka added. "Let's do or die."

"No," Arnie answered. "If we lose our control we will die. Hold to the battle plan. Should the manu moana breach the windhover defences, our second line of bellbirds, parakeets and pigeons will be waiting. And if they breach that, we will have the rails, robins, fantails and saddlebacks at the third. At every seabird advance, they will find our troops. If we have to, we will field a running battle all the way back to the inlet." He gave the signal to Chieftain Parera of ducks: "Time for you to make your diversionary move."

"Come on, boys," Parera quacked. "Let's do our thing."

Large and goose-like, the paradise shelducks took wing like bomber squadrons. Quickly they closed on the seabird front. All the way across, however, the shelducks were complaining:

"Why can't we continue on our flight path and engage the enemy? Do we really have to pretend to be afraid and break to the right, boss?"

"We must follow Chieftain Arnie's instructions," Parera ordered. He kept his squadron in V-formation, maintaining their flight path for as long as he dared.

"They're getting too close," Arnie said to Tui.

"Now," Parera called. In front of him was Tarara of terns.

The paradise shellduck clan stalled in the air and set up a clamour loud enough to wake the dead: "The enemy is too strong for us! They will overpower us! Head for the hills, boys, head for the hills –"

With that, Parera's troops banked and fell away, flying towards the sacred mountains.

Elated, Tarara took the bait. "Come on, troops, they're sitting ducks."

"No, maintain your position," Kawanatanga said.

But it was too late. To a bird, the terns followed Tarara's impetuous lead. Further and further away from the seabird army they sped, gaining on the fleeing paradise shelducks. Over the flanks of the sacred mountains, around the corner they flew, across a large reed-filled lake. The shelducks descended lower, skimming the water and turned as if to make a last-ditch stand. Tarara led his terns in for the kill.

From among the reeds, the 100-strong mallard duck clan leapt up in a hail of white-feathered fury. Hissing and quacking, they grabbed the terns by throat, leg or wing and pulled them down into the water. A second contingent of ducks leapt into the fray, kicking up in single springs.

"*Glink-glink,*" they cried. "Come to your deaths, terns."

"It's a trap," Tarara yelled. "Retreat!"

As he said the words, he felt himself being dragged down through the air. There was a splash. He tried to struggle, but it was no use. Held firmly underwater, he knew he was going to drown.

"It's working," Arnie said. The diversionary attacks by Chieftain Kahu and Chieftain Parera had softened the front-line attack of the manu moana. But not for long.

"Call my seashags to the front," Karuhiruhi ordered.

Wheezing, whining, writhing, the seashags advanced like a horde of black striking snakes. With a sudden push they broke through the neck of Manu Valley.

"This is bad news," Tui said. "Ka oti te kakati e te kawau waha nui. A shag which flies up a narrow valley cannot be turned back. Once its big throat has closed on a fish, its beak closes firm and the fish has no hope of escaping it. It will be the same with us."

Arnie turned to Kawau. "Take a message to Chieftainess Skylark. Tell her that Manu Valley has been breached. We shall hold the seabirds off as long as possible and then make a controlled retreat. We shall make our stand at the lagoon. Tell her to be ready for my signal."

Skylark turned her head, alarmed. Although the wind was blowing away from her, she could hear the clash of beak on beak and strike of claw against claw.

"We must hurry," she said to Ruru.

Chieftain Ruru remained puzzled over the role of the shotgun. In following Skylark's orders on how to install it, he had been basically working in the dark. No problem, he was used to that. Even so, he was still none the wiser about the function of the "cannon", as Skylark called it now.

Would it work? Only one way to find out.

"Open the shotgun," Skylark ordered.

With a sharp click, Ruru flicked the lever, and the double barrels were exposed.

"Load," Skylark commanded.

Working in groups of four, owls placed two cartridges on the mats Kotuku and the other women had woven. Taking a corner each, they flapped their wings, ferried the cartridges up into the air and hovered over the shotgun. There, the beaks of other owls nudged the cartridges off the mats and into the two barrels of the gun.

"Close the shotgun," Skylark said. Her voice came out as a small squeak. Her nerves were getting to her.

The owls put their backs under the barrel and raised it. Click.

"So what now, Chieftainess?" Ruru asked.

"We wait for the signal from Arnie," Skylark said.

Hopping down from the shotgun, she checked the system of winches, pulleys and ropes which Arnie had arranged so that the shotgun could be fired. Six of Ruru's strongest owl warriors were ready to take the rope in their beaks and pull.

But Skylark was bothered. She was sure that one item on her checklist was missing. What was it? It was something important.

Then Kawau came flying out of the sun. "The seabirds have breached Manu Valley," he said.

With a cry Karuhiruhi urged the seabird army forward. "Charge! Take no prisoners!"

The ranks of landbird defenders buckled and broke apart.

"They're through,"Arnie said "It will only be a matter of time before they overrun us."

"We can hold them a while longer," Tui answered. "Ara! Look –"

He pointed his wing at a birdfight between six seashags and three aggressive kaka; and the seashags were coming out much worse for wear. Arnie remembered Flash Harry and the kaka colony on Joe's island.

"He kaka kai uta, he mango kai te moana," said Tui as he watched one of the kaka warriors deliver the *coup de grâce*. "The kaka feeds just like the shark."

Throughout the sky, the battle had broken up into individual and desperate birdfights: kea against albatross, shoveler against gannet, parakeet against petrel, bellbird against prion, cuckoo head to head with fulmar, crow with mollymawk. Darting in between were the valiant remnants of the swifts, joined by the smaller birds – rifleman, robin, silver-eye, thrush, tit, grey warbler, waxeye, wren, yellowhead – squeaking and chirruping, trying to divert attention so that their bigger cousins could make the fatal thrust, the lethal slice of claw or cut of beak.

Chieftain Kea and his stocky warriors were right in the thick of it. Arnie well understood why they had earned a fearsome reputation as sheep killers. This time their target was a flock of albatrosses who were braying across the sky in an attempt to shake their kea attackers off.

Elsewhere, Arnie saw Chieftain Kuruwhengi and his shoveler tribe entering the fray. Working in pairs, and in tandem, the shovelers used their speed and body weight to slam the seabirds to smithereens. Flying very fast with short, rapid wingbeats, they closed on their targets, banked, rocketed and *bang*: another gannet went to the Great Bird Heaven in the sky. Using similar tactics, Chieftain Kotare and the kingfisher clan joined the melee. Flying at considerable force, with a churring noise like a jet plane descending, they speared their opponents in skilful rapier thrusts of beak to beak.

But the seabirds were unstoppable. "How can you turn back the tide in full flood?" Tui asked Arnie in despair. "How can you stop a forest fire when it is raging through the trees? How can you stop the coming of the night? This is our twilight –"

Arnie sounded the retreat. He hoped that Skylark was ready.

"Fall back! Regroup at the inlet."

Skylark was anxious. The noise of battle was drawing closer and closer. All around her, the birds who had been assigned to protect the lagoon were growing nervous. "E kui, will the seabirds kill us? Will they take us as their slaves? What will they do to our children?" Te Arikinui Kotuku, Te Arikinui Huia, Te Arikinui Korimako, Te Arikinui Parera and Te Arikinui Karuwai walked among them, soothing their fears.

"Hush," they said. "Trust in the Lord Tane."

"There will still be time for a treaty," Chieftain Titi interjected. "I told you all right from the start that to fight the seabirds was the wrong thing to do. Now we shall suffer for it."

Kotuku turned a baleful yellow eye on him. "Kra-*aak*. Kra-*aak*," she warned, waving her beak back and forth as if she was sharpening it. "Enough of your talk of a treaty, Titi. All of you, kia kaha, kia manawanui. Have strength. Be of brave heart."

The landbirds settled down. The robins began to sing a beautiful waiata of comfort. As the strains drifted across the lake, others joined in. With hope and faith restored, the song grew fierce with passion. Seizing the moment, Te Arikinui Kotuku, eyes blazing and feet stamping, began a women's haka. Her strength and conviction reminded Skylark of Hoki. *Things of value must always be fought for.* "Ka whawhai tonu atu, ake, ake ake! We shall fight on forever and ever!"

Skylark was so stirred, she didn't notice that Te Arikinui Huia had come up to her side. "Tell me, Skylark, you who come from beyond a thousand birdsong mornings, do great things happen to the landbirds?"

A deep pang of sadness came over Skylark. How could she tell Huia that by the year 2003 AD at least fifty of more than 100 native birds species would have disappeared? That the huia clan itself would become extinct and that the only place you could see a huia was as a stuffed bird in a museum? How could she tell Huia that the noble moa, New Zealand eagle, laughing owl, Eyles' harrier, bush wren, New Zealand crow, Chatham Island fernbird and New Zealand coot would also become extinct? That at the very last moment the black robin, stitchbird, saddleback, takahe and kakapo would be brought back from the brink to live their lives on protected sanctuary islands?

Skylark decided to answer the question like Hoki and take the long way round.

"Great things do happen for the landbirds," she said. "For a time, you become the rulers of the Great Forest of Tane and your progeny is as numerous as there are stars in the sky."

"For a time?" Te Arikinui Karuwai of robins asked.

"Yes," Skylark nodded, "until the coming of the Lord Tane's next great creation – man. He is born far beyond the horizon and his seed spreads far and wide across the world. It is one of these seeds – that sown at Raiatea in French Polynesia – which spawns the race who eventually come by many canoes down to these southern islands at the bottom of the world. It is a bird, the long-tailed cuckoo who, during regular migratory flights from east of Fiji, leads man here. With man the birds create a partnership."

Skylark turned to Huia. "For instance you, Te Arikinui Huia, are elevated to high status by the First Man. They call you the bird of Whaitiri. Because of your beauty, they honour you as a bird of the gods."

"My beauty?" Huia asked. "You flatterer you."

"Not only that, but because you have twelve tail feathers you are revered as a sacred bird. Twelve is a sacred number and you are regarded as looking after the twelve appearances of the moon every year. Your feathers are therefore much desired because they give prestige and power to the owner. They are used as barter and passed from tribe to tribe. Land, women, greenstone could be exchanged for one such feather. However, with the arrival of the Second Man, all things change –"

That was the beginning of the end of the time of the birds. This second man cut down the native forest, logging it and farming the land. He sprayed chemicals across the trees and killed off native species – birds, mammals, flora as well as fauna. He brought with him his companions – mice, rats, wild cats, dogs, stoats, ferrets, weasels, hedgehogs, possums, deer, goats and the marauding honeybee, which competed with the birds for food. When that food diminished, man's companions turned to the eggs, chicks or the adult birds of the Great Forest. Slowly but inevitably the bird species diminished. Picked off one by one by man himself. By gun. By car. Often for the fun of it.

Man, the toxic being.

"And will this thing, this man, look like the ghost that appeared to burn down the sacred tree?" Huia asked.

Skylark drew a human in the dirt.

"What? No wings?" Huia laughed. "Where are its beak and claws? How could the Lord Tane think of creating such an ugly creature!"

"You and your stories, Skylark," Karuwai scoffed. "They are cautionary tales of the kind mother hens tell their chicks."

Kotuku saw the sad look on Skylark's face. She caught the intimations of mortality contained in her words. She turned to Huia and scolded her. "You ask such difficult questions, Huia. Like all things, the fortunes even of manu whenua wax and wane. We may rejoice today but what about tomorrow? All depends on the will of the Lord Tane."

The mood was interrupted by Chieftain Ruru who, giving the alarm, pointed to the trees. Darkness was cutting a line across their tops. "The sun is going out," he said.

"It is a solar eclipse," Huia gasped.

"The Lord Tane himself comes to punish us," Titi cried.

"No," Skylark answered. "The seabirds are coming." She turned to Ruru. "Quick, get your warriors to take up their positions."

Before she could draw another breath, Skylark saw the forest shivering. It exploded as manu whenua in retreat came flying through the trees and across the lagoon.

"The seabird army is not far behind us," they cried. Some were limping. Others were ferrying back the wounded and the dead. The air was whirring and chittering as the retreating landbird army landed and reinforced the defensive positions all around the lagoon.

Oh my God, Skylark thought. It's all up to me now.

She went through her checklist again: Angle of trajectory, check. Shotgun's loaded, check. Barrel closed, check. Owl warriors in place, ready to pull the trigger, check. Then she remembered:

"Chieftain Ruru," she yelled, her eyes wide with fright, "we have to cock the shotgun, otherwise it won't fire –"

"How do you do that? Oh me oh my, what a cock-up."

Skylark knew the fault was hers, not Ruru's. "No offence, Chieftain Ruru," she said, "but it would be really nice to have birds around you who understood what you wanted."

Quickly she flew up to the shotgun. "I need another rope up here," she said. Immediately three stocky owl warriors lifted a rope to her. She took it in her beak, but nervousness was getting to her and she couldn't lever it over the two cocking levers. "Sometimes it is so inconvenient not to have fingers and thumbs," she wailed.

With a roar like a hurricane, the battle between the opposing armies smashed through the trees. The wind of a thousand beating wings began to stir the surface of the lake, lashing it into fury.

"Done," Skylark said as she finally slipped the rope into place. "Now pull!"

At her command, the owl warriors heaved at the rope. "Hii haa! Hii haa!"

Skylark took a quick look across the lagoon. Was that the war council in retreat? Yes: Chieftains Kuku, Kaka, Kea and Piwakawaka. Oh, where was Arnie?

Then she saw him.

"Arnie!" she screamed.

He was fighting a rearguard action. His opponent was Kawanatanga – and Kawanatanga was winning.

"Quickly now," Skylark urged the owl warriors. Her heart was pumping with fright.

"Hii haa! Hii! Haa!"

It seemed to take years before the cocking lever double-clicked into place.

"Now back to your positions!" Skylark yelled.

The owl warriors scrambled over each other to return to the ropes that would pull the trigger.

Meanwhile, Kawanatanga was closing on Arnie. "I was told in that other world we come from, that in this world I would meet my nemesis," he laughed. "I never thought you would be such a weakling. Prepare to die –"

Kawanatanga slashed with his claws. At the last moment, Arnie spun out of the way, folded his wings and dropped to the lagoon. As he did so he yelled at Chieftain Kahu, Chieftain Kawau and Chieftain Tui. "Disengage with the enemy." He wanted to leave Skylark with a clear shot at Kawanatanga, the black bastard.

"Now, Skylark. Now."

Skylark heard Arnie's sharp cry curling towards her. The owl warriors were waiting, ropes in beaks, arms pumped.

"On my order, fire from the first barrel . . . fire!"

With an almighty heave, the owls pulled at the ropes. The trigger moved. But nothing happened. Oh no. What was wrong?

"Skylark, fire!" Arnie called again.

"It's the safety catch," Skylark realised. "It's still on."

The seabird army began cruising across the lagoon like conquerors. They reached the halfway mark, coming closer. Dreams of victory flared in Karuhiruhi and Kawanatanga's eyes. The Great Division was about to be overturned.

"Skylark, quickly, before it's too late –"

Skylark's mouth was dry. She needed a drink of water. She could hardly speak. "Te Arikinui Kotuku, there's a tiny switch up there –"

Kotuku cocked her head, saw the switch on the shotgun. She put her strong bill against it. "You mean this little thing?"

Skylark nodded. Heard the tiny click as the safety catch was unlatched.

"Fire!" Skylark said.

The shotgun roared. The owls were thrown to the ground by the recoil. Arnie ducked. A shell whizzed over his head and exploded. Pellets scattered through the air.

"E hika ma," Ruru said, picking himself up and dusting himself off. "He aha tera? What the hell was that?"

His shock was nothing to the pandemonium in the first ranks of the seabird army.

"Get back to the ropes!" Skylark yelled. The recoil had kicked the shotgun off its cradle of rocks. Already Ruru was on the case. He knew his owl warriors were bruised, but he ordered them to get under the barrel and to lever it back up.

"Don't worry about us, Chieftainess Skylark," Ruru said.

"Second barrel . . . fire!"

Another shell left the shotgun. The owl warriors were again kicked to the ground. No time to waste.

"Reload! Reload!" Skylark screamed.

This time, the shell exploded right in front of Karuhiruhi. Caught in a hail of pellets, the only thing that saved him was a quick-thinking corporal who flew to his protection. With horror, Karuhiruhi saw the corporal's body disintegrate. He felt a wet lash across his face and realised it was a spurt of blood from the dying corporal.

Karuhiruhi completely lost it. "The Lord Tane has returned to the side of the landbirds!" he yelled. "Retreat! Retreat!"

In fear for his life, he turned and wheeled away from the lagoon. The bewildered seabird army watched. Then, one by one, they banked and followed him. After all, was he not their leader?

"Come back, come back, you fools!" Kawanatanga raged. "We must press on with the attack –"

But from all corners of the Great Forest of Tane, the manu whenua, led by Arnie, came flying.

"*Kik-kik-kik-kik!* Don't even think about it." Arnie said.

It all happened so quickly. One moment the sky had been filled with seabirds. The next they were turning, wheeling away, following Karuhiruhi out of Manu Valley. Only Kawanatanga and his squad of seashags remained.

Kawanatanga was insane with rage. He hissed and spat at Arnie. "Next time, boy," he said, "it will be just between you – and me." With contemptuous ease, he flicked a wing and was away, soaring on the wind, back to the sea and the offshore islands.

On his return to his island fortress, Karuhiruhi dismissed his troops and sought the sanctuary of the royal nursery where he would find the solace of Areta and his baby son. The mood on the flight back had been sombre. Karoro, Taranui and Parara had joined him from the corners of the sky, and when they reached their destination fights broke out between those lieutenants who were loyal to him and those who questioned the order to break off the fighting. "For the second time we have flown the field of battle," Karoro shrilled. "Yet we were winning –" Turmoil was in the air, as great as that which Cleopatra, the Egyptian Queen, had faced when, leaving the sea battle of Actium to her consort, she gave victory to the navy of Octavian.

"Live to fight another day," Areta soothed. But she was bothered by Karuhiruhi's obvious tiredness and despondency. With foresight she realised the psychic diminution which had come upon him since Kawanatanga had turned up. Her husband's star was in the descendancy, and Areta suspected Karuhiruhi knew it. Visibly aged by his conscience, his mana had been tested in battle, and for the second time he had not come up to the mark. Kawanatanga's mana, on the other hand, was on the rise. Not only that, but Areta had seen the lustful way Kawanatanga looked upon her and had felt her own passions responding. Perhaps it was time to consider, she mused, the artful and political business of changing birds, of using her feminine wiles to ensure that in the changeover she still maintained her position.

So it was that when Kawanatanga whirled down the corridors seeking the place where his ancestor had taken refuge, Areta had already placed herself on the perimeter of the nursery.

"Do not include me in any revenge you are about to enact," she said. She gave him a sideward glance, hinting that she was prepared to consider other offers.

"You fool," Kawanatanga raged when he confronted Karuhiruhi. "Do you realise how humiliating your running away was?"

"Don't touch me," Karuhiruhi answered, grabbing his son as if he was a shield. "From my child's loins will come the line from which you are descended."

Kawanatanga sighed. "Put the child down," he said. "Don't cringe before me. How do you think it makes me feel to see you hiding behind your child? The weapon that was fired against you was a shotgun, nothing more, nothing to do with the Lord Tane. Nor will it be of any use to the landbirds again, now that we know they have it. Should they fire it again, we will keep out of its range –"

Karuhiruhi heard a noise in the corridor. Areta was there, and with her were Karoro, Taranui and Parara. He realised he was without allies or friends. "How was I to know?" he whimpered. "I am ignorant of the marvellous magic that comes from the future. When it happened, what was I to think?"

Karuhiruhi hugged his son closer. But Areta made her move. She came across the floor and soothed her husband. "Give me our son, Lord," she said.

Nodding, Karuhiruhi delivered the child into her arms. When she had him, Areta slipped past Kawanatanga, accidentally caressing his loins as she did so and giving him the glad eye. "Make it quick," she said enigmatically.

Karuhiruhi began to sob. Kawanatanga walked towards him and took him in his arms. He was surprised at how small Karuhiruhi was. Small, ineffectual, a harmless bag of bones. "What am I to do with you, my ancestor?" he said. "All my life I grew up hearing of your great deeds. None of it is true, is it? All of it is lies. Ah well, you did your best –"

He turned quickly and kissed Karuhiruhi on the forehead. "He aha ma te rora. What use is a coward to anyone? There can be only one leader here –"

With a quick movement Kawanatanga slashed at Karuhiruhi's jugular, and pulled. Areta watched, horrified. Her son squirmed in her arms.

"You are weak, my ancestor," Kawanatanga said. "I must take over from you, can't you see that?" He listened to Karuhiruhi's death rattle, his chest heaving. Then Kawanatanga stabbed at the old bird's breast and ripped out his heart. The blood spurted out in fast jets. Kawanatanga arched his throat, flipped the heart out of its cavity and swallowed it whole. The blood spilled out of Kawanatanga's mouth.

Kawanatanga called Karoro, Taranui and Parara forward. "Tell the army that my beloved ancestor Karuhiruhi is dead. His consort and I are taking an appropriate hour to mourn his death. After that we will resume the battle. This time there will be no retreat." He smiled across at Areta. "Put the child to bed, my lady," he said. "Attend to me, for you are mine now."

– 3 –

It was Chieftain Ruru, who had maintained warrior scouts over the sea, who reported the developments at the late Karuhiruhi's island fortress.

"Kawanatanga has taken over leadership of the seabirds," he said.

Up to that moment, Chieftain Tui had been leading the landbirds in a celebration of victory, and this time he had made appropriate thanks to Lord Tane. He realised the import of Ruru's words and, alarmed, flew to the highest branch of the paepae. He raised his wings for silence. "We have had grave news," he reported. "Our intelligence tells us Kawanatanga has murdered his ancestor and taken his widow as wife. Our celebrations are premature. The war is not over yet."

"You worry too much," Chieftain Kawau said. "I haven't even been touched in the fighting so far."

"He koura koia, kia whero wawe?" Tui asked. "Are you a crayfish that you turn red so quickly? Do not assume that just because we won this morning the same will be the case this afternoon. We won the battle, but we have not won the war."

Te Arikinui Kotuku agreed. "Are you always so smug, Kawau?" she asked.

Kawau took even greater offence, and very soon a squabble developed. The raised voices escalated.

"Do something," Skylark said to Arnie.

Arnie quickly took the paepae. "It is a proper thing," he said, "to debate the news of Kawanatanga's plans, but let us not fight each other. We must retain our solidarity. If we don't, we will lose focus on winning the war. On that count, I agree with Chieftain Tui. A first win does not mean a final victory. It's not a done deal."

"Ka tika, ka tika," the landbirds agreed.

"Nor should anyone think," Arnie continued, "that the next battle will be easier than the last. The next time we'll be fighting the birds from the future and Kawanatanga himself. They have strengths and strategies you haven't even dreamed of. They will stop at nothing to win. All must be prepared to fight to the death."

Chieftain Tui took command again. "In that case, tend to your wounded," he said to the manu whenua. "Get some rest. Eat. We have gained a breathing space, so let's enjoy it while we can. It is as like a lull in a rainstorm."

The celebrations broke up. Skylark watched as Arnie spoke with Tui, Kahu, Ruru and Kawau on preparations for facing Kawanatanga. There was much nodding and shaking of wings – and then Arnie's head came up as if he was looking for somebody.

"I think you're wanted," Kotuku hinted.

"Me? What for?"

Kotuku gave a secretive smile. She saw Arnie's gaze light on Skylark, the broad grin of relief and happiness that flooded his face, and his eager flight to join her. However, halfway across to her, the beautiful Kahurangi somehow blundered into Arnie's flight path and fell, prettily, to the ground.

"The brazen hussy," Kotuku said to herself as Kahurangi accepted Arnie's wing, helping her up. However, Kotuku's irritation turned to glee when Arnie, unaware of Kahurangi's obvious wiles, simply said to her, "See ya." Either the boy had common sense or was blind or incredibly dumb. Whatever, Kotuku was very happy to see him approach Skylark.

"I think I'll leave you two alone," she whispered.

"Let's get out of here," Arnie said as soon as he reached Skylark's side. "I need a break. Do you want to go for a walk by the lake?"

"Are you sure? You can go with her –" Skylark indicated the scowling Kahurangi – "if you want to."

"Who? No, it's you I want to talk to. Come on." Skylark shrugged her wings and followed. For a while, they picked their way around the mossy edge.

"I'm parched," Arnie continued. "Feel like a drink?"

Together they hopped towards the water, put their beaks into it, and drank. Skylark went to take a second sip, and for a moment was confronted with her reflection. She had been expecting her own face – and Arnie's – to stare back. She couldn't help it. She burst into a peal of laughter.

"I know the feeling," Arnie said. "How do you like me best? As a human or a falcon?"

"I'm not sure," Skylark answered. "You're just Arnie. It doesn't matter what you look like. And you're doing a great job here, oh chieftain."

"You really think so? That's a big compliment coming from you. It wasn't so long ago that we couldn't stand each other." He stared at Skylark with his brown and blue eyes, and she felt her heart do a little flip.

"We've been through a lot, haven't we!" Skylark said quickly. "It's not every day that a boy gets the chance to change into a bird and save the world. I mean it, Arnie, I'm really proud of you."

Arnie bobbed his head and kicked his claws together in an "aw shucks" way. "I couldn't have done it without you," he said. "If you hadn't fired that shotgun, we'd all be slaves to the seabirds by now. I knew you would come through."

"I almost didn't."

"That doesn't matter. The fact that you did it is all that counts. And it saved the day. One second more and we would have been yesterday's toast."

"But the seabirds will be back," Skylark shivered. "So it's just as well we stayed, isn't it. You're the only one here who knows Kawanatanga and how to stop him."

"Actually I'm clean out of ideas," Arnie said. "That's why I've come to see you. You've always been more resourceful than me. You have this habit of thinking laterally. Can you think of anything?"

Skylark grinned. "Well, you could phone for help again. Who knows what else Hoki might throw through the ripped sky." Then she grew serious. "Whatever happens," she said, "we've only got two more days to do it before we have to think of returning to Tuapa."

Arnie nodded. He heard Chieftain Tui whistling for him. "I'd better get back. But hey," he gulped, "you wouldn't mind taking another walk like this when we get back home, would you?"

He had nothing to lose. She'd either say yes or no.

"Sure," Skylark answered.

Arnie tried to be nonchalant. "Cool," he said.

And Auntie Bella said he couldn't get a girlfriend? Ha.

He flew back to the paepae. Chieftain Tui was in deep conversation with a deputation from Chieftain Kakapo of ground parrots, Chieftain Takahe and Chieftain Pukeko.

"We may not be windhovers or forest birds, but we are here to assert the mana of all ground birds," said Kakapo, puffing up his chest. "Just because we have no wings it doesn't mean that we are not fighters."

"Ka tika, ka tika," Takahe agreed. "How do you think we feel, sitting here on the ground while the fight is happening up there in the sky?"

"In other words," said Pukeko, "and to cut to the chase, bring the seabirds to our level. If you birds with wings can get the seabirds down to the ground, leave them to us. We'll finish them off, eh boys?"

"I don't know," Tui said, unconvinced. "Are you ground chieftains suggesting that we bring the fight to our forest home? Where our nesting places are? Our wives and children? I don't like the sound of it. No, it's too dangerous."

"The proposal has merit," Arnie intervened. "The seabirds have the upper hand only when they have a clear sky to attack from or a target that is in the open air."

"You like what the groundbirds are saying?" Tui answered.

"Somehow or other," Arnie said, "we've got to beat the seabirds' odds. This is a way of doing it. The sky is their battleground. The trees are ours. Down here we'll have the greater advantage." He was liking the idea more and more. "Let's change the rules. Use the forest as a trap. Give our wingless brothers the chance to do their job. Adopt guerrilla tactics. Hey, now there's an idea."

"Guerilla tactics?" Kahu echoed, puzzled.

Arnie was jumping around with excitement. "They were perfected by a man called Te Kooti," he answered. "As the seabirds advance to the inlet, we should get the windhovers and the forest birds to lure them into the forest. I know Kawanatanga and his followers. They won't be able to resist. They'll follow and, in our world, they will lose formation. They won't be able to move in squads so easily. The ground birds will be able to pick them off one by one. It's really the best chance we've got."

The Council of War waited for Tui to make the decision.

"Okay, Chieftain Arnie," he said. "You've been right so far. You may be right again. Let's do it."

And then it was time for war again.

Kawanatanga appeared on the ramparts with his new consort, Areta. "I will bring you the whole world," he promised her, "and I will lay it at your feet." He leapt into the air, and, as one, the seabird army lifted from the unholy Sea of Feathers. Slapping his breastbone, Kawanatanga, the new Supreme Commander, set up a ferocious haka.

"Ka eke i te wiwi, ka eke i te wawa,
Ka eke i te papara huia –
Breach the outer defences, capture the inner palisades,
storm the very centre of the manu whenua domain,
scrape the land clean of them –"

The words burst across the sky with ominous foreboding. To Skylark, Arnie and the manu whenua, the words sounded like thunder rolling from the east to the west across the sky. They were dissonant, filled with dread, skulls, rattling bones, portents of death and destruction. Some among the waiting warriors felt their bowels loosen, their courage desert them. Many would be killed this day. But what else could they do except continue to fight for their land, their hens and chicks, history and culture?

Chieftain Tui stepped forward. "Oh Lord Tane," he prayed, "look down upon your subjects the landbirds in our hour of travail. Forgive us our past trespasses and, if it be Thy will, let Thy Great Division, which we fight to protect this day, stand forever and ever, Amine."

From the Great Forest of Tane came the chorus, "Amine."

There was a disturbance. Te Arikinui Kotuku craned her neck and peered across the sacred mountains. "Chieftain Arnie," she said, excited. "I think the reinforcements I sent for have arrived."

"They couldn't have come at a better time," Arnie answered. "Where are they?"

Kotuku pointed to the clouds, where a string of stately cranes was silhouetted like a kite in the shape of a Chinese dragon. As they came nearer, Arnie's face fell. "Only ten of them?" he asked.

Kotuku chose not to hear Arnie's disappointment. Instead, she called out to the incoming birds. "Welcome, cousins, come to ground and take your place amongst us."

The cranes circled the paepae. They were gorgeous to look upon with giant filamentous kimono wings. They carried wooden staffs in their feet. When they landed, they prostrated themselves before the landbirds.

Kotuku introduced the cranes to the Great Council. "Sirs, as you are aware, my species is a rare one in this land. Indeed, I live at Okarito with my colony, only by your leave and the blessing of Lord Tane. But my clan is worldwide and loyal to each other. They have sent us my cousin, the Great White Egret, who lives in China. She has brought with her crack Chinese fighters adept in the martial arts."

The Great White Egret gave a slight grave nod. "My name is Yu Shu Lien," she said. Her voice was soft, lyrical and warm. "My fighters come from the Wudan mountains. We may not be many but we respect the ideals of honour and selfless duty. It is our obligation to support our cousin, Te Arikinui Kotuku of these southern islands."

Kung fu cranes from China, Skylark thought. Great.

Arnie's response, however, was extraordinary. He prostrated himself before the Great White Egret. "The honour is ours, Shu Lien," he said. "E ai o harirau, hei rere mai. What wings you have with which to fly here! In your country, long after you are gone, monks from the Shaolin order will create a society of martial arts fighters based on your ideals."

"What on earth are you talking about!" Skylark whispered. "Sometimes you just don't make any sense at all."

"I can't help it if you don't go to martial arts movies. Think Michelle Yeoh –"

The Great White Egret hid her face in modesty at Arnie's praise. "The things you speak of are to do with hidden dragons, crouching tigers. Let us turn to the immediate present and your current dilemma. We unreservedly join you in your battle against ambition, avarice, theft, murder and the wish of the seabirds to become conquerors of the world."

And the hour of battle was again upon them.

With a sudden uplifting of wings, the seabirds advanced like a weather front broiling up from the south.

"This time we will not retreat," Kawanatanga cried.

Boom. The shotgun, which Arnie had ordered brought forward, sent its shells whistling through the seabirds.

Boom. Under the instruction of Chieftain Ruru, the second shell soared through the air and exploded its pellets.

The front lines of the seabirds faltered, but Kawanatanga urged his army forward. "Get through before the landbirds have the chance to re-load! Toroa, advance with your albatross squad and take out that shotgun."

The seabirds pushed – and, as they had done that morning, entered again into the throat of Manu Valley.

"Manu tu, manu ora, manu moe, manu mate," Arnie cried. "If you stand you live, if you lie down you die. Hold firm. Be steadfast."

Again Chieftain Teretere led the swift clan. White undertail coverts dazzling, they rained across the sky as if fired from a thousand crossbows. On their tails came Chieftain Kahu and his hawk battalion, Chieftain Parera and the paradise shelduck iwi, and other windhovers of the open sky. Meanwhile, Chieftain Ruru was having his own desperate battle as the albatrosses descended on his owl warriors.

Boom.

A quick re-loading gave the owls some respite. The Great White Egret whispered to her kung fu warriors and approached Arnie. "Chieftain, may I lead my fighters into the fray? These are ideal fighting conditions for us."

"The sky is yours," Arnie answered.

Yu Shu Lien and her nine warriors advanced. They held their staffs in their claws. The Great White Egret bowed her head before Kawanatanga: "Enemy lord, turn back or face us."

Kawanatanga gave an incredulous laugh. "What can ten do against a thousand?"

"Actually," the Great White Egret answered humbly, "quite a lot."

She gave a sharp order. "Hai. Hohooo." Next moment, the kung fu warriors were jumping, flying, circling, tumbling, somersaulting in and out of the ranks of seabirds. Every time they made a move they slashed with their staffs, slicing three seabirds at one blow. They wove in and out, under and above, stabbing and jabbing giant holes in the approaching army. At the end of their first feint, they retreated and bowed.

"Wow," Skylark whistled.

With a roar of anger, Kawanatanga urged his army forward. Next moment, the Great White Egret and her warriors were fighting for their lives. Together with the windhovers, they were pushed backwards, ever backwards, over Manu Valley. Watching, Arnie was trying to calculate the moment when the maximum number of enemy were engaged. In particular, he was waiting for the black seashags from the future, the greatest threat of all, to enter the envelope of air immediately above the Great Forest of Tane.

They were in the zone. "Yu Shu Lien, windhovers," Arnie yelled, "dive, dive, dive —"

On the order, the windhovers folded their wings and dropped like stones toward the green canopy of the forest. Would the black seashags follow them? Would they take the bait?

The seashags swooped after their descending prey. The windhovers dropped through the forest and disappeared.

"Come on, you black devils," Arnie whispered to himself. "Follow the windhovers through. Go through —"

It was Kawanatanga himself who sealed their fate. "Kill the cowards. Bring back to me their heads as trophies. Especially bring back that Chinese bitch!"

One by one, the black seashags banked, and in a trice the forest swallowed them. They founds themselves in a maze of sky-splitting trees and ferns, a glowing forest which took their breath away. Soon, all of this would be theirs. All this beauty. All this awesome taonga. All this virgin land. But where were their prey?

"They've gone to ground! They're playing hide and seek! Where are you, my little lovelies."

Lower and lower the seashags descended. They fluttered through the dense canopy, weaving this way and that among the dense branches. At last, they broke through into the space between canopy and ground where they were able to cruise, wings outspread, between the trunks of the trees.

But why was it so quiet? Why was it so silent? And such a humid, oppressive silence too. The seashags began to grow uneasy.

"Do you still pursue us?" the Great White Egret asked.

She was swaying on a slender branch. In a sudden movement, she swung her long bamboo staff, decapitating an attacking seashag. Next moment her kung fu warriors were flipping from branch to branch, knocking down the enemy birds.

This was the moment Chieftain Kaka had been waiting for.

"Pokokohua! Taurekareka!"

He sprang the ambush, and his tribe of parrots came out from the holes in the trees. They leapt in twos and threes onto the seashags, riding them like cowboys, forcing them to stall and fall to the ground.

The seashags hissed and bucked trying to dislodge their unwanted riders. No sooner were they grounded than Chieftain Koreke of quails and his tribe came running fast on twinkling legs. They rose with a whirr, aiming themselves like bullets at the downed seashags. Desperately the seashags snapped at their attackers.

The Great Forest was silent no longer. Everywhere, the ground birds were hastening to the attack – all the woodhens, pukeko and kiwi, as well as the pheasants, partridges, rails, coots, crakes, moorhens, pipits, and wagtails.

"It's a trap! Get out while you can!" the seashags yelled.

But once the trap had closed, nothing could save them. The air at ground level was dead, still, without any underwing airflow to provide lift. Even if they managed to become airborne, their manoeuvrability was limited and there was not enough air space to achieve a fast getaway.

"Aue, my canoe is done for," a seashag cried as he clipped a tree and fell to the ground again. All around him the smaller birds were waiting and whirring. Flashing their crimson or green feathers, red or yellow crowns, and orange fronts, they attacked like swarms of brightly coloured avian piranha.

"Ma iro kite," the ground birds shrilled. "We will see the maggots when all of you lie on the ground after the battle."

High in the sky, Kawanatanga finally understood what was happening. He saw his seashag battalions disappearing into the forest canopy and not returning.

"Why didn't you warn me?" he asked Karoro. "The entire forest is a great Venus fly-trap. Re-group! Keep out of the forest! Return to your battle formations!"

Seething with anger, Kawanatanga waited for the restoration of his birds' attack configuration. He counted himself lucky that he still had half his seashag battalion. "The victory can yet be mine," he said.

"So what do we do now, Chieftain Arnie?" Kahu asked.

"We're outnumbered but we're just going to have to fight on with every beak and claw until it's all over," Arnie answered.

Te Arikinui Kotuku stepped forward. "Even ours?" she asked. "No use standing on ceremony. In war, gender doesn't matter, right?"

"Right," Arnie said.

"Here we go then, girls," Kotuku called. She led Huia, Korimako, Parera and Karuwai into the air.

"E, i, kia whakatane au i ahau. Now we play the men –"

At the sight of so much desperation, Skylark began to lose heart. The onslaught was inexorable. Manu whenua were falling from the sky.

"Why is this happening?" she asked Arnie. "Why can't we get everybody out of this mess?" She felt hot tears brimming in her eyes and huddled closer to him.

"You mustn't give up, Skylark," Arnie said.

"I'm not," she replied. "After all I'm still not the kind of girl who goes 'Save me, save me, I'm so helpless.' It just pisses me off that here we are, back in a time before even humans were around, fighting a really crucial war for survival – and we're losing!"

"Attagirl, Skylark," Arnie answered. He loved having an excuse to comfort her so that he could cuddle her under his wing. "Our situation is not all that hopeless. After all, Kawanatanga is only a bird, for goodness sake and –"

Arnie took a sharp intake of breath.

"That's *it,*" he said. "Where's the penknife Hoki sent us?"

"Over there by the box of matches."

"I want you to tie it to my raking claw with some flax. It will give me an extra extension."

"What for!"

"It's a trick I saw in a James Bond movie," Arnie said. "The villainess had a shoe with a blade in the sole. It gave her a longer reach. Who knows? It might work."

"Might work for what!" Skylark asked.

"Look, Skylark," he said gently, "there's only one way to win this battle."

He shook his leg to make sure the penknife was tied on securely. "Ahakoa he iti te matakahi, ka pakaru i a au te totara. Although the wedge is small, by it the totara tree will be shattered."

Before Skylark could stop him, Arnie had taken to the air.

"But where are you going!" she yelled.

"I have to take Kawanatanga out," he called back.

– 4 –

"No, Arnie, wait –"

Skylark cried out after Arnie but he was already beyond hearing. She hated having shown her vulnerability. Now she had to prove herself all over again. Not only that, but she had also come up with a good idea – one just as good as Arnie's and less dangerous.

"Typical, typical, typical," she said to herself, stamping her feet. "It's just typical of a man to assume all the decisions and hare off into the unknown, without even discussing it, as if he were the only one around to save the world. Why do men always think they know best? Why do they always think everything depends on them? And leaving me here, like some ditz, as if I've got nothing better to do than wait for him to get back. Well, think again, pal."

Skylark looked around for the box of matches, picked it up between her claws and whizzed up through the embattled sky to talk to Te Arikinui

Kotuku. The white heron was engaged in a particularly vicious bill-fight with an albatross. The albatross lunged; Kotuku deftly parried and delivered the rapier thrust. The albatross fell from the sky.

"Hello, Skylark dear," Kotuku said. "Enjoying yourself? Is Arnie all right?"

"Arnie's off doing this boy thing. He's gone after Kawanatanga. He thinks that if he kills him the seabird attack will falter."

"Why didn't I think of that?" Kotuku said. "The battle goes against us. Let's hope he can dispatch his job quickly."

"Well, I've got a little mission of my own on the boil," Skylark continued, trying not to let her temper get the best of her. "It's just as good as Arnie's. I need you to help me, together with one of your crack platoons."

"Oh? Is it really necessary to withdraw some of my troops? Everyone's needed at the front. Are you sure it's not just a hen thing?"

Skylark glared at Kotuku. "What do you mean?"

"You're not just doing this to show Arnie you know better?"

"No," Skylark answered. "I'm really serious about this mission. Whose side are you on anyway?"

"Okay." Kotuku nodded, not quite convinced. "But there are no sides in love, Skylark. You're going to have to learn not to win all the time. If you can't do that, try at least to pretend to lose."

With that Kotuku yelled out to The Great White Egret, Te Arikinui Huia, Te Arikinui Karuwai and Te Arikinui Korimako. "Can you all keep the manu moana busy? Skylark and I have something to do, okay?"

"Go," Huia answered, her eyes wide with anxiety. "But don't be too long."

Kotuku signalled eight of her fiercest troopers to follow her. "Kra-*aak*! Kra-*aak*! We are under Chieftainess Skylark's command." She turned to Skylark. "Where are we going?"

"To the offshore islands," Skylark answered.

"Let me through, kik-kik-kik-*kik* –"

Arnie headed for Chieftain Kahu. All around him were astonishing displays of aeronautical prowess as landbirds clashed bills and struck claws in duels across the sky. Arnie himself had fended off a fulmar here, a southern giant petrel there, and had almost been gutted by a particularly dexterous frigate bird, which came up behind him, its long, angular tail opening and closing in a menacing scissor action. Luckily for Arnie a whirling pigeon and a prion intervened in battle between them, and the petrel sheared off, screaming with anger at being denied its kill.

Kahu just had to be right in the thick of it. His beak was covered in blood and when, from the corner of his right eye, he saw what he thought was another seabird closing on him, he whirled and struck with his left claw.

Arnie danced out of the way. "Easy, chief," he said. "I'm on your side, remember?"

"Oops!" Kahu smiled, relieved. "So how goes it, my young warrior from the future?"

"The battle hangs in the balance," Arnie said, "but I fear the worst. Although the odds have gone down, we are still outnumbered. Even if we win, the seabirds from the future are still coming through the ripped sky."

"We will never be taken by the seabirds," Kahu cried, "never. Even if they enslave our world, we will escape to the mountains and carry on reprisals. We will never submit to their rule." Kahu cocked a curious eye at Arnie. "You've got something on your mind, Chieftain?"

"I'm going after Kawanatanga," Arnie said. "But he's surrounded by his own personal guards and they'll kill me before I get within spitting distance of him. Could I borrow you and your hawks for a while? If they can keep the guards engaged, you and I will be able to get past them. If we do that, I want you to engage Kawanatanga, pretend you're wounded, and decoy him away from the battle. Can you do that?"

"Consider it done."

Kahu nodded and gave three piercing whistles. Immediately three of his sons came flying down with the wind. "Yes, Dad?"

"Follow after us," Kahu said. "Leave Kawanatanga to me and Chieftain Arnie, but do what you like with his guards —"

Arnie turned and looped low, looking for Kawanatanga. Kahu and his boys moved in on either side of him. Arnie used his binocular vision, found Kawanatanga and zeroed in.

Further over on the far side of the battle, Arnie saw a slight movement. White feathers sparkled in the sun, drifting down Manu Valley, beating seaward.

In front was a small brown bird.

Was that Skylark?

"Are we being followed? Surely the seabirds are after us."

Skylark was gliding the offshore winds, afraid to look back. If she did so she might see that Kawanatanga had noticed her and Te Arikinui Kotuku slipping away. He would guess what she intended to do and would send seashags, like avenging harpies, to stop her.

"No," Kotuku answered. "We've got away undetected."

Skylark followed the coastline, hoping to blend in with the landscape. Who knew what scouts Kawanatanga might have left on guard of the outer islands? Or maybe Kawanatanga felt so confident of victory that he had left the door wide open. Well, if he did, she intended to fly right through it.

"Are we not going straight to the islands?" Kotuku asked.

"No," Skylark answered. "Not yet."

The islands were like three jagged teeth jutting out of the glistening sea. Skylark recalled Arnie's description of them. The closest island was the late Karuhiruhi's pah, a jagged crown of tall crags and eyries fortified by military parapets and launching pads. The two outlying islands were nurseries, one low-lying with nests scattered over a high plateau, the other high with holes in cliffs for mollymawk chicks. Above and around them, Skylark could see female seabirds wheeling and circling in the bright sky. Now what had Arnie said?

By the way, Skylark, did I tell you there's oil down there? The stuff is just oozing out of the ground.

Okay, so where was it?

Kotuku gave a slight grunt of distaste. She had guessed where their mission was heading. "Just follow your nose, Skylark dear," she said. Already, the sharp acrid smell was permeating the air.

"Oh no," one of young troopers said. "That place is evil. To fly over it is to lose consciousness and fall into the bubbling black mire beneath. Once you land in it, you are trapped there forever. Must we go there?"

"I want to create a diversion," Skylark answered. "But to do it, I need some straw."

"Straw?" Kotuku asked.

"The stuff you make your nests with."

"Would abandoned ones do? There's bound to be plenty of those on the beach."

"Perfect," Skylark said. She followed Kotuku down to the sand dunes. "Can you carry one in each claw?" she asked the troopers. "Okay? lets go."

The mission took off again, heading for the place where the oil seeped and boiled above the ground. Skylark skirted the black sludge, but even from a safe distance the toxic fumes affected everyone as large bubbles of gas were expelled. Caught in one of them, Kotuku started coughing and vomiting.

Skylark saw a small outer pond where landing looked safe. She signalled the mission to go down. "Soak the nests in the oil," she instructed. "Now, take them with you, fly a safe distance away and wait for me. I'll be with you soon."

"Why are you staying behind?" Kotuku asked.

"There's something else I want to do before I join you," Skylark said.

"Then I'll stay with you," Kotuku answered.

"No," Skylark ordered. "I said go, and I mean go."

Skylark's head was reeling from the toxic fumes. "If I can set the oil alight," she said to herself, "the smoke is sure to bring the seabirds back." She tried to light a match. "But what if I catch fire myself, or don't leave enough time to get away?" She tried again. Still no flame from the match. Worse, she felt herself being overcome by the fumes, becoming disoriented. She sank down on the sand, her head whirling. "I've got to do it," she gasped. "I've –"

There was a whir of wings as Kotuku returned. "Why do you think you always need to do things by yourself?" she asked.

"Oh don't get me started," Skylark coughed. "Can you hold this box firmly for me?" She took a match in her beak and struck it against the box. Again the match failed to flare.

"Give it to me," Kotuku said.

She took the match from Skylark's beak and struck it against one of her claws.

Skylark was dumbfounded when it burst into flame.

"Now what do you want me to do?" Kotuku asked.

Skylark threw the match into the oil. There was a small plop as the surface of the oil ignited. A blue flame began to spread toward the main oilfield.

Quickly Kotuku and her troopers dragged Skylark away to safety. When she revived, the oilfield was ablaze.

"Oh, you naughty, naughty girl," Kotuku said.

"Do it now, Kahu –"

"Okay," Chieftain Kahu answered. Leaving Arnie at his high surveillance point, he led his three sons down to engage Kawanatanga and his personal guards. Kawanatanga laughed, contemptuous of Kahu's vain attempts to lock on, claw against claw: "Is that the best you can do?"

Arnie's heart was thudding fast. He was alarmed by the way Kawanatanga was slashing at Kahu. It would only be a matter of time before he inflicted a real blow – and it could be mortal. Before that could happen Kahu finally kicked in with the plan of action, clutched at his left wing, and twisted and fell away from Kawanatanga. Would he take the bait?

He did. With arrogant ease, Kawanatanga left the protective circle of his personal guards. Immediately, Arnie folded his wings and followed in free fall.

"Go go go," Arnie cried under his breath to Kahu. Kawanatanga, more heavily built, was gaining on his prey. Ground zero was coming up at them. Kawanatanga was getting ready to strike. He made his move – and Arnie made his. He dived out of the sun, sounding his charge. *"Kik-kik-kik-kik!* Arnie's small head was erect, his feathers tight and smooth against his body. His eyelids flickered fractionally. He was totally turned on by battle lust.

Kawanatanga was lucky. Startled, he saw the shadow settling above him, sheared off to the right and just managed to escape Arnie's notched tooth. Arnie turned after him, passing Chieftain Kahu as he stabilised.

"Have fun," Kahu said, as he beat his way back to the battle.

Only then did Kawanatanga realise the trap had sprung. But was he worried? No, he felt the thrill of destiny. "Ah, so I face my nemesis again," he said to Arnie. "One on one?"

"You got it," Arnie answered. "You're from the future. So am I. There's not enough room in this world for the two of us."

"Then prepare to meet your Maker," Kawanatanga said. He stretched out his neck and struck. Arnie's raking claw came up, past the striking neck. With surprise, Kawanatanga caught the flash of sunlight and a glimpse of steel. He managed a quick avoiding flick. Even so, the tip of the penknife riffed through his skin. "That's not fair," Kawanatanga complained as he back-pedalled.

Airborne and intent on the kill, Arnie didn't give a shit. "Use it or lose it, Kawanatanga," he said. "Nothing's fair in love and war. Time for you to go. Hasta la vista, baby."

Kawanatanga dived for the sea. The gap between him and Arnie lengthened. Arnie expected him to level out but, instead, Kawanatanga crashed cleanly through the water – and Arnie had just enough strength to pull out of his dive.

"Damn, damn, damn," Arnie swore. "I should have expected that." Obviously, Kawanatanga was swimming underwater. He could be anywhere. If only Arnie could calculate the place where he would come up, he could be waiting for him. "Where are you, you seashag submarine?" Arnie called. Backwards and forwards he flew, trying to locate the wake caused by Kawanatanga's propelling feet. He decided to break to his left.

Wrong choice. Far on the right, Kawanatanga re-surfaced. His powerful wings elevated his body out of the sea and, before Arnie could get a chance to head him off, Kawanatanga was flying towards an area honeycombed by coastal cliffs.

"Catch me if you can."

Arnie gave a cry and wheeled after Kawanatanga. As he did so, he saw wisps of brown smoke on the horizon just above the offshore islands.

Something was on fire.

Skylark must have something to do with it.

"Come on, girls," Skylark said. "Our job isn't over yet."

"So what's next, Chieftainess?" Kotuku asked.

"It's time for our mission to split up," Skylark answered. "We're going to attack the two nursery islands. You, Kotuku, take four of your troopers, set fire to the nests you're carrying and drop them onto the first of the outer islands, the one where mollymawks raise their young in the cliffs. I'll take the other troopers with me to the second island where the seabird mothers nest on the plateau. You must make the drops strategically."

"Strategically?"

"Drop the nests wherever there is dry grass or straw, where they have the maximum opportunity to catch fire and spread. We want both islands to catch fire."

"What about the nests you're carrying?" Kotuku asked. "You've always got to leave the best for the last," Skylark grinned. "They're for the fortress island."

Kotuku wheeled with her squad and, with the oil-soaked nests in their clawed feet, made for the first of the two nursery islands. Galvanised, Skylark led her own squad to the second island. As they approached, female gulls rose up in clouds. Territorial as ever, they had a lot to defend. The entire plateau was dotted with mothers and recently hatched chicks.

"Oh no, all those baby chicks," Skylark said and, for a moment, her resolve wavered. "I don't want to harm you, darlings. All I want is for your daddy seabirds to come flying back to rescue you."

Then she found herself in a birdfight with seven attacking prions. She looked into their dark, furious eyes, and saw their beaks snapping at her. That changed her attitude. "It's either you or us," Skylark decided.

Battling desperately, Skylark and her troopers pushed through the attacking gulls. They were still over the ocean, but gradually they were able to make it to the edge of the plateau.

"Quick," Skylark yelled at the troopers. She struck a match against her claws and set fire to the nests they were carrying. "Make the drop –"

The troopers closed their wings, descended through the gulls and aimed the nests at a patch of dry grass on the plateau. "Bombs away!" A puff, the grass caught fire and began to spread. The flames drove the seabird mothers into an absolute frenzy of anxiety.

Suddenly, there was a dull crack and a flash as a sheet of fire flickered in the sky above the other nursery island.

"How did Kotuku manage that?" Skylark asked herself. Then, "It's the guano," she gasped. "It's a powder keg. The ammonia from the guano creates an inflammable gas. It fuels the fire, reaches flash point and everything goes up." In panic she looked at the flames dancing beneath her. "We've got to get out of here," Skylark cried. "The same thing's going to happen to this island." She took to the sky, urging her troopers to follow quickly after her. Higher and higher they soared.

Flash point.

The air cracked apart. A white sheet of fire leapt through it. The flames and heat sizzled and crackled around Skylark as she flipped and rolled out of danger.

"Well, Skylark dear," Kotuku said when she rejoined the mission, "if the seabird army doesn't hear that and see the flames and smoke, they would have to be deaf as well as blind."

"And we haven't finished yet," Skylark said.

"What the heck –"

Arnie and Kawanatanga had been sky dancing and Arnie was blinded by two bright flashes cracking across the sky. "No!" Kawanatanga cried. Clouds of mother gulls were fluttering above two of the offshore islands. Their wailing rolled inland on the wind.

Arnie tilted his head and, when his sight returned, focused his gaze seaward. What was happening there? Sure enough, he saw a little brown bird and nine white-winged cranes skimming the crystal sea. So it was Skylark after all.

"Brilliant, Skylark," he yelled. "Just awe-some!"

She had caused the seabird army's drive to the inlet to falter. Attracted by the flames and smoke and the screams of seabird mothers, they began breaking off from the cut and thrust of the attack.

"Something else has happened," Arnie realised. A loud chorus of horror and consternation came from the battlefield; it was followed by a tidal wave of air flowing inward from the ocean and up the Manu Valley, as if some huge hole had opened up which needed to be filled. More seabirds fled in terror back to the sea.

"I must return to my army," Kawanatanga said to himself. "My fight with the falcon from the future will have to wait for another day." He sensed an upward ascending wind and turned into it.

Arnie, however, was not about to let him go so easily. He flew into Kawanatanga's path, blocking him. "Going somewhere?" he asked.

"The gods favour you today," Kawanatanga sneered. "Let me pass."

"Like hell I will," Arnie answered. "My elemental mission is to defend to the death, to the last sinew and feather, the manu whenua. You're going nowhere."

"Then die," Kawanatanga said.

He attacked, his eyes alert and feral. But his impatience to return to the battle acted to Arnie's advantage. When he stretched for the kill, his wings dipped and he dropped below his foe. Parrying with finesse, Arnie lifted, mantled, and dropped on Kawanatanga's back.

"Who's going to their god?" Arnie cried. He thrust his legs down and forward, and the talons of his right leg bit, dug, flexed and hooked. Holding on with that leg, Arnie manoeuvred the penknife that Skylark had tied onto his left leg into a strike position.

"Mess with the best," Arnie yelled, "die like the rest."

Too late. Kawanatanga, in a reflex action, lunged forward. He tore away from Arnie's talons – and as he did so, pulled the penknife out of its binding. Arnie watched helplessly as it spiralled toward the sea.

Kawanatanga could only see red. "I have the upper hand now."

Arnie spilled air. His only hope was to put enough space between him and Kawanatanga and, in the interim, think of some strategy to change the balance of power. Alternating gliding with bursts of powered level flight, Arnie made a desperate bid for sea level.

"We'd better hurry," Te Arikinui Kotuku said. They were fast approaching the late Karuhiruhi's fortress island. Already the jagged crown was spearing into the sky, the ramparts rushing up like spears to meet them.

What was it that had happened on the battlefield? Skylark asked herself. She had felt a sudden lurch and kick in the dynamic of the world when the two outer nursery islands had reached flashpoint and dazzled the sky with blinding white light. She wracked her brains for an answer.

"Prepare to repel the royal guard," Kotuku warned. Areta's crack squad of prion marines had taken to the air and were planing across to meet them.

"Keep them busy, will you?" Skylark asked. "I have the two remaining nests. I can do this job on my own."

"Okay," Kotuku nodded. "But don't take too long, will you?" With a cry she and the troopers engaged the prions.

Skylark dived for the ramparts. She was following a hunch of hers that somewhere there'd be a main shaft going right through the middle of the fortress.

"If I plant the burning nests there, I'll be able to bring the castle down – and its Queen and new King with it."

But where was the entrance? She heard a scream and saw one of her troopers fall from the sky. She was wasting time –

Then Skylark saw it. A grand hallway, just behind a tall balcony from which the late Karuhiruhi had saluted his military.

Skylark dropped, and before Areta's bodyguards could stop her, she was in. Three doorways appeared before her. Unsure which one to take, she flew through the left doorway and found herself in the army barracks. Oops. She backed out and, this time, chose the doorway in the middle.

Behind the doorway was a stairwell. A jink, a swerve, another swerve – man, there were so many passageways. From one of them, however, came a lovely updraft of wind, sufficient to fuel a fire. Skylark followed the draft to its source: a large bedroom, palatial, drapings all over the place. Just the ticket. She settled. Put the nests down. Lit a match.

"How dare you enter my royal chambers!" Areta came flying through the room. Screaming with rage, she knocked the match from Skylark's wing. Skylark feinted to the left, then returned as Areta surged past. Her breast feathers pulsing with exertion, she swung sideways and extended her left foot.

Years of royal living had robbed Areta of physical fitness or dexterity. "Oof," she said as she tripped, lost balance, and went head over heels through the air. She hit a wall and fell to the ground, moaning. Her baby son began to wail from its cot.

"This is no time to be sentimental," Skylark said to herself. She struck a second match. Threw it. Its flame caught on the drapings and in a second the whole room was on fire. "Time to get out of here." She braced and leaned forward. Her tail approaching horizontal, she pushed off from the floor, heading for the exit.

Areta gave a demented wail. "My son!"

The fire spread to his crib. Quickly, Areta pulled him out and headed for the secret trapdoor. Below was a passageway leading down and out of the fortress at sea level. Using her last reserves of energy she opened the trap-door with her beak. Before she could take another step with her son, the flames whooshed past her and down the vent.

"You can't get away from me. I have you now."

Kawanatanga had completely forgotten about returning to lead his troops in the war. Taking out this falcon from the future had become his obsession, and he was determined to relish the chase, enjoying the certainty of the kill. He would play with Arnie as a cat does with a mouse. He wanted to feel the ultimate power. "I'm in control, now," he called. "You live at my leave. You will die when I choose to kill you."

His mocking laughter followed Arnie has he hydroplaned across the sea. But was Arnie worried? The longer you play with me, Arnie thought, the longer you'll be kept away from the battle. Nor am I about to give in without a good fight.

Mustering his energy, Arnie dipped between the troughs of the waves, hoping that the pursuing Kawanatanga might make an ill-judged move, be caught by a curling wave and dunked.

No such luck.

Panting with exertion, his velocity decreasing, Arnie decided to make a break for the land. Maybe he could lose Kawanatanga along the shoreline, among the smoke drifting across the sea from the offshore islands. Yes, that was it.

"I'm so bored now," Kawanatanga sighed. He locked onto Arnie and swooped.

Bird turned missile, his wings extended a fraction for the sake of steerage, Kawanatanga hooked and grappled Arnie's left wing in his beak. Holding the wing, Kawanatanga lifted one of his feet and raked Arnie's back, slicing it open. At close quarters, Kawanatanga was ruthless. He had the advantage of a longer bill reach. Another jab and he tore Arnie's shoulder.

"Prepare to breathe your last, Arnie," Kawanatanga said. "I will open you from head to tail. I will rip you apart from head to sternum so that your entrails will spill out and fall to the sea."

In agonising pain, Arnie stabilised with his right wing. His mouth was dry. He was losing consciousness. The blood was running like a river from his wounds. Bobbing his head to clear it and to sharpen his wits, Arnie turned and prepared himself for Kawanatanga's killing thrust. "Game's over," Kawanatanga said. "I've won."

Screaming, Areta turned away from the vent. With that exit closed to her escape, there was only one way out – and that was to ascend the main stairway.

"Don't worry, son," Areta soothed her wailing child. "I'll get you out of here and away from danger."

Away from danger?

Alas, poor Areta. The fire which Skylark had made in the royal nursery had really taken hold. It was roaring down the vent, a huge fiery jet stream travelling through the volcanic composition of the island. Some of the flames flicked through other vents, other veins, other channels, other cracks in the subterranean foundations.

Areta reached the open air with her son. "Thank God, oh Queen, you're safe," a prion royal guard said.

At that very moment, a tongue of fire flicked and reached down and found an underground channel. There, in the channel, streamed a huge river of oil right at the very centre of the fortress island itself.

Areta heard a rumble, deep beneath her feet. "What is that?" she asked the royal guard.

Before he could answer, the island fortress exploded.

"No! Not Areta! Nor the son from whom I am descended –"

A huge ball of fire erupted into the air. It boiled higher and higher, burning a hole in the sky. The heat from the blast hit Kawanatanga, and with it came the smell of death.

"Chieftain Arnie! Defend yourself. We're almost there –" From the corner of his eye Arnie saw Chieftain Kahu and Chieftain Tui coming to his rescue. But he knew they would be too late.

Kawanatanga was like a maddened machine, his eyes bloodshot with anger, his face glowing with insanity.

"You. You –"

He prepared to deliver the death blow.

He slashed with his claws at Arnie, but the thrust went right through without having any effect.

Kawanatanga's eyes popped with puzzlement. "You should be dead."

He slashed again. But he had no claws to slash with. They disintegrated before his eyes.

"What's happening to me?" Kawanatanga screamed as his feet disappeared. Then his thighs. Now his wingtips. And his tail feathers.

Whimpering he grabbed for Arnie.

"Keep away from me," Arnie yelled as he backed away in horror. Kahu and Tui fluttered down beside him. They caught him in their wings.

"Don't be afraid," Kahu said. "This same thing has been happening to many of the seabirds. When the offshore islands started to catch fire, they began to disappear before our very eyes –"

"Kua riro ki wiwi ki wawa," Tui added, awe-struck. "A third of the seabird army has gone. They have fled into the unknown. Kawanatanga will soon join them."

Kawanatanga cried out in fear. "I don't want to die," he sobbed. His body was wavering, blanking out, as if someone was erasing him. He was disappearing piece by piece. Finally, all that was left was his neck, beak and eyes.

"Please save me," his beak said. "The Lord Tane will listen to you –"

At that moment Arnie felt a great surge of pity. "It was either you or me," he said. "Goodbye, Kawanatanga."

Kawanatanga was no longer there. Where he had been was an empty space of air.

Arnie crumpled, sobbing with relief. Of course! Skylark had decimated the rookeries. She had destroyed the descent lines for the seabirds from the future. Without their descent lines, those seabirds ceased to exist.

They, and their leader Kawanatanga, were gone forever.

–5–

"Skylark, you did it," Arnie said.

"Yes, but you're hurt," Skylark answered, concerned. She had just arrived back at the lagoon.

"No, no. I'm fine," Arnie protested. But when he put his wings around her, he winced in pain. His left wing was seeping blood.

"Take Chieftain Arnie down to the lagoon and bathe his wounds," Kotuku said. "And don't forget, Skylark, try not to win all the time."

"Okay," Skylark answered, slightly puzzled at Kotuku's hint.

She supported him down to the water's edge and, while he slipped in, prepared a poultice for him from the mud.

"Did you know what would happen?" Arnie asked as he sat in the lagoon having a birdbath.

"That the enemy would disappear? Of course I did." But as soon as she said the words Skylark understood what Kotuku had been getting at. *There are no sides in love, Skylark. If you can't learn not to win all the time, try at least to pretend to lose.* "But," she added hastily, "you gave me the idea."

"Did I?" Arnie sounded pleased. But before he could ask any more questions, Skylark had changed the subject.

"Okay," she said, "you can come out of the water now."

With a hop and a skip, Arnie flipped out of the lake. He gave a vigorous shake and the water sprayed off his feathers. Skylark began to preen him. From the corner of her eye she saw Kotuku watching and nodding with approval.

A blissful look came over Arnie's face. His eyes rolled up and he gave a deep sigh of contentment. "I could get used to this," he said.

Skylark blushed. Having never been in this position before, she didn't know how to reply. Instead, she concentrated on the job at hand. "That will just have to do for now," she said. "It's a pity they don't have bandages around here. But that's the way it is in birdland."

Chieftain Kahu came flying towards them and broke the spell. Skylark saw that all the manu whenua at the inlet had lifted and were flying in their hundreds back to the cliff face where the sacred tree was.

Kahu bowed low before Skylark and Arnie. "Tui has asked us all to the paepae for the victory celebration. It is my great honour to escort you there." His voice fell to a whisper. "Confidentially, you have saved the day, Chieftain Arnie, and we wish to give you the greatest honour."

"But it's really Skylark who did it," Arnie protested.

It was too late. Kahu had already launched himself into the air. As Skylark and Arnie followed him, Kotuku joined them.

"Do you mind, dear, all this fuss over Arnie?" she asked.

"No, of course I don't," Skylark answered. "I was never any good at being centre stage. Let Arnie take the credit that is due to him."

"You're learning fast. After all, we know who was the real hero of the battle, don't we? I salute you, Chieftainess."

Skylark heard a huge cheer as they approached the sacred tree. Waiting for them on the highest branch were Chieftain Tui, Chieftain Ruru and Chieftain Kawau. Every branch was filled with birds. To one side perched Te Arikinui Huia, Te Arikinui Karuwai and Te Arikinui Korimako. To another were Chieftain Piwakawaka, Chieftain Koekoea, Chieftain Parera and Chieftain Kaka. The Great White Egret and her crack troops from China were sitting on the branch reserved for respected visitors. Chieftain Pekapeka was in his usual place, hanging upside down. On the ground, the wingless birds – Chieftain Weka, Chieftain Kakapo, Chieftain Kiwi and Chieftain Titi among them – were still settling down.

Young women, led by the comely Kahurangi, were dancing and twirling their pois for all they were worth.

"Come down from the sky, noble hero," Kahurangi sang. She was shimmying and bopping in a way that wasn't quite traditional, and totally ignoring Skylark. "Come into our midst and receive your reward."

Huh, thought Kotuku. She's so obvious. Throwing herself at Arnie.

Young warrior birds, winged and wingless, leapt forward in an eye-bulging, muscle-popping haka.

"Ka mate, ka mate! Ka ora ka ora!
It was death, it was death! But now it is life!
It is life . . ."

Gesticulating, they called Arnie, Skylark, Kahu and Kotuku down to the paepae.

"Whakarongo ake au ki te tangi a te manu nei a te ma tui! Tui! Tuituia!" Chieftain Tui called everyone to attention.

A hush fell over the audience. It was spellbinding. Filled with anticipation. Sweet. Tender. Arnie gulped, looked at Skylark and held his wing out to her – and Skylark took it. "You'll be okay," she said. But her heart was thumping too.

Tui cleared his throat. "As the tide of the ocean recedes, so the tide has turned against the manu moana and takes them back to the sea where they belong. Let peace again prevail between us. Let the seabirds be happy where they are. Let them not try again to usurp the border."

Pandemonium erupted. Birds tumbled and flipped in the air. A chorus of jubilation rose among the congregation. Tui lifted his wings to restore order. "Come forward, Chieftain Arnie, saviour from the future."

But Arnie hung back and Skylark rolled her eyes and kicked him in the shins. "Ow! What did you do that for?"

"Go on! Everybody's waiting! This is your moment. It was your destiny to do this. Everyone needs a hero. You are theirs." She pushed him again, and there was nothing else he could do except grin stupidly, kneel before Tui and bowed his head.

"Chieftain Arnie," Tui declaimed, "all the manu whenua thank you for your services. We wish to bestow upon you the highest honour any bird can receive. We dub thee, Sky Rider. Arise, Sir Arnie."

The air rang with thunderous applause. Skylark felt a glow of pride, but couldn't resist teasing him.

"What's it like being Lord of the Wings?"

"I'm getting my own back," Arnie replied. Before Skylark could stop him he turned to the audience. "I thank you all for this honour," he said, "but I am only a garage mechanic from Tuapa. The honour you have bestowed on me really belongs to Skylark."

Arnie knelt in front of her. "You are my lady," he said. "I am simply your knight. You are the wind beneath my wings."

A loud gasp arose from the manu whenua. A cock acknowledging a hen? During the formalities of the marae? Why, it was unheard of.

"Get up, Arnie," Skylark hissed. "Oh please, Arnie, you're embarrassing me."

Arnie remained on his knees, and his gesture spurred Kotuku into action. After all, it had been Skylark who won the battle and been the cause of the manu whenua's victory. Who knows? In her own world she was probably just an ordinary being, but look at her accomplishment in this world. Kotuku flew up to join Tui, Ruru and Kawau on the paepae. A yelp of protest came from Kawau.

"The Chieftainess from the future needs to be recognised, Tui," Kotuku said. "Do it."

Tui harrumphed, startled. He looked at Ruru who, remembering Skylark's leadership at the inlet, nodded. "So many strange things have already occurred to change our world," Ruru offered. "Another will not break the back of the camel."

"Camel?" Tui shook his head. Sometimes Ruru could be so arcane and mysterious.

"Well?" Kotuku prompted.

"Don't rush me," Tui answered, his white collar bobbing. He looked down at Skylark. "Chieftainess, your love for your mother, and for us, has brought you on a journey that many of us would tremble at."

And Skylark let go. All her life she had only counted on herself to get her through anything. She had never asked anything of anybody. She started to weep.

"Although you are just a small and ordinary bird, lacking in extraordinary powers –"

Kotuku stared hard at him with steely eyes. "What do you want to say a thing like that for?"

"–you have nevertheless proven courage beyond the call of duty. Who would have thought such a little bird could do so well? Ka mahi te tawa uho ki te riri. Well done, you whose courage is like the strong heart of the tawa tree."

The manu whenua, swayed by Tui's words, began to whistle their approval. Kotuku hadn't finished with Tui yet. "Not so fast, Tui," she said. "Down on your knobbly knees."

"You're asking too much, Kotuku –"

"Down I say!" Kotuku repeated, her beak slashing wickedly close to his manhood, "or else –"

Tui knelt on the paepae. There was a moment of suspense. Then Ruru went down on his knees too.

"I will not do it!" Kawau said. "I will not –" Ruru tripped his left foot and Kawau crumpled also.

One by one, all the manu whenua followed suit. Silence fell across the Great Forest of Tane.

"We will never forget you, Skylark," Tui said, "nor you, Arnie, valiant champion."

Swayed by the rightness of it all, the manu whenua finally erupted with throbbing cheers and shouted hurrahs. Some surrounded Skylark and Arnie, and many began to fly around the sacred tree. They made of it a whirling bright multi-coloured carousel of joy. Tui warbled with happiness. He saw that the wingless birds were bringing berries and fruits for the feast, and signed for the celebrations to begin. "Eat! Drink! Be merry –"

Right in the middle of it all, Arnie stood up and hugged Skylark in his wings, and was about to peck her – when something shifted, *changed.* Something came like an invisible fist and smashed all the flying birds to the ground. Everywhere birds were falling, and Skylark would have fallen too had Arnie not been there to hold her.

"It's happening again," Skylark said. "Time has begun moving forward."

Acid rain began to fall, burning Skylark's feathers. In alarm, the manu whenua sought deep shelter among the leaves of the sacred tree. Looking out Skylark saw the rugged mountains becoming dusted with hoar frost, glacial ice and snow. The surface split and crumbled, forming a corrugated patterns of hooks and chevrons like an ancient nightmare.

"It's like a nuclear winter," Arnie said.

The wind came up Manu Valley and in a trice all the birds of the forest were doubled, coughing and vomiting.

"What is causing this?" Tui asked.

Skylark searched the Heavens for an answer. She saw a huge ominous stain spreading from the rip in the sky.

"The poisonous gases of our world are affecting yours," she said. "In our Time, our world is polluted. All the gases are pouring through the ripped sky."

"Then it's time for you to go back," Kotuku said. "Although I will miss you, Skylark, your task is not over. Return to your own Time and tell the guardians of the future that they must close the ripped sky – not just against the pollution but anything else that might come through. Who knows? Another leader like Kawanatanga may arise, similarly obsessed with world domination. You did well to come here with your message and to help us. It is time for you to return now with mine."

"Skylark and I should get moving," Arnie nodded. "We've only got a day before the Time Portal closes."

"Must you really go?" Kahu asked, looking for Kahurangi and motioning her to join him.

"I'm afraid so," Arnie answered. "The sooner the better. The sun is sinking and the clouds are lowering."

"What shall we do with the shotgun?" Skylark remembered.

"We'll just have to leave it here."

He was so cross with himself for forgetting the time, and now he was getting worried.

Skylark grinned. "That'll set the cat among the pigeons. What on earth will a future archaeologist think when he comes across this artefact embedded in the Palaeolithic age of birds and dinosaurs."

But Kahu was still persistent. He sidled up to Arnie and whispered to him. "Are you sure you wouldn't want to stay behind with us? You are the son I never had. You could marry and bear me strong grandsons. Now, on that score –" he coughed – "I have a lovely daughter. You've seen the way she looks at you –"

Kotuku cut Kahu short. She took him aside. "You should know better!" She glanced at Skylark and Arnie. "Love doesn't work that way."

"Eh? What?" Kahu asked.

Sometimes, Kotuku sighed, Kahu could be as dumb as. "Kua eke ke taumou na tetahi, kauaka hai raweke," she scolded him. "Do not interfere with those whose hearts are already reaching out to each other. You may be able to see into the corners of the sky, Kahu, but you are blind at seeing into the corners of the heart. Although they do not know it yet, Skylark and Arnie are as if already betrothed."

In a last-ditch effort, Kahurangi threw herself into Arnie's arms, and Skylark herself spoke out. After all, Kahurangi was really pretty and, well, she wasn't Winona Ryder. "Arnie, if you want to stay, then stay. You've done your job, and I'm grateful. I'll be able to make it back by myself."

Arnie's face blanched. He stared at Skylark as if she didn't know anything.

"How can you say that to me, Skylark?" he asked. "Don't turn your face away from me."

"Don't you want to keep on playing the hero?"

"Skylark," Arnie answered, "where you go, I go."

– 6 –

After that, it all happened so quickly. The Runanga a Manu set up a loud trilling farewell. Chieftain Ruru and his owl clan began a series of sad, lugubrious poroporoaki. Skylark found it difficult to leave them.

"We must go," Arnie said. "Now, Skylark."

"Goodbye," Skylark cried. "Manu whenua, live forever –"

She lifted into the air, Arnie beside her, and they began their return journey to the Time Portal.

"Don't look back," Arnie said. Even so, long after they had left the twin mountains, Skylark could still hear the trilling birds.

Kotuku and Kahu escorted them as far as Cook Strait. The Great White Egret and her kung fu warriors also accompanied them, and then turned to the east for their flight back to China.

"It has been an honour," Yu Shu Lien said. "I will take back with me to my side of the world the story of the extraordinary exploits that have taken place, here, at the end of the sky." Then she led her warriors from that place, flying fast and in a pefect V-formation, falling like feathers into the setting sun.

"We must hurry," Arnie said. He turned to embrace Chieftain Kahu. "I have travelled under the protection of the white hawk," he said to Kahu, who couldn't disguise the tears at the corners of his eyes. "When I return to the future, I promise that your descendants will travel under mine."

"Farewell, Chieftainess," Kotuku said to Skylark. "I will carry you in my heart forever."

Skylark and Arnie flew up into the sky. The emotion was too much for Te Arikinui Kotuku. Her filamentous wings glittered in the sunlight as she sang a waiata of farewell:

"Haere ra e te hine, farewell, Skylark, farewell, farewell, oh farewell . . ."

Skylark and Arnie climbed towards the clouds. The sky was empty, oh so empty, and Skylark felt very alone. At least Arnie was there. No matter that she had offered him the chance to stay in this world, she was glad he was coming back to hers. But she was worried about him too. The blood was seeping through the poultice from his injured wing. All the way up, Skylark tried to find thermals, any little upward current that would make flying easier for him.

"As soon as we get home, I'm taking you straight to a doctor," Skylark said.

"That won't do my wing any good," Arnie quipped. "I need a vet. Actually, speaking of home, it's sure going to seem pretty quiet after all we've been through, isn't it? No one will believe us of course, but the things we will have to tell our children –"

"What! Our children?"

"Oh." Arnie blushed, trying to cover his tracks. "Well, after all, one of these days you'll get married and, uh, I'll probably get married, not to each other of course, and um –"

"I'm never getting married," Skylark cut in. "I've been a witness to one bad marriage and I'm not about to repeat their mistake, thank you very much." Having feelings for Arnie was one thing, but marriage? Whoa!

They reached the cloud ceiling and stilled, gaining their breath. "After you." Arnie said.

"No, after *you*. From now on I want to see where your hands – I mean wings – are at all times."

But when Arnie took the lead he began to tire. Skylark was alarmed to see that he was operating mainly on one wing. He was going so slowly she was soon overflying him.

"I'll play leader," she said in the end. It would be easier for Arnie to cruise in her slipstream.

The journey through the clouds was like going through candyfloss. Wisps of it kept breaking across Skylark like a dream. When she penetrated the upper atmosphere the sky was azure blue, beautiful, with tall cloud pillars like castles. But Arnie was lagging far behind and – oh no – the poultice had fallen off, and blood was streaming from his wing.

Desperate, Skylark searched the air and saw that a stratospheric windstream was pouring from the south, a river of cold wind which had come up from Antarctica. She sped back to Arnie and pointed it out to him. "There's our train," she yelled. Once Arnie was in it, all he'd have to do was open his wings and glide.

"Great." Arnie nodded with relief. It wasn't just his wounds that were worrying him. Although the sun was still in the sky, the heat was going off the air and the edges of the cloud cover below were turning crimson. Time too was ticking by. They'd make their rendezvous with the Time Portal only by the skin of their teeth. But where was it?

"There it is!" Skylark cried.

Hanging on the horizon was the Southern Cross. Right in the middle of it was a dark plughole, studded with gem stars. The stars were winking as if the Time Portal was already on a countdown to zero.

"We'd better hurry," Arnie said. Although he was flying on his reserves, the sight of the Time Portal gave him renewed energy. However, rather than let Skylark take the lead again, he surged ahead, sensed what he thought felt like a short cut warming his underwings, and crossed into it. "Oh no," he groaned. It was a cross-thermal, like a rip, and it began to pull him away from the stratospheric windstream.

Skylark flew quickly after him and recognised the danger. "What's happening, Arnie?"

The air was shimmering. The atmosphere was heating up. "There's a rogue thermal cooking," he said. "We're right in the middle of it. We have to get out of it quick, otherwise we'll miss that ride home."

It was too late. With a sudden whoosh, the air around them erupted into rising columns of heat. Arnie tried to stabilise himself but his left wing wasn't up to it and he began to spin away in a giddying ascent.

"Arnie!" Skylark screamed. She soared after him, reached – and locked claws. "Hang on!"

Hydraulic elevator winds exploded all around them. There was nothing else for Skylark to do except maintain her own wing configuration for both herself and Arnie – wingtips upthrust for balance and steerage – and ride with him to the top floor. Sometimes she just couldn't maintain her trim and they would tumble and twirl out of control, the winds trying to tear them apart. But despite the bone-jarring effort, Skylark held on to Arnie for dear life. She knew if she let go he'd be swept one way and she the other, and how would they find each other again?

Not only were they going higher, they were also ascending into a world of ever-increasing blackness. Soon they reached the realm that lay above the sky. A few seconds later they had gone beyond the stars. Suspended above an inky universe, they were swept into the belly of the Primal Night. The light blinked out completely.

When the elevator stopped, Skylark's heart was thundering in her ears. Everything was so pitch black. She couldn't even see Arnie. But she could hear him whimpering as he clung to her: "Skylark? Where's the button that will make the elevator take us back? I don't even want to know where we are –"

Arnie was going out of his mind with terror. He stared wide-eyed into that black universe and began to sob.

"What's wrong, Arnie?"

"The darkness," Arnie whispered. "Have I ever told you that I've always hated the dark? My foster parents used to throw me into a cupboard and lock the door and –"

"Sssh now," Skylark soothed. "Don't worry. I won't let anything harm you."

But Arnie was rigid and sweating with fright.

"I can hear things moving around us," he whimpered. "They've come to get us. Can't you hear? Can't you hear them?"

Indeed, Skylark could hear the sliding, the hissing, the scraping as things with scales slid closer and closer. Quickly, she fumbled among her feathers, found her prize, and struck it. The match flared, a glowing light of comfort. The darkness erupted with screams as creatures with thousands of blind eyes shrank away from the light. When they screamed, Skylark screamed too. But Arnie began to gibber with gladness.

"Skylark! You brought the matchbox!"

"No, but I've got six matches. They're under my wings. So hold on tight, Arnie, because I'm getting us out of here – and quick."

Holding the match in her beak, Skylark closed her wings and hoped that gravity worked here. How could you tell with all this blackness? As she descended, she pulled Arnie down with her. His imagination was still working overtime. When the match went out, he gave a moan of horror and clung to her like a drowning man.

"I dreaded being put into the cupboard," he said. "I used to yell and cry but nobody came to get me out. And then spiders, snakes and scorpions came to crawl all over me –"

"Sssh," Skylark soothed. All around her the whispering had started. The blindworms were talking to each other. *What are these two birds doing here? This is not their domain. Are you hungry, my sisters? When was the last time we ate, my brothers? Oh, let us keep them here with us. Grab them while they are unaware. Do it now.*

Skylark struck the second match.

"They're all around us," Arnie screamed.

"Coming through," Skylark roared. Down and down she pulled him, slashing out at the thousands and thousands of blindworms with their opaque shining eyes. The second match winked out. The creatures made a rush at them, and again Arnie started to blubber.

With quivering hands, Skylark lit the third match. Arnie had grabbed her around the neck and his tight hold was strangling her. "Arnie! Arnie –"

"We're never going to get out of here, never. We'll be lost in the dark forever."

They were still descending, but there were no lights anywhere below them. And the creatures in the darkness were bolder now, coming closer, sliding after them, crowding in, taking away the air.

"Get back! Get back." Skylark yelled.

A few seconds later, she struck the fourth match. Then the fifth.

One of the blindworms came close, pursed its scabrous lips and blew it out.

Now's our chance. Attack, my brothers. Ambush them, my sisters. Cover them, weigh them down, go into all their openings and eat them from the inside. Quick.

"One more match to go," Skylark said. She stopped herself from saying aloud the obvious next question: "And when it goes out, what then?" Instead she started to sing:

"Mud, mud, glorious mud, nothing quite like it for soothing the blood,
So follow me, follow, down to the hollow, and there let us wallow
In glorious mud."

It was such a silly song and Arnie couldn't understand. "How can you sing at a time like this?"

Then he saw stars below.

"We've made it, Skylark!" Arnie yelped. "We've made it!"

The blindworms gave a loud scream of anger. *Grab them. Pull them back. Don't let them get away.* Shuddering, Skylark fought her way through them and plummeted down, dragging Arnie with her.

"I wouldn't want to do that again," she said. She looked around, taking her bearings.

They were back in the universe and way over on the horizon were five stars. The Southern Cross.

"It's still there!" Arnie cried.

"And the Time Portal hasn't closed yet!"

The lights were still winking on and off, on and off.

Before Skylark could stop him, Arnie went hurtling across the universe, dropping through the well of the night sky. All he wanted to do was be in the light.

"Wait for me!" Skylark laughed. Boys were all the same. Always in a hurry. She folded her wings and dived after him. Caught up in the thrill of the chase, she registered only dimly at first a shadow that cut across the Milky Way, looming out from behind Pluto. It looked like a dark island, spinning in space, coming closer and closer out of the luminous sea of the universe. As it approached, the whole universe began to vibrate. Warning bells began to clang in Skylark's head. Something that Lottie had said to her, just before she pushed her out of the plane:

Whatever you do, do not let the winds of the Heavens take you up into the uppermost reaches of the sky. If they do, pray very hard. And, above all, don't go anywhere near the volcanic island where the giant pouakai lives. Otherwise . . .

Skylark's heart began to pump very hard. "Please God, please make the island just a nice, cute, desert island with a palm tree on it and no sign of anything that looks remotely like a volcano, please God –"

But the island wasn't nice or cute, and there were no palm trees in sight. Instead, as it loomed closer it revolved and, as it rolled, a huge volcano loomed out of the dark side. Sometimes in life, luck runs out. As the volcano came closer, Skylark saw something looking over the rim. Two crimson eyes with cruel black facets, watching Arnie as he fluttered erratically by. The face was straight out of *Aliens 1, 2* and *3* and *Alien Resurrection.* With a terrifying rush, the creature slithered and scrambled up to the rim to take a better look.

Skylark's heart stopped. The pouakai. She back-pedalled like crazy, knowing that it had not seen her.

Standing on the crater's edge, the giant ogre bird was a terrifying sight. In that world of birds it was the size of a jumbo jet. Its body was entirely covered with scales. Iridescent colours flashed off its metallic hide.

Through its multi-faceted eyes it calibrated Arnie and locked on to him. Silently it opened its wings, became a tattooed pterodactyl, a terrifying flying alligator. It smelt Arnie's blood and began to hunt.

Terrified as she was. Skylark moved in behind the pouakai. Her brain was racing. What could she do? She couldn't stand by and watch Arnie being eaten, not when they were so close to home.

"Arnie, watch your back!"

But he was too far ahead and did not hear her warning cry. Nor did he know he was being hunted until the raptor was right onto him. He felt its breath, heard its clamouring hide. He turned, saw the pouakai and its cruel wide-open beak, and knew it was certain death.

Then Skylark came speeding from behind the pouakai.

"No, Skylark, don't," Arnie yelled. "Save yourself."

All I have to do, Skylark thought, is lure the pouakai away. That will leave Arnie time to reach the portal. Then I can make a U-turn and join him just before it closes. Yes, that's what I'll do.

She zoomed in front of the pouakai, faced off, and stopped it in its tracks. "Touch him and you're dead."

The pouakai looked at Skylark, astonished.

Skylark darted at it again. "It's me you want, you feathered orange predator creep!"

Arnie saw the danger. The pouakai had an extendable neck. "You're too close," he shouted.

Skylark tried to get away. The pouakai lunged. Missed. It lunged again, its beak opening wide. Missed again. But the third time the pouakai's neck suddenly elongated. There was a sudden jab, a clamp –

Why, that didn't hurt at all, Skylark thought.

The pouakai snatched Skylark in its jaws. Gave a short vicious shake.

"Goodbye, Arnie," Skylark whispered.

"No!" Arnie cried. Helpless, he watched as the pouakai closed its wings, turned and carried Skylark back to its volcanic island. Next moment, like a bowling ball, the island rumbled past him and away, receding into deep space.

Weeping with shock, Arnie limped to the gateway. "Oh, Skylark, Skylark," he cried.

Then he rallied a moment.

Maybe Skylark had managed to wrest herself free of the pouakai's jaws. Maybe, even now, she was speeding across the sky towards him. "Come on, come on, you can do it," he urged through the empty sky.

The lights stopped winking. The portal had run down to the end of its timing sequence.

Skylark wasn't going to make it.

There was a click. The portal started to close. At the last moment, Arnie rolled and went through. "Hoki will know what to do," he said to himself. "She's just got to know what to do —"

Part Four

[CHAPTER FOURTEEN]

– 1 –

And all at once Arnie found himself being buffeted by huge gravitational forces. Some were pulling him one way. Others were pulling him another. Foolishly he tried to stabilise himself; he screamed as his damaged wing was pulled from its shoulder socket and he lost consciousness.

The Southern Cross winked out. Arnie's body tumbled head over heels in a dizzying descent through a primeval sky. Planets whirled around like pinballs. Comets trailed fiery tails from north to south. Above him a worm hole opened, sucking him in. Regaining his senses slightly, Arnie was dimly aware of galaxies being born, of exploding supernovas and golden suns as he rolled and spiralled through a giant intergalactic hydroslide until there, in front of him, was the opening back to the future and his own universe.

Time was ticking past. Arnie saw the sun rising on the green globe of Earth below. It was bathed in auroras of beautiful light – and Arnie was falling again. Another portal opened and he fell through it. He had a minute to get through the inner lock and back into his own Time. On the other side, he saw the Cathedral of the Birds and the seabirds in suspended animation, stationary, in mid-air, frozen at the moment when he and Skylark had escaped them.

Time began to run again – and Arnie dived through. He was in the zone. Bones were spinning in the air. The entire cathedral was collapsing around him. Arnie fell through the inner lock onto the cavern floor. Seabirds were screaming all around him, their wings creating a huge turbulence. He put his hands to his head to protect himself and, closing his eyes, huddled into a ball.

The tumult settled. A huge cloud of dust rolled through the cavern. Arnie waited for the seabirds to shred him. But nothing happened. When he looked up, the seabirds had disappeared as if they had never been there at all. His feathers had moulted and he had turned back to his human form. He tried to move and knew he had a broken shoulder. He scrambled for his clothes, still lying where they'd fallen on the cave floor.

No time to waste, he thought. I've got to get help. I've got to get back to Hoki in Manu Valley. He stood up and blew some of the remaining feathers off his chest.

Someone tapped him on the shoulder. Somebody else shone a torch in his eyes. "Well, what have we here?" one of the rangers asked.

"Looks like a Kentucky fried chicken," said the other.

"Nah, it's Big Bird."

"Whoever he is, all I can say is he's in one big heap of trouble."

– 2 –

When, later that afternoon, the telephone rang at Hoki and Bella's house, Hoki answered it immediately. She'd been waiting.

"Good morning Ma'am," she heard. "This is Sergeant Pilkington. I'm the duty officer at Nelson Police Station."

Hoki dropped the receiver with fright. "Something's happened. Something's wrong."

Bella hurried over. "Yes, Officer?" she asked.

"Would you know of a young man by the name of Piwaka?"

"You mean Arnie? He's my nephew. Is he with you?"

"So you do know him?" Sergeant Pilkington sounded disappointed. "You can verify his identity?"

"Of course I can. What's he done!"

"Well, Ma'am, the doctor's with him. He's got a dislocated shoulder and some other wounds that are being attended to. We're holding him here for questioning. He's being charged with trespassing on government property."

"Is he all right?" Bella asked. "I would like to speak to him please."

"Yes, well, hang on, I'll put him on." Bella heard muffled noises at the other end and then, thank God, Arnie was on the line.

"Arnie? Is that you, nephew? Did you do it? Were you able to get back in time to tell the manu whenua about the seabirds?"

"Yes, Auntie."

Bella smiled with relief. "They did it, Sister!" she called. "They did it!"

Hoki gave a whoop and snatched the telephone from Bella. "Put Skylark on the phone, Nephew. I want to speak to her."

"I can't," Arnie said.

"Why not! What's happened to Skylark?"

"We had an accident. We were attacked and Skylark –"

"Please don't say it, Arnie." Hoki began to tremble. "Please tell me that Skylark made it home with you."

"She's still back there," Arnie said. "And it's all my fault. If we'd come back when we should have, we would both have made it. But I wanted to stay to help the manu whenua win their second battle with the seabirds. Then, when we were coming home, the winds took us right to the top of the Heavens."

"Oh no."

"Skylark got us down again but I lost my cool, Auntie. I really lost it. I was so glad to see the portal that I rushed to get there. That's when the pouakai saw me and came after me. Skylark tried to save me and –"

"Yes, Arnie?"

"The pouakai got her."

Mitch and Francis were on duty at the cliff face when Bella told them the news.

"Only Arnie got back? Not Skylark as well?" Mitch asked.

"No, Skylark didn't make it," Bella answered. "As for Arnie, I'm driving to Nelson to collect him. Will you two be all right while I'm away?"

Mitch turned to Francis. "You go with Bella. I can keep guard myself." Then, quickly, so that Bella wouldn't see his tears, he raised his rifle and began rapid firing at the seabirds. "Damn you," he cried. "Damn you all to hell."

Bella and Francis hit the road with Francis in the driver's seat. Actually, Bella had wanted Hoki to make the trip but Hoki was too distraught, huddled in her chair and moaning to herself.

"Arnie blames himself, but I'm the one to blame," she kept saying. "I shouldn't have let Skylark go up north with him."

"You weren't to know they'd both actually go through the portal," Bella said. "They did that of their own choice and their own free will."

"No, no, no," Hoki wailed. "I could have stopped them. If I'd been there, none of this would have happened. If there was a price to pay, I should have paid it, not Skylark."

"I will not have you talking like that, Sister," Bella said. "You hear me? Do you hear me Hoki?"

The atmosphere in the car was tense. In an effort to break the silence and lighten the mood, Francis switched on the radio: Crowded House. But although he sang along with the lyrics, Bella clearly wasn't up to it, so Francis switched the radio off. Anyhow, he had a question. "Auntie, what did Hoki mean when she talked about the price to pay?"

"You never want to take notice of everything that Hoki says," Bella said, "but sometimes, when the gods have granted you something, a payment has to be made."

"Skylark's the payment?" Francis asked, shivering.

They arrived in Nelson. Bella had to post bail for Arnie before the police would release him into her custody. She was shocked at his appearance. He was trembling, feverish, and although his arm was in a sling and he managed a one-armed embrace, he wouldn't look her in the eyes.

Immediately she had signed for him, Arnie began to go over and over his sorrow. "I shouldn't have left Skylark there, Auntie. When the pouakai grabbed her and took her back to its nest, I didn't go after her and save her. If I had been the one taken, that's what she would have done. I failed her."

"No," Bella answered. "Don't even go there, Nephew. Don't blame yourself."

"But I've got to get back there," he yelled. "I have to try to save her!" He snatched the car keys from Francis, who'd been jiggling them nervously, and stormed toward the carpark.

"Stop him," Bella said.

By the time she arrived at the carpark Francis and Arnie were fighting. Francis had managed to wrest the keys from him, but was nursing a bloodied lip after Arnie socked him in the mouth.

"He's gone mad, Auntie," Francis said, and threw the keys to Bella.

Eyes bulging, Arnie approached her and raised a fist. "Give me the keys, Auntie. Give me the goddam keys."

"No. And if you hit me, I'll hit *you* with my handbag." Bella was cruel. She looked Arnie in the eyes and didn't try to make it sound pretty. "Face facts, all right? Pray very hard that the pouakai broke Skylark's neck as soon as it caught her."

"No, Auntie." Arnie lunged for the keys again. "Skylark may still be alive."

"Not after all this time," Bella said. "You mustn't hope. Instead, you should pray that she had a quick death and not the slow death of being taken back to the nest and being eaten alive piece by piece, or being fed to the chicks. Do you know what the chicks will do with Skylark if she is in the nest? They'll play with her at first, like a cat does a mouse."

"She was alive when I saw her last. Even in the pouakai's beak I could swear she was alive –"

But Bella was relentless.

"The chicks will think it's great fun to have this screaming little plaything running around in their nest. After a while they'll get bored – and one of them will accidentally jab her with its beak and taste her – mmm, yummy. It'll jab her again. The other chicks will join in the fun. Then they'll dismember Skylark a piece at a time. She may even remain conscious for a long while. Hers will not be an easy death."

Such horror took Arnie over the brink. "No. *No.* So help me, Auntie, I'll hit you if you don't give me the keys. I've got to go back. I've got to." Arnie gave a shuddering moan, his eyes rolled up and he collapsed, unconscious, into Bella's arms.

By the time Bella, Francis and Arnie arrived back at Manu Valley, Arnie's condition had worsened. He was drawn, shivering and incoherent. Immediately, Hoki put him to bed and gave him two sleeping pills. Even so, his mind was filled with images of Skylark being pecked at by ravenous chicks and he thrashed about on the pillow.

"Skylark! Save yourself! No, oh no –"

For a long time, Arnie lay sweating and screaming out Skylark's name, over and over again. And every time he did it, Hoki was stabbed with remorse. Then gradually the sleeping pills took effect and he quietened down.

"You mustn't keep on blaming yourself, Nephew," Hoki whispered to him as he drifted off to sleep. "If anybody failed her, it was me. You two were just the messengers. I was the one who really should have delivered the message."

When darkness fell, Arnie was still sleeping. Hoki prepared dinner for Bella, Mitch and Francis – corned beef and mashed potatoes, Mitch's favourite. After dinner the men went to the bach. The women began to do the dishes. Bella could tell that Hoki had something on her mind. "Okay, Sister, spit it out. What's eating you now."

Hoki was in between washing and rinsing. "Cora is being brought out of her coma tomorrow. Somebody has to tell her about Skylark. Somebody has to tell her that Skylark is dead."

"You sure pick your moment," Bella said. "Well, don't ask me to do it. That's your job."

Hoki was holding the remaining plate from the last lot they had bought at The Warehouse. "I can't," Hoki answered. "I loved her –"

"What about me? I loved Skylark too, you know. Just because the chips are down and the going is getting rough, don't you start piking out on me now."

Hoki was too busy blubbering to be able to answer.

"All right, then," Bella said angrily. "I'll do it."

Just to make herself feel better, she grabbed the plate that Hoki was rinsing and threw it on the floor. After all, why should her sister always be the one to send plates to the great heaven for broken crockery in the sky?

The next morning, Bella dressed in her formal black dress and tied a black scarf around her head. Mitch and Francis were up at the ripped sky. Hoki was seeing to Arnie, giving him some soup.

"Everybody's got somebody to get them through this," Bella grumbled to herself, "and I've got nobody. Great." She drove fast down Manu Valley and into Tuapa. "Ah well, better get it over with." She had never felt so lonely in all her life.

Cora was lying in the bed, attached to monitoring equipment. Dr Goodwin and his team were there. So was Lucas, face wan with concern.

"Hello, Bella," Dr Goodwin said. "We're just about to bring Cora back to us, so you're just in time. Isn't Skylark with you?"

"No," Bella said. She didn't know what else to add. In silence she stood next to Lucas and waited.

"I've been coming to see Cora every day," Lucas said. "I've been watching her while she's sleeping. She's so . . . beautiful."

Bella looked at him. This was the time when Cora would spit out the poisoned apple. When Sleeping Beauty would awake. As for the rest –

Lucas's dreams and the restoration of happiness to the kingdom, well, life wasn't that simple, was it?

Dr Goodwin began the induction procedure. He kept checking the monitoring equipment and Cora's vital life signs. A few suspenseful moments passed, before he gave a grunt of satisfaction. "It shouldn't take too long," he said to Bella. "Will you be here when she recovers?"

"Yes," Bella answered.

Dr Goodwin and his team left the room. After a few minutes, Lucas, too, left to go back to work at the garage. "Will you tell Cora I've been here? Tell her I'll be back." Twenty minutes later, Cora gave a deep indrawn breath. Her eyelids began to flicker. Bella took Cora's right hand in hers, not for Cora's comfort but for her own.

"Is that you, Hoki?" Cora murmured.

Cora's forehead was beaded in sweat. Her eyes opened. She was trying to focus, looking around the room, and Bella thought she was looking for Skylark.

"Oh, hello Bella," Cora said.

The moment Bella had been dreading had arrived. "You must be wondering why Skylark isn't here with me," Bella began. "Well –"

"Skylark? Skylark?" Cora was sighing. She started to form the words. "I know about Skylark. Of course she's not here. She's in that other place."

Bella's heart stood still. "That other place? What do you know?"

"I have a message." Cora began coughing. "From Skylark."

"A message?"

Cora's voice was soft and calm. "She's trapped in that other place. You know, that place where she and Arnie went. It's big, dark and horrible. And a huge bird, it kind of looks like Godzilla, a giant ogre bird, has taken her to its nest. There are eggs there. Skylark's all wet and shivering."

"But she's alive?"

"Yes. Her message is 'Mum? Will you tell Hoki and Bella to send somebody to get me?'"

Bella gave a hoarse cry.

"I haven't got a bloody clue what's going on," Cora said. "But when you see her will you tell her that –"

"That?"

"I know what she did for me. Tell her thank you and that –" Cora began to drift away into unconsciousness – "I love her."

– 3 –

The pouakai clamped its jaws around Skylark. She kicked and screamed, trying to wriggle loose. "Let me go, you big bully –"

The pouakai was amused at first but then became irritated. It gave a sudden flick, not quite enough to break Skylark's neck but enough to render her senseless, and she fainted.

Skylark had no idea how long she was unconscious. When she revived she was so disoriented she didn't know whether she was dreaming or awake. Had she really become a bird and flown through the gateway all the way back through Time to help the manu whenua? Nah, get real. Surely, she was still dreaming.

"In which case," Skylark said, "it's time to wake up. On the count of three I'll awake in Tuapa and I'll make Mum a cup of coffee and –"

Skylark counted, one, two, three, but nothing happened. She went to pinch herself. Oh no, where were her hands and fingers? What was she doing with a beak, feathers and claws?

It was dark. It was raining. Lightning crackled overhead. At every flash her memory came back to her. The pouakai had captured her. It had brought her back to its nest on an island orbiting deep space. The nest was conical, as big as the Auckland Skytower, and attached to the inside of a volcanic rim. The pouakai had woven the nest out of thorny branches and plastered it over with mud.

"I'm not dreaming after all." Skylark squinted her eyes and wiped the rain away. Where was the pouakai? Flying somewhere looking for other food? The lightning flashed even whiter and Skylark saw, far on the other side of the nest, three giant eggs.

The horror began to sink in. I've seen a movie like this, she thought. The pouakai is like the Mother Alien. Soon her eggs will hatch, crack apart, and horrible things with great big razor teeth, snapping jaws and dripping in goo will come out – and I'm their first meal.

Whimpering, Skylark scrabbled around looking for a way out. The sides of the nest were high and impenetrable and, when she tried to climb over them or even fly, she found that she had been tethered to the ground with a piece of twisted rope. After repeated attempts she fell back. She tried to climb again, grabbing at the mud plaster. The mud came away, revealing that skulls and bones of previous victims had been used to seal the nest.

Screaming, Skylark scrambled away. Lightning forked overhead and she saw that the entire nest was latticed with bird bones. For a while she went completely berserk, pecking desperately at the rope, yanking at it with her beak and trying vainly to unpick the knot. She realised she was losing her head.

"Skylark O'Shea," she said sternly to herself. "Calm down, get over yourself, and think this through. The worst case scenario is that you'll die. Actually, you should be dead by now, but you're not." That thought made her feel better. "Where there's hope there's life," she continued, echoing the kind of optimism she'd always scoffed at in her mother. "So although your situation is desperate, it's not entirely hopeless . . . is it? Do you really intend being anyone's dinner? No you don't –"

The thought of her mother had jolted her. An idea slipped into her brain.

"I'm not going to give up without a fight," she said.

She sent her message to Cora.

"So she's alive –"

Overcome, Hoki swayed and her eyes filled with tears.

"Could be," Bella answered. But she was having serious reservations about what Cora had told her. "Maybe Cora was just dreaming. Can we rely on what she saw or heard?"

"Yes," Arnie yelled. "After all, I managed to get a message to Auntie Hoki from that place, so why can't Skylark?"

Still feverish, he leapt out of bed and began pulling a shirt over his head and shoulder sling. He was hyper, going out of his tree, talking to Skylark as if she could hear him: "You have to hang in there, okay? I know how alone you feel. We've been through so much, so just hang on 'cause I'm on my way –"

Bella tried to restrain him. "Just where do you think you're going?" she asked as he headed for the door.

"I'm on to it," Arnie answered. "Don't you see? I know the way. I've been before. I know where she is. I'll go through the portal and –"

Bella looked at him as if he was crazy. "Haven't you forgotten something?"

"Don't try to stop me, Auntie,"

"The portal doesn't exist any more, even if it did, how could you fly with your shoulder like that!"

Arnie's face paled. He slumped against the door. "The portal is closed? What's wrong with my shoulder?" His face became dark with despair. "There's got to be another way in. We can't just leave her there."

A long silence fell. Then Hoki gave a deep gasp.

"What is it?" Arnie asked.

"Actually, there is another entrance to the past," she said. "And there is another way of getting back, another way of putting this right."

Bella froze. She folded her arms. "I don't want you to talk about it or even think about it," she said.

Arnie's hopes mounted. "What is this other way?"

"Through the ripped sky, of course," Hoki answered. "The same way as the seabirds have taken to get back to the past."

"I'll go that way then," Arnie said.

Hoki shook her head. "I know you really want to go, Nephew, but you can't. You haven't got a chance. And there's another problem." She slid away and went to the sitting room. When she returned she held in her hands the Great Book of Birds. She opened it at Revelations Chapter Four Verse Six:

"Verily, all that is written will come to pass. The battle of the birds will be fought again. And the outcome will hang in the balance, and many birds on both sides shall perish or be sorely wounded in the fight. Then will be heard the voice of the Hokioi and her flight across the sky –"

With a cry of fear, Bella pushed the book out of Hoki's hands and it fell to the floor.

"Forget what the book says," she yelled. "The option you're considering just won't work, Hoki, and you know it. I refuse to discuss it with you."

"You can't bury your head in the sand like an ostrich," Hoki answered. "Skylark has to be rescued and there's only one way to do it."

"Would someone explain what you two are talking about?" Arnie interrupted. But Bella and Hoki were too busy arguing to hear him.

"If there was a ninety-nine per cent chance that Skylark was still alive, yes," Bella said. "But it's been almost two days since Arnie last saw her. If she wasn't dead then, she must as sure as eggs be dead now."

"Listen to me, Sister," Hoki insisted. "As long as that one per cent chance remains, we have to risk it. And the best chance we have to rescue Skylark lies with the flight of the Hokioi."

"The Hokioi?" Arnie asked. Thank goodness his two old aunties heard him this time.

"In the old days," Hoki explained, "when the Lord Tane made the Great Forest, not all the birds left the Heavens to come down to the Earth. Some stayed in the upper reaches of the Sky. They became birds of immense supernatural and psychic power. You encountered one of them when thermals carried you too high."

"The pouakai –"

"The giant ogre birds, like the pouakai or his cousin the poua, circumnavigate the world," Bella cut in. "Some of them have sworn eternal vengeance against man for what he has done to the world. If hungry or enraged, they have the awesome power to devastate entire territories. They prey on man and devour him wherever he settles."

"This doesn't explain the Hokioi," Arnie said, his patience wearing thin.

"I'm coming to that," Hoki continued. "The realm of the supernatural birds can only be negotiated safely by supernatural birds themselves. Whoever goes through the ripped sky has to be one of these birds, one who is not only able to survive the perilous winds and currents of space, but also has the leave of the manu Atua, the God birds, to whom the Lord Tane entrusted this realm. The Hokioi is one of these birds sanctioned to travel through the upper sky realm. It was known as the Spirit Messenger of the Gods and of Immortal Life."

Arnie's face set with determination. "Then we have to find this bird."

Hoki looked at Arnie as if he was dumb.

"You're looking at her," she said.

Darkness, rain and forked lightning.

On an island rolling through deep space, Skylark was busy trying to break free of her tether. She was chattering away, talking to herself, and it helped her because it made her feel as if she wasn't so alone. Mind you, some of her dialogue was inane, but who else was around to hear her? "No pain without gain," she said as she hopped the length of her tether, her sharp eyes looking for some weakness, some flaw. She found one: a spot where the tether was frayed and most thin, connected by seven strands loosely bound together. "Aha! When one door closes another opens." Oh, if only she had that penknife! There had to be something else she could use. She found it: the sharp edge of a long curved beak, the remnant of some earlier meal enjoyed by the pouakai. "Waste not, want not," she said.

At the same time Skylark noticed a small subsidence in the floor of the nest. She hopped over to investigate: Yes! Scraping away with her tiny feet she saw that with a little bit of work she might be able to squeeze through.

If I can't go over the top or sides, I'll go through the bottom, Skylark thought to herself, but first things first. She went back to the curved beak and looked at it intensely. "I know you belonged to a bird which didn't escape the pouakai," she said. "Please help me to do what your owner couldn't."

Skylark took the beak in hers and began to saw. "Time to get down and dirty," she said. Her progress was agonisingly slow. She had no idea how long it took her to cut through one of the strands. "Six to go –"

An ear-splitting shriek interrupted her work. She yelped and ran for cover. From out of the darkness came the pouakai. "Fee fi fo fum," Skylark said. "I'd forgotten how gigantic you were." As the pouakai circled the nest, Skylark saw a clutch of wriggling blindworms in her claws and remembered the dark uppermost Heavens. "So that's your happy hunting ground."

With a dizzying swoop, the pouakai glided down to the nest. She flapped her wings, causing a swirling whirlwind, stalled and landed. Brought back to reality, Skylark managed to saw through another strand. Five strands left. But she was as firmly tied as ever.

The pouakai released the blindworms into the nest. She didn't bother to tether them as she had done Skylark. After all, they had no wings and they were blind. The pouakai cocked her head and checked out Skylark. She gave a low growl and opened her beak menacingly – and her breath was absolutely foul. "You need to see an orthodontist immediately," Skylark said. The pouakai gave a menacing cluck, hiss and rattle.

Close up, she was terrifying. Her face was massive. The eyes were black slits surrounded by red orbs, like a devil's, and surmounted by triangular patches of white. She had large ear orifices. Her razor-like beak was conspicuously long and covered with horny plates; at its base were quill-like whiskers. All this was surmounted by a crest of three crimson horns.

"Pretty, aren't you?" Skylark murmured.

The pouakai seemed to be sensitive to aspersions about her looks. She opened her beak and gave Skylark a closeup of her sharp teeth.

Take a look, little one.

Skylark backed away. "Okay, okay, I get the message," she said. Satisfied, the pouakai began to preen herself, as if she had all the time in the world. No reason to hurry.

Around the pouakai's throat was a collar of bright red feathers. Her plumage, black and bronze, looked like reptilian scales, shaggy, falling down and around her monstrous body to muscular hindquarters. The wings were awesome, spreading out like knives, black-tipped as daggers and diaphanous as a bat's. Her legs and feet were heavy and powerful. When she moved her tail swished, long and tapered like a dinosaur's.

"You're an alien queen all right," Skylark said, a hint of admiration and awe in her voice. "No doubt about it."

Skylark's attention was taken by the blindworms. They knew they were in deep trouble. There were twelve of them, shining, luminous, wriggling and wrapping themselves around each other, trying to be the one in the middle.

Dear oh dear oh dear, my sisters, what have we come to? Dear oh dear oh dear, my brothers, is there no way to escape our unhappy fate?

"No," Skylark sighed. "We're all in the same basket."

The blindworms heard Skylark and came sliding over to her, sniffing her with their nostrils.

You're not one of us! What are you?

"Another burger for chicken dinner," Skylark answered. "Something nice, warm and tasty for the pouakai's little kiddies."

Is it that bad, stranger?

"Yes," Skylark answered, "and it's just about to get a lot worse."

From the corners of her eyes, she had picked up a slight movement. The pouakai noticed the movement too. With a cry of joy, she waddled over to the three eggs, the nest creaking and quaking at her footfalls. She inclined her head, listened and purred.

From one egg after another came a faint peeping. The first egg developed a hairline crack as the chick inside jabbed at the shell and prised it open. Stretching and cracking noises followed, and the chick emerged, squealing, as it broke through the albumen and blood of its amniotic fluid. The second chick came too, a nightmarish vision of pink pulsing flesh through wet congealed down. With a scream, the third chick smashed open its shell and fell out, bawling, thrashing its feet and wings. Eyes not quite open. Ugly as.

The blindworms went crazy. They smelt and heard the chicks and knew their goose was cooked.

Something is hungry, sisters. Something is squealing for food, brothers.

Sniffing the air, the baby chicks advanced on the blindworms. Skylark watched them coming and, seeing that they were only interested in the very interesting white wriggling worms, sidled away into the shadows. As for the blindworms, they acted as if they were rabbits and a python was in the room. They simply gave up.

Ah well. Ho hum. Fiddle dee dee. What goes around comes around.

They knew they were done for.

Watching from the sideline, the pouakai gave a lightning swift downward kick and decapitated one of the blindworms. Its stomach and guts cascaded in a steaming heap before the three chicks.

Yes, babies, food.

The chicks pounced on the dead blindworm and demolished it. Horrified, Skylark pressed herself further into the dark. Was that how she would be eaten? Whimpering, she began to saw again at the tether. Another strand snapped. Four to go.

The three chicks were yelping and screaming at the mother pouakai.

More, Mummy, more.

The pouakai shook her head. Nonchalantly, she picked one of the other blindworms up and threw it at the feet of her chicks.

Get your own dinner, children.

The chicks scrambled after the blindworm. They gave it some tentative pecks.

Mmmn, yummy.

In a frenzy, the chicks shredded the worm to pieces. The nest became a butchery site. The chicks exploded into violence, hissing, spitting, crashing and fighting each other over the other blindworms. Very soon, another six blindworms were massacred. Then one of the chicks saw Skylark.

What have we here? Dessert?

In space, nobody can hear you scream.

Back in Manu Valley, day had ended and Mitch and Francis had gone to Tuapa for the night. Hoki knocked on the door to Bella's room. Bella had stormed off in anger, refusing to even think about Hoki going back to rescue Skylark. When she opened the door she was grim-faced.

"I should never have told you what I heard from Cora," Bella said. "It's only given you and Arnie false hope. Look at you both: away with the fairies. There's another way. I'll go. I'm stronger than you –"

"But when you change," Hoki answered, "you'll only change into a bellbird. I'm the one who will become the Hokioi. I'm the one whose name is imprinted with the genetic code of the Hokioi. I'm the one who can fly in the upper Heavens. It looks like all my pigeons have come home to roost, ne? I cannot escape my destiny. It's already written, Sister. You and I always knew this day might come."

"Not like this, though," Bella said. "Not with this crazy brainless foolishness you seem insistent on carrying out. Look at you. A cripple who has to use walking sticks to get around."

"Thanks for the vote of confidence."

"You're so hopeless, Hoki," Bella continued. "When it comes to physical things, you haven't a show! If you can't walk without aid, how are you going to be able to fly!"

"I know what you're saying, but –"

"You've never been able to do anything right. Sometimes I wonder whether you know which side is up."

"You don't have to rub it in."

"You're dead in the water even before you start. No, Sister. No. I won't let you do it. No."

From his bedroom Arnie heard the two women arguing. He got up to find out what was happening and was just in time to see Hoki walking out of the house followed by an irate Bella.

"Does everything I say always go in one ear and out the other?" Bella yelled.

Arnie went after them.

Outside, the sky was already turning red from the sunset. Hoki had paused at the back of the house where there was an old armchair under some apple trees. Arnie caught up with his aunties there.

"What's going on?" he asked.

Hoki had that look on her face. "Bella has been trying to persuade me not to go," she said, "but I have no alternative. I'm going." She took a deep breath. "And I'm leaving right now."

"Now?" asked Bella, taken aback. She looked at Arnie as if it were all his fault.

"By my calculations, the pouakai's island is due to come orbiting back towards our planetary system tonight. I need to be waiting for it when it is closest to earth. If I miss it, there won't be another chance for Skylark. It's now or never."

"You haven't heard a word I've said, have you," Bella said, compressing her lips. "Well, go then."

"No word of love, Sister? No word of good wishes?"

"Why should I waste my time wishing you well," Bella shouted, "when all the odds about Skylark being alive and your chance to get her and return are so slim? She can't have lasted this long. You're going on a fool's errand –"

"I'm not giving up until I see Skylark's body," Hoki answered. "If you won't give me your blessing, I'll go without it. Goodbye, Sister."

She began to walk towards the cliff path. Bella turned her back and folded her arms.

"Aren't you going to see her off?" Arnie asked.

"And condone this madness? No."

"Hoki will be all right, won't she?" Arnie persisted. "She and Skylark will get back, won't they?" Waiting was a torture to his loving heart.

His question went right to the crux of the matter. Bella began to shake with emotion.

"Although the Great Book of Birds prophecies this flight," she wept, "it ends at the point where Hoki begins her journey. It doesn't tell us what happens next –"

"That settles it! I'm going, not her. Damn it, I'll take her place."

Bella slapped him hard. The welt reddened his cheeks. "Wake up, Nephew," she screamed. "Nobody should go back there! Not even Hoki."

Hoki was halfway up the cliff face. All around her the sky was deepening into crimson.

"Oh, how's she going to get on?" Bella wailed. "I'm the one who has always done the dangerous stuff. I'm the one with the legs. She's always been the scaredy-cat. And her sense of direction is hopeless! Even when there are signposts she often takes the wrong turning. I tell her to go left and she turns right. Sister! Sister! Wait!" Bella and Arnie started to run. Up and up they raced. The sun was going down into the sea. The dusk chorus was beginning. They were going to be too late. "Sister," Bella cried again.

Hoki was standing at the edge of the cliff. She was chanting an incantation.

"E nga manu Atua o Te Wao Nui o Tane
Homai ki ahau te mana, te ihi, te wehi
Oh God birds of the Great Forest of Tane,
give me your strength, your dread, your powers . . ."

At her words, the manu whenua responded with a frenzied song. It came strange and wild from the north, south, east and west. It seemed to swirl around Hoki like a whirlwind.

"Equip me with strong wings for my journey
fighting claws, a fierce beak, acknowledge me
Let the Hokioi's voice be heard again in the skies
The Spirit Messenger of the Gods themselves . . ."

The whirlwind and the birds' chorus reached a crescendo. Bella and Arnie put their hands to their ears. Far to the north Birdy clutched her heart with anticipation, knowing something profound was happening. In the east, Joe felt the wind begin to blow and realised that the time had indeed come for the flight of the Hokioi. Down in the south, an image came into Lottie's head of an old woman ready to embark on her last journey.

"For the last time," Bella wept, "please don't go, Sister."

The birdsong stopped. Just like that.

In the Manu Valley, nothing except the wind. The sunset blossomed red and glorious, like a benediction.

"You're such a softy," Hoki said to Bella. "I knew you would come to say goodbye." She gave a brave smile. Leaned forward. Gulped at the sight of the valley far below. "It's sure a long way down," she said.

Before Bella and Arnie could stop her Hoki stepped over the cliff and was falling. The wind was flapping at her black gown. Her black scarf came loose and fluttered away like a ribbon. She was holding on to her walking sticks for dear life.

"She's going to kill herself," Arnie cried out, alarmed.

The ground was rushing forward. "Heeelp —" Hoki screamed.

"Oh my giddy aunt!" Bella sighed. She cupped her hands to her mouth and shouted. "Open your wings, you stupid idiot!"

Arnie saw Hoki spread her arms. And that's when it happened. All that was falling was Hoki's clothes, shoes, scarf and walking sticks. But where was Hoki? Arnie heard a screech of triumph, and flying out of the neck of

Hoki's black gown came a gorgeous dark bird. The bird whistled and sang and soared in the morning currents.

"Is that Hoki?" Arnie asked.

"Yes," Bella said. "Can't you recognise her?"

Sure enough, when Arnie took a closer look he saw that one of the bird's legs was withered.

Hoki began to dive bomb her audience, whistling and giggling at every pass. "I could get used to this!" She came in for a landing on Bella's right shoulder, stalled, made contact, almost slipped off but managed to steady herself on her good foot. She began to preen Bella's hair.

"Hmmn," Hoki said. "Guess who didn't wash behind her ears this morning."

Bella reached up to Hoki and enclosed her in both hands. She brought Hoki face to face so that they were looking at each other eye to eye.

"Oh what's the use," Bella sighed. "You always do exactly what you want to! Are you ready for your great journey, Sister?"

"Yes," Hoki warbled.

Bella was weeping, rubbing her cheeks against Hoki. "I love you, Sister."

"Stop crying or else I'll get too waterlogged to fly," Hoki said.

Bella smiled sadly. "Now there's an idea." She kissed Hoki on the beak, took a deep breath, opened her arms and, shouting to split the sky, launched Hoki into the air. "Go now."

Hoki flew up to the ripped sky, stilled, waited for her moment, then went in – and vanished.

– 4 –

Yes, darlings, the mother pouakai said, *pudding.*

Cheeping, stumbling, cawing and slashing at each other, the pouakai's three chicks advanced on Skylark. But they were hesitant, because unlike the blindworms this strange bait darted across to the other side of the nest. "You bite me," Skylark threatened, "and I'll bite you right back." The baby chicks looked up at the mother pouakai, puzzled. She purred to them.

Food is like that, children. Sometimes you have to catch it on the wing.

Reassured, they started to hunt Skylark again. "Stay away from me you skinheads," she said. The baby chicks were thrilled at the fun of it all, especially when the strange bait again leapt over their heads and flew out of their reach. And when the strange bait did it a third time, they chortled with glee. What a great game this was.

It wasn't a game to Skylark. Whimpering, with heart pounding, she resumed sawing at the tether. Another strand gave way. Three left. But how much time did she have left? In desperation, Skylark looked up at the mother pouakai. "If I promise not to eat another Kentucky fried chicken," she asked, "will you let me go?"

The pouakai roared with anger.

"I didn't think you would," Skylark said.

Skylark wiped at her tear-stained face with a wing. The baby chicks were right on top of her now, glaring down. One of them made a sharp jab with its beak and Skylark yelled in pain.

"Do that again and I'll sock you in the eye," she yelled. The pouakai pushed the chicks forward irritably.

Why are you afraid, babies? It's just a little brown bird.

The chicks advanced once more. Skylark tried to get away. The tether would not stretch any further. "This is it," Skylark said to herself. "Bye bye world. Goodbye Mum." She closed her eyes tight. Who wants to see Death approaching? As she did so, however, she seemed to see Cora tossing and turning in her hospital bed. And what was Cora saying to her?

"Skylark O'Shea, you've forgotten everything I've told you, haven't you! A girl should never leave home without a Broadway tune in her purse. A show tune is just the thing when you're in a jam! Whenever that happens, sing, Skylark, sing."

Sing? What a joke. Or shall I give it a try anyway? Skylark thought.

She cleared her throat, opened her beak and remembered some of Cora's dreadful Broadway show music.

"The hills are alive with the sound of music,
With songs they have sung for a thousand years . . ."

The notes were like a string of pearls, cascading across the velvet sky. *I didn't realise you had such a terrific voice,* Arnie had said. The notes shone, gleaming with lustre and loveliness, carrolling out of that terrifying desolate place. *When you open out the throttle Skylark, you can really soar.* But was it working? No. The chicks were on top of Skylark again, and this time there would be no stopping them.

But what was this? The mother pouakai began a throbbing growl. The song seemed to have penetrated into the dark maze of her brain, whizzing across the synapses and short-circuiting all the usual connections until it hit the pleasure centre in the left hemisphere. There, a small explosion sent warm signals back to the mother pouakai. Her eyes widened with joy, she swatted her chicks away and peered down at this surprising little bird. Swaying to the song, she opened her mouth:

Da heels ar aloiv wiv da sarn or moozeec . . .

The voice was like a trumpet, brazen and baritonal, and so powerful that it knocked Skylark backwards. What had happened? Some long-ago writer had said something about music having the power to soothe the savage beast. Was that what was happening?

Yup and yessirree. "Oh Mum, it worked," Skylark sobbed, frantic with relief. Bewitched by the beauty of Skylark's voice, the mother pouakai gathered her chicks to her and prodded Skylark with a wicked claw.

More! More!

"So you want a monster karaoke sing-along, do you?" Skylark asked. "Okay, you've got it."

With that, she began going through her repertoire of show songs. From *Sound of Music* she went on to *My Fair Lady.* The chicks imitated their mother, bobbing their heads and swaying along with the words. It was weird. It was awful. Like the mother pouakai, they opened their throats, trying to imitate Skylark's sounds. What came out was a cacophony of brays, yells, trills and howls.

"Orl oi wont ees a woom sumwear
far awoiy frum da coal noit ear . . ."

The mother pouakai gave a gasp, crowed with joy, decapitated one of the last remaining blindworms and fed it to the chicks.

Sweeties, aren't you just clever little things?

Skylark took the opportunity to saw through the tether again. Only two more strands to go, and then a sudden dash for that hole in the nest, and –

She was exhausted, but she knew that if she stopped singing she was a goner. From *My Fair Lady* she went on to *Oklahoma,* thankful at last for her mother's musical tastes. When the chips were down, Mum's show songs were coming in handy after all.

Except that while Skylark knew the tunes, she didn't know all the words. "Oh Mum, why didn't I listen to you more closely when you were singing your songs? I promise you if I get out of this alive I'll pay more attention and never laugh at you again." Ah well, she'd just have to make up the lyrics.

Did the mother pouakai notice? A flicker of suspicion shone in her eyes, and she showed Skylark her fanged teeth.

Worse was to come. Skylark was ready to drop with fatigue and she was running out of tunes.

She had no choice but to repeat herself. The mother pouakai cuffed her sternly with her sharp claws – and, oh no, some of her high notes went sour, curdled and decidedly flat. The pouakai became very cross.

You'll have to do better than that, dearie.

Quickly Skylark sawed through the last two strands of the tether. Just in time. The mother pouakai recognised "Do-re-mi", and as everybody in the whole world knows, there are only so many repetitions of that song anybody can take. Ruthlessly and with glittering eyes, the pouakai nodded to her chicks.

Party's over, babies. Go get her.

The chicks were ravenous. Hopping, snapping and half flying they rushed over to Skylark for the kill. With a cry, Skylark lunged out of their way. The tether snapped and she was free. The mother pouakai spread her wings to stop the little brown bird from gaining flight, and looked bewildered to find herself outwitted. Where had she gone?

There! Wriggling down through the floor of the nest.

I don't think so, sweetheart.

The outraged pouakai started to demolish the nest. She elongated her neck, pulling the thatching of bones, mud and branches apart. At every beak thrust she got closer and closer to Skylark.

"Help!" Skylark cried. Screaming for her life, panting and crying, she burrowed further down. The thorns and protusions of the nest scratched at her, tearing her feathers and skin. But she kept on pushing deeper and deeper until she was falling out of the bottom of the nest. Seconds later, she hit a small outjutting ledge. The fall winded her but she managed to crawl into a small crack. Gasping for breath, she manoeuvred herself inside. She heard the pouakai approaching. Maybe if she flattened herself against the wall, her protective colouration would save her from being seen.

No such luck. The pouakai's very angry eye looked into the crack. Blinked.

Come out of there, you little bitch.

The pouakai's wicked beak slashed back and forth, trying to winkle her out.

And Hoki was falling through a crimson sky.

Seizing the opportunity, a few seabirds sneaked through with her. As soon as they were on the other side, fierce revolving winds swept them down an elevator shaft to the world below. But Hoki was swept in another direction, into a part of the sky where water spouts were being created. The forces at work were cataclysmic, thunderous.

"I haven't even got a pilot's certificate, yet," Hoki wailed.

The water spouts coiled and spiralled like liquid snakes across the sky. Every now and then, one would crash into another and a bigger water spout was formed from the collision. With alarm, Hoki saw two headed her way.

"Time to get out of here," she yelled.

She snapped her wings close to her sides and plunged like a sky diver – she'd seen people doing it on television and hadn't realised it was so much fun.

A few seconds later, all light disappeared. Hoki increased her wing surface, stabilised, and found herself approaching a gateway to a region of absolute and awful blackness. Her first test was about to begin.

"I am at the threshold of Te Kore, The Void," she said to herself. "The place where all things began. The Great Abyss at the beginning of Time."

The gateway was ebony. Carved spirals, black on black, covered the gateway with curvilinear petroglyphs. Hoki's blood ran cold as she saw three awesome manu Atua, guardians of the gateway, coming to confront her.

Who are you, you who dares to trespass the highest Heavens? The three God birds were six storeys high, heavy bodied with contorted mask-like heads and three-digit hands and feet.

"I'm Hoki," Hoki answered, scared as hell. "I'm fifty nine, my address is Post Office Box 2, Tuapa, my social security number is –"

The manu Atua computed Hoki's response. Their faces swivelled towards her, examining her closely. Their paua eyes glowed with supernatural light, and Hoki knew that her answer wasn't acceptable. But the God birds were forgiving.

The correct answer is that you are the Hokioi, the Spirit Messenger of the Gods. But we know you like to play tricks on us, favourite bird of Tane. Pass by.

"Sorry," Hoki answered. "I won't do it again."

Bowing and scraping as she went through the gateway, Hoki dropped through Te Kore. How long her descent took her, she didn't know. It could have taken a minute, a year, a thousand years, a million years. When you are negotiating a realm where there are no signposts to time or distance, Time itself ceases to exist. Hoki was so anxious to get to Skylark that even a minute of utter blackness was a minute too long.

Then Hoki saw a second gateway looming out of the darkness and knew that she had reached the threshold of Te Po, The Night. This time, the gateway was studded with geometric kowhaiwhai, abstract representations of the galaxies of the universe.

"Here we go again," Hoki said as another three manu Atua came forward to mediate the threshold between one world and the next. They were glorious creatures of light. They had fabulous wings, webbed with astrological motifs – suns, moons, shooting stars – and, when they approached, Hoki was prepared.

"I am the Hokioi, the Spirit Messenger of the Gods," Hoki intoned grandly. "By virtue of the powers vested in me, I bid you to let me pass."

We know who you are, you who belongs to the Lord Tane, the three God birds answered, amused. *But if you wish to pass by, even you must state the nature of your mission.* Their voices contained the music of the spheres.

"The nature of my mission?" Hoki asked. "What is this? A quiz show? I am here to save Skylark. I haven't got much time."

The three manu Atua shimmered and scintillated, smiling among themselves. The Hokioi had always been short tempered. *Then pass by, bird of the Lord Tane, you who determines the fate of all.*

"Thank you," Hoki answered. Goodness, this was worse than getting your eftpos number wrong at Big Save. She didn't dare ask for Fly Buy points as she passed through the gateway.

And Hoki was dropping again, this time through Te Po. As she descended, she passed through the many gradations by which night became transformed into light. Aurora after aurora began to brighten the darkness until, with a triumphant flourish, the First Day dawned.

Again, Hoki didn't know how long her descent was taking but she was really relieved when she saw the third gateway, standing on the horizon at the threshold of the dawn. After all, she hadn't come for the view.

Hoki sent a prayer ahead of her. "Can you hear me, Skylark? I won't be long now."

The gateway was ablaze. It was golden, fiery, a living representation of Te Ra, the sun. Beyond it lay the twelve Heavens, Nga Rangi Tuhaha.

For the third time, Hoki sought permission from the manu Atua to pass. Their forms of pure light dazzled and blinded her.

"I am the Hokioi," she said, "I am the bird of Tane, and I seek permission to cross your threshold on a matter of life or death."

The three God birds blossomed with fiery sunspots and eruptions of flames. They seemed to be taking an agonisingly long time to consider Hoki's request.

You speak truly, Spirit Messenger of the Gods, they said, finally, and their words were sad and inevitable. *Whose life is to be saved*?

Hoki's mouth was dry. "The life of my niece," she said.

The manu Atua twirled in a kaleidoscope of blazing, molten beauty.

And who will pay the price?

Hoki bowed her head. "I will." There was nothing else to say, really. "Can I be on my way now?"

The God birds sighed with sadness. *Yes, pass by, bird of the Lord Tane, and fulfil your destiny.*

With gladness, Hoki soared through the gateway and sought a swift river of air that would take her south. Once in midstream, she searched ahead for her bearings. Oh, the sky was such a huge place with so many Heavens to it and so many unfamiliar constellations. But fate was on her side and guided her wings to a point where winds met, clashed and created huge turbulence. All of a sudden, elevator winds took her upward and she found herself in the realm of blindworms. She saw glowing eyes and spectral creepy-crawly shapes pressing in on her.

"Advance on me no further," Hoki ordered. "I am the Hokioi —"

The bird of infrequent flight? We have not seen you, oh queen, not for a timeless Time. Let her pass, brothers. Let her go, sisters.

"Thank you," Hoki said. All she wanted to do was get out of there. But then she heard one of the blindworms complain:

Boy, there's sure been a lot of traffic coming through our skies lately.

Traffic?

Immediately Hoki put on the brakes. "What do you mean by that?"

Two birds have recently passed our way, the blindworm said. *One of them was caught by the pouakai.*

Hoki tried to still her thudding heart. "Is she still alive?"

Who knows? The pouakai herself has harvested our skies and taken some of our brothers to feed her chicks. The eggs have already hatched.

"Oh no," Hoki answered. "I'd better get my skates on."

She went absolutely vertical, hurtling downward through the blackness. What was a little vertigo when there was a matter of life or death to deal with? It seemed a thousand years went past before she emerged again into the light. But this time she knew she had made it.

"I'm here! I have reached the paepae o te Rangi," she said. "I am at the edge of our universe."

Before her eyes she saw the magnificence of the Earth's planetary system, a place centred by a radiant sun and circled by familiar planets. She recognised Venus, Vega, Antares, Canopus and Orion's Belt. Third planet out she saw the Earth, a beautiful green and blue orb with a circling moon. As the Earth revolved, she saw the sparkling corona called the Southern Cross.

Heart beating fast, Hoki dived for the Southern Cross. She was going so fast that she looked like a comet streaking through the stratosphere. When she arrived she stilled, staring squarely and intently deep into space. She was at the right coordinates, in the right quadrant.

"But have I come too late?" she agonised.

No. There was a rumble. A roar. From out of the menacing sea of the universe, where things go bump in the night, the volcanic island appeared, making its regular rotation from the dark side of the sun.

"Here we go." Hoki beat her wings faster and faster. They blurred as she reached the same speed as the rotational circling of the volcanic island. As the island passed by, she hitched a ride. The centrifugal forces did the rest, pulling her in and then spitting her out.

Right below her was the pouakai's nest. Three chicks were in it.

But where was the mother pouakai? There, at the base of the nest. It was trying to get at a tiny bird huddled in a small crack in the rocks. Hoki widened her irises and her long-range vision clicked in. The tiny bird was fighting back.

Skylark.

Hoki didn't even take time to think. She opened her mouth and a tremendous screeching cry came from it.

"I am the Hokioi –"

Skylark had almost given up when the screeching cry split the heavens apart. Surprised, the pouakai, pulled her beak away.

Flying down through space, coming straight at her was a strange bird. The pouakai had never seen anything like it. But as soon as Skylark spotted the way the bird trailed its legs, as if it was lame, she knew it was Hoki. "Oh Hoki –"

Hoki flew around the pouakai's head, trying to entice it away. But the pouakai was undeterred – it had the raptor's advantage of size and strength, after all, so it bent again to rooting out its prey.

"Are you deaf?" Hoki screamed. "Did you not hear my name? I am the Spirit Messenger of the Gods."

The pouakai roared in response.

Then go about delivering your messages. You have no business here.

"Oh no?" Hoki answered. "Watch this space."

She flew up to the pouakai's nest and disappeared over the rim. When she reappeared, she had one of the squawking chicks in her claws. Furious, the pouakai half scrambled, half flew towards her. Calmly, Hoki reversed out of the way. She and the pouakai eyeballed each other. The pouakai rattled and hissed.

Don't even think of harming my child.

"You took one of mine," Hoki said, "so I am taking one of yours. Don't like it do you?" She indicated Skylark. "You wanna do a trade? Then back up. Back up, I say!"

The pouakai understood the deal and nodded.

Hoki turned to Skylark. "What are you like at the sprints, the hundred-yard dash?"

"Hopeless. Me and school sports never worked out."

"Well, hitch up your skirts, girl," Hoki said, "because I'm going to persuade the pouakai to follow me. I'll use her chick to lure her as far away as I can from you. While I'm doing this, I want you to to fly as fast as you can to the place where the sky hangs down to the horizon. That is where the ripped sky is, at the paepae o te Rangi. We're going out the way the seabirds came in."

The plan confirmed, Hoki continued her reversing movement, the pouakai's chick in her claws. The pouakai followed her. Across the sky they went, feinting, attacking, fending like boxers. The pouakai roared and hissed with anger, but Hoki kept her cool. From the corner of her left eye she saw a black hole forming. It began to swell, then widened below her, an inverted cone leading into infinity.

"Go, Skylark!" Weak and exhausted, Skylark crawled out of the crack in the volcano and began to fly in the direction of the ripped sky. Seeing this, the pouakai could not retain her rage.

We had an arrangement. Honour it now.

"Okay," Hoki shrugged. She dropped the chick into the black hole. Screaming, the pouakai went after it, trying to save it before it disappeared forever.

My baby.

"That'll keep her busy," Hoki said. She tensed, wheeled and used a turbo-boost of speed to catch up with Skylark.

"I'd almost given up hope," Skylark wept. She had crossed almost halfway to the ripped sky.

"You didn't think I'd leave you out here all alone in the dark, did you? Hush, Skylark dear, don't you cry. Switch your booster rockets on and let's high tail it out of here."

All of a sudden, Hoki heard a distant roar. The mother pouakai had rescued her chick and was placing it back into the nest.

"Don't worry about her," Hoki said. "She won't be able to catch us up now."

Oh yeah?

The pouakai had an ace up her sleeve. She did a curious thing. As the volcanic island revolved, she revolved with it, like a satellite orbiting the Earth.

"The pouakai is using the speed of the revolving island as a slingshot," Hoki said, alarmed. "Once she reaches escape velocity, she'll be able to catch us up."

Sure enough, there was a series of loud reports as the pouakai broke free of the island and began to accelerate after them. So fast was her flight that she closed in very quickly on Skylark and Hoki. Her talons were braced for deadly duty.

Coming ready or not.

"Just keep on my left wing, Skylark," Hoki yelled. "Conserve your strength. Glide along in my wake. Cruise in my slipstream. We're almost there."

Skylark was whimpering. Ahead was the vertical wind shaft leading to the ripped sky, so tantalisingly near. But the pouakai was crashing through the stars, roaring through meteor showers like a train, getting closer and closer.

Hoki took a gamble. Calibrated the distance. Stalled and sideslipped.

"What are you doing?" Skylark shouted as Hoki fell behind.

"Don't worry about me. It's you the pouakai's after!"

Hoki was right. The pouakai wasn't about to hunt another supernatural bird. It went for the easier catch. Ignoring Hoki, it grabbed for Skylark. Extended its neck. Snapped its jaws. Missed. Roared with rage as its quarry made it up the wind shaft.

I'm coming to get you.

That's when Hoki made her move. "Not if I have anything to do with it," she said. She knew she was no body match for the heavier bird, but as the pouakai went past her she threw all her strength into a powerful side thrust. "Yeeargh!" Body-slammed the bugger. Saw the pouakai's look as it was pushed off course. Went for the slam dunk.

"Hhhuuuuhhh!" Excreted a stream of splashing and blinding shit into the pouakai's eye.

Having bought valuable seconds before the pouakai could recover, Hoki sped up the wind shaft after Skylark. Not far above them was the jagged edge of the ripped sky.

"We're going to make it!" Skylark cried.

But lumbering behind them came the pouakai.

"Go through," Hoki shouted.

– 5 –

And Skylark fell through the ripped sky.

There was a *crack* as she did so. It scared the living daylights out of Bella. She fell against Arnie, who grabbed Francis and Mitch to keep his balance.

"What the heck is that –"

Mitch's shotgun went boom, the bullet whizzing through the air, causing further confusion among the seabirds still trying to get in. To make things more puzzling, a little bird was trying to get out. When Arnie saw the bird coming through the rip, his heart leapt. But she was out of control, rolling over and over, trying to stabilise herself.

"Skylark, oh, Skylark –"

She was going too fast, in danger of going over the cliff. Arnie leapt for her and caught her. Skylark felt his warm hands around her. Saw the bright sunlight. Everything was a kaleidoscope of sky, sea and Manu Valley.

"Arnie –"

Dazed, Skylark looked up and into his eyes. Then the whole world began to whirl around.

"Put her on the ground," Bella told Arnie. "Quickly!"

With awe, Bella, Arnie, Mitch and Francis watched as Skylark changed slowly back into her human form. Mitch and Francis stared open-mouthed at her transformation.

Skylark looked up at the ripped sky. "Where's Hoki? She was right behind me."

The sky bulged and the huge head of the mother pouakai came through the rip, blinked and looked around, surprised. She tried to push her way through.

What have we here?

"Holy smoke!" Mitch shouted.

Arnie's wits were about him. He let the pouakai have it with both barrels. "Take that, you cyborg freak."

Roaring with pain, the pouakai fell back through the rip. As she did so, she chomped on some of the seabirds and pulled them with her.

Bella shivered with anxiety. Where was Hoki? She closed her eyes. An image came to her of a small crippled bird buffeted by the currents of Time, trying to get the pouakai's attention, trying to coax it away from the ripped sky.

"Here kitty kitty kitty," Hoki called. "Come to Mama."

The pouakai tried to clear her eyes. Tiny pellets of shot had lodged there like grit. When she saw Hoki she gave a snort of irritation.

Get a life.

After all, the pouakai had found a new paradise, a great new hunting ground. Lots of new food for its chicks. It tried to clamber back through, presenting Hoki with the unseemly sight of its posterior.

"What's a girl to do?" Hoki asked herself. With a grimace of distaste – Hoki had always been fastidious – she closed her eyes, hoped that her tetanus shot would protect her, and bit the pouakai on the bum.

That did the trick. The pouakai fell back again, lost its balance and began to twist out of control down through the wind shaft. Roaring with rage, it locked on to Hoki and pulled her down with it.

Helplessly caught in the pouakai's claws, Hoki didn't have a chance to free herself until they had reached the lip of the universe. And was the mother pouakai angry? Was she what! Staggering in the air, fierce eyed, she looked at Hoki:

Whoever or whatever you are, I don't give a shit. This time you've really pissed me off.

The pouakai attacked. Hoki sideslipped and followed with a sudden upswing and a hover.

"You want to mess with me?" Hoki asked, facing off. "Even on your best day you're not as good as I am on my worst."

Wings back-paddling, Hoki turned at right angles and beat across the universe, striking out for the higher thermals.

"I've got to keep in front of her," she said to herself.

She dropped into a jetstream. Smaller and lighter, Hoki set a cracking pace with a fast deep-pumping wingbeat. Her short wings and long tail configuration, designed for speed and manoeuvrability, allowed her to keep just a little ahead of the pouakai, but it took all of her effort. The pouakai made a bone-cracking lunge, and managed to flick at her. The motion was devastating, and Hoki began to tumble out of control.

Is that your highest speed? the pouakai asked scornfully.

Luck was running out for Hoki. The pouakai closed on her, menacing, positioning itself for the kill. Hoki looked desperately for a way out. But she was in a No Exit street.

"Ah well, I've had a good life," Hoki said. Far below was the green and blue orb of earth. "But I'm definitely not going to die out here in the universe," she continued. "If I have to go, let it be in the embrace of Papatuanuku, the mother of us all." Defiant to the last, she yelled at the pouakai. "If you want me so bad, then damn well come and get me."

Proudly, Hoki tipped, felt the G-forces and let them pull her down. The speedometer went into the red. Reaching 200 kilometres an hour, she dived through the space. The pouakai dived after her. As for Hoki, she had decided that if she had to go, she'd make sure everybody knew about it.

"Hokiiii-oiii! Hokiii-oiii!"

She hurtled across the Heavens. She was the Bird of Destiny. She was the Bird of Fate. She hit the Earth's stratosphere and her feathers warmed up and burst into flames. Behind her, the same thing was happening to the pouakai. From Earth, they looked like two meteors flaming across the sky, one small, the other large – and gaining.

"Hokiii-oiii! Hokiii-oiii!"

Below, the manu whenua heard the call of the Hokioi. They gathered around Te Arikinui Kotuku, Chieftain Kahu and all the birds of the paepae.

"Remember this day," Kotuku said with awe. "On this day, after our second war with the seabirds, remember that you saw the Hokioi."

The pouakai opened its jaws. It extended its neck. Hoki felt its hot and fetid breath. She waited for the pouakai's beak to make its quick jab, slide through the intersection of bone and skull and impale her brains.

"Oh Lord Tane," Hoki cried. "I offer my spirit up unto you. All I have ever wanted to do was to serve you in life and unto death. Receive me –"

In her last moments, Hoki thought of Skylark. She also thought of Bella, and wondered how her sister would get on without her.

"Goodbye, Sister."

But something extraordinary happened. From everywhere in the upper sky came the manu Atua, the supernatural ones of the bird kingdom, God birds of indescribable magnificence. Some of them looked like immense flying dragons. Others like darkly gleaming bats with pearl-veined wings. Some were heavy-bodied, grotesque with mask-like heads and three-digit hands and feet. Others were beings of pure light, of such surpassing beauty, that they took Hoki's breath away. As they hovered, they wove a screen of incredible brilliance around Hoki so that the pouakai could not get through to her.

But she is mine, the pouakai roared.

The manu Atua stilled, held court, made a collective decision. The pouakai waited for the affirmative. The manu Atua uttered judgement.

Foolish, arrogant pouakai, they said. *This one is yours, you say?*

The pouakai knew she was lost.

No, of all the Lord Tane's creatures, this one above all others is his.

The manu Atua swirled in a gigantic carousel, faster and faster, individual birds blurring into one gigantic phoenix. Their wings touched. Lightning crackled, and a skein of death wove around the pouakai. She began to shudder and scream. The electric bolts pierced her carapace, sheeting and sizzling through every vein, reaching to her heart. A sudden discharge, and the pouakai exploded.

For a moment there was silence. Hoki dared not move. Dared not look up on the faces of the manu Atua. When the voices began to speak to her, she nodded in assent.

And now, you, bird of Tane, will you pay the price?

"No!"

On the other side of the sky, Bella heard the voices of the manu Atua. Then she saw Hoki in her mind's eye. Sometimes Hoki was a bird with wings, sometimes an old woman stabilising herself on her walking sticks.

"Bella? Sister? Can you hear me?" Hoki's voice whistled in Bella's mind.

"Yes. And I can see you, Hoki."

Hoki was hastening across the sky and up the wind shaft. "The manu Atua have agreed that the Great Division may stand. I have to close the ripped sky so that never again will it be challenged."

"You know what this will mean?" Bella cried. Her voice was like a whirlwind screaming along the corridor of past and present.

"Yes," Hoki said. "It's the price, and the time has come to pay it."

"I won't let you," Bella yelled.

At that moment Hoki herself appeared, darting through the ripped sky and fluttering over Bella's head.

"Please don't make this difficult for me," she whistled.

Bella's face began to stream with tears.

"Why are you crying?" Skylark asked, afraid.

"Hoki has to do her job," Bella said. "She has to close the sky."

Arnie, Mitch and Francis gathered around.

"So what's the problem?" Skylark asked.

"She has to do it from the inside."

And Hoki flew back to the ripped sky. She became a bird of blinding light and awesome beauty. Suddenly she extended her wings. Her feathered pinions struck at the top right and left edges of the rip. Flames burst out where the pinions had pierced through, soldering the bird firmly so that she could not move. At each strike Hoki arched her neck and crooned with pain.

"Sister –" Bella sobbed.

Hoki closed her eyes. Her head drooped with the exertion. Then she opened her eyes and smiled at Bella. "You know I have to do this. Maybe I'm not so hopeless, after all."

She cried out again, a scream of anger, and she was an old woman balancing on her walking sticks in the middle of the air, trying to grab the edges of the sky with both hands. She took three deep breaths and, when she cried out again, she was a dazzling bird, pulsing with energy.

The bird began to move its wings, backwards and forwards, faster and faster. The valley filled with light and the roar of the wind. The air blurred.

With a roar, Hoki nailed it.

She began to pull the ripped sky together.

"What on earth was that!" Flora Cornish asked.

She heard a roar and ran outside the diner to see what was causing the commotion. She shaded her eyes and looked up in the direction of the noise. Some Korean sailors from the massage parlour joined her, and cowered in fright.

"It looks like something's happening up at Manu Valley," Lucas said. The noise had brought him out of his garage. He saw smoke and a mushroom cloud of dust hurtling into the air. "Maybe one of the road gangs is using some explosives to clear the bush."

At Tuapa College, Ron Malcolm felt the ground tremble. Fearing an earthquake, he yelled out to his class, "Get under your desks!" The students screamed, but when there wasn't a second shockwave they calmed down. "Sir, look –"

Ron saw a crack in the sky. He gasped in astonishment. How could that be? Then a bright light poured like molten silver into the rip. In that moment Ron thought he saw something incredible – an old woman, pulling at the sky with her hands. For a moment she seemed to falter in her task. Then, with another agonised cry, she flexed her feet, became incandescent, and pulled the seams together. The sky joined together with a roar.

Down in the main street, Flora Cornish shook her head and closed her eyes. When she opened them she knew she had been dreaming. This was Tuapa, as sleepy as ever. There above Manu Valley was the sky, as seamless as ever. Yet, when she blinked again the ripped sky stayed printed on her retina. And she knew she had heard somebody screaming and seen somebody dying. Her thoughts went to Hoki.

More people came out onto the street. They stood reassuring themselves for a few minutes. Old Mrs Barber said she had just put her washing on the line and was glad a thunderstorm wasn't on its way. Harry

Summers said that it must have been a freak local weather event, which he blamed on global warming. Lucas said he'd take the truck up the valley later to find out what it was.

The sun was hot and the sky was clear and it was good to have a bit of a chinwag. Suddenly, a strong hurricane-like wind began to blow from the Manu Valley. The air was filled with an unearthly silence.

The sun went out.

From the main road, the townspeople saw them coming. Seabirds were beating out of Manu Valley, retreating back to the sea.

Tears were streaming down Bella's face. She looked up at Hoki. "I don't want you to go, Sister. I don't want you to do this. There must be another way."

"No there isn't. The sky must be closed forever."

"Come through the sky," Bella pleaded. "Let's try to figure out how we can close it from the outside."

"You know that can't be done."

"I'm giving you an order," Bella yelled. "You just do as I say!"

"Please, Bella," Hoki begged her. "You know I don't want to leave you. But there's no other way." She began to weep. She had joined the sky with her wings but the seams at her feet were still opened. "Sister. Help me. My feet have no strength to pull the sky closed."

Skylark and Arnie were hugging each other. "Don't go, Auntie Hoki," Arnie cried.

But Mitch and Francis knew this was the way it had to be. Mitch began a wild haka:

> "Ka mate, ka mate, ka ora ka ora
> It is death, it is death, it is life, it is life . . ."

That's when Bella stepped forward. She took Hoki's right foot and positioned it. Then she took Hoki's withered left foot, kissed it, and put it into the sky's left overlap.

Sighing to herself, Bella nodded. "Finish your job, Sister."

With a hiss, Hoki struck at the right bottom seam. With another cry she struck again at the left bottom seam, her withered claw welding into the sky.

Shouting with rage, Hoki began to pull the bottom part of the rip together with her feet.

"Move, damn you," she cried.

In her death throes she pulled the seams together.

The sky joined with a roar.

[CHAPTER FIFTEEN]

– 1 –

A week later.

In the bright summer sunlight, Tuapa looked the way it had always been. Flora Cornish opened her diner, as always, at five in the morning. Fishermen came in for a hot breakfast at six before heading for the harbour and setting out to sea. Around seven, the girls from the massage parlour ended their night shift and headed home to hit the sack. Lucas came roaring through the main street half an hour later to open his garage. Right on eight, Ron Malcolm clocked in at Tuapa College. The buses bringing rural students to school started to arrive at eight-thirty. Over at the medical centre, Dr Goodwin had started his morning rounds. Nothing about the tranquil scene would have suggested that anything out of the ordinary happened there. Nothing, that is, except for the splash of media excitement when Cora Edwards had fallen from the stage in *Bye Bye Birdie.* For one brief moment, Tuapa had its five minutes of fame. Now, it was back to normal.

Skylark snapped Cora's big suitcase shut.

"How are you doing, Mum?" she asked.

Cora was in her usual muddled state. She sat in the middle of Bella and Hoki's bach, trying to pack the other suitcase. She was taking back more clothes, personal toiletries and shoes than she had brought with her. Not only that but there were all the telegrams, letters and gifts received from fans and well-wishers.

"Why do you need them all?" Skylark sighed.

"Honey, I just can't leave all these signs of affection behind. I have to answer every letter personally and, after all, they prove my fans still love me and that I am still a star. Just wait till my agent Harold gets a load of all of this. He'll be on to South Pacific Pictures and I'll be back at the top."

Skylark smiled to herself. It was just great to see her mother on the way to recovery. Of course there was a long way to go, but Dr Goodwin had organised Cora to be admitted to a programme of drug rehabilitation when she returned to Auckland. It had also been good for Cora to have had her summer romance with Lucas. Now that she was leaving, however, he had realised that a bird in the hand was better than one who was flying away and had made up with Melissa.

"I'll tell Bella you're ready to go," Skylark said.

"But I need you to help me!"

"No, Mum," Skylark answered. "From now on, you must help yourself."

She left the bach and knocked on the door of the homestead.

"Is anybody home?" Skylark called. When there was no answer, she walked in.

The house was quiet, shadowed. Once upon a time two sisters had grown up and lived in it; now only one sister lived there. The physical impact of the loss could be seen everywhere. Hoki had always been the one to keep the house tidy. Now, dishes were piled in the sink. Clothes were waiting to be washed. The sitting room was a mess. And Bella was drinking like a fish. Vodka bottles, gin bottles, beer bottles and whisky bottles were everywhere.

One room, Bella's bedroom, however, was perfect: the bed was made up; everything was in place on the top of the bedside vanity. And why? Ever since Hoki's death, Bella had taken to sleeping in her sister's room, pulling the sheets and blankets around her as if that would help her get over her grieving.

Through the window, Skylark saw Bella silhouetted against the sky at the top of the cliff. She walked out into the sunlight and up the cliff path. Bella was looking out across Manu Valley to the sea. The forest was mysterious, shining with beauty. Far away, the sea was like a sparkling emerald.

Skylark took Bella's right hand and kissed it. The old lady pulled her into an embrace. She reeked of alcohol.

"So I was the one after all," Skylark began. "But why did Hoki have to die for me?"

"She did it gladly," said Bella. "For you, me, everybody, the landbirds. She did it to keep the order of things." She was trying to focus with her eyes. "Did you know I didn't want her to go to rescue you?" she asked, slurring her words. "I thought that surely you must already be dead. But Hoki has always been so stubborn." Bella let out a bellow of raucous laughter. "She knew it was her job, her responsibility. After all, you were her mokopuna. How could she leave you there! My sister Hoki had a long and wonderful life. Yours is just beginning."

Skylark saw a seashag and, for a moment, felt a clutch of terror.

"Is it all over now?"

"Better be!" Bella laughed again. She swayed, made some drunken steps to the cliff edge and raised her fist to the world. "But the manu whenua face an even greater threat today than the seabirds ever posed. It comes from men now, you bloody buggers!" Bella pointed in the direction of the logging trucks. "I had another fight with the road builders today. Those beggars, they take liberties with us. They don't only want what's theirs. They want what's ours too. Greedy. Like the seabirds, they eat everything up. When will it stop? Someone has to be around to tell them to stop. Me and Hoki may have been just a couple of crazy ladies to them, I know, but at least we drew the line. Someone always has to be here to draw the line. And the line, Skylark must be drawn at the valleys that are left to us. Someone has to keep the boundaries in place. Someone has to say no to the bulldozers. Someone has to drive them back to the sea. Someone has to say no to the pollution. Someone has to say yes to the Earth and the people of the Earth."

Bella raised a defiant fist in the air. "I may be drunk," she said, "but I'm not down for the count. The line will always be drawn here, Skylark. At Manu Valley."

Then it was time to leave.

Skylark was wearing one of her favourite badges: PLEASE LEAVE ME A GREEN AND PEACEFUL PLANET.

Bella had recovered somewhat from her drunken state and, shamefacedly, had put herself together to say goodbye to Cora. "Where the heck is that nephew of mine!" she scolded. "He knows you're going north today."

Skylark coloured. At first, on her return from the other side of the sky, things had been really good between her and Arnie. But, after a few days, he'd stopped coming up to Manu Valley to see her. He seemed embarrassed and withdrawn, offering excuses about how he was busy at the garage, as if he couldn't get away quickly enough.

Well, Skylark thought, if he won't come to me, I'll go to him. "I'll stop by the garage on the way out."

Bella hugged Cora. "Your daughter, Skylark, she's a wonderful girl."

"She's always been a good girl. I don't know why she puts up with me."

"You're her mother. The only one she's got."

"Yes, well, some people don't know when to give up, do they."

"Will you be all right back up north by yourself?"

Cora gave Skylark a rueful look. "I guess I'll have to be." With that, Cora stepped into the ute.

Skylark drove down Manu Valley, and they were soon in Tuapa. She stopped outside Flora Cornish's diner.

"I won't be long," Skylark said to Cora. "Why don't you go and have a cup of coffee."

If there was a problem with Arnie, Skylark wanted to have it out with nobody around. Her heart was beating nervously as she approached the garage. What if he wasn't there?

He was. When he saw Skylark, his face fell. "So you're on your way then."

"Yes."

"Well, thanks for coming around."

Skylark wasn't going to let him get away as easily as that. "Arnie, what's wrong with you? I could never have done it without you. I thought I could, but I was wrong. You got me around the country, up to Parengarenga, down to Tauranga and across to Nelson. You came with me through the portal and I don't know how I would have got on when I had to tell the Runanga a Manu about the seabirds. If you hadn't been my warrior –"

Arnie had a spanner in his hand. At Skylark's words he threw it across the garage. It clanged against the breakdown truck. He turned to face her and there were tears in his eyes. "Please don't do this to me, Skylark. Please, just go, will you? I let you down. I mean, I was the one who left you there. I shouldn't have done that."

Skylark stared at Arnie. "Is that what all your silence is about?"

"Don't you understand? I was supposed to look after you and I didn't do my job. When we were flying in the upper Heavens, I lost it, and I went running across the sky, and that's when the pouakai saw me. And you saved me. You! Some sidekick I turned out to be. Some intrepid hero –"

Skylark felt herself going numb. She didn't know what to do. "Well, that's that," she said quietly. Then she put out her hand. "Would you like to give me the keys to your wagon?" she asked. "We left it at Wellington airport, remember?"

"My keys? What for?"

"Didn't Mum tell you? I'm taking her across on the ferry as far as Wellington. While I'm there I thought I'd pick up your wagon and drive it back. That is, if you don't mind. If you do, I'll just catch a bus back."

"You're coming back? You're not going away for good?"

"I thought you knew," Skylark answered. "Didn't Mum tell you?"

"Tell me what?"

"You can't trust her to do anything properly," Skylark said crossly. "I told her she's on her own now. I've got my own life to get on with. Do you remember what Lottie said? There are some things that you have no choice about. When Bella goes, who will look after Manu Valley? It's going to have to be me. And you know what?" Skylark's heart was beating fast.

"What?" Arnie asked.

Boy, he wasn't making this easier. "After all we'd been through," Skylark continued, "I was kind of hoping that –" She took a deep breath. How could she get it through his thick head! Then she thought she heard Te Arikinui Kotuku's voice: *This would be a good time to pretend, Skylark.* Rolling her eyes with irritation, Skylark struck a pose and said in a girly voice:

"Arnie! Save me, save me, I'm so helpless!"

Arnie couldn't help it, he burst out laughing. "What did you say? I didn't hear you!"

Skylark put her hands on her hips and wagged a finger at him. "You heard me. I'm not saying it again."

"So is this the part where the hero gets the heroine?" Arnie asked. He strode over to her and took her in his arms.

"When who gets *what*?" Skylark was still trying to get over the shock of Arnie's arms around her.

"Oops, I'll rephrase that. When the heroine is lucky enough to get the hero?" He pulled her in to him. Tighter. Tighter.

"That's better. Maybe." Hmm. Arnie felt more muscly as a boy than as a bird.

"Good, that means we can – uh –"

"Uh? Can what?" Arnie's eyes were confusing her, but Skylark wasn't about to give up everything.

"You can kiss me, and now that we've destroyed the evil avian empire, we can ride off into the sunset."

Skylark pursed her lips. "I wouldn't push my luck if I was you," she said.

– 2 –

Three days later, Bella awoke at 3 a.m. The curtains were billowing across her face like gossamer in the darkness. She knew something wonderful was going to happen.

She had been coming home in the afternoons to find berries on the floor and window sills. One night she dreamt of fluttering wings and feathers caressing her cheek.

"Uh oh," Bella said. "Time to stop drinking and destroy the evidence."

Over the following days, Bella tidied all the rooms, swept the floors, did the dishes, cleaned the kitchen and washed the clothes. Most important of all, she made two trips to the dump to get rid of the vodka bottles. She bought some household deodorant and went around spraying it so that not one hint of alcohol lingered.

The seventh day.

Two in the morning. Bella couldn't sleep. She put on her dressing gown, said her usual morning prayers, went down the hallway and looked accusingly at the kitchen. Hoki had always been the first to rise, make the breakfast and to call, "Sister? It's time to get up." Bella missed hearing her thump down to the kitchen on her walking sticks, thump, thump, thump.

Her eyes glistened at the memory. The house was so silent now.

Bella made a cup of tea and took it back to the bedroom. She was just about to get back into bed when she saw something strange lying on her pillow.

A feather.

Bella gave a gasp. She looked around the room. Went to the open window and looked out. She thought she saw a shape flitting its way up from the house, along the pathway to the clifftop.

"This is it," Bella said. "The time has come."

Heart beating fast, she pulled the quilt over her shoulders, shuffled her feet into her slippers until her big toes stuck out the holes in the front, and walked through the house and out the door.

The stars were sparkling like the eyes of Heaven. The moon was a crescent of beauty. The valley was rustling and sighing with the wind, alive and free from the caprice of man.

"Is anybody out here?" Bella called.

The wind was cold as she left the house and walked up the cliff path. She thought she heard someone chuckling, but realised it was only the distant sound of the waterfall. When she got to the halfway point where the old bench was, she sat down to rest. There, she saw another feather.

With a smile, Bella picked it up and continued up to the cliff top. She looked up at the night sky, and understood the enormity of the universe. She felt even lonelier, closed her eyes and fell asleep.

How long she slept, Bella never knew. It must have been at least an hour because her bones felt stiff. But she was woken by something falling on her head. At first she thought it was a twig; then she felt something else go plop and bounce off her hair.

Bella kept her eyes closed, not daring to hope. She could hear warbling and whistling in the air above her. When she could resist it no longer, she opened her eyes to see that the ground all around her was covered with berries.

"Are you awake now?" a voice said. "I've been using you for target practice for ages. You can sure sleep, Sister."

Bella's heart was really pounding now, and she had to take a deep breath to regain her composure. "So you've finally decided to come home, have you?" she asked.

"Yes," the voice said. "I thought I'd better see how you were doing without me."

"I knew it was you. Berries on the kitchen floor. Bird droppings all over the house."

"Now there's a thought."

With that, there was a soft whirring of wings as a dark-plumaged bird flew out of the crimsoning sky and tried to settle on Bella's head.

"Ouch!" Bella exclaimed.

"Oops," Hoki said. "I'm still trying to get the hang of this."

"So I can see."

"My withered claw doesn't help either."

Bella put her hands up to steady her sister and, at the touch of feathers, her tears flowed like a stream.

"There, there, Sister," Hoki warbled. "There, there."

She hopped down onto Bella's shoulder and nestled herself close to the crook of her neck, softly preening her sister's hair and crooning a comforting song.

"Me he manu rere, aue,
Kua rere ti to moenga . . ."

"Just as well I'm waterproof," Hoki said.

"I've missed you, Sister," Bella answered.

"I'm sure," Hoki said. "Nobody to order you around."

"Nobody to growl."

"Nobody to make breakfast for you."

"Nobody to break any plates."

"Nobody to talk to."

"Nobody to dress you either, by the looks of it," Hoki whistled. "You look dreadful."

"You would too, if you had to do all the work by yourself. The place has been going to the dogs since you left."

"I'll say," Hoki said. "You've been on a drinking binge, haven't you! You were never good at cleaning up your vodka bottles. No amount of deodorant is going to get rid of the smell that quickly."

"At least I tried to tidy up for you."

"You should have spent more time on yourself! Look inside your ears! Atrocious. When was the last time you washed them? Forget about growing spuds in the paddock. In your ears would be better."

Bella felt Hoki pecking her ears and then, hop, Hoki was back on top of her head again.

"The manu Atua were compassionate, Sister. They asked the Lord Tane to have mercy on me and he heard their plea. He allowed me to come back."

"But as a bird?" Bella asked. "Did that have to be the price?"

"Be careful, Sister," Hoki said. "One should never question the compassion of the gods."

Bella nodded. "I'd much rather have you in my life, Hoki, than not in my life at all."

There was a pause. "Are you sure?" She had a wicked gleam in her eyes. "This is going to be so much fun! I can sit here on your head all day while you work. I can perch on your shoulder whenever you go around the farm. And instead of breaking dishes when I'm mad at you, I'll poop on you instead."

"You wouldn't dare. Just because you're a bird, don't think that you'll be able to get away with anything."

Hoki whistled and flew into the air. She executed a few fancy sideslips and tumbles before returning to Bella's head. "That's how I escaped the great pouakai," she said. "By comparison, you'll be a breeze! How's Skylark?"

"She's fine – and things seem to be developing between her and Arnie."

"Oh no! Poor Skylark."

"Poor Arnie, you mean!"

"But the good news is that she'll be staying with me, here in Manu Valley. She wants to take over when I am gone. Meantime, you and me have to keep going on, Sister. As long as we keep paying the rates and keep a look out to repel all invaders –"

"I can be the scout for us," Hoki said. "Nobody will know it's me at all. Wheee!"

She did some somersaults in the air.

"Show-off," Bella said.

"Will you get used to me like this?" Hoki asked, as she launched herself again into the air.

"No," Bella answered, "but I suppose you can still help me in the valley even if you are a bird. And will you stop treating me as if I was an aircraft carrier?"

Whistling with delight, Hoki plummeted and circled around Bella, teasing her.

"Stop that," Bella laughed. "If you don't, I'll put you in a cage."

"This beats using walking sticks any day!"

Bella had a sudden memory of Hoki's crutches leaning against the bedroom door. She closed her eyes with sadness.

"Don't cry," Hoki said. She fluttered herself against Bella's cheeks.

"As long as you're with me, I suppose that's all that matters," Bella answered.

Hoki made soft comforting noises. "Got you!" Bella yelled. She grabbed Hoki with both hands and imprisoned her, lowering her so that the two sisters were looking into each other's eyes.

"Gee you're cunning," Hoki objected. She pecked at Bella's fingers, trying to make her open her hands.

"Just so long as you know who's going to be boss," Bella said, giving Hoki a stern look. "Okay?"

"You were always a big bully," Hoki answered. She cocked her head to one side and spat a seed into Bella's face.

Startled, Bella opened her hands and Hoki flew free. "Let's go home now," she warbled. "I'm hungry. Got any worms for breakfast?"

Bella stood up and looked across Manu Valley. The bush clattered and sighed in anticipation of the dawn. Suddenly the thought came to her:

"Oh Lord Tane, most of your great forest has gone, the land has gone, and man whom you created has changed the order of things. Please bring to man the understanding that he needs to save himself and his world."

The sky began to lighten, the sun's first rays shimmering across the dome of Heaven. Then it struck the twin mountains.

Birdsong. The mara o Tane.

The birds of the forest strained their throats in celebration. The wild music was like small bells. The sounds, pure and full like those of a glass harmonica, rose in a crescendo of sweetness. It was a melodious chorus. A triumphal ode. A hymnal to Tane. A gloria to light.

Hoki flew back and landed on Bella's head. "Oh, I'm going to ruin your reputation now!" she carolled. "The first time we go down to Tuapa I'm going with you. Everybody will say, 'Look at that Maori lady with the bird on her head!'"

The birdsong swelled with indescribable beauty.

The dawn flooded across the sky.